Shadows Awoken

Beshadowed
Darkness Unknown
Blood Bound
Shadows Awoken
Everdark Cursed

Published by Fairies and Fantasy Pty Ltd 2021
ISBN: 978-1-922390-24-0 (paperback)
ISBN: 978-1-922390-25-7 (hardcover)
Shadows Awoken (Beshadowed Book 3) copyright © 2021 Selina Fenech.
All rights reserved. www.selinafenech.com

www.selinafenech.com

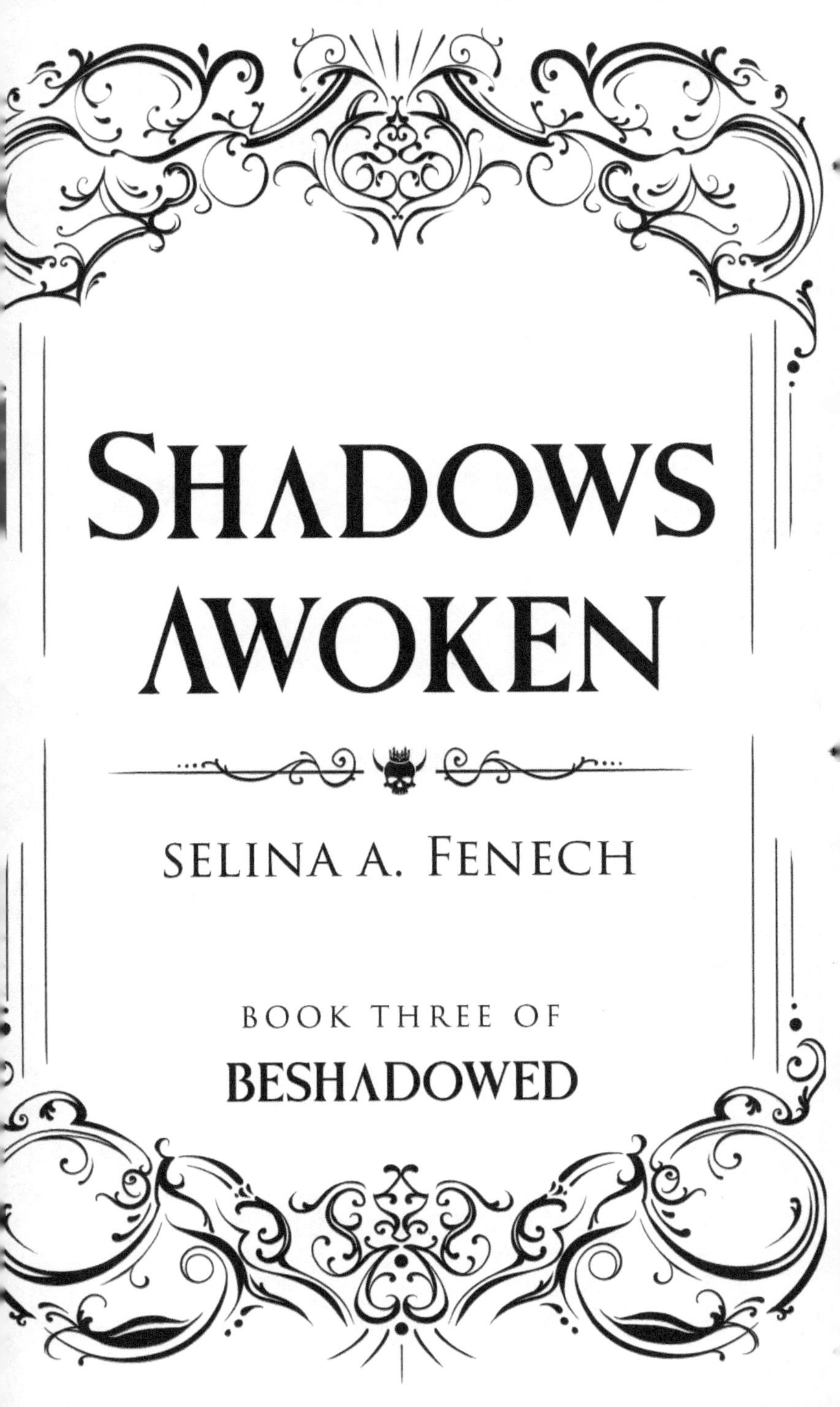

Shadows Awoken

Selina A. Fenech

BOOK THREE OF

BESHADOWED

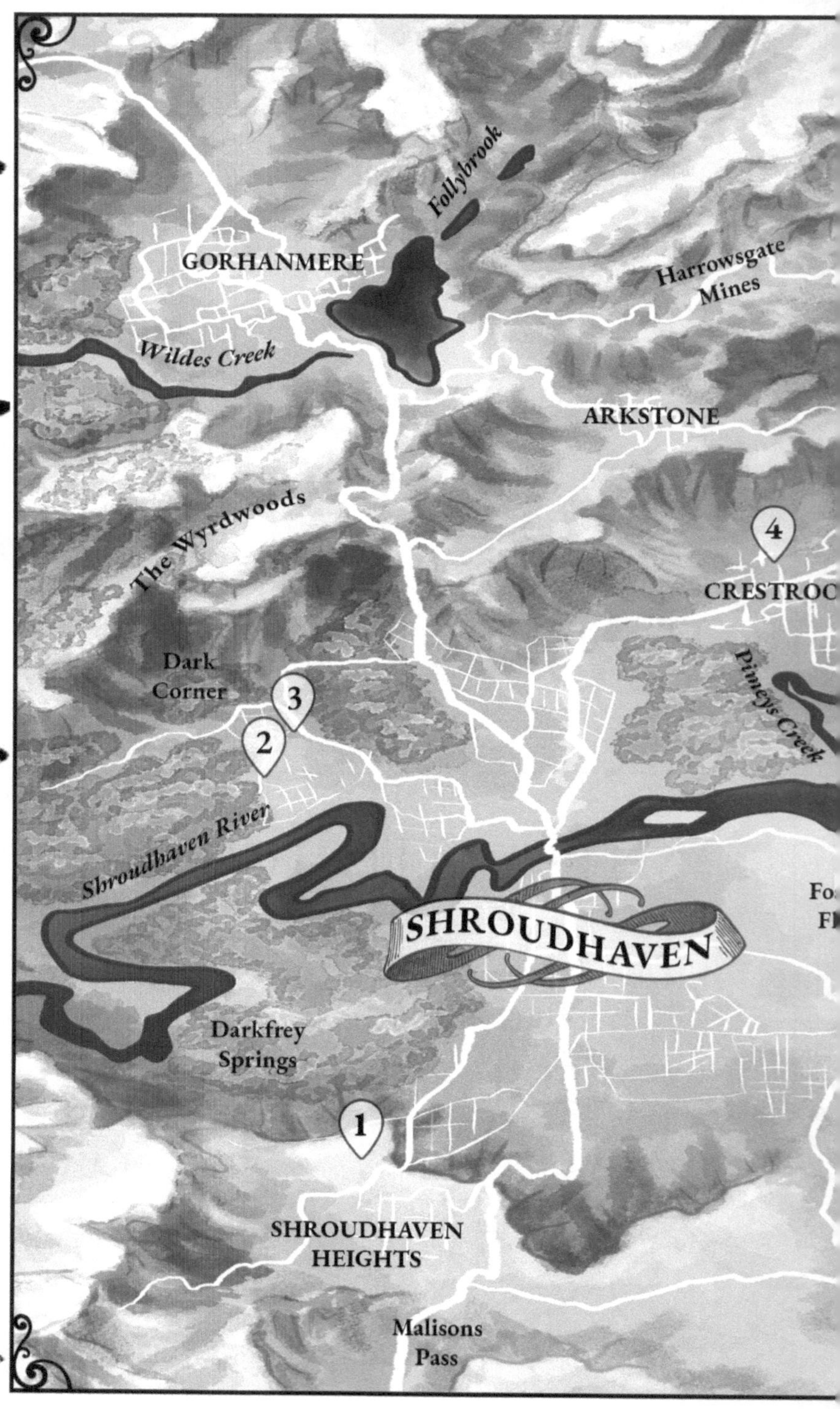

GORHANMERE
Follybrook
Harrowsgate
Mines
Wildes Creek
ARKSTONE
The Wyrdwoods
4
CRESTROO
Dark
Corner
3
2
Pimeys Creek
Shroudhaven River
SHROUDHAVEN
Fo.
Fl
Darkfrey
Springs
1
SHROUDHAVEN
HEIGHTS
Malisons
Pass

lfgrounds
Bright
Corner
6
HARTLEYDALE
Terras Beach
eys
k
CRYBELS
COVE
RESTON
Myrkur Lake
Bakers
Marsh
Sanctuary
Point
CARNOCK
ISLAND
5
KEY
1. DARKFREY ESTATE
2. BODERLETH
ANTIQUES
3. HOWELL HOUSE
4. CRESTROOK
UNIVERSITY
5. CARNOCK
LIGHTHOUSE
6. ROOKS HOTEL

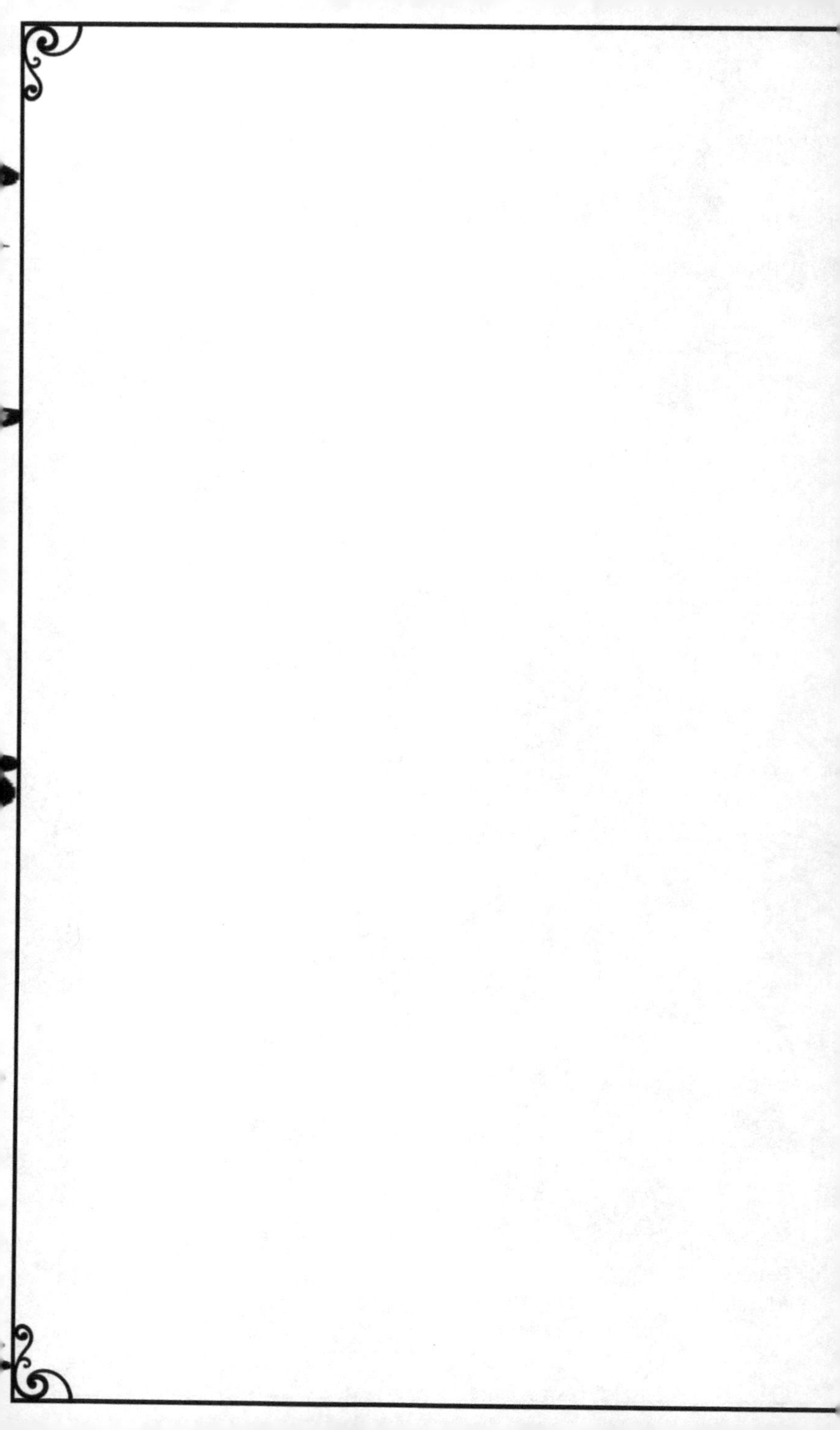

CHAPTER ONE

For all of Rylan Howell's years as a Darkfrey, only the mission mattered. Fighting the darkness, keeping the world and those he loved safe. No matter the cost.

Now Rylan's world had been turned upside-down, but it felt right.

Being home at Howell House felt right.

Reuniting with his mother felt right.

Heading out on a hunt with his brother by his side again felt right.

Seeing Everly again, outside of her dreams … was temporary. Rylan had made sure of that.

His new team—a band of runts and outcasts by Darkfrey standards—chatted noisily in the back of Lian's SUV as Rylan pulled over on Main Street of downtown Shroudhaven.

Fog shifted and parted as they came to a halt. He could hardly see five paces ahead of the vehicle, even with the headlights shining bravely into the night.

The asphalt was wet from an earlier rainstorm and drops flecked the windshield. Rylan twisted the key to turn off the engine, and the headlights extinguished. He shushed the others and they responded instantly. Maybe they weren't as hopeless as he thought.

The eerie silence of the early hours greeted them. A flickering illumination pierced the mist from the direction of their target location, causing strobing effect.

In the passenger seat, Callan eyed the flashing light with nebulous shadyr eyes, his dark hair feathering around his face. It was already longer than Rylan considered suitable back when they were both still at Darkfrey Estate, and it had been allowed to grow even longer since.

Callan smirked. "The Boutique All seems like a weird place for a beshadowing. What ghast wants to hang out in a dollar store?"

From the very back seat, Denny leaned forward to the middle row where the girls sat. "Come on, we all want some booty call action now and then. I'm open to it any time, just so you know."

Light flashed off his blond beard as he grinned toothily and waggled his eyebrows.

Tammy's grimace shuddered through her whole body.

She'd tucked herself into the corner of the seat so that her lean face was half in shadow and her shaved, dark hair looked like a bruise spreading over her skull.

Everly's friend, who Rylan didn't even think should be there, finished applying some lip gloss as though nothing had been said.

Cherry, sandwiched between the girls, whipped around and snarled, "Read the room, you deluded swine. No one thinks you're booty call material, no one thinks you're funny, no one will ever want you until you quit being such a selfish bigot."

Woah. That was not the Cherry that Rylan remembered.

There was pain and a level of viciousness in his voice completely unlike how he'd behaved while still a Darkfrey. He'd been more subdued back then, shy even, before he came out. Things changed after that.

Rylan figured he'd be bitter about it. He was right to be. But the way Harper patted Cherry's shoulder supportively, it seemed like something more was going on.

There's so much I don't know. How are we supposed to be a team?

Harper flung the side door open like a cannon blast in the silence. "Come on. Let's get this party started! I want to be done and dusted before Everly wakes up."

And how did this bliv end up on our hunt?

Harper had shown up at Howell House in the middle

of the night, just as the team had stepped out to deal with the weroth report. She carried a bundle of shiny gardening tools under one arm and wore an even shinier smile, and an apron.

"Bellsy? What are you doing here?" Cherry had greeted her with matching enthusiasm.

Rylan glared at those smiles and the out-of-towner. Surely she'd experienced enough of Shroudhaven to know she shouldn't be wandering around at night on her own.

"Just returning these to Lian. I've cleaned and sharpened them all for her, too."

"It's almost two in the morning?" Callan said it like a question, one Rylan was wondering as well.

"Is it? Time got away from me. Everly went to bed early, I think she's still feeling a bit off, you know."

Rylan's teeth ground against each other.

Harper shrugged in a jangle of saws and secateurs. "So, I thought I'd get a few more things done."

Tammy's eye roll could be heard in her words. "Why are you wearing an apron?"

"Oops, I forgot to take it off. I was just baking some muffins."

The whirlwind of a woman left Rylan confused. "I thought you were packing to leave?"

"Yeah, I was packing, too. The muffins are for the drive tomorrow." Harper hummed with energy, vivid green eyes bright and alert. "Hang on, if it's 2 a.m., where are you all off to?"

"Shadyr business," Rylan said at the same time Callan said, "Weroth hunt, at The Boutique All."

Harper's grin turned supernova. "I'm in! I'm coming, I'm coming too!"

"Well, there's a sound bite for the spank bank."

A chorus went up.

"Gross!"

"Inappropriate."

"Denny!"

Harper ignored him, dashing over to put the gardening tools on the porch. "One last dose of Shroudhaven spookiness before it's all over. It's perfect!"

Rylan grunted, "That's not—"

"Cool," Callan said over him. "Did you bring your axe?"

"No," she pouted.

Turning back to the tools, she plucked out some hedging shears and tested them with a few quick clips. *Sshhhckt Sshhhckt.*

Her grin twisted up and her eyes narrowed wickedly. "These should do."

"I don't think—" Rylan tried again.

"Bellsy gets what she wants," Cherry snapped.

Harper bounced on the spot, then filed into position

with the rest of them. "You know, I don't normally wear an apron when cooking but thought I could get one more photoshoot in. I was trying a more cottage-core look. Turned out super cute. Repainting the cupboard doors really helped. I'm going to miss shooting in that old house …"

Right. Yeah. That's how she ended up with them.

Rylan didn't like the idea of a bliv he barely knew tagging along. Everly trusted her, and so it seemed did Callan and the others, but trust wasn't enough to save her from being turned inside out by an eidolghast.

Rylan gritted his teeth and opened the driver's side door, stepping out into the cool night. Misty rain wet his skin, and he ran a hand over his shaved head, glancing at the SUV as Harper stepped out like a star arriving for a Hollywood premier. Perfect makeup, perfect silky hair, perfect warm-brown skin, perfect Pilates princess figure.

Rylan couldn't see how this *influencer* fit into shadyr business. Even if his brother vouched that she was capable.

Capable or not, Harper was a human, and as far as he was concerned, she had no place joining the team on a hunt.

"You're going to stay close and keep your head down," Rylan told Harper as he stepped onto the sidewalk to join her and the others. "We can't be responsible for keeping you safe while we take down the eidolghast."

"Save your over-protective 'keep you safe' bullshit for

Everly. I'm here to hunt. I'm not weak." Harper shrugged and tossed her dark tresses over her shoulder. "And neither is she, FYI."

"Roast his ass," Denny guffawed.

Cherry high-fived Harper.

Rylan clenched his jaw. If this team showed him no respect, how was he supposed to lead ...?

I'm not, he reminded himself. *This isn't my team.*

All eyes were on Callan, who was diligently checking over the street and shop front while the rest of them squabbled. His little brother had grown a lot, and leadership suited him. But Rylan was left feeling lost. He had no idea who these people really were, or what his place among them was. They seemed to have accepted the bliv more than they accepted him.

"Just don't let your human need for 'one last adventure' get you killed, all right? Or we'll see how strong Everly is when I deposit your corpse back home."

Harper glared him down, tall enough to meet him eye to eye. "I do *not* know what she sees in you."

A pang lanced through Rylan's chest, and he battled to keep his expression even.

Cherry's bright-red hair flopped over his eyes in a blunt fringe, matching the red and white leather jacket he tossed back into the SUV.

He draped an arm around Harper's shoulders. "Leave

Bellsy alone. She's already been through several missions. She knows the game. Just chill already. You aren't a Darkfrey anymore so quit with the arrogant asshole attitude."

Rylan frowned and turned away from them, shrugging out of his jacket and shirt and chucking them back into the car before closing it up. All the shadyrs now wore only their flexible body armor and tactical pants, prepared for what was to come.

Everything Rylan knew told him that Harper was a human and a liability.

But doubt stirred within him. How true was what he'd been brought up to believe by the Darkfreys?

That deep-seated certainty that humans were weak, and that shadyrs in a hunting brace, shadyrs like him, were the best, the strongest, the only hope for the safety of their world from ever-encroaching darkness. Top of the food chain. But recent events left him questioning everything.

Maybe those Darkfrey biases he was only now starting to acknowledge ran deeper in him than he knew. Maybe he *was* being an asshole.

He'd still keep an extra eye on the human, though. A dead best friend wasn't the going-away gift he wanted for Everly. The pang in his chest returned.

There was a moment when trapped with Everly in her sleeping mind that Rylan had thought maybe they could be together. That all his self-imposed rules of the living world could be ignored, and he could just *be* with her, in her dreams, forever.

Then his soul had been hurled back into his body and he'd woken to screams, and blood, and Everly, cold on the floor.

She'd come back to him from that death-like faint, but it was the real wake-up call. Everly couldn't be part of Shroudhaven, and shadyrs, and danger. He couldn't handle seeing her hurt like that. She couldn't be part of his life.

The mission remained. And there was no room for anything else.

Rylan checked his watch: twenty to three. Still several hours till dawn, but they didn't have time to dawdle. The eidolghast—a weroth, according to Cherry who had sensed it during a late walk and returned for backup—needed to be taken down before sunrise when the street would be filled with potential victims.

He cut himself off halfway through thinking they should just report it to the Darkfreys and let them handle it.

That's how Darkfreys think. I'm not a Darkfrey anymore, but I'm still a shadyr. I still have my mission.

The Boutique All had a wall of glass windows and doors on the first floor of the building that gave passersby an internal look at the chaotic madness of the emporium. Normally there would be holiday-themed scenes and mannequins wearing *I Dropped a Call in Shroudhaven*

T-shirts, or a view of dozens of packed metal shelves leading off out of sight.

Tonight, though, an eerie, strobing light pierced outward, silhouetting everything inside so the shapes juddered like possessed shadow puppets.

Callan returned from his recon down a side alley. "All set? We have potential access down here. Let's move in."

The team followed quickly and reached a locked metal door beside two dumpsters overflowing with broken-down cardboard boxes.

Rylan was used to the privileges of being a Darkfrey, one of which was having access to almost anywhere in Shroudhaven if needed for a hunt. Having to force their way in seemed wrong, but he put his shoulder up beside his brother's and the door gave under their combined strength. Callan grinned at him, then ushered everyone inside.

Rylan's boots squeaked on the white linoleum, scuffed by years of foot traffic. He kicked them off, as did the other shadyrs, leaving them in a pile by the door. The pull of his change already churned within him, and of any shadyr form, the weroth transformation was the least kind to clothing.

The door brought them inside where a divider wall separated a basic kitchenette from the main store. They emerged from the alcove between shelving piled in wicker baskets of all shapes and sizes, and drooping, floor-to-ceiling synthetic flowers that seemed to be rotten.

The store was deathly quiet except for the low, musical bars of "There's a Mermaid in My Lighthouse" playing over crackly speakers.

There's a mermaid in my lighthouse, and her heart belongs to me.

There's a mermaid in my lighthouse, she keeps staring out to sea.

Up ahead, the aisles seemed to stretch onwards into infinity. The more Rylan stared, trying to see the end, the more they wobbled and twisted in his vision. Thick, flickering fog pooled around his bare feet.

All the signs of an eidolghast in residence.

The weroth's presence prickled over his skin like hot embers. It was close but not too close—somewhere farther in the depths of the labyrinthine store.

Rylan had no doubt it could sense them, too.

CHAPTER TWO

At the first intersection of aisles, they stopped. Something cold and smooth touched Rylan's foot, and he reached down to pull it from the heavy mist so he could identify it. A loose fluorescent tube. It buzzed incessantly, light strobing, despite having no power source.

Across from him, Callan gently kicked another one, and it swirled beneath the low fog. The lights lay scattered throughout the store.

"Watch out for broken ones," Callan told his team.

Cherry and Tammy had already become engulfed in the black, cinder-spotted smoke of their shadyr transformations. In gaps between the dark magic, their arms and legs jutted through, lengthening. Claws pierced from the tips of their fingers like curved blades.

Wiry fur sprouted from every inch of their bare skin,

and by the time it covered them, it would be thick enough to protect them from the weroth's slimy acid. Or broken glass.

Tammy and Cherry were still young, less practiced at containing their shadyr forms. The rest of them—Callan, Denny, Rylan himself—wouldn't change until they chose to.

The potential for standing on a fluorescent tube with a bare human foot made Rylan consider changing now, too. But in the highly competitive Darkfrey braces, it was a point of pride to see who could hold off their change the longest.

Callan, though, nodded in solidarity to Tammy, and began his change, too.

Denny, whispering a mini wolf howl, followed.

The shadyr form when in the presence of a weroth had birthed the age-old legend of the werewolf. For good reason, too, since when the transformation was complete, they looked exactly like the beast of lore.

"I feel like I should have brought some doggy treats," Harper muttered.

"You changing already?" Rylan asked.

As his change stabilized, Callan's snout-like mouth twisted into a wolfish grin.

"We do things a bit differently." He elbowed Rylan, strong enough that it almost knocked him down. "Hey, just want you to know, it's good to have you back."

Rylan hesitated, suddenly feeling awkward as the only shadyr left in human form. "Glad to be back."

"Feels great to be hunting together again, doesn't it? As long as you're feeling up to it."

Rylan rolled the kinks out of his shoulders and shrugged. "Yeah. I'm feeling better by the minute."

"You were in a death-like coma for weeks," Callan pointed out. "It's okay if you're a little rusty."

Rylan didn't miss the sly smile, even on the wolfish snout.

"Could kill more ghasts than you in my sleep, little brother." He returned the smirk.

"Wanna bet who takes this one down first?"

Harper stepped between them. "My money's on Callan. Soldier boy here is too busy pretending he doesn't want Everly around to have his head in the game. He hasn't even suited up yet!"

Rylan hid his grimace, trying to keep it light. "Who invited you into our smack talk?"

Callan barked a laugh. "She's got you there though."

"She doesn't, because I'm not pretending anything."

Harper pushed past them and took the lead, poking through the shelves as she went. "Methinks he doth protest too much!"

Rylan eyed Harper as she plucked items from the shelves around them, arming herself with a thick canvas raincoat, leather work gloves, and a plastic face shield.

She laughed flippantly at how ridiculous she looked, but she clearly knew enough about what they were up against to be planning ahead. She didn't have a shadyr's natural protection against weroth acid, so she was making her own. Maybe she did know what she was doing.

"She doesn't know what she's talking about," Rylan grunted to Callan as they broke into a fast stride to keep up as Harper continued around acorner, Denny, Cherry, and Tammy close behind.

"Sure. Suuure." Callan grinned, all fangs. "I for one liked having Everly around again and I'm totally comfortable admitting that. You know I had a crush on her as a kid too, right? Hot older friend of my brother's? Maybe I'll ask Everly to stay."

Rylan's fists clenched and he smiled over equally clenched teeth.

He's just having a go at you, ignore him, you did the right thing telling Everly to leave.

In a shadow nearby, Tammy grunted. "Are we going to kill a ghast or fight over a woman who could literally suck your soul out of your body? To be honest, I'm in either way. Both sound like a great chance to opt out of this mortal meat-suit."

Anger swirled out of Rylan's control, and he spun toward the goth girl.

Restraint slipped away, and his change exploded around him violently. Flames of pain scorched his fingertips as his claws extended, and the entire expanse of his skin itched and burned as the fur burst from his pores. He grunted in pain and frustration.

When he emerged from the change, Callan stood between him and a wide-eyed Tammy, a concerned, warning look on his face.

Hot air puffed from Rylan's wolf-like mouth, and he shook his head, denying his anger. He hadn't lost control of his change since he was fifteen.

I must be weak from the coma, that's all.

He held Callan's gaze and muttered, "Everly's safer far the hell away from Shroudhaven. End of story."

Callan's expression calmed, and he let out a slow breath. "I dunno. Look, jokes aside, seems to me life can take away what we love—"

Rylan shot the darkest of looks at his brother.

"—at any moment for all kinds of reasons. So, why should we be the ones that push them away?" Callan turned as he spoke, his gaze falling for a second onto the sullen wolf-girl behind him.

"Come on, let's hunt already!" Harper all but yelled from up front, snipping her garden shears. "Which way? This place is a maze."

Callan slapped a clawed paw onto Rylan's shoulder.

"You want to take the lead on this? You know … if you're up to it."

Rylan snorted a laugh, sighed, then nodded. Best to focus on the hunt. Closing his eyes for the briefest moment, he opened his newly enhanced senses and tried to home in on the sensation of the weroth lurking somewhere in the store.

"This way," he said, inclining his head as he took off to his left.

The team fell into line behind him, moving past school supplies and a wall of greeting cards. The occasional sound of a toe-claw tapping the floor or Harper's sneakers squeaking marked their passing.

The next section held cleaning supplies: bottles of bleach, brightly colored containers of detergent, and more brands of floor cleaning fluids than seemed necessary. The lids on some had popped, and black fluid oozed and bubbled out the tops. The temperature grew colder the farther they moved into the store.

The aisle took a right-angle turn, then another, turning left, then left, then left and left again in an ever-shortening spiral, before branching out impossibly into seven different paths that cut out at strange angles. The beshadowing was already messing with space and dimensions, turning the cluttered store into more of a labyrinth than it normally was.

Still the song played, warbling over the tinny speakers.

Hungry light shines over the waves and my mermaid she yearns,

When will I return, when will I return?

With a squeal of static, the music cut out, and a pre-recorded voice chirped, "Don't forget to join our frequent buyer club for The Boutique All bonuses! Enjoy your time at The Boutique All, and remember, no matter the deed, The Boutique All has everything you need!"

Rylan always wondered if the name was intentional or a naive mistake.

They must know how it sounds.

He could hear muffled chuckles from Denny farther down the line.

The recording ended in a glitchy crackle, and the mermaid song began again.

Somewhere nearby, something hard clattered to the floor.

Rylan stilled, his entire body going on alert. He held up a fist.

The strobing light made it hard for his eyes to adjust to their natural night vision, but his sense of hearing had sharpened until he could hear even the mice roaming through the walls.

And the weroth's six needle-pointed feet tapping on the linoleum. It was on the move.

Signaling the others, Rylan put on a burst of speed and bounded along another aisle filled with pet supplies, shelves piled high with metal food and water dishes. The floor seemed to slope downward, and as they passed through, the bowls jumped off the shelves like popcorn in a skillet, clattering down into the distance.

The clang of each dish hitting the floor ached in Rylan's ears. "I've lost the trail. Can't hear which way it's gone."

"There's something," Callan said, pointing.

What seemed to be a pile of mannequin legs that had merged into a strange, flesh-colored plastic insect, ambled past them in jerky, disjointed steps. Harper squeaked at the sight and skidded to a stop.

"Woah." Her phone was out of her pocket in an instant and she snapped a couple of photos, the flash merging with the strobing light around them.

"What? I'm not going to post them! Just for my personal mood board, I swear."

Rylan growled. "This isn't a game."

"I *know*. But that doesn't mean life has to be spent as grumpy Mr. Serious Pants a hundo percent of the time, either. Tammy, can you eye-roll at him for me? You do it best." Harper poked at her screen, blue light reflecting off her face shield. "Aw, they turned out all weird and blurry."

"Sorry, babe." Cherry patted her gently on the back. "Beshadowings are almost impossible to capture."

Harper pouted.

"Hurry up," Rylan snapped, speeding up again. "We have to find this thing."

A large, black silhouette stepped into the aisle ahead of him.

"I think it found us," Denny said.

Rylan slid to a stop on his clawed feet.

The weroth balanced on six legs, each tapering to a point so thin it seemed physically impossible for the monster to be standing. Though it had no visible eyes, Rylan knew it had no trouble "seeing" him and his team in the foggy darkness.

It hissed in deep, undulating syllables. A disturbing green glow emanated from inside a toothy mouth, opening so wide it split its entire body in half.

Then it charged.

Its strange legs bent at unnatural angles as it slithered in a rush at Rylan. The force of impact threw him off his feet. Gravity vanished as he rolled through the air, and then he bounced off the unforgiving floor.

He rolled twice before coming to a bone-jarring halt against an endcap of dryer sheets. Two dozen boxes that smelled like eucalyptus rained down on him, and he batted them away irritably, surfacing from the overwhelming scent with an immediate headache.

I am off my game. This is embarrassing.

Cherry, Tammy, and Denny leaped over his body and bounded toward battle with the weroth. As a team, they well outnumbered the ghast, so Rylan wasn't too worried about Cherry and Tammy's novice abilities or Denny's tendency to preen and prance when he should be fighting.

Callan didn't seem worried either as he casually helped Rylan up.

As Rylan stumbled back to his feet and fell into a loping run to join the party, he caught sight of Harper.

She let out a powerful battle cry and wrenched the garden shears in her gloved hands. They snapped right in two, and the bolt that joined the halves pinged onto the floor. The feverish glint in her eye and confidence in her shoulders was ... not normal. Not for a human coming face-to-face with an eidolghast.

Surprised by the brutality in her expression, Rylan found himself slowing. Watching her.

Harper dashed into the fight, keeping speed with the werewolf-shaped shadyrs beside her. Her twin shear blades flashed in the strobing lights.

She was under the beast first. She swirled the shears elegantly, each slice accompanied by a tennis-player's grunt. One, two, three legs, cut out from beneath the beast.

What the ...

That wasn't paper she was chopping through. No matter how spindly they appeared, a weroth's legs were all bone and sinew, hard as steel.

Black acid spurted from the wounds, and the eidolghast staggered and stumbled, smashing into the shelves beside it. An avalanche of basketballs and tennis rackets rained down. Harper dodged back, landing as spry as a cat.

Cherry, Tammy, and Denny reached the weroth next, each targeting a leg of their own.

Rylan and Callan followed, racing in time. As mirror images, they leaped into the air, flying for the monster's bulbous body.

Rylan slammed into the beast, digging his claws deep into the ghast's black-hole-colored fur as its filaments waggled around his hands. Callan landed beside him, shooting him a grin. Rylan found himself smiling back.

The creature wobbled wildly on half its remaining limbs, bucking and trying to throw them. Rylan reared back, slicing his razor-tipped claws across the black expanse beneath him. Slimy, deep-green blood appeared, and the weroth let out a short, sharp cry of fury.

Callan swiped next, dislodging a hunk of acidic flesh that splattered onto the low ceiling.

"You trying to steal my kill?" Rylan scoffed.

Callan got another swipe in first. "Gotta show my team I'm as cool as the legendary Rylan Howell."

Rylan's wolf-like mouth turned up on one side, and he dug faster into the oozing flesh of the monster.

A crash came from the other side, and Callan looked down. Another smash clattered as the weroth rammed one leg and the shadyr attached to it against the shelving. Tammy cried out.

"Careful!" Callan hissed at her.

"I'm fine!" she snapped back.

"How do we finish this thing off?" Harper called from below.

The sound of a blade slicing was followed by the spatter and sizzle of acid.

The weroth kicked out, shaking Cherry free from another leg. It stabbed that same limb forward, attempting to skewer him on the floor.

Cherry skittered out of range, then yelled, "There's a weak spot, deep in its back! That's what those two are digging for."

Rylan thrust both arms into the hole they had created, tearing backward in an attempt to wrench the gash wider. Callan shouldered into him, jostling for the best position to get his claws into the kill spot.

A figure appeared, flying toward them, silhouetted in the stirred-up fog and strobing lights. In a flurry of flying, silky hair, and sizzling raincoat, Harper landed with a ferocious cry. Both shear blades plunged deep into the hole the brothers had made.

The weroth stilled. A harsh, susurrus gurgle escaped its

glowing maw. Then its remaining legs crumpled beneath it. It slammed down onto the floor.

Callan and Rylan jumped off to the sides. Harper tumbled in a backward somersault, skidding on all fours on the blood-slickened floor.

Her chest heaved as she grinned and panted, straightening herself up. "Did you see that? I did it! I took it down!"

"I think it was really a team effort," Rylan muttered.

With the eidolghast defeated, he brought forth his shift, swirling in shadowy magic until he'd returned to his human form. Callan and Denny followed suit, but Cherry and Tammy remained changed.

"Don't diminish this for her!" Cherry snapped, giving Harper a furry high five. "You were amazing, but I never had any doubt."

The weroth corpse sizzled, melting in its own acid. The shear blades oozed upward out of the gore, worn and pockmarked from the caustic onslaught.

"Aw, I liked those. I think dual wielding is definitely a good look for me. Remind me to replace them for Lian."

Harper shed her outer protective layers and brushed herself down. Her cheeks were flushed and her eyes gleamed bright with a strange mixture of excitement and something that looked a little too like bloodlust. As she took her gloves off, a faint scar line shimmered on her wrist in the low light. She pulled her sleeves down again, covering it.

Tammy rolled her shoulder, wincing and tugging at her body armor that was too tight for her. Rylan frowned. She must still be wearing the same Darkfrey armor she had from when she was kicked out years ago.

He was so used to having access to new resources whenever he needed them, but he realized now that the armor he wore, that he'd left the Darkfreys with, might be the last he'd ever own, too. At least he wasn't still growing, like the goth teen.

Callan moved closer to her. "You okay?"

"Ugh, I'm not a baby. Go check on Denny or something for once."

"I'm fine, thanks for asking," Denny yelled from a pile of sports drinks nearby. "Except for this raging boner from watching Bellsy in attack mode."

"I swear he makes me want to barf out my ovaries," Harper grunted, and Tammy snorted a laugh that left the others shocked.

She quickly schooled her animalistic face back into a scowl. "What? I mean, she's right."

Harper squealed in glee at Tammy's approval and skittered over with a hand up for a high five from her, too.

Tammy folded her wolf claws, just as black as her normal hands, under her crossed arms. "No."

Smiling regardless, Harper let out a long, satisfied sigh.

"What next? We left this place in a real mess. Should we clean it up for them? I can fit on some cleaning. Won't take long at all."

Cherry sniffed. "I think we should call in the Darkfreys and have them handle clean up. They have to be good for something, after all. Plus, I'm wiped."

Rylan's muscles also held an aching tiredness despite the enhancements of the werewolf form, but he wasn't about to admit weakness.

"Sounds like a good plan to me," Callan nodded, punctuating it with a yawn.

Tammy lifted her snout to the ceiling. "Do you hear that?"

Rylan shook his head. "Hear what?"

As if to answer him, police sirens wailed to life.

Rylan groaned. "Ghast dammit. I bet this place had a silent alarm. We gotta get out of here before the cops show up."

"What about the body?" Harper asked. "Won't they find it?"

Rylan turned back to the corpse, but it had mostly melted into a disgusting black puddle by that point. "I'm more worried about them seeing a couple of werewolves running around than what's left of that."

The group headed for the exit at a quick clip—easier now that the beshadowed fog was dispersing and aisles ran in straight lines again. The fluorescents had ceased their strobing, plunging the store into darkness.

The shadyr night vision kicked in properly for Rylan and the others, and he checked for Harper in the gloom, but she seemed to move with as much confidence of sight as the others. Something weird was going on there ...

But it didn't matter.

He'd already done his duty in chasing Everly, which meant Harper too, out of town. Tomorrow, they'd both be on their way, and whatever Shroudhaven weirdness had taken root in Harper would likely fade away. Even the entity inside Everly had only shown itself when she'd returned to Shroudhaven. Hopefully, it too would die off, outside of this darkness-tainted town.

Reaching the back door, Rylan snatched up his boots, and still the song played on an eternal, eerie loop.

There's a mermaid in my lighthouse, and her heart belongs to me.

There's a mermaid in my lighthouse, to her I own the key.

Chapter Three

The ice-and-fire adrenaline crackling through Harper's system was heightened by the arrival of flashing blue and red lights that shone down the alleyway to meet them.

Rylan and Callan, who'd been ahead of her on their journey through the store, came to an abrupt halt several feet out from the exit. Still pulling their boots back on, they checked up and down the alley.

Harper stepped toward the main street and lights. "Want me to go hold them off? I can distract them."

Callan grabbed her arm and twirled her around before she could walk any farther. "No. I think there's another way out down here. Better if we can all get away unseen."

"Especially the young'uns with their shadyr hangover," Denny said.

Tammy's shimmering galaxy-eyed gaze landed on him,

and her face—barely recognizable in werewolf form—contorted with effort. A hint of blackness swirled around her, then faded again without any change. She groaned fiercely. She and Cherry carried their boots with them, clutched in their front paws.

"You'll get there," Callan offered.

She eye rolled.

"But for now, let's get out of here."

The store exit wasn't far down from the main street, and the flashing lights were way too close to the left, so the group turned right and jogged along the grimy, narrow path between buildings. Sodden, slimy scraps of cardboard and newspaper slipped under their feet, and rodent-shaped shadows darted away from them up ahead.

Harper knew the team was fully visible as long as they were in the alley. The moment an officer appeared at the entrance, they'd be seen, and there was nothing they could do about it.

She didn't exactly relish the idea of being arrested for breaking and entering, but the excitement of running from the cops, and being so close to being caught, made the situation that much more exhilarating. Power rippled through her veins and made her feel capable of *anything*.

What I could have done with this power six months ago…

Maybe her entire life wouldn't have been blown to bits. When Bryce had doxed her and all the internet had access to her home address, she could have done with a magic boost.

She wouldn't have felt so vulnerable in her own home. She wouldn't still have nightmares about how close the gap was between her fleeing what should have been her safe haven and the moment when that random man showed up with a gun.

She could have fought back, not felt so … powerless.

But then you wouldn't have moved in with Everly, she reminded herself.

She disliked the idea of life without her bestie. But she refused to be powerless again. Refused to get anything wrong, do *anything* below the highest of standards. Refused anything other than total control.

Finally, a turn in the alley showed itself up ahead.

But not before a gruff, angry voice called out, "Hey! Stop! Stay where you are!"

The group ignored the directive and put on another burst of speed. Harper followed Callan around the corner, her blood pumping as fast as her sneakers on the ground. Excitement pulsed through her, and she smiled broadly even as heavy boot falls chased after them.

The dingy alley was crisp and bright in Harper's eyes, and she kept pace easily with the three soldier boys and two werewolves by her side. Their sheltered path ran out quickly, expelling them onto a brightly lit street.

At that time of night, the street was still and empty, and it would be a long run to the shelter of the next alley. There were barely even any parked cars to hide behind.

Harper still didn't know the town as well as the others. "Which way?"

"Where can we hide?" Cherry asked, wide-eyed as he scanned the relatively bright and barren view.

Callan's eyes searched the roof tops, settling on the lowest. "You think you two can get up there? The rest of us ... I don't—"

"Running from something?" A voice muttered.

From the shadows of a shop entrance beside them, a figure stepped out.

Tall, lanky, with a hint of a potbelly beneath his black skull-and-lightning T-shirt. The older man had a beard that hung down his chest and ended in a thin braid, and his eyes were surprisingly blue. Harper had met this Shroudhaven legend once before.

Barry.

Tucked under a streetlight a little way down the block was his ever-present cardboard box.

Everyone seemed too nonplussed to reply.

To their credit, Tammy and Cherry attempted to hide their werewolf forms behind the others, in complete futility. But Barry didn't seem at all surprised at their monstrous appearance.

"Go on. Quick. Into the box."

"Um. What?" Harper managed.

Barry's cardboard box sat against a red brick wall with a tarp and a floral sheet dangling over the opening. He grabbed the corner of both and ripped them back, exposing the inky abyss inside. There was no way it would be big enough to hide them all, not even if they lay on top of one another like they were piling into a coffin.

No one moved until a glance back showed three police officers turn down the alley their way.

"Get in," Barry hissed, one pale hand flapping erratically.

With a shrug, Callan dove in first. Cherry and Tammy went next. Harper expected to see a furry elbow or foot jutting out, but somehow, they all fit. Denny and Rylan shared a look and followed as well.

"You have got to be kidding me," Harper muttered, getting down onto hands and knees.

Only seconds after Harper crawled in, Barry's lighthearted voice filtered through behind her. "Good morning, officers! If you're seeking the children who passed through, they've gone down that street and around the law office."

The odd old man really *had* protected them.

With hardly a grunt of gratitude, the officers stomped off into the distance.

Harper expected to come to a quick halt and need to climb into someone's lap—*not Denny's, please not Denny's*—but instead, the darkness kept going.

And going.

And going.

Until the cardboard above her head vanished, and a space tall enough to stand opened around them.

Harper straightened, and a flashlight popped on behind her as Barry joined them.

He stood up with a wise smile beneath his fluffy gray mustache. "Welcome to my box."

Callan arched his neck, looking all around. "This … is some box."

Barry chuckled and joined Callan at the front of the group. "Damn straight, boy. My box is a special box."

Denny coughed, but even he was apparently too shocked to pick that low-hanging fruit.

"But you kids are a bit special too, aren't you?"

Tammy cowered, hiding her werewolf form behind Callan. "You're not scared of us? Of how we look?"

Barry gave a raucous laugh. "I know about *everything* going on in this town. I'm not scared of you scamps."

Rylan returned to them, having walked off a little ways. "How far does this thing go?"

"Woah, woah, slow down. Don't go wandering off without me. You could get lost forever down here."

"It's a straight tunnel," Rylan said flatly.

"That's what you think. Follow me. Let's lay low for a bit to make sure the cops are gone, then we'll pop you back out wherever you need to be."

"Wherever?" Callan raised his eyebrows. "So, this is how you always show up everywhere."

"Did you know?" Harper asked, wondering why he'd been willing to lead his team into the box for shelter.

Callan shrugged. "I'd heard some weird rumors that made me think it was worth a shot in the squeeze we were in. Figured it was regular Shroudhaven weirdness but didn't quite realize the scope of the weirdness. Does this system extend all over town?"

Barry nodded and combed his fingers through his beard. "Only a few places I can't get into, or don't want no truck with."

He pointed a finger at the straight tunnel ahead of them and made a gesture as though selecting a direction to take. Waving his flashlight like an airplane conductor, he walked away at a slow, leisurely pace.

With a few shrugs and wary glances, the team followed along. There was enough room to walk two abreast, and Harper ran her hand along the wall to her side.

It was cardboard, all of it, scrappy squares and torn-off sheets layered over each other with staples and tape. Disconcertingly, it gave under her fingers, just like being within a cardboard box, rather than some solid tunnel through the earth. She shivered, wondering what might be on the other side if it tore.

In the middle of the group, Cherry and Tammy's shadyr hangover must have expired because they swirled up in magical smoke and emerged again as themselves. There was a large acid burn on Cherry's pants, and he poked at it, muttering how he hated weroths.

The memory of the man in nice slacks crawling out of Barry's box and giving Barry a hug came to Harper, and the time he approached Harper during her argument with Everly. "Um, Mr. ... Barry?"

"Juuust Barry."

"You've helped other people too, right? You do this a lot, don't you?"

"Ah well, I got a good setup here for avoiding danger, which never seems far off in this town. Filthy with monsters, as I bet you know." He trailed off, his blue eyes going unfocused for a moment.

Then he shook off the reverie, his braided beard swishing as he took long-legged strides. "Figured I could put this place to good use."

"This place ... Just how did you get it?" Rylan asked, frowning at the cardboard around him as though it could attack them at any second.

Barry tilted his head and hummed. "It was so long ago.

I collect things, you know."

Like that explains it.

Harper shook her head. "Why'd you help us? We were being chased by cops, not monsters."

"Not monsters?" Barry guffawed.

When everyone only stared back, he cleared his throat. "Well, I'm not much of a fan of law enforcement. Whose laws, anyway? Nothing more than a system of oppression …"

Barry's muttered rantings continued as the single long tunnel went on. From time to time he would pause, seem to ponder which direction to take, then follow along the only available route again.

He moved too slow for Harper's liking. Adrenaline arced like electricity through her veins, heightened by the Bane's magic.

The first time she was cut by the ancient blade was an accident when she'd snatched it away from Everly. The rush of power was so intense she'd almost pulled a door off its hinges in her panic. But then the cut healed, faster than possible. And Harper tested the effect of the Bane on her skin again.

She'd lost count of how many times since then she'd refreshed the magic with another small slice … She'd been on a high of productivity and strength and energy.

Now the eidolghast was dead and the cops were long

gone, the lack of exciting things to do made her itch for more.

The rush of her pounding pulse when she'd sliced into the weroth's tough skin …

The exultation that sung in her veins when she'd cut off three of its gross, spidery legs …

Fighting monsters and crawling into magical cardboard boxes—how was she supposed to go back to normal after this? Back to a life she'd been so powerless in.

It will be different this time.

This time, she'd have the Bane. It had been agreed by the Howells that it should remain in Harper's care. Because it was somehow related to the Beast of Teeth and Stars, they decided it should stay close to Everly, but not *too* close.

Since Harper had already taken possession of it, the decision was easy. Lian also liked the idea of how Mordan Darkfrey would react when he found out they'd allowed an ancient shadyr artifact to be taken out of Shroudhaven by a bliv. She'd chuckled about it for hours.

Still, having the Bane didn't feel like as much fun without also having monsters to hunt. As much as Harper would love to dismember some of the human monsters in her life, that was generally frowned upon.

"I'm going to miss all of this so much," Harper said with a pout. "I feel like I just got a taste of the good stuff, then was told, 'No more monster hunting for you, little missy!' and sent back to my room."

Up ahead, Rylan grunted. "Don't go getting any ideas. You're leaving Shroudhaven. Everly, too. Neither of you belong here. It's not safe."

"Not safe for the eidolghast," Harper retorted. "Remember who took the kill tonight?"

"You got lucky. Most of that luck being that you had five shadyrs backing you up," Rylan said.

Harper stomped over a fold of cardboard. "You're lucky I respect Everly's decision to go because I would otherwise be staying just to spite you."

She glared at his back to show him she meant it, but he didn't turn around. He'd been grumpy since he woke up from his strange coma. Harper studied the subject of her best friend's uber-crush. He could no doubt be considered hot. Strong brow, chiseled jaw, darkly good looks, about three of every muscle.

She didn't really think Everly would be into that broody alpha personality though. Maybe he was different when they were kids, before the Darkfreys got their hooks into him.

But Harper couldn't see the appeal in him at all. The more she thought on it though—and Bryce's betrayal gave her plenty of time and reason to think on it—she couldn't seem to remember the appeal of any of the men she'd ever had in her life.

In front of her, Cherry caught her eye over his shoulder.

"We're going to miss you too, Bellsy. I don't know what I'm going to do, losing you as well—" he choked on the last words.

Harper reached forward to take his hand and squeeze it. "You're going to call me. And I'm going to call you. As much as Shroudhaven reception allows it."

Up ahead, the tunnel stopped at an apparent dead end. Barry pushed against the cardboard, and a door that had been unevenly cut into it popped open. Flakes of kraft paper shed from the rough edges.

Stepping through the narrow doorway, they emerged into a cavernous room. Flattened cardboard and pegged-up sheets broke the space into sections. To the left, ragged old mattresses with bedsides made of boxes created a rough dorm area. Lamps of all shapes and sizes sat beside beds and in corners, brightening the patchy brown space with warm light.

Harper couldn't tell how they were being powered. A large dining table with eleven mismatched chairs could be seen down another path. Straight ahead, a range of threadbare armchairs sat in a circle, over which on a long rope hung an asymmetrical, arty, single-piece crystal chandelier, glowing softly.

Various oddities clearly straight off garbage collection piles filled every other space, from old bicycles to boxy television sets. Stacked tinned food and old soda bottles filled with water created trip hazards in between.

Harper turned on the spot, taking it all in. "You really have been collecting."

Callan raised his eyebrows. "This is some setup."

"My uncle Teddy would love this place," Denny agreed. "If it had more firearms."

Tammy gave him a distasteful look.

Barry shook his head, making his long beard swing. "Not really my groove. I'm a pacifist through and through. Anyway, welcome to the heart of my maze. Stay as long as you want."

"Thanks, but I think we can probably get back to the street now we're all, um, ourselves again," Callan said.

"No problem, I can let you out round the block from where we started." He waggled a finger at them, leading them through the center of the cardboard bunker.

As Harper moved between the armchairs, she paused to admire the light fitting hanging there, not far over her head. Light sparkled prettily from its intricate forms. She'd been reading up on crystalware for the antique sales and wondered whether it had a maker's mark on it. She reached out a hand to turn it and check.

Barry slapped her fingers away with a roughness that made her gasp. "Don't touch that!"

"Okay!" Harper stepped back beside Cherry and hissed,

"So much for being a pacifist."

Barry walked them in a small circle, then back out the same doorway they had come in. The path they followed led as straight as before, and soon grew smaller until they had to move on hands and knees. Like a strange caterpillar conga line, the group crawled out. They emerged from the cardboard box through the floral bedsheet and tarp curtains in a completely different location than where they'd first entered.

Getting to his feet, Callan held out a hand to Barry. "Thanks, man. We appreciate your help."

Barry stared at Callan's arm as if he didn't understand social niceties, then placed the very tips of his fingers around Callan's thumb.

He gave one floppy shake, then released the shadyr. "You're most welcome. I typically don't help ... well, your type. Only the normal folk. But I've been watching you. Lian's kids," he added with a nod. "You're better than the other lot."

"The other lot?" Rylan asked.

Barry's blue eyes gleamed, and he looked beyond Rylan into the night. Without another word, he ducked back into the cardboard box. A second later, the sheets and cardboard folded in upon themselves like an origami magic trick and vanished without a trace.

"No matter how weird things get, Shroudhaven always

finds some new way to surprise me," Harper muttered.

"Let's aim to get back to the car with no more surprises tonight," Callan said, taking the lead down the footpath.

Shroudhaven's usual dark mist pressed in on them, and the street stretched into the eerie fog, silent and empty this late at night.

Harper wondered how many monsters were roaming the fog out there, and her fingers twitched. But her energy levels were dropping. The walk back to the car left her exhausted.

A deep yearning grew inside her. She needed to get back to the Bane soon. She needed ... more. The sensation concerned her, remembering the glassy-eyed gaze of the more-scars-than-skin Gorhanmere cultists.

She knew the risks, but she needed this. She needed the power, the control. Would she be strong enough to keep herself from crossing that line?

CHAPTER FOUR

Jasper tugged the hood of his jacket up over his head against the cold of the night, then checked his phone again.

Six days.

Only six days since he'd lost Cherry, and each one had been more interminable than the last. Every second that passed was pain, and that pain was a failure of his ability to move on.

Why won't it stop hurting?

Even though they'd had to keep their relationship hidden, he'd had something good with Cherry, but part of him knew it could never last, not if he wanted to remain a Darkfrey.

I knew. I should be able to let it go.

But without Cherry in his life, everything that had felt

right now felt wrong. Before, he could be a good Darkfrey and be secretly in love. Now, it seemed he could be neither.

Jasper tapped the icon for his text messages. Before he could get his emotions in check and stop himself, he chose Cherry's thread.

Cherry's last message drew his attention like a magnet.

Seven letters. That he couldn't stop looking at, no matter how they made his heart sting.

TTYL. ILY.

"Eyes up, Jasper," Vonny said in her clipped, bossy tone. "I'm not going to die because you feel the need to check your socials while on patrol."

Only the hood hiding his face gave Jasper the nerve to roll his eyes in reply. He dropped his phone back into his pocket without a sound. Arguing with Vonny Mesman was like doing a round in the ring against a tornado. It wasn't worth the damage.

Beside her, the newest member of their team, Nilson Darkfrey, did have the nerve to visibly roll his eyes. He never missed a chance to make it clear he was above everyone and everything around him. Entirely too big, too violent, too casually cruel, and Jasper had no doubt that if the brute found out he was gay, Nilson would kick his ass into the Everdark without blinking twice.

There were half a dozen shadyrs who could have replaced Rylan in their brace, yet somehow, they ended up with Mordan Darkfrey's son.

Life just kept piling on lately.

Jasper focused on the thud of his sneakers against the asphalt as the four of them moved briskly along the main street, marching two by two. To his side, Annabeth pressed both her fists to her lips, huffed breath into them, then rubbed her palms together. She seemed to suffer the cold more than others, just like Cherry did.

Fall in Shroudhaven wasn't picture-perfect. Winds howled and buffeted, and rain left everything soggy and gray. When discussing the approach of winter, Jasper had told Cherry he'd be there to keep him warm. But now ...

Jasper managed to stop an inch away from ramming into Nilson's brick wall of a back, where he'd come to an abrupt halt in front of him.

Get over all of that and focus, Jasper scolded himself, taking a step back into formation.

Only a huff came from Nilson as any indication as to why they'd stopped.

Several people approached through the fog. A few familiar faces, a few that were slightly less familiar.

And one that was Cherry.

Sweat broke out across Jasper's skin and his chest stung as if someone had planted a knife in his solar plexus.

Like the other Howell shadyrs, Cherry wore only his body armor and acid-burned pants. Battle-worn, exhausted, and entirely gorgeous.

Their eyes met and under his red hair, Cherry's gaze was as brittle and icy as the weather.

Jasper wanted to reach for him, to yank him into his arms and try to ease the suffering between them.

But he remained silent. Frozen.

The two groups faced off against each other in the misty darkness.

Vonny spoke first, her voice harsh in the quiet night. "You're awake?"

Huh? Jasper blinked, dragging his eyes from Cherry to see Rylan standing at the front of the Howell pack.

Annabeth leaned to the side for a better look.

"Rylan?" She took a step forward.

Vonny swiftly raised a fist. "Awake, and went out on a hunt with this lot? He's clearly chosen his side."

Annabeth stepped back into place, her expression turning hard and blank.

Rylan stared the Darkfreys down, animal rage in his eyes. He made no move to rejoin them, to argue his case, or to explain.

Jasper had seen the braver side of Rylan when they were on the same team. He was a soldier, through and through. His every action had a purpose, his every movement was calculated and strategized. He didn't do or say anything without a reason.

But there was also something new to Rylan. A kind of jagged edge or shattered piece to him that wasn't there before his coma. Something had changed. It weighed on him, visible even to Jasper. He was a Darkfrey no more.

Cherry, Callan, and now Rylan too? So many choosing to leave the Darkfreys. Not that Cherry had a choice, really. But the Howell brothers were on equal footing with Mordan's own offspring as some of the best shadyrs at the estate.

Could I leave too? Could I be beside Cherry, instead of stuck on the other side of party lines?

It felt too hard, too much. Cherry had always been the brave one. Jasper had drawn on that courage when Cherry was by his side, but even if he did leave the Darkfreys, he doubted Cherry would take him back.

Nilson crossed his arms over his barrel chest. "When are you runts going to stay out of shadyr business? I found the stinking mess you left at The Boutique All."

Denny coughed from the sidelines. "Sounds like what your girlfriend says about you."

Not a hint of humor or understanding crossed Nilson's face as he turned to Denny. "You? You should be there with the cleaners now, slop boy."

"You know I'm not a cleaner! You know I deserved a brace rank," Denny snapped back.

"You'd be better off as a Darkfrey cleaner than as

a Howell runt. Dregs and outcasts from *our* training, pretending to be something you're not. You're all nothing."

Jasper tensed as Cherry caught his eye, then dropped his gaze to the ground.

"Oh, they are something, all right." Vonny's voice was low and hard.

Her eyes were fixed on the small goth girl skulking at the back of the group. "Two half-breeds, a moronic pervert, a useless misfit, some random human pet."

She cut a scathing glare across Callan, Rylan, Denny, Cherry, Harper, and back to Tammy. "And last but not least, that stain on existence."

All the color drained from Tammy's face—which wasn't much, considering how pale she already was.

Callan put a hand on her shoulder, but she flinched away.

"How dare you stand there after what you did to my son?" Vonny stalked forward, closing the distance.

"I—" Tammy's lips wobbled.

"*You* are a curse that stole my boy from me!"

Callan stepped into Vonny's path. "What happened to Blaise was an accident. We all wish things could have been different, but—"

"Do you?" Vonny shoved him, but he remained solid.

Rylan, Cherry, Harper, and, to Jasper's shock, even Denny, closed in, forming a wall between the young shadyr and Vonny's rage.

She stilled and glared through the protective line as though she and Tammy were the only ones there. "Do you wish it was different? Would you wish it with all your heart that you could bring my son back? Would you wish to take his place?"

"I do, I would," Tammy replied in a small, frightened sob.

"That's enough," Callan barked.

Tammy gasped at the air as if it were drowning her.

Then she vanished.

Jasper blinked at the space where she'd been standing. *What in the Everdark?*

Beside him, Annabeth sucked in a quick breath, and she reached out to grab Jasper's arm. It wasn't just him seeing things, then.

Cherry sighed and pulled his phone from his pocket, taking a few steps away from the crowd as he dialed.

Vonny's irritation faded, and she raised an eyebrow at Callan. "Did she just ... disappear?"

Callan scowled back darkly, and there was a sharp danger in his tone that Jasper had never heard before. "Wouldn't you be happy if she did? She's been through enough. You have to leave her alone."

Vonny's bitter laugh rang through the night. "*She* has been through enough? No, only I get to decide that."

Cherry's low voice drifted over as he murmured into his phone, "Hey, Rush. We need a Dark Corner pickup."

Vonny took a step back as though struck. Her eyes narrowed.

Jasper clenched his teeth. Dark Corner was the shroudpool that Vonny's son, Blaise, had fallen into. Was that where Tammy had ended up, and how? He stared at Cherry as he ended his call. This seemed like an everyday occurrence to him but was something they'd never discussed when together.

Why did he keep this a secret? This is the sort of thing the Darkfreys should know about, it could …

Jasper's chain of thought cut off with the blunt recollection of how his relationship with Cherry ended. Because he'd passed along information about the Howells that Cherry had provided him to the Darkfreys. It hurt that Cherry hadn't told him everything. As though Cherry never truly trusted him all along.

I did the right thing. The Darkfreys needed that info. For the mission. For the good of all against the Everdark.

Cherry moved closer to Callan but didn't quiet his voice when he said, "Come on, let's go. They don't deserve any more of our time."

"We're not done here yet." Nilson stalked forward, putting himself into Rylan's personal space. "We know you're in possession of stolen Darkfrey property. Lucas told us. The artifact belongs to us."

Rylan opened his mouth, but before he could say anything—

"Like hell it does," Harper said.

Nilson turned to her as though to a yapping puppy.

He grinned, the smile stretching his meaty face. "Shut it, bliv. You've got nothing to do with this."

She stepped up to him.

Tall as she was, he still dwarfed her, but fire filled her eyes. "I have everything to do with it. The Bane is where it belongs, which isn't with some entitled sock stuffed with rocks like you."

"Harper," Rylan growled in warning.

Nilson thrust a hand toward her chest in a shoving motion. She snatched it from the air, faster than sight, and twisted it away from her.

With a grunt of disgust, Harper dropped his arm and raised her fists.

"I'm not afraid of you," she spat, and swung.

Jasper held his breath. He'd already spent the last hour and a half hoping tonight would go smoothly so he could go home and get some sleep, forget his feelings for a while. Now, there was about to be a brawl between the Howell and the Darkfrey teams.

Jasper couldn't honestly say which side he'd fall on. Not with Cherry's big dark eyes watching him.

With a smack, Vonny caught Harper's punch in her grasp.

She put up a hand to warn Nilson back, and wrestled Harper's arm downward, grimacing with the effort. "You're a strong one."

"You have no idea," Harper snarled.

Vonny grinned, her profile skull-like beneath her blond, bobbed hair. "The shadyrs at Gorhanmere were especially strong, too."

Harper inhaled sharply and snatched her hand away. Callan reached for her, and she let herself be pulled back into the protective circle of Howells.

"Wow, you runts never fail to surprise me with the trouble you get into." Vonny shrugged, then motioned with two fingers to her brace. "Come along. Someone has to keep the town safe while this lot falls apart from the inside."

Nilson snarled at her for edging into his role as leader, and at everyone else for merely existing. He took the lead away from the other shadyrs.

Letting loose a ragged breath, Jasper whirled on the ball of his foot to follow his brace leader. At least it was over.

But it wasn't, because he was powerless against the urge to look back.

To see Cherry staring at him, with all that pain, and judgment, and loathing.

Jasper cursed between gritted teeth and turned away again. He trudged after Vonny and Nilson as they muttered under their breaths about the Howell team. Their brace had once been a family, but that family had been broken then broken apart again.

Jasper did his best to now separate the working aspect of hunting eidolghasts from the emotional aspect of being a part of the team. They weren't a family anymore, but it didn't matter if they could still get the job done. As long as he held brace rank, he was someone, worth something.

He may have to live a lie to remain part of the Darkfreys, but at least there he made a difference in this dark world. Even if he could never truly belong.

Chapter Five

Blearily, Everly rolled her sleeping bag up off the couch. Only the softest hint of morning light showed in the sky through the living room windows, but after waking in a panic, Everly only wanted to leave, and leave now.

A knee-buckling sting shot through her arm as she tried to push the silky fabric into its stuff sack. She exhaled through clenched teeth, trying not to whimper.

Peeling back the sleeve of her shirt, Everly eyed the damage the Bane had done to her, disheartened to see that it looked even worse than it did last night.

She'd cut her right forearm to free Zozo's soul, then cut her left to free Rylan's. She'd managed to release them both, but not without consequences.

Those two cuts had done a lot more damage than expected. Thin red lines spider-webbed beneath her skin, cracks marring the pale expanse of her arm as if she were fractured glass, waiting to shatter. It felt like she was breaking apart from the inside. Every movement sent more pain shooting along her nerve endings.

I just have to get out of here, out of this house, this town, and then I'll have time to heal.

Moving more carefully, she gave up on the sleeping bag and left it flopped loosely on top of her already-packed duffle bag. She tiptoed out to collect the last of her toiletries. Even the walk down the short hallway left her breathless and sheened in sweat. The door of the bathroom swung open to reveal Harper leaning in close to the mirror, wiping something dark green off her neck.

"Sorry, I didn't know you were up already."

"No probs, I'm all done in here if you want the bathroom," Harper said. "I wasn't expecting you to be up so early either, sleepyhead."

They shuffled past each other in the doorway, switching places. Everly leaned heavily on the basin, ran the tap, and splashed her face with water.

Harper hovered in the hallway. "Are you okay? You look pale."

"Yeah, just didn't sleep well." Except she had, deeply, so deep she couldn't wake herself from the terrifying and vivid nightmares that plagued her.

Everly stood up straighter and put on an *I'm fine*

smile. "It's good you're up, I'd like to get going soon. I have a few more things to pack, then I'm ready to leave whenever you are."

Everly scooped her toiletries into their case in one handful and zipped it closed.

Harper's face fell. "Oh. I was kind of hoping you might have changed your mind about leaving."

"Staying was never the plan," Everly said firmly.

"Yeah, I know, but I kind of like it here. We could totally make this our home."

"No!" The word dropped between them with explosive power.

A rush of heat and nausea washed over Everly, and she swallowed hard. This place wasn't home. It was good they were leaving. She carried a lifetime of bad memories of Shroudhaven—her mother's mental and emotional abuse, her father's death, plus Rylan pushing her out of his life, twice.

There was nothing more for Everly here.

As soon as they were ready, she intended to lock the door and never return. She'd already found a team of movers willing to come in and pack up the antiques shop, and she'd also found a good storage place back home where she could rent a garage for it all as they continued selling it off.

Her time in Shroudhaven was *officially* over.

She should have been ecstatic to get out. Away from there, the dragon would remain firmly locked away. She could live a normal life. Forget about eidolghasts and shadyrs and the man with the nebulous eyes who'd stolen her heart only to break it.

Instead of feeling happiness or relief, she felt hollow, slowly shattering apart.

Reining in her emotions, Everly murmured, "This isn't my home. It hasn't been for a really long time."

Harper's long lashes fluttered and her lips lifted in a smile. "Then we leave. I go where you go. You know that. The only thing I need to grab is the you-know-what and then we can hightail it out of here."

Everly's mouth popped open. "Really? You're all set?

"Mm-hm."

"Your makeup and camera gear?"

"Done."

"Final sales we need to post out?"

"Done."

"Fridge emptied?"

"Done."

"Did you even sleep last night?"

Harper tittered a high-pitched laugh and skipped off down the stairs.

Everly took a deep breath and let it out slowly, slumping over the sink again as she waited for a wave of dizziness to pass. Then she grabbed the last of her belongings and hauled her duffle bag downstairs, sleeping bag dangling under her arm.

Harper was waiting with her laptop bag over her shoulder and one small rose-gold suitcase by her side.

"Is that it?"

Harper nodded. "The rest is all loaded, ready to make our escape."

Everly wasn't sure when Harper had done everything but was grateful it meant no waiting. Maybe she really had been up all night, although she certainly didn't look like it.

Following Harper down the entrance hall, she did one quick doubletake back through the kitchen doorway. "Um, when did you repaint the cupboards?"

Out on the back porch, Harper just shrugged.

Stepping outside, Everly dug in the pocket of her blue jeans, pulling out the bundle of keys the estate attorney had given her. She reached back into the hallway and flipped the switch, extinguishing the candle-shaped lights. She needed no greater ritual than that to farewell the haunted abode. Turning the key, she listened to the lock tumble on her life in Shroudhaven.

"Goodbye, spooky house," Harper sang.

Not one for goodbyes, Everly just walked away, as she had once before.

In the backyard, the swing set was still overgrown

because she'd never had a chance to tackle the worst of that jungle. Maybe the next owners would.

A plate tucked into a small clearing in the weeds held only the barest dredges of watery blood from the raw meat left out the night before. She hadn't seen Zozo in real life or her dreams since she'd freed him, so had to hope it was him who'd consumed the meal. Maybe leaving the plate there would give the next owners the hint to put food out, too. She hoped Zozo would be okay.

Everly's duffle bag weighed a ton by the time she'd walked around the house. At least the front yard had cleaned up well since Everly first returned. Much less overgrown and wild than on the night when everything had gone to hell, right there, and her whole world changed.

She would never be able to rid herself of the vision of Rylan being torn apart. Of how she'd run to him, taken him in her arms, seen his blood glistening on his broken body. Of how something had also split open inside her, releasing the dragon. That *thing*. The soul-eater.

Her friends, the Howells, they'd all heard it. They had all heard Crowea call the thing inside Everly a soul-eater. Yet they went about as though it was no big deal. Maybe none of them truly believed it. None of them could *feel* the thing inside her like she felt it, its hunger, how close they were to becoming its next meal.

For all they knew, Rylan was the only soul that had

gotten caught up in any *eating* business, and she'd gotten him back out okay. No harm, no foul, right?

They had no idea how hard it was to stay in control, or the cost of extracting souls back from the being's grasp.

And they wouldn't know. Soon, Everly would be too far away.

Everly glanced up the street, shuddering at the way the fog drifted like ghosts beneath the dim light of dawn.

"I'll drive," Harper said as she unlocked the campervan and tossed her bags in, "so you can rest."

"Thanks." Everly grunted in pain as she set her duffel bag on top of Harper's matching suitcases.

She climbed into the passenger side as Harper took her seat behind the wheel.

The campervan's engine rolled over and Harper gently pulled away from the curb. "It wasn't all bad though, right? I think I'd like to come back sometime. To visit."

Everly slouched further into the chair and shoved her hands into the pockets of her red bomber jacket. "You'll have to come without me."

A beat of silence fell over them.

At the end of the block, Harper took a right turn, and Everly sat up, confused. "You're going the wrong way. The highway's the other way."

Harper squeezed the steering wheel between both hands, her green eyes glinting in the backwash from the headlights. "We've got farewells to make."

Everly's skin prickled. "Harper, no."

"You seriously thought we were going to zoom out of town at the crack of dawn without saying goodbye?"

Everly rubbed the growing tension between her eyebrows. Escaping without a word was *exactly* what she wanted. She didn't have the energy to deal with goodbyes, or the strength to listen to Lian telling her she should stay. Her arm hurt like crazy, and she felt hot and cold at the same time.

She just wanted to *go*. "We said everything that needed to be said yesterday."

"Did you say *goodbye*? No? Then you didn't say everything."

Everly turned to the window, avoiding Harper's eyes. "I don't want to wake them up."

"I'm sure they're still awake."

"Huh?"

"We're going. Driver's rules! And look, we're already here."

What was a short walk between the Boderleth residence and Howell House was even shorter by car. The campervan trundled down the long drive lined by silvery birch trees, and Lian's ancestral home emerged at the top of a low hill, all the porch lights shining in welcome.

The glow illuminated the weathered siding and flaking

ivory paint on the trim. The hundred-plus-year-old house hulked against the pink-blushed sky, still quite lovely in its decay.

In the shadows beyond the porch lights, something moved and rustled in the underbrush, and Everly's head whipped toward it. A curved, tan tail that looked suspiciously like Zozo's poked above the bushes but vanished almost instantly.

It seemed the Howell gang was awake, and a few of them sat on the porch. As the campervan drew closer, they rose to meet it. Callan, Cherry, and Lian came down the steps, but Rylan remained at a distance.

And there's the instant regret. Everly groaned pitifully.

Harper shut off the engine and leaned over, giving her a one-armed hug. "You can do this."

"I'm not sure about that." *Emotionally or physically,* Everly thought as another wave of nausea left her head spinning.

"Look, I'm not saying that this is my last-ditch effort for Rylan to pull his head out of his sculpted ass and beg you to stay, but I'm not *not* saying that."

"You just said it!"

Harper sighed, then squeezed Everly one more time before reaching past to open her door, practically pushing her out.

As Harper hopped out her side and they walked up

the path together, the door to Denny's trailer slammed open and he appeared in his tiny porch light, shirtless and carrying a beer.

"Ugh," Harper said.

"We could have avoided him entirely," Everly pointed out.

"Stop dodging your issues. These people love you. I mean, maybe not this guy, not in a way we want, anyway," she amended with a glare at Denny's leering grin. "But the rest of them do."

Lian reached them first and wrapped her thin arms around Everly, tugging her in for a hug. Her long cardigan sweater was as gray as her hair, and the fabric smelled like a mix of citrus and eucalyptus.

It was the smell of home.

Well, Everly's surrogate home, anyway.

Everly raised her arms to return the hug, wincing at the pain it caused.

When Lian released her, the older woman stepped away and studied Everly with worried gray-brown eyes. "You're not off already, are you?"

"Yeah, making an early start." Everly studiously kept her eyes from turning up toward the porch. "We just stopped to say a quick goodbye."

"Oh, I thought we might have more time! We haven't even properly celebrated you bringing Rylan back to us.

Can you at least stay for breakfast?"

Before Everly could refuse, Callan said, "We've got waffles! We can do a farewell feast. Don't leave without waffles."

He reached for her, and Everly let him bring her into a brotherly hug. Her chest ached at the thought of never seeing him or his mother again. They'd been her family when her own hadn't been capable. Them, and Rylan.

Everly could see Rylan's feet up on the porch through the corner of her eye. He was just standing there, wouldn't even come close to her. Shame and queasiness heated her face.

"That's okay, I don't want to trouble you with all that. We should keep moving." Everly thumb pointed back to the car, then reminded herself through gritted teeth to restrain the hand gestures.

"I'm going to miss you two." Cherry leaned in and hugged them both, adding in a whisper, "My confidants."

"Oh, but Rush and Tammy aren't back from Dark Corner yet!" Lian declared. "You have to say goodbye to them, too. And you might as well grab a coffee for the road while you wait."

Everly could feel prickles of sweat breaking across her forehead, and stars floated in her eyes.

She needed to get back into the van, to sit down, to be leaving. "I don't think we have time ..."

Lian raised one thin eyebrow. "Are you on the clock or something? Another twenty minutes won't hurt anything."

Everly wobbled on her feet, shaking her head.

Lian's shrewd eyes locked onto her. "Are you feeling okay? You still look unwell."

Swallowing, Everly put energy into her smile. "Oh, no, I'm fine, it's just that the Bane is in the van."

"Well come inside away from the thing!" Lian waved them on and led the way back up into the house.

Everly's gaze followed her for too long, catching Rylan's eye for a moment. She hastily turned away, but not before seeing the seething distaste there. Maybe the others didn't look at her like the monster she was, but he knew.

Harper hooked arms with Callan and Cherry and like the traitor she was, she followed Lian up to the front door.

"No, Harper, we really should—"

"Maybe a beer for the road, too," Denny crowed.

Twenty minutes, I can do twenty minutes.

Everly took a step forward, crunching the gravel under her boot. Her feet were heavy, and the heat that had been radiating in waves from her arm seemed exceptionally hot. Her eyesight wavered, blurred, and a tiny chill of panic snaked up her spine. Nausea swelled inside her. Her head pounded and swam.

I can't do twenty minutes.

"Harper—" her voice failed.

She stumbled.

Black edges pressed in on her vision.

Then her legs gave out and she collapsed.

Through dimmed vision and thunderous agony, she saw Rylan, his face like white marble, close to hers, his teeth long and sharp. She felt as he caught her in his unyielding arms.

Voices surrounded her as all went dark.

"Evie!"

"What happened?"

"What is that on her wrist?"

Chapter Six

Everly's eyes fluttered open to a cool, dim room.

Shock rushed through her, chasing away the last of the cobwebs from her dreamless sleep. She swallowed through a cotton-dry mouth. The shapes of people moved nearby, but her vision remained blurry. She blinked to clear it.

Four navy walls cradled her, each of them dotted with dozens of stars—glow-in-the-dark stickers that she'd helped put up a lifetime ago. A vintage television still hunched on the small dresser next to the equally aged gaming console they'd once spent hours playing.

She could still recall the theme song of their favorite platformer so clearly.

The room, Rylan's room, was like a childhood dream, at once achingly familiar yet so distant. Much like the man her childhood sweetheart had grown into.

As her sight cleared, she realized that the poster of their favorite anime show that had been taped to the wall—that had been there when she'd last been in the room—was gone.

Rylan had only been back in his childhood bedroom for one night, and that was the change he'd chosen to make.

Did Rylan tear it down because it reminded him of me?

The thought brought hot tears to her eyes, blurring them again.

"Shh, it's okay." Lian appeared at the side of the bed, holding out two little white pills as she reached for a bottle of water on the nightstand. "Here. Take this."

Everly considered refusing them and saying she'd just had a panic attack, but the way she felt, she needed whatever pain relief she could get. Propping herself up on her better elbow, she accepted them.

Her other arm burned as she popped the pills in her mouth and took the water bottle. She gagged as she washed the pills down her dry throat, then tried to hand the water back to Lian.

"More," Lian ordered. "Drink at least half."

Everly made a petulant face but obeyed.

Lian waited patiently, then took the bottle back and set it on the table.

Everly spared a glance at the clock on the nightstand. Barely ten minutes had passed since she showed up at

Howell House then fainted, but she felt as though she'd been under for days. She tried to get into a more upright position.

Lian stepped closer to the edge of the mattress, crossed her arms, and her motherly concern morphed to a glare. "You're not going anywhere."

"I'm fine, really." Her entire body felt like it was running several degrees too hot.

All it took was a light push from Lian on her shoulder to send her flopping back against the pillows.

The glaring continued.

Meeting Lian's icy gaze, Everly asked, "What?"

"Why didn't you tell us about your arm?"

Everly's cheeks heated even more. "What about it?"

"Ev. We know." Harper's disapproving tone drifted from the doorway.

Everly found Harper standing in the glow of the hallway light, and beside her, Rylan.

All three of them looked at her as though she'd been caught kicking an orphan's kitten.

She was used to that disappointed distaste from Rylan, but the vampire form he was in made it more vicious. His lips were spread, revealing his fangs beneath, and his bone-white skin made him seem like an ancient, judgmental statue.

Generally, shadyrs didn't take that form unless there

was a vasmire close, but not in this case.

In this case, Everly was the problem. Since releasing his soul, Rylan's shadyr senses now reacted to Everly like they would an eidolghast.

And nobody knew why.

But it gave him yet another reason to not want to be near her.

Lian, clearly tired of waiting for Everly to own up to the situation, sighed. "Were you going to tell any of us about this?"

She brushed her fingers lightly over Everly's wrist.

Everly intended to keep playing innocent and ask, *About what?* since the last she'd looked, the damage from the Bane was hidden beneath a bandage beneath her sleeve.

But a quick glance showed that the red cracks had spread downward, creeping over her wrist and into her palm. "Oh."

"Oh? That's all you have to say?" Rylan's voice was gravelly.

Everly shrugged, the movement awkward in her prone position. "It's nothing. Don't worry about it."

Harper stepped closer. "That wasn't there yesterday. I saw the bandage you put over the cuts from the Bane. Whatever is going on, it's coming from those cuts and it's spreading."

"I'm sure it will heal," Everly said, frowning at how it

had grown.

"It's clearly getting worse," Rylan grumbled. "There's more than there was even ten minutes ago."

Lian gently picked up Everly's hand, studying the strange pattern. "It looks as if you're cracking apart from the inside. Like a broken mirror."

"We have to fix this." Rylan took a step closer, and his skin rippled, black smoke swirling around him as he shifted away from vampire and toward werewolf.

With a grunt, he stepped back again. "From what I understand of what Crowea said, the being inside Everly is only a piece of something that had been broken in the past by the Bane."

He pointed an accusing finger at Harper. "And you let her hack into herself with that same artifact? No wonder she's falling apart."

Harper gasped. "Let her? As soon as I saw what happened the first time, I tried to stop her the second. You're the reason she was dead set on slicing herself up again."

"What's done is done!" Lian snapped. "Let's focus on a way to fix it."

Harper harrumphed and folded her arms, a begrudging pout on her lips. "Look, I think Rylan's probably right. This isn't just about the Bane, it's about the thing that's inside Everly, how it is reacting to it. Cutting normal humans with the Bane doesn't do this."

"How do you know?" Lian asked.

Harper's mouth twisted and she huffed, "Okay, fine, so I might have scratched myself with it while trying to wrestle it away from our stabby martyr over there."

Everly's mouth dropped. "You said that didn't happen."

"I didn't want you to worry! You'd been through enough. Anyway, it was fine, completely a nonissue."

Everly knitted her brows. There hadn't even been a mark on Harper's skin ...

Harper continued briskly, "If it's the dragon that's breaking and taking Everly's body with it, we need to somehow strengthen and heal it. Find another piece of it maybe."

A chill ran down Everly's spine. "That sounds risky. I already have trouble controlling the thing. If it were even stronger ..."

Staring down at the floor, Rylan said, "If making it stronger will save you, then we need it."

A loaded silence filled the room, and Everly fidgeted with the blanket between her fingers. All three of the others stared at her expectantly. She sighed.

"Fine. But how would we even do that? We're at a dead end with whatever my dragon is." Other than *soul-eater*, a term Everly noticed everyone had been skirting around. "Or how and why it's in me."

Harper perked up. "If monsters are a thing ... is necromancy? Is there any way to speak to the dead, maybe bring back Mr. or Mrs. Boderleth? They might know something about why Everly is this way?"

Rylan let out a short, sharp laugh. "Even if they knew something, which I doubt, that isn't possible. Any secrets they may have had died with them."

Lian reached over and gave Everly's hand a gentle squeeze. "Our only other info is what the eidolghast referred to: the 'Beast of Teeth and Stars.' We're in possession of the *Bane* of Teeth and Stars, but as far as I'm aware, there are no other artifacts associated with that very specific phrase."

Harper gasped. "Oh! What about *other* artifacts? Surely there's something at Darkfrey Estate that can heal? I'm all in for round two of raiding that place."

Lian shook her head. She still hadn't released Everly's fingers, as if she knew how much her helping hand had eased the shame inside her.

"I'm unaware of any 'healing' artifacts," she said regretfully. "But I do think there is one other clue we've overlooked."

Everly tensed, expecting *soul-eater* to finally come into the conversation.

"The being inside you is made of *light*, while the eidolghasts are creatures of darkness. That seems relevant, don't you think?"

Everly *hadn't* thought of that before. She'd always assumed that the creature in her was a monster, an eidolghast of some kind.

She asked, "What does that mean? I thought the Everdark was just that, all darkness. Could a creature of light come from there? Or does that mean it's from somewhere else entirely?"

The floorboards creaked as Rylan shifted position, leaning against the doorframe. "Actually, the Everdark wasn't always dark."

"I mean, it's in the name," Harper muttered. "It's not like they called it the *Recentlydark*."

Rylan shot her a glare.

She rolled her eyes. "But what do I know?"

"A lot for a bliv," Rylan said, sounding more frustrated than approving. "Honestly, most shadyrs would think the same. Only history nuts like Annabeth really talk about how the Everdark didn't start out as a realm of darkness and monsters. She would always go on about that, along with all the other pre-crossover history theories and religious studies most shadyrs aren't interested in."

"Too busy fighting monsters to care where the monsters came from and why," Lian said.

Rylan continued, "Anyway, the point is it was the ghasts that *made* it that realm dark."

"How?" Everly asked, not sure she wanted to hear the

answer.

"That's what eidolghasts do—they come to a dimension and slowly take all the light away until it's entirely beshadowed. That's why it's so important we fight them back. That's why our shadyr ancestors from that dimension fled to this one when all the light was gone. Annabeth lectured our brace on it all the time." Rylan's voice grew stronger as he talked, more excited and intense.

While he'd been lying in his strange coma, Annabeth had shown up at the Boderleth residence and asked to see him. During her visit, she'd revealed to Everly not only that she had a thing for Rylan, but that she believed his heart belonged to someone else.

The way Rylan looked as he spoke now, Everly wasn't convinced it didn't belong to Annabeth.

"So there may have been creatures of light like my dragon in the Everdark at some point? It might still have come from there?" Everly wanted to feel some relief, that she didn't have an eidolghast possessing her body.

But regardless of what label the being had, she knew deep in her gut that it wasn't *good*.

Lian nodded thoughtfully. "That would make the Beast of Teeth and Stars an enemy of the eidolghasts. Which tracks based on what we know. Still, the ghasts won that realm, with no other trace of creatures of light having survived. We can only make guesses. They predate our history."

"Which means," Everly said, her voice sharp with irritation, "that we haven't gotten any closer to knowing what this ... *soul-eater* inside me really is."

The name hung heavy in the room. Holding back a grunt of effort, Everly sat up, pushed the blankets away, and swung her legs over the edge of the bed.

"Look, I'm fine, really. We don't know that the wounds won't heal themselves in time. I'm sure they will. I just need to leave, and recover, away from all of ... this."

Rylan caught her eye on the last word. He opened his mouth to speak.

A light trilling sound shot through the room, and Lian jumped, then shoved her hand into the oversized pocket of her cardigan. She extracted her phone, glanced at the screen, then frowned.

"It's Rush," she informed them as she accepted the call. "Hello?"

Lian listened intently for a moment, her expression changing, and all the color faded from her so that she was nearly as gray as her cardigan.

"We'll be right there." She hung up, face grim. "We have to go. Tammy's missing."

CHAPTER SEVEN

Rylan clutched the handle above his head as his brother careened the packed SUV through the empty, early morning streets of Shroudhaven.

He was half-transformed into his vasmire form, thanks to Everly's presence at the very back of the vehicle, which heightened his senses and made his brother's wild driving hurt his head.

"Do you have to take corners like that?"

Callan didn't spare a glance at him, all attention on the road. "We might not be a brace in the Darkfrey's sense, but we are a team. They are *my* team and my responsibility. And unlike the Darkfreys, I care about losing one of them."

"Ouch. Point taken, right to the heart."

Lian, who sat directly behind Rylan, leaned forward. "Keep up the pace. She's not just team. She's family."

Rylan turned and caught her eye. Yesterday, when he'd risen from apparent death, she had been all motherly love and welcoming arms, but now, there was something harsh about how she stared him down.

She spoke in a low voice, close to his ear. "I know it's only been a day, but you need to start shaking your Darkfrey habits. We do things differently."

Yeah, I'm getting that impression, Rylan thought, but before he could say anything his mother continued, "And your misguided hostility to Everly has to end."

Rylan tensed, a million arguments and excuses firing through his brain. But he didn't owe those to anyone, even his estranged mother.

"I know what I'm doing."

"No, you don't."

Rylan spun in his seat, staring the woman down. "Don't treat me like a child."

"Then stop acting like one."

Beside him, Callan coughed a laugh, but quickly schooled his face and gave his brother a sympathetic look.

So this is what it will be like being back at home, is it?

"Ha, sick burn from your mom," Denny chortled from beside Lian.

She smacked him on the shoulder.

Callan leaned across and not subtly whispered, "Not sure if you noticed, but Mom is hardcore now."

"Well," she muttered, "losing your kids will do that to a person."

Callan's grin failed. "We're back now."

Rylan nodded. "Both of us."

In his youthful hot-headedness to become the best monster hunter there was, in his bitter anger in the belief that it was his mother who had kept him from that path, it had been easy to distance himself from the pain he caused her when he left and took Callan with him. She had changed because of that. They all had. He could only wonder what sort of family they would be now.

"And I'm so glad you are. But let's not lose anyone else," she said sternly.

Callan refocused on his driving, putting on a boost of speed, but Lian held Rylan's gaze.

Rylan's eyes turned to Everly, who was sitting in the back between Harper and Cherry. She still looked so pale, wearing that rigid smile that wasn't fooling anyone.

No, I can't lose her. That's why she can't stay in this dark and deadly town.

He already couldn't forgive himself that she was now falling apart from what she did to save *him*. He would fix that. Save her. And then say goodbye. This little excursion was just delaying the inevitable.

Dark Corner shroudpool was close to Howell House, in a section of thick forest that butted up to the

Wyrdwoods—a place full of eidolghasts and other things that prowled beneath a sunless canopy. Rylan didn't think anyone went there, until he learned about Tammy's curse when the Howells used it to escape a beshadowed nightmare in Rook's Hotel.

Rylan hadn't known Tammy prior to waking up, but she seemed like a good kid. A little younger than his brother, on the darker end of teenage attitude and sullen, but considering what he knew of her past, he couldn't blame her.

He didn't know the details but remembered when Tammy had been exiled from the Darkfreys. She'd had some part in the death of the Mesmans' boy. Her Everdark-blackened hands had been seen as the visible mark of her guilt. He'd only learned later that this was the price she paid for trying to reach into a shroudpool to save her friend.

She'd only been around thirteen. Rylan had been secretly glad when he heard Lian took her in. The way the kid looked when she left, he wasn't sure she would've survived otherwise. It was clear some Darkfreys hoped for that outcome. That had been the first time Rylan ever questioned his place there. It took him another three years, and an attempt on his life, to finally break from that establishment himself.

Callan pulled to an abrupt stop behind Rushelle's yellow sports car and cut the engine. The buxom blonde leaned on the back bumper of her car, fire-engine-red lipstick glowing in the darkness. Her beehive hairdo and the sharp black wings on her eyes made her look like a vintage pinup.

She straightened as the team piled from the SUV, her usually cheerful face drawn and tight.

"I've tried to call her five times," Rushelle greeted them, her hands twisting with worry in front of her tight yellow tank top. "It rings, but she's not answering. Poor duck, I hope nothing's happened to her."

Lian glanced at the tree line. "Did you go in?"

Rushelle nodded, and the typewriter charm on her gold necklace clinked against the chain. "Nothing looks out of place. The signs are all still up on the fence, and the opening in the chain-link where Tammy comes through is still hidden. I did a quick turn around the shroudpool, and it hasn't changed either. She's just ... not there."

"She always teleports here," Callan said. "She's never gone anywhere else."

Lian ran her fingers back through her graying hair, her gaze darting over the forest.

"I'm not sensing any ghasts nearby. So something either happened to her within the beshadowed area, or she somehow teleported somewhere else. Okay." She puffed out a breath, rubbing her eyebrow. "Okay, we're going to split up—"

Before she could complete her thought, a chorus of tinny sounds chimed within the group. Rylan watched as Lian, Rushelle, Cherry, and Callan each checked their phones.

A group text. A group Rylan wasn't yet part of.

Rushelle perked up. "It's from Tammy."

Lian's voice shook as she read, "Don't worry about me—I'm off to see about making a wish."

Harper, who had been fussing over Everly, glanced up, confused. "That's it? What does that mean? Is Shroudhaven harboring a genie?"

Cherry shook his head, his voice haunted. "No. No genies."

Harper lifted her palms upward. "I feel like I have to ask these things, you guys are always holding out on me."

"No genies," Callan agreed through gritted teeth. "But we do have an island in the middle of a dangerous lake with a rock that supposedly grants wishes."

Lian stared past them all, unfocused and pale. "*If* you survive the swim."

Phones were pocketed again, and they were back on the road within seconds.

Rylan understood the rush—Myrkur Lake was a death trap. But he also detested that they were on this trip in the first place. This was an unwanted distraction. Everly was fading by the second.

Rylan forced back his anger before he put his fist through the passenger door. Tammy didn't know, had no reason to know she was stealing time from Everly. The kid must have been in a bad state to be heading in a direction nobody came back from. She must know that. Every shadyr knew that about Myrkur Lake.

It was a legendary place among Shroudhaven teenagers. In a small town, there wasn't much to do except hang out and make their own fun. Some of the more daredevil teens liked to do that by challenging each other to take a harrowing swim across the black depths.

The legend stated that if you survived the dangerous swim to the island in the center, you'd find a strange stone there. Touching it was said to grant a wish.

The problem was that the island was a known shroudpool location, and the beshadowing that accompanied it had spread throughout the lake. The water was inky black and frigid, full of currents that seemed to have sentience, and twisted, possessed sea creatures looking for their next meal.

Thankfully, most kids chickened out after dipping their toes in the water.

Most.

Rylan had heard of at least three drownings during his lifetime, and not a single report of anyone who made it to the island and returned.

Morning had broken, but the sun was hidden behind

heavy black clouds and thick fog. The SUV zoomed down the highway as Rushelle followed in her coupe, headlights shining into the rearview mirror.

Callan slammed his palm on the steering wheel. "Vonny put this into her head, the way she was digging in this morning, telling Tammy she should wish things were different."

"She did?" Lian asked. "I'm going to need a word with that woman. She knows damn well there're no wishes to be granted in this town."

Harper leaned forward from the back.

"But how do we know for sure the wish thing isn't real? 'Cause maybe that could help, you know ..." She flicked her gaze across to Everly beside her.

"I'm fine," Everly said with a crackly voice.

"I know because that's why I left the Darkfreys in the first place." From her spot in the middle, Lian turned from Harper to stare out the side door.

"I grew up training there like most shadyr kids, alongside my best friend. Sidney ... She was different, you know? People used to put a whole bunch of harmful labels on others back in the day. Still do, I guess, and I don't feel like it's fair for me to slap a label on her now without an approval from her I can never get. But for a place that kicked someone like Cherry out, Darkfrey Estate was *bad* for her."

Harper tutted and looped an arm over Cherry's

shoulder. He grumbled something incoherent, still sullen since the run-in with Rylan's old brace.

Lian continued, "Still, being a shadyr was everything to Sid. She fought against every true part of herself to fit in there."

Rylan swallowed. He'd never had the full story on why his mom split from the Darkfreys back before he was born.

From the distracted look in Callan's eyes, maybe he hadn't either. "What happened?"

"No matter how Sid tried to hide herself, the in-crowd took a disliking to her," Lian said sadly. "She was kicked out, on a technicality, like Cherry, but everyone knew why. She was exiled. She swam Myrkur Lake because she wanted to wish herself 'normal.' She just wanted to be accepted by her own, and she ended up getting dead, when there was nothing *wrong* with her!"

The last words burst from her.

Rylan's hand twitched to reach out to his mother, but Everly reached forward first, putting her hand on the older woman's shoulder. "I'm sorry you lost her."

"Loss ... happens. But I didn't lose her. They killed her, them and their awful, unfair, hateful ways." Lian took a shuddering breath and smoothed back her hair with one hand. "That's why I left the estate and never looked back. She's why I take in anyone who defects from the Darkfreys. Anyone."

All eyes in the van turned briefly to Denny, who seemed completely oblivious to any shade thrown his way.

"Shame that they're no better now," Cherry grumbled from the back, this time just loud enough to hear.

Lian shook her head. "A damn shame. Thirty years have passed and *nothing's* changed. You either fit the Darkfrey mold, or you suffer the consequences. Some of you more than others."

Cherry sunk further into Harper's embrace. Rylan knew the consequences were many. He knew Cherry's parents. Both shadyrs, both fully indoctrinated Darkfreys.

As were Tammy's.

And now the two young shadyrs had been disowned for who they were, not just by their kind, but by their own family.

Rylan's shoulders grew tense with tangible contempt for the Darkfreys. Did the others still see him as one? He had been until so recently that part of him felt like he was. He'd had similar concerns and disagreements about Darkfrey ways, too, but had always been—he could hardly admit it—too scared to say any of it out loud.

His voice wavered as he said, "If anything, they've gotten worse."

Callan shot a glance at his brother, then returned his eyes to the road. "The whole world is changing, for the better. The Darkfreys can sense that they're a dying breed and they're digging their claws in deeper, screaming louder in denial. You're not like them. Just so we're clear though, I made the right decision to get out first."

"I hope I'm not going to regret this." Everly's voice drifted up to the front, low and a little strained. "What about you, Denny? Why did you leave the Darkfreys?"

There was a soft sympathy in her tone that twanged a string in Rylan's chest. That her heart was big enough to even care about that tone-deaf meat sack ... even when she was suffering herself.

Why does she have to be like that? Why can't she just think about herself for once?

Cherry cracked a grin for the first time in a while. "Because he's too big of a jerk even for them."

"That's not why!" Denny said gruffly, as though Cherry had offered the reason seriously. "Those asshats put me on a cleaner team. Me! Refused to give me a spot on a brace. I'm better than that. I chose to leave."

Callan scoffed. "You're such a liar. Everyone knows you were hitting on Alexis, and she tattled to Daddy that you were harassing her."

Harper gave a desperate-for-gossip gasp. "Who's Alexis?"

"Alexis Darkfrey," Callan clarified. "As in Mordan Darkfrey's only daughter."

"No way!"

"That's right, no way," Denny said hotly. "You've got the story wrong. What me and Alexis had was mutual."

"Could you be more deluded?" Cherry snapped. "She's an eleven—"

"So we're right in each other's league," Denny said, gesturing to his body.

"—And she's married. With children. To someone who isn't you."

Denny smirked and shrugged. "Forbidden fruit is *always* better."

"Oh look, here I am, regretting it," Everly muttered.

"Gross!" Harper squealed, and the rest of the van burst out in insults.

Rylan exchanged amused glances with his mother, who remained silent.

For a moment, things felt almost normal.

Unfortunately, there was nothing normal about their situation. Rylan was exhausted. He'd wanted to shower and hit the sack after the hunt but had been waylaid by Everly's collapse. Now they were driving all over town to try to help Tammy, who clearly didn't want their help to begin with.

Being stuck in the SUV with Everly, which kept him in a constant state of half-transformation, was wearing him down. Her injuries were clearly wearing on her, too.

Callan swung off the highway onto a rough service

road. Rylan knew it well, having done patrol out there in the past. Much like the other known shroudpool areas, the Darkfreys had worked secretly within the community to have the lake marked unsafe for public access, with some story about hazardous chemicals.

Not that it stopped everyone.

Sneaking in and scaring each other on the water's edge was something of a teenage rite of passage. That's why the Darkfreys kept the lake on their regular beat.

Rylan half hoped there would be a Darkfrey brace out there now, to have already stopped Tammy from entering the water.

But when the end of the road and the tall chain-link fence came into view, there were no other vehicles.

Once the SUV stopped moving, Rylan hopped from the passenger side as the others piled out around him. Callan, Denny, Lian, Cherry ...

The other two were taking their time.

Rylan hovered uncertainly by, fighting against the change as best he could, as Harper reached back into the vehicle. Everly leaned heavily on her as she climbed out of the back seat.

The headlights of Rushelle's car coming to a stop behind them washed over Everly.

She looked ... rough. Shadows grew beneath her eyes, purple against too-pale skin. Back in his bedroom, she'd piled her silvery hair into a messy bun and demanded to join them. Even though he and his mother had attempted to convince her to remain behind and rest, they'd failed.

He wished she had *listened*. She was in no shape to be out, much less on this wild goose chase to stop Tammy from doing something terrible.

Everly met his gaze and she straightened, linking arms with Harper.

She rolled her eyes, likely at the hard look on his face, and hissed, "I'm fine."

Tammy needed to be stopped before she became the lake's next victim, there was no doubt about that. But her recklessness pissed him off since it could be dangerous for Everly. Not just for her *being here* and insisting to help, but for the fact that her injury needed to be the top priority right now.

She wasn't fine.

Rylan didn't want her there, but he also didn't want her to be alone, out of his sight. Not until she was better. He'd only just gotten his arms under her when she'd fainted that morning ...

If it happened again, would he be there to catch her?

CHAPTER EIGHT

Tammy hadn't expected the water to be *so* cold.

Granted, Shroudhaven and its surrounding areas weren't known for sun-kissed weather, but Myrkur Lake wasn't just cold—it was bone-numbingly frigid.

As soon as the water reached her knees, she began to shiver, which made moving forward harder and slower than it should have been.

Not a lick of morning sunlight pierced the heavy sky to offer her warmth, and a soup of fog swirled over the surface of the lake. She'd left her boots back on the bank, and her bare toes sank into deep, squelchy silt as she trudged farther into the water. After several moments, she couldn't feel her toes at all.

But what was a little frostbite if there was *any* possibility she could bring Blaise back? She was coming away from this with him, or not at all.

Either way, the rest of the world would be better off.

Vonny's hardened face and verbal assault were seared into Tammy's mind. She could take the hatred. It was the pain beneath that cut her to the quick.

The guilt Tammy lived with on a daily basis had built into a painful throbbing in Vonny's presence. When her curse brought her again to Dark Corner, right to the scene of the crime, she knew Vonny was right. She did wish things were different.

Vonny and her husband, Kole, wanted nothing more than to have their son back.

Tammy would give anything for the same.

When the water level reached up to touch its icy burn to her ribcage, she pushed off and fell into a shivering, painful swim.

The wind cut over her face and shaved head like thousands of tiny knives.

She jolted as something like bony fingers brushed against her leg, and her heartbeat pounded madly as she imagined a dozen terrible monsters beneath the black water.

She put on a burst of speed to get away from whatever it was.

The island sat dark and silent ahead. Her limbs burned and ached. It still seemed so far away.

A strong current passed beneath her, tangling her legs.

Tammy let out a yelp and lost her buoyancy, bobbing beneath the choppy surface.

The dark water swallowed her like a hungry weroth, sucking her down. Tammy kicked and flailed her arms, swimming furiously for the surface. She was in total darkness—not even the barest hint of morning light from above penetrated the water.

She managed to splash back into the air, gasping frantically for oxygen.

Turned around, she saw the headlights of two cars arriving.

Before they'd even fully stopped moving, doors opened and slammed, and several familiar silhouettes lined up on the shore.

Two led the charge, both of them jogging for the edge of the lake faster than the rest of the crew. A blinding spotlight popped on and swept the water.

Tammy threw up a hand as the beam landed on her face.

"Tammy!" Callan yelled. "Get out of there!"

"Come back," Lian called. "Please!"

Tammy pursed her lips in irritation, then turned around and started swimming again.

She'd already come this far. She intended to finish the journey.

The light jerked madly for a minute, and over the

splashing of her arms, she thought she heard arguing on the shore.

Then the sound of more splashing joined hers.

Tammy halted and turned to see Callan, illuminated by the flashlight now in his mother's hand. He swam with Olympic swiftness toward Tammy.

"What the Everdark are you doing?" Tammy shrieked. "Don't follow me."

Callan kept swimming, so Tammy turned away, trying to get away from him. But she couldn't outpace his longer limbs.

As soon as he surfaced within arm's reach, she lashed out at him, splashing water his way. "Get *out* of here, Callan! I don't need you to babysit me."

"That's not ... Just stop, you have to go back, it's not safe." He eased forward, treading water with an irritating finesse—like everything else he did. *Infuriating.* His long hair was plastered to his face, putting his sharp cheekbones on display, and Lian's spotlight danced over him, making his concerned features sharper.

"Ugh, I told you not to worry about me. Just go."

Water dripped from his eyelashes as he stared her down. "I'm not leaving without you."

Tammy's heart fluttered, but she firmly shoved it down and away. "I've got to do this."

"What, die? Because that's all that's going to happen."

"Who cares?" Tammy said hotly.

She lifted her hands from the water, brandishing her blackened fingers. In the flashlight's beam, they looked even more charred and horrific than usual.

"I'm already cursed. Who cares what happens to me?"

"*I* do."

Tammy blinked the water from her eyes and a shiver ran from the nape of her neck to her toes.

Her teeth rattled as she spoke. "No, you don't. You just want to be a good little team leader. Just let me do this. I *have* to do this."

She whirled around and swam for the island once more. Hard fingers snatched at her arm and dragged her back. Tammy thrashed against Callan's grip.

Their legs tangled beneath as they both treaded water, and Callan didn't release her arm. His irises, shadowed by his brows, appeared black, but they sparkled like tiny universes.

"You aren't at fault for what happened to Blaise."

"I'm not? Gee, how dumb of me to think it was me, there, in my body, being at fault." Tammy attempted to yank her arm from his grasp to no avail.

His gaze landed heavily on her. Devastating. Judging.

He tugged her closer until their chests brushed together. Tammy froze, legs and arms going weak as his warmth came through their body armor.

"What happened to Blaise was an *accident*," Callan said softly.

"I couldn't hold on!" The words burst from her, raw and ragged as tears stung the back of her throat. "*We* went to Dark Corner. *We* started a ritual thinking we could close the shroudpool. *We* wanted to be big damn heroes. But *I* lost Blaise. *Me*."

"So, what? You're just going to give up? Swim head-on into a beshadowing?"

"It's worth it." If there was a chance, any at all, she would sell her soul, she would trade places, she would *not* be careful what she wished for.

Nearby, the water splashed.

Callan and Tammy both whipped toward the sound. Tammy held her breath as her gaze swept the black surface.

"That wasn't you?" Tammy clarified, turning her wide eyes on Callan.

He shook his head and released her arm. "No."

Another splash. This time from behind Tammy. She turned around, arms knifing through the water as she searched wildly across the lake. Lian's spotlight pierced through the fog all around them, but under the glittering surface, the lake was a total blackout.

More movement—behind Callan.

His back bumped against hers. "We need to get out of here."

Lian's voice drifted from the shore. "Cal? What is it?"

Before he could respond, the water separated next to Tammy's elbow and a slick form crested over the surface. The water churned. Tammy let out a startled cry and darted back—into the empty space where Callan had been.

"Callan?" Tammy cried, whipping her head side to side.

There was no sign of him. She dove. Headfirst, down into the inky, skull-chilling water.

A burst of released air bubbled up against her face. Fingertips brushed against hers. She grabbed on, tight.

A slimy, snake-like thing wriggled past her, sliding across her lower back. Tammy pulled at Callan's hand, but could only feel them being dragged farther down, faster than she thought possible. The water whipped past her like a strong wind.

Something wrapped around her thigh, smooth and slippery but with a vice-like grip. It jerked at her body, pulling against the bond between her and Callan. She clung tight, adding her second hand. He squeezed back in return.

Lungs burning, Tammy kicked out with her free leg, trying to detach the creature, but she couldn't find the body beyond the tentacle. She didn't even know what the creature was, but considering she hadn't transformed into one of her shadyr forms, she knew it wasn't an eidolghast. Too bad, since if it had been, at least she'd have some way of defending herself.

A second slithery tentacle tangled around her foot, and something sharp sunk into her calf. A gasp of precious air escaped her mouth.

Don't panic. Don't panic. Don't panic.

If I vanish out of here and leave Callan alone, if he dies here because of me ... I could never ...

Her renewed kicking and struggling made no difference. The creature had an iron grip, and she was quickly losing feeling in her leg. She was losing feeling everywhere.

Oh my ghast. I'm going to die.

She wasn't afraid of death—not really. Not for her.

But she didn't want *him* to die.

Callan's fingernails dug into her skin and her small, blackened palm slipped through his. *Not again.*

She fought against the crushing emptiness of her lungs, putting all her energy into holding on as her senses faded. *I can't do it. I can't hold on.*

Blinding light flashed all around her, turning her eyelids pink.

Tammy's stomach lurched, and her eyes popped open. Golden illumination filled the underwater world around her, fading off into a murky horizon. The glow highlighted the shiny, ghost-pale hide of two oversized, squid-like creatures wrapped around her and Callan. Gaping, beaked maws detached in shock from their victim's flesh. Their bulbous eyes were a strange, milky white.

The squid things released Tammy and darted away, disappearing into the darkness beyond the light with a high-pitched squeal that sounded like a cry of pain.

Her gaze darted down, following them, and she watched, horrified, as dozens of hideous silhouettes beneath Callan swam away from the light in a cacophony of alien moans and screeches. Through the water, she could feel their screams in her bones.

Callan kicked up to her level, grabbed onto her, and together they swam for the surface. It was so far away. She flailed, real panic setting in as her lungs burned for oxygen. Callan gripped her arms and yanked her upward, dragging her alongside him.

Tammy breached the surface and sucked greedily at the air, her chest feeling like it was on the verge of exploding. She took two more deep breaths before Callan urged her forward with a gentle shove.

"Swim for the shore," he said, coughing out water.

Tammy blinked at him—he was glowing golden from beneath. Her eyes dropped to the water, which only moments before had been blacker than midnight, and realized it wasn't some spotlight up above shining into the water.

The lake was lit up from *within*.

"Tammy, go!"

The second shove woke her up, and she whirled around,

throwing her already-tired, aching body into the fastest swimming she'd ever done. She swam without looking ahead, arm over arm, sucking in air between bursts of energy.

Her feet hit the ground, and she surged forward, digging her toes into the muck for more speed. Water splashed wildly around her body as she pumped her arms and legs for the shore, only turning briefly to check that Callan was still behind her. Once her feet were on solid ground, she managed to raise her head and look at the Howell team waiting on the banks up ahead.

Even though they were all there, they were entirely eclipsed by Everly.

She stood on the shore, her body a kaleidoscope of shimmering, white light. Her silver hair floated on an invisible breeze, and her eyes beamed like two small flashlights through the last remnants of morning fog.

Her feet hovered several inches off the ground, her body supported by multiple tendrils of light. Those same tendrils arced out of her fingertips and into the lake—the source of the glowing.

Tammy sloshed through the last of the shallows, a prickle of awe opening inside her. Everly looked otherworldly and magnificent. It wasn't the first time Tammy had seen her wield the strange power, but it would never be something that didn't leave her awestruck. She was like a goddess.

The light vanished before Tammy and Callan had fully left the water. The tendrils sucked back into Everly in a flash, and she dropped. Her legs crumpled beneath her. Rylan leaped forward, grabbing her before she could fall face-first into the lake.

Shivering in a way that made her eyeballs ache, Tammy prepared for an onslaught from the team about her behavior. But all attention remained on Everly.

Everly was attempting to get her feet under her and push Rylan—whose body was mid-shift between vampire and something scaly—away. But her legs didn't seem to want to hold her up. Rylan kept his arms around her, and Lian stepped forward to peel back Everly's collar, exposing something red on her shoulder beneath the jacket.

"The cracks are spreading."

Harper gasped.

"Cracks?" Tammy asked, taking several more steps along the muddy bank in her bare feet. She noticed her shoes were clutched in Rushelle's arms like a teddy bear.

Everly coughed. "I'm fi—"

"Don't you dare say it." Rylan swept Everly into his arms, one arm behind her shoulders and the other behind her knees.

As he straightened, he glared at Tammy, looking even more dangerous in his strange, combined form. "I'm taking her to the car."

Then he stomped off with Everly.

Tammy watched them go, her stomach roiling with upset and swallowed water. Everly had saved her life. Callan's too. What had she paid for that?

Neither of them would have been in danger if Tammy hadn't come here.

It's always my fault. I'm the curse ... always.

Lian fussed briefly over Callan, who waved her off.

Then her brown eyes zeroed in on Tammy. "What in the Everdark were you thinking?"

Callan watched her as well, and Tammy turned away, staring down at her bare, mud-caked toes. "I'm sorry. I just ... I thought if I could make a wish to bring Blaise back, I could make everything right again. I could fix all the mistakes, not steal the artifact, not try that stupid ritual, not lose him. Then maybe they could forgive me. All three of them. Vonny, Kole, even Blaise ..."

Callan shook his head and turned away from her.

Rushelle appeared by her side and wrapped her in a blanket, adding a warm hug over the top. "Glad you swam back to us, little duck."

Tammy clung to the blanket, but it did nothing to warm the frost in her heart.

Lian's gaze narrowed. "Wait, what artifact? Something from Darkfrey Estate?"

Tammy shook her head, her heart fluttering from Lian's

intense gaze. "It belonged to the Mesmans. Blaise took it from their home the night of the … the night he died."

Lian cocked her head. "You're telling me Vonny Mesman had a shadyr relic?"

"Blaise said they had a few. I sort of always thought he was just lying to seem special, until he actually brought that one with him, that night."

Lian exchanged glances with Callan. "That seems a bit strange."

"It does."

Harper stepped up beside them but seemed to ignore their conversation. Her gaze was fixed out over the water, and her forehead crinkled.

When she opened her mouth, Tammy didn't expect her to start singing. Her voice was strong and rich against the wind cutting over the lake.

"Hungry light shines over the waves and my mermaid she yearns, when will I return, when will I return?" She paused, then turned to her gaping audience. "Hungry light shining over the waves. That's what we just saw, wasn't it?"

"I suppose?" Callan said. "But it's just a song."

Harper shook her head, her bright green eyes flashing. "There's also the last verse that references a star: My star shining bright, in love under the light. It's very teeth-and-stars-ish, don't you think? It has to mean something."

Rushelle, who had applied a blanket and hug to Callan,

perked up. "I've never thought about the lighthouse that way, but it does sound a bit like that, what with how it works."

"How do you mean?" Lian asked.

"Oh, I sometimes forget I'm not with the Crybel's Cove crew anymore. Most shadyrs assume they keep the lighthouse going, right?"

Tammy, Lian, and Callan nodded.

"Nope!" Rushelle grinned. "The lighthouse has no keeper, isn't even hooked up to electricity. It just does its own thing. Has for a long, long time. Maybe fifty years. The bulb, if that's what it is, is powered by some kind of magic."

Harper spoke up. "Some kind of *light* magic. Like a piece of a hungry star!"

Lian frowned. "Maybe. What else do you know about it?"

Rushelle shrugged. "Not much. Don't know if anyone does. It's a kind of a 'if it ain't broke, don't fix it' situation, cos nobody wants to set foot on that island if they don't have to. What's this about, anyway? After more clues about Everly's glowy dealeo?"

Lian chewed at a thumbnail. "Yeah. And we need clues fast. Harper might be onto something. We don't have any other real leads."

"I agree it could be worth following up. Harper's got

good instincts." Callan shoved his foot into his boot, despite the fact he was still dripping wet.

Several red marks marred his arms where the beshadowed squids had come for him, and Tammy realized with a terrible sinking feeling that tonight could have been so much worse.

Lian's gaze was heavy with concern as she watched her son. "I'm going to let the rest of you take point on the lighthouse excursion. I have an errand to run myself."

Rushelle stepped over by her side, dangling her car keys in one hand. "What are we doing, ma'am?"

"I've been thinking about the other missing shadyr artifacts since they didn't show up at Gorhanmere. If Vonny and Kole had one, maybe they have more."

Callan's eyebrows lowered. "The question is, why?"

Lian grabbed the keys from Rushelle. "I'd like to find out."

Chapter Nine

Lian yelled into the intercom at Darkfrey Estate's front gate for a solid twenty minutes before deciding that Vonny truly wasn't there. She didn't even consider talking to Kole. He'd been a lost cause for years.

Where could that woman have snuck off too?

She wasn't with her brace, apparently, not on duty, but not at the estate. Sounded shady as the Everdark to Lian.

Back on the road, Lian rubbed her eyes. She was exhausted. In all the turmoil of the last few days, she'd hardly slept a wink. She'd thought last night, with both her sons alive and under her roof again, she'd be able to get the rest she needed.

Then they decided to go out on a hunt. And every raw, motherly nerve ending inside Lian screamed for the duration of their absence. She'd paced the entire time, with

Rushelle kindly topping up her teacup and insisting she wasn't tired, either.

Lian had only driven Rushelle's tiny yellow sports car once or twice, but the thrill of having the engine purr beneath her was just as exciting as the last time. Having raised two sons, she'd never had the option of a little two-seater with a speedometer that went all the way up to ludicrous.

Lian had sent Rushelle off with the rest of the team to prepare for the next mission, despite her insistence on sticking together. Rushelle was their only in with the Crybel's Cove crew, the offshoot of the Darkfreys that had jurisdiction over the sea.

And if the Howells were going to need a boat and access to Carnock Island, they needed an in with Crybel's Cove. Lian hated putting Rushelle in that position, but she hated the idea of not doing everything they could to help Everly even more.

Tammy's revelation that the Mesmans once had an artifact in their home crawled underneath Lian's skin. For as long as Mordan's lineage had ruled over Shroudhaven, they'd insisted that any shadyr artifact belonged in the estate's possession. Mordan was especially protective of them, keeping them under lock and key in his special, temperature-controlled storage area.

Although Lian didn't care for Mordan and his fascist

ways, she had never truly been bothered by his decree. Most of the relics were either useless or too hazardous to fall into *anyone's* hands, human or shadyr. As long as they sat in their glass cages at Darkfrey Manor, they weren't in dangerous hands.

Until she found out that they were.

All those empty cases ... The Bane, they'd found. Her sword, she had by her side as always. Tammy had revealed that the Mesmans definitely had one, maybe more.

But ... why?

Only an answer Vonny herself could give.

Shroudhaven was just coming to life when Lian rolled into the downtown area on her way home from the estate. It had been her home forever, and would likely continue to be home up until the day she died and could be buried alongside her husband in Shroudhaven Cemetery.

Pimeys had settled this town since the beginning, and they came from original shadyr stock, though not every Pimey carried the shadyr gene. Lian had happily traded her ancestral name to take her husband's, but she'd always be a Pimey at heart.

She passed Pimey's Diner—owned by one of her cousins—and a few blocks later, she rolled by Pimey's General Store, owned by her great uncle but run by one of her nephews who wasn't much older than Rylan.

She'd wanted a simple, safe life like that for her boys.

But the world had other plans.

The sports car hummed along the street where the abandoned Rook's Theater rested. The old movie theater had closed a while back after a tragedy more than likely brought on by an eidolghast. The theater was usually empty, doors boarded and locked, the entire facade covered in graffiti.

Lian was surprised to recognize Harper's campervan parked at the curb in front of it. She slowed and whipped the tiny coupe over to park on the other side. The kids should all be back home, cleaning up from what just passed, and getting packed and prepared for what was next. She had to go check that everything was okay.

Lian moved to leave the car when Harper appeared from around the back of the theater, walking with a bit of a skip in her step as she jingled her keys and rounded the front of the van to the driver's side. She was alone.

But the street wasn't empty.

The moment Harper's van pulled away from the theater, Vonny Mesman appeared from the shadows. She wore her usual uniform of a Darkfrey jacket and tactical wear. Even though the hood was up, Lian easily recognized Vonny's platinum bob swinging freely.

Vonny was also alone.

Lian shoved open the driver's side door and jogged toward the front of the theater, heading Vonny off on the sidewalk. "I want a word with you."

Vonny drew up short, a flash of annoyance crossing her sharp features before she grinned pleasantly. "Whatever about, Howell?"

"Tammy almost died this morning."

"Only almost? What a shame." Vonny shrugged and attempted to walk around her.

Lian tossed out an arm, nearly clotheslining the shorter woman. "We're not done. You hurt one of my kids. You sent her racing to certain death."

"Your 'kid' deserves whatever is coming to her," Vonny seethed, knocking Lian's arm away. "If some harsh truth sends her over the edge, then she knows it too."

"She's a wounded child!" Lian snapped.

She drew a breath and rubbed the bridge of her nose. She'd come to get info out of Vonny but her anger over Tammy was taking control.

She soothed it away, trying a new tack. "I knew you long before the accident that took Blaise. You weren't like this before. You used to have compassion. You used to care about Tammy. Can't you stop blaming her? Blaise's death was a tragic accident."

Vonny lunged forward, getting in Lian's face. She was several inches shorter than Lian, but no less threatening.

"He's not dead!"

"Either way, he's gone," Lian replied, careful to

maintain her composure. "Tammy mourns him every day, just as you do. She carries the weight of her own guilt for not being able to save—"

"I don't give a shit about Tammy's guilt." Vonny sliced her palm through the air as if to cut off Lian's words.

Lian said, "If I hear you've spoken to her again, there will be consequences."

Vonny cocked her head. "It's cute you think I'm scared of your threats."

This time, it was Lian's turn to step closer. She lorded her height over Vonny and tightened her jaw, putting the full force of her 'mother bear' fury into her eyes. "Don't you remember sparring class, Mesman? Or was the way I beat you into a pulp so humiliating you wiped it from your memory?"

Nothing but their breaths fell between them for several long seconds.

Then Vonny took a single step back—relenting.

Dear ghast, miracles do happen.

Vonny glanced away, her eyes on the street rather than on Lian. "Look, I have places to be—"

"One more thing," Lian interrupted.

Vonny sighed, tucking her hands into the pockets of her jacket. "What?"

"I know shadyr artifacts are missing from Darkfrey's private collection."

Vonny's eyebrows drew together. "And how might you know that?"

Lian considered her next words. She didn't want to come out and accuse Vonny of taking them. That wouldn't get them anywhere. Lian had to try another strategy to get her to drop some clue about where they were and why.

"I was told the Gorhanmere shadyrs had them, but they only had one. Do you have any idea where the rest might be?"

"Apart from the ones you stole, no. Why are you looking for them?"

Lian hedged her bets—how much could she tell Vonny without compromising the situation? She couldn't imagine the Vonny Mesman she'd once known had turned *completely* evil in the interim, even with her son's death tossing her into existential denial.

"Everly's in trouble," Lian said carefully. "We're running out of options to help her, so I'm investigating every possible path."

Vonny blinked, then coughed a short laugh. "Everly? The human?"

"Not *only* human."

"Whatever she is, she's not a shadyr. Quit wasting your time trying to fix a cockroach."

A pang hit Lian straight in the chest. "Is that what you think? Anyone without shadyr blood is nothing more than a bug?"

"We're the superior species, Howell, whether you like it or not."

Lian clenched her hands into fists and carefully took hold of her emotions. There was no getting through to this woman. But Lian would make sure she didn't hurt her kids again.

"We're done here. I'm going to be keeping an eye on you. Because if you're happy to stand by and watch people die, if you're driving kids to their death, who knows what else you're up to."

Vonny bared her teeth.

Lian remained silent, planted to the sidewalk in front of Rook's Theater. Vonny glanced past her, then back, then past her again before grimacing. She whipped her phone from her pocket, the screen glowing to life as she marched away.

Lian glanced at the theater as well, before following Vonny down the street.

Because as little information as she'd gotten out of that discussion, she was now certain of one thing.

Vonny Mesman was up to *something*.

The wind on the docks at Crybel's Cove was furious, as if the ocean was trying to warn them away. Everly gingerly climbed from the back of the Howells' SUV onto the asphalt. Stray strands of hair whipped against her cheeks in the gale. She glanced up at the clouds, nervous at how dark they'd become.

The team had taken an hour at Howell House to pack supplies for the journey. Everly's small daypack held a flashlight, extra clothes, a few tools, some non-perishable food, and a water bottle.

She hooked her arm through the strap and fell into step with the rest of the team. Their packs looked like something elite special forces would carry, filled with survival kits, paracord, flares, and first aid kits—the kind with tourniquets and sutures rather than Band-Aids and cotton balls.

Everly kept pace, determined to prove she could walk and function on her own, no matter how weak she felt. Back at the house, she'd wanted desperately to crawl into bed and stay there, to sleep, to not feel the constant burning pain in her arm and hand, but the whole purpose of this journey was to figure out answers to her affliction.

If she let the Howell team venture into any kind of danger without her, and something bad happened, she'd never be able to live with herself.

So she'd splashed water on her face, double-fisted two

energy drinks, and shoved her exhaustion as deep as it could go. The pain from her cracking arms, however, she couldn't do much about. Ibuprofen wasn't even touching it. It had spread all the way up to her shoulder on the side with Rylan's cut. Zozo's spread slower but was still larger than before.

Rylan's boots creaked on the dock's wide planks as he walked nearby. Since Everly had collapsed at the house, he had stayed close, but his expression remained remote.

Now they weren't stuck in a car together, he seemed to be hovering on the edges of her effect on him. Far enough away that he remained in human form, but close enough that holding his form clearly took some effort.

He looks as tired as I feel.

The whole team did. But Everly's condition had already worsened. They didn't have the luxury of waiting. Another reason why she refused for them to make this journey alone.

Everly had learned on the way over that Crybel's Cove—the small township seated between Shroudhaven and the ocean—had a Darkfrey team put in place specifically to keep shroudpools from forming out at sea.

Two members of the team waited at the edge of the pier next to a small fishing boat. Their waders and linen shirts were more suited for deep-sea fishing than ghast hunting, but they wore the standard Darkfrey jackets.

One man was older, closer to Lian's age, with salt and

pepper hair and a wind-weathered face. His skin was deeply tanned, and the bronzed color made his icy-blue eyes glow. The younger man was closer to Everly's age with blond hair that hung shaggy over his forehead.

Rushelle took the lead as the team crossed the splintered planks of the pier.

She grinned as she greeted the two men. "Hey, fellas."

"Rush," the older man replied, a hint of sheepishness in his gruff tone. "Been a while."

Rushelle turned her sunny smile back to the Howell team. "This is my uncle, Flint, and my cousin, Layton. They've agreed to take us to Carnock Island. They tried to kill me once, so they owe me a favor."

Everly shot a look at Tammy, who returned the astonishment by mouthing, *"What the ...?"*

Flint cleared his throat awkwardly. "It wasn't really like that. It was meant to be a teaching moment."

"And hoo boy did it teach me!" Rushelle said. "Now, we're on a pretty sensitive time crunch. Are we all set to board?"

"All set. And listen, we're sorry about how things went down. But this is a one-time deal. We aren't meant to be running joy rides out to the island. Not for anybody. Including whatever you lot are meant to be." He widened one eye as he took them in.

Rushelle, still in pinup makeup. Rylan, clearly

struggling to hold human form. Denny and Cherry squabbled about something over to one side. Tammy was trying to look the shadyr soldier part but seemed to be barely holding it together, and Callan seemed more interested in keeping a worried eye on her than on the conversation.

Everly could only guess how rough she herself looked. She'd already had to take her small pack off and put it at her feet because it was making her tired.

"We're in a hurry, is what we are," Rylan grumbled, heading toward the boat.

Everly spoke up. "Can't leave yet. We're still waiting on Harper."

As if summoned by her statement, the rumble of vintage engine announced the campervan as it pulled in behind them. Harper bounced out of the driver's side seat, shouldered her pack, and locked up. She sashayed along the docks like she'd stepped off a photoshoot. Even Everly did a double-take.

Where did she get rose-gold hiking boots from? Are they new?

Everly didn't see Harper pack, so could only guess what filled the well-stuffed backpack. She could see Harper's personalized axe hanging from her belt holster. She'd also taken the time to freshen her makeup—probably in the car on the way, something she often did that terrorized

Everly in the passenger seat.

Callan raised an eyebrow at Harper as she joined them. "All done?"

"Yup, should be safe and sound."

They'd decided it wasn't a good idea for the Bane to sit in the camper while they were gone, or unguarded in one of their homes. They also didn't think keeping it too close to Everly was for the best, either, in case it exacerbated her condition. Harper had ducked away while the others packed to hide it somewhere safe.

She clapped her hands and bobbed on her toes, looking entirely too energized compared to the rest of them. "Is it time? Are we going?"

The dull hum of a vibrating phone came from Cherry, and he fished it out.

"BRB," he said, his brow furrowed as he hurried off to answer the call.

Rushelle checked her own phone, then caught Rylan's eye. "I'm worried about your mom. She's a tough lady, but nobody should be alone in Shroudhaven. Ever."

Callan smirked at his brother. "You would know, wouldn't you, sleeping beauty?"

Rylan made no reply, but color rose in his cheeks. A sensation Everly too was experiencing. Rylan wouldn't have told Callan about what happened in her dreams, would he? No. Everly couldn't see him sharing that particular experience any time soon. But he clearly still remembered it himself.

"What are you thinking?" Rylan asked Rushelle. "You want to go after her?"

She nodded. "Now I've sorted out your passage, you think you kids can handle this without me?"

"Of course." Callan handed over the SUV keys. "We've got Harper's van."

Cherry returned, his face twisted in confusion and his phone dangling from one hand. "You sure? Because you're another shadyr down. That was Jasper asking for my help. It seemed kind of urgent."

Harper stepped closer to him. "Everything okay?"

Cherry ran a hand up through his red hair. "I ... have no idea. I wouldn't leave if it didn't seem important. Rush, can you drop me downtown?"

"Of course, sugar. I'll drive you." She turned back to her cousin and uncle and in a low, dangerous voice, she added, "You're going to take care of my friends, now, aren't you? You're not going to leave them to die like you did me?"

Harper and Everly exchanged wide-eyed glances.

Flint nodded. "We'll get them to the island safely. You have my word."

Rushelle brightened again, did a quick round of hugs, and headed off with Cherry to the SUV.

Rylan glanced around at the remaining team. "Looks

like it's just us. Let's get moving."

Everly picked up her backpack of supplies, but before she could toss it over her shoulder, Rylan snatched it and put it on his with his own pack. He shimmered into vampire form through a gust of black mist, then stomped away to the boat without another word.

Everly didn't hate that he was being protective of her, but he acted so put out by having to do so that it only made her feel worse. After the incident at the lake, and her second collapse, Rylan had told her in no uncertain terms that she wasn't to use her powers again. No matter what.

Even she had to admit that the cracking spread much faster when she did.

The fishing trawler swayed on the waves as Everly stepped onto it from the dock. Harper came after her, carrying a bag of her own, and the two of them were directed to go into the cabin by the stoic Layton.

"I'm loving this whole sailor slash shadyr aesthetic," Harper murmured, glancing over her shoulder as she stepped through the narrow door. "But what the heck did Rush mean when she said they left her to die?"

"I'm still wondering that myself." Everly followed her into the claustrophobic aisle.

They passed a small corridor with a pair of bunkbeds on each side and bathroom access, dumped their packs, and headed up front to the cabin.

A bench ran the length of the room and wrapped around one corner where a table was anchored to the floor, walled in by a small kitchenette and bar situation.

The far wall held a bank of windows that looked out over the sea, lined underneath with high-tech screens and controls. Rylan had taken a seat up there beside Flint. Everly eased onto the bench near Tammy and Callan, and Harper plopped down next to her, squeezing in tight.

Denny sauntered in like he owned the boat, heading right for the mini fridge. "What, no beer?"

Harper let out a sound of disgust. "We should've left him behind."

Callan sighed. "As annoying as he is, he's also a relatively capable shadyr. Sometimes. And we need numbers. We don't know what we're walking into."

Denny snatched a soda and popped the top.

"Booyah! 'Capable shadyr.' You hear that? Don't you forget it, either," he said, then tossed back a big swig and climbed into a bunk.

Callan winced. "I should not have said that loud enough for him to hear."

"Yet he didn't seem to hear the 'relatively' or 'sometimes,' did he?" Tammy said.

Layton finished up on the exterior deck as rain began to spatter on the windows, and headed in to join Flint at the steering wheel.

As the boat's engine whirred and they pulled away from the dock, Harper leaned over Everly and said, "Psst. Cal. What's the sitch on Rush and these guys? They tried to *kill* her? Are we safe with them?"

Callan's mouth twisted. "It's no secret that Rush has never been interested in the shadyr mission. All she wants to do is work on those weird fantasy romance satire novels she's always tapping away on her laptop."

Denny snorted from around the corner. "Like a woman could write a *proper* novel."

Tammy, slouched on the bench next to Callan with her black hands shoved into the pockets of her hoodie, leaned up to say, "They're really good, actually."

Harper gasped, her eyes glittering. "You've read them?"

Tammy shrugged bashfully. "I was bored."

"Oh Em Gee! Can we fangirl for a sec? 'Hunted for the Far King' is my absolute fave. How about you?"

Tammy's jaw dropped, as though the idea of interacting with Harper over a shared passion horrified her.

Callan lowered his voice and side-eyed Tammy. "Wait. Aren't they, um, erotic?"

"Kill me now," Tammy groaned and slouched deeper into her hoodie.

"Don't be a child," Harper scolded him. "And yes, they are super hot. The spice, it's just, chef's kiss!"

Everly squinted and shook her head. "And what do her

books have to do with these guys?"

"Right, that." Callan dropped his voice to a whisper as Layton trudged by on his way out of the cabin. "Rush was part of the Crybel's Cove team before she came to us. Apparently, they got fed up with her attitude toward her duties and left her alone in a deadly situation. Luckily, Mom saved her."

Harper sighed. "Sounds like Rush got double lucky getting away from these guys. And now she's free to bring her gift of delicious smut to the world."

Callan chuckled. "Yeah, and the irony of it is, Rush has been more than happy to help Mom out with shadyr stuff when needed. And she's a natural, have you seen her fight?"

Everly nodded, remembering her ferocity at Rook's Hotel.

"She just doesn't want to be fighting all the time. Which is fair. Some shadyrs don't understand that, though. For some, there is only the mission, and if you don't stick to it, you're a traitor."

Layton banged through the door into the cabin, swiping water off his face and ruffling his wet hair. "It's getting sketchy out there."

Flint spoke up, though he didn't turn away from the rain-darkened view outside. "Weather turns on a dime out this way. It's not abnormal for a gale to rise up out of the blue, or go away just as fast."

Sleet pelted the window, and Everly could hardly see outside.

Rylan glared at the gray sky. "Should we be worried?"

"Probably not," Flint replied, punctuated by boat-shaking thunder. "Maybe."

Twenty worried minutes later, Carnock Island formed from the stormy darkness ahead, a hulking silhouette that rose from the sea. High above, the lighthouse beam slowly circled like a shooting star, sparkling through the lashing rain.

The wind whipped around the boat, battering at the sides like fists while the waves tossed them about recklessly. Everly sat on the edge of the bench, clinging to the seat beneath her so she wouldn't be thrown to the floor. Her heart had lodged in her throat, and fear chilled her spine as the storm gained potency.

An anxious atmosphere filled the cabin. Everyone stared ahead of the boat as if they were heading toward certain doom. Flint and Layton stood at the helm, Layton assisting with gadgets Everly didn't understand while Flint's attention remained focused on steering through the rain.

The sense of impending doom only intensified when, as the boat drew ever closer to the dark shore, Flint muttered, "Well. That's not good news."

Rylan stood, one hand latching onto a railing. "What is it?"

Flint and Layton exchanged glances, and Flint met Rylan's gaze. "The lighthouse dock's gone."

Rylan's brow furrowed. "What do you mean, gone?"

"Absent, no longer there, vanished—"

Rylan's growl cut Flint off.

The old man shrugged. "Anyway, we can't set you down here. In this weather, I'd recommend not letting you out anywhere, but if you insist, there's a small bay back along the island that might be calm enough that we don't all get smashed to pieces on rocks."

"That will be a lot farther from where we want to be, won't it?" Everly asked.

"We came prepared to cross the island if we needed to," Rylan said.

"I'm not sure we were quite prepared for this." Callan gestured to the weather. "We could try again tomorrow, bring Cherry, Rush, and Mom along for backup."

A large wave smashed the side of the boat, rocking it violently.

Flint flashed an irritated glare over his shoulder. "We brought you to the island like we promised Rush, but one time only. We can't dock here, and in this weather, it's not safe for us to remain on the sea. So I suggest you make a decision—are you staying or are you coming back with us?"

CHAPTER TEN

The storm had eased in the shelter of the bay, but the water was still beyond choppy. Everly stared down at the restless surface of the ocean and the dinghy bobbing there. The shore wasn't that far away from Flint's fishing trawler, but the tiny rowboat looked rickety enough to turn into toothpicks the minute a wave slammed into it.

And all six of them were meant to ride the thing through four-foot waves?

Harper and Tammy descended first, keeping their weight low and balanced as they crawled into the rocking boat.

Flint handed Rylan a satellite phone. "I have no idea what it's going to be like on the island, if this will even work. But if you can get a signal to us when your mission is complete, we'll try to come back for you."

A muscle ticked in Rylan's jaw. "That's a lot of ifs."

As they were all standing in a group around the ladder, he was back in vampire form again, making his expression more vicious.

Callan placed a calming hand on his brother's shoulder and addressed Flint with a stoic nod. "We appreciate your help. Hopefully we won't be long."

Layton stared through the rain at the island. "From what we've seen, the established shroudpools are mostly on the north side of the island. If you keep south, hopefully you'll avoid the worst of it."

Callan and Denny headed down next, then Rylan stepped onto the short ladder and reached back for Everly's hand. Biting her lip, she took it. Even though the ladder was only three rungs, both the trawler and the dinghy rocked about wildly, and she didn't trust her arms to have the strength to hold on. They stepped down the ladder together, one of Rylan's arms around her waist to keep her from slipping.

The team piled shoulder to shoulder into the small rowboat, balancing packs between them.

Once everyone was seated, Layton leaned over to toss them the rope. "Try and get to the beach fast. Nyevmers are rare, but still a threat. Best to stay out of the water."

"Nyevmers?" Everly asked, a slight catch in her throat. She clutched Harper's leg. The seasickness hadn't bothered her much on the larger fishing boat. The smaller dinghy was like a buoy in the middle of a hurricane. The constant up and down was liable to make her vomit before they reached the shore.

Rylan picked up one oar and thrust the other at Denny beside him. "Water-dwelling eidolghasts."

"Oh. Good," Everly replied, blinking fast against the rain. "Sea monsters. Coolcoolcool."

Silence fell over the rowboat, broken only by rumbling thunder that Everly couldn't tell was coming or going. Denny and Rylan paddled with efficiency, gliding the rowboat over the waves. Every few feet, a wave would slap into the prow and send water splashing over the occupants, soaking them more thoroughly than the rain already had.

All the while, high above the mountainous island, the lighthouse beacon rotated. Circling. Circling. Circling.

The rowboat scraped against the sand with a jarring thud. The island stretched ahead and above. Menacing. Ominous. Shrouded in fog, with the illuminated lighthouse up above like the lure on an angler fish.

Lowering his oar, Rylan slid over the side and splashed into water up to his knees. Callan half-stood to join him, but with one hand Rylan grabbed the prow and tugged the boat and its occupants onto the sand.

"You know, I can almost see an upside to being shifted all the time," Callan said as he stood up, shouldered his pack, then hopped out of the dinghy.

Rylan bared his sharp fangs at his brother. "Yeah, means I can beat your smart ass whenever I want."

The rest of the team loaded up and followed, then Rylan finished dragging the boat well out of reach of the ocean.

Rylan halted on the sand in his Goldilocks distance away from Everly and shook off the vampire form as if to make a point. Everly couldn't be sure, but it seemed like he was closer than before. His olive-green eyes roamed the dark wall of trees that covered the steep hill.

"I wonder what we're going to find in there."

Harper pumped her arms in the air like a cheerleader. "Everly's cure! Everly's cure!"

"Jeez, save some optimism for the rest of us," Tammy grumbled. "'Cause I am fresh out."

Callan crunched over the sand to stand beside her. "Come on, let's treat this as an island holiday."

"Ugh, you too?"

Rylan wiped water from his face. "We're going in. Stick close together. Keep your eyes on the dark. The place could be crawling with eidolghasts and who knows what else. Cal—can you take the lead? Denny, can you handle the rear?"

"Don't say something like that to him!" Harper hissed.

Denny smirked and nodded.

"Tammy, you're up with me," Callan said and marched forward.

She grumbled about babysitting but hustled to catch up. Harper scurried forward, probably realizing she didn't want to be *the rear* directly in front of Denny, which left Everly and Rylan in the middle together, no doubt as he'd intended. As he took his place behind her, he returned to vampire form.

The group set off over the narrow strip of beach toward the woods.

Everly glanced back at Rylan. "I'm sorry. About all of this. About ... what I do to you."

He remained silent for a moment, then in his gravelly voice muttered, "You have no idea ..."

Everly winced. "Is it bad? Hard I mean, transforming involuntarily?"

"Not too bad. I've been able to at least direct my form into something familiar like vampire or werewolf, which means it's not much of a strain. But there are other eidolghast energies coming from you as well. Rare ones. A bit of nyevmer. Some auerdax. Even some I have no idea what they are. Forms I've never experienced before, trying to come out."

Cold wind whipped around Everly, driving raindrops into her eyes. "So, I'm just overflowing with eidolghast energy. Great. Great. Good to know."

Fog drifted in and out of the thick trees like a tide. An overgrown path marked by a weathered wooden sign came into view. A carved impression of a lighthouse sat above a blood-red arrow pointing straight ahead.

The minute the trees closed around them, the howling wind, crashing waves, and steady rain all vanished. The forest was like a vacuum, sucking up all sound so thoroughly that it couldn't be natural. Everly rubbed her ears to make sure she hadn't suddenly gone deaf.

Beyond their footsteps on the ground, there was nothing. No birdsong. No insects. No hint of the storm raging around the island.

Just empty, eerie stillness.

It was also dark. Much darker than it should have been.

One by one, flashlights winked on, dispelling some of the gloom. Outside their bright bubble the darkness was a deeper black than physically possible. Like the shadows were no longer a trick of the light but living, sentient beasts.

As much as Everly wanted to keep her head down and pretend there was nothing to fear, she followed Callan's instructions and eyed the darkness around them, watching for danger.

Which was how she saw the woman.

A tattered white dress trailed around her as the woman paced slow, awkward steps through the trees in the distance. Everly's breath caught in her throat, and she came to a sudden stop.

"Over there," she whispered.

Also hushed, Harper said, "Is that ...?"

Callan hissed, "Shh!"

The woman turned toward the sound.

She had no face.

Where her eyes should have been were only smooth, empty sockets covered by dark skin. Her nose and lips protruded slightly but were smoothed away as if someone had stretched an ebony veil over her face. Long, dark hair tangled in strands around her, soaking wet.

Her head angled and twisted toward them in jerky movements.

Callan kept his hands up, signaling them all to stay still, stay silent. The whole team froze, mouths closed, barely breathing. Long moments later, the ghostly woman turned and walked away. Where her feet touched the ground, glowing spots sizzled. Dark shapes shifted around her like a crowd of transparent people, rippling and darting, as if she were tiptoeing among an army of shadows.

Then, just like that, she vanished.

The Howell shadyrs relaxed and turned back to the path, but Harper and Everly remained wide-eyed.

"Was that a ghost?" Everly said.

Harper let out a long, shaky breath. "And more importantly, where was her *face*?"

Callan replied, "You never know what you're going to find in a beshadowing. Ghostly, undead, twisted remains of human victims aren't uncommon. You're lucky she had no face and didn't see us. For all we know, she could hurt us. Stay vigilant if she returns."

Harper made a puppy-dog expression. "Human victims? I wonder what her story was."

Everly matched her pout. "Aw! Are you being sympathetic to a ghost? If I hadn't told you recently, I love you."

Harper reached back for Everly's hand as they returned to their march.

Along their line, heads turned side to side, keeping all angles around them monitored.

Softly, the quiet of the forest changed. Distant at first, a long, low groan broke through the silence. The team exchanged glances, but the source of the sound couldn't be identified.

Another whine started up, this one louder and with an almost human-like resonance behind it. Then a third, higher in tone, joined it, and then another, until a chorus arose within the forest, like a hospital ward filled with pain.

"More ghosts?" Everly asked.

"It sounds like someone being tortured," Harper added.

Tammy grumbled, "It's coming from the trees. The one at Dark Corner does this sometimes."

Denny reached around to his pack and drew out a wicked-looking machete. "As long as they don't start moving."

Harper tapped the axe by her side, as though reassuring herself it was still there. Everly squeezed her hand lightly.

"I'm getting the hint of a weroth stalking around out there somewhere," Tammy muttered.

Callan said, "Yeah, not close though. Hopefully it stays that way."

The ground turned steep beneath Everly's boots. After several moments, she and Harper were forced to release each other and walk single file as the undergrowth crept out of the trees and onto the path. Everly's calves burned from the effort of climbing, and her injured arm throbbed in time with her heartbeat. Her head swam and she focused on the solid ground beneath her feet.

The trees kept up their mournful cries until a sudden rustling cut them off. Callan threw his arms out to stop the team.

Everly clutched her flashlight, ready to turn it into a weapon if required.

She recognized the familiar leaping gait of deer. She let out a sigh of relief, glad it wasn't more creepy faceless ghosts, until one of them passed through the beam of her flashlight.

Tawny body, four spindly legs ...

But where its head should have been, instead there was an octopus.

The cephalopod parts were pale pink and slimy, fading into their fur-covered bodies like some kind of twisted centaur. Long, curling tentacles dangled down the creatures' chests, whipping around as they leaped over the undergrowth, directly toward Everly and the others.

"Move," Rylan yelled.

As one, the team turned, running along the path from the swarm of grotesque chimeras.

The creature at the lead lifted its cephalopod limbs and released an ear-splitting, high-pitched squeal like the cry of a wounded rabbit. The trees joined in, howling dreadfully.

Everly kept her sore arms tucked in tight, and her eyes darted between the pursuing monsters and the path. Her chest ached, each breath hard to draw. She pushed through the pain, running her fastest.

The crash of bodies through bushes came from ahead as the path narrowed. Denny moved to the front, swinging his machete to clear away plants as he ran.

A protruding root caught Everly's foot, and she stumbled. Rylan grabbed her jacket and hoisted her back to her feet before she could hit the dirt. He moved in front of her, taking her hand and dragging her through the ever-thickening foliage. Small hooves trampled the ground behind them.

The touch of a tentacle brushed the back of Everly's neck.

Then the path disappeared.

Even with Denny going berserk up front, their pace slowed significantly. Rylan swore then put Everly in front of him again, turning to confront the pursuing beasts.

"Look," he called out.

The others slowed, glancing back.

The octopus-headed deer had stopped. They stood eerily still, staring with bulbous white eyes. Then they bounded away in the opposite direction.

"When the monster chasing you gets scared and runs the other way ... That's always a *good* sign, isn't it?" Harper muttered.

"We're for sure going to die here," Tammy agreed.

Harper's flashlight blinked on and off, and she let out a short, sharp curse, then banged the heel of her hand against it. It blinked a few more times, then extinguished entirely.

Callan and Tammy's lights went dark, too. Within seconds, only Everly's was left, and then it sputtered out, plunging them into darkness.

The trees went silent all at once.

Callan cleared his throat. "If this isn't the beshadowing that keeps on giving."

Everly reached for Harper, her heartbeat racing in her throat. She couldn't see anything. Even the shadyrs, who had better dark vision, seemed unsure, unable to tell where to move next.

"I could try to use my powers, give us some light."

"No," Rylan said from somewhere nearby.

"Just a bit, just enough to see."

Harper sighed from her left. "Gotta agree with Rylan on this one. It's not worth it. You keep those powers closed up tight. No matter what. We can't have you shattering to bits before we even get to the lighthouse."

A bright beam flashed over the canopy, and the team squinted away from it. It turned the forest a dull, eerie gray before it circled away, and everything went dark again.

"Speak of the devil," Harper sang.

"We must be close," Rylan said. "Wait for the next pass, then move."

A long, grim moment later, the lighthouse's strange glow circled back around. As the light fell on Everly, her skin tingled.

"Go," Callan called, and they jogged forward.

The pale illumination gave the whole forest a kind of underwater ambiance. Aiming for the source of the beam, they pressed forward until they lost visibility again.

At least the darkness gives me a chance to catch my breath.

Everly's entire body ached, and even the slower speed at which they pressed through the undergrowth left her gasping. She had all the symptoms of a full-blown panic attack but knew it was the Bane wounds spreading the weakness through her.

Every time the lighthouse beam came around, Everly got an eyeful of the forest around them. The trees were spaced farther apart in this area of the woods and draped in thick vines as large around as Everly's thighs. And each time the beam washed across Everly, it roused the dragon.

It liked that light. It *wanted* that light. Everly shivered.

In darkness once more, Tammy whispered, "What's that?"

"What's what?" Callan replied.

"Look off to the right and upward when the light comes back around."

Everly trained her gaze on the area Tammy had indicated and waited. The light returned.

A huge, oval shadow hung from the vines in the trees.

"What *is* that?" Callan squinted at the shape.

Nobody moved, too busy taking in the looming silhouette and trying to determine its risk.

Everly was able to make out a rounded, canoe-like shape, longer than a train carriage, but little else.

Denny, on the other hand, gasped. "Well, I'll be an eidolghasts uncle. It's a submarine."

He took off into the underbrush, crashing over the forest floor.

"Dude! What are you doing?" Callan called, lurching

around the women and leaping over a fallen tree trunk to snatch at Denny's arm.

He missed.

Rylan hissed, "Get back here, you idiot!"

Denny ignored them both. The lighthouse beam illuminated him trampling through the forest on a trajectory for the hanging submarine.

Callan sighed. "We have to stick together."

"Do we though? We could just leave him," Harper suggested.

"Dark," Tammy said. "I like it."

"Come on." Callan moved off after Denny, the others falling in behind.

Everly watched the canopy for glimpses of the sub, surprised at how large it was, and how delicately it hung from the thick vines.

As they joined Denny beneath the craft, he said, "Son of a ghast. It's a U-boat."

The lighthouse beam left and Everly blinked at the darkness overhead. Even without the glow to silhouette the monstrosity, she could sense it there. Heavy. Choking.

"Those bastards tore up the Atlantic Seaboard. They hunted Allied shipping vessels in packs. A heap of 'em went missing after World War II."

"But how did it end up here? Up *there*?" Harper asked.

The light came back around as Denny shrugged, his

gaze still on the craft. He pointed at a gaping hole in the vessel.

"See that? Bet an Allied sub took it down, Nazis and all. Otherwise, it looks untouched. Can you imagine what treasures are inside that thing?" Denny let out a whistle. "I'm going in."

"Are you kidding?" Rylan grabbed the back of Denny's jacket. "We're in the middle of a beshadowed forest. You are *not* climbing into the ruins of a Nazi submarine."

Denny groaned, trying to shake Rylan's grip. "Aw, come on. You never know what we'll find. Those guys were up to all kinds of wild stuff. The Holy Grail could be in there for all we know. That'd be a way to fix up your girlfriend."

Rylan pulled Denny in close, the light flashing on his stone-cold vampire face. "We've been here too long already."

"Let's keep moving," Callan said.

Something pungent hit Everly's nose and she gagged.

Beside her, Harper said, "Oh my ghast, *warn* a girl before you let one rip, you neanderthal."

"It wasn't me!" Denny replied.

"That's not gas," Rylan said. "That's death."

The smell grew stronger.

Metal groaned like a whale's song, and in the eerie gray light, a horde of humanoid figures poured from the cavernous hole in the side of the U-boat.

Then the light left them again.

Chapter Eleven

The inky black between rotations of the lighthouse beam held no ambient light at all.

Just chilling darkness, filled with rustling and stomping, strange grunts, hissing sounds, and the squelch of wet fabric.

"Everly?" Rylan called out.

"I'm over here," she yelled back.

Footsteps pounded her way.

Callan's voice covered the sound. "Tammy, to your left!"

"I know!"

Disturbing, gurgling growls filled the air.

Denny shouted, "At least a dozen of 'em! More still coming!"

A dozen of *what*?

The shadyrs could see at least something in the low light. Everly blinked, trying to take anything in.

I might as well be blind.

She still held her flashlight, so she whipped it up and shook it, desperately hoping the bulb would come back on. When that didn't work, she beat it against her thigh.

Come on, come on!

Nothing. It was dead.

A pained cry came from across the space, sounding like either Tammy or Harper. Rylan grunted and a hailstorm of fist-meeting-flesh sounds came from nearby.

I need to see what's going on. I need to help.

Holding her least shattered arm up in front of her blind eyes, she focused on the dragon inside her. It was wounded, angry, hungry, but she felt almost like she was getting a grip on it and its powers. The sulking state of the being inside her seemed to make it easier to control.

A bright glow emanated from her fingertips, and agony shot along the length of her arm, right up to the base of her skull. Everly cried out.

"Stop it!" Rylan barked at her.

The pain in her hand and the fury in his eyes made her pull the dragon's power back inside herself. Before the light faded out again, she could see at least five human figures encircling him, limbs thrashing. Then darkness again.

"I have to do something!" Everly yelled back.

"Just stay safe." Harper's words were punctuated with a loud *oof* and the chop of her axe. "We've got this."

The lighthouse beacon circled around again, casting a pale beam across the scene as the light filtered in between the twisted trees. Everly's eyes widened.

When the things had come out of the U-boat, they'd appeared humanoid. Now Everly could see that they weren't *living* humans, and they weren't *entirely* human either.

They had dripping, bloated bodies covered in barnacles, and eyes cloudy from death ... where they hadn't rotted away entirely.

Rather than normal noses and mouths, they had sloping, fish-like snouts of scaly, pallid skin. Several had missing limbs, or limbs where the skin had been torn away to the bone. Some of their uniforms had remained eerily intact, though. Light passed over familiar red armbands, and Everly froze, shocked to see something in real life that she'd only ever seen in historical photographs.

The crew of the U-boat, beshadowed back to a twisted semblance of life, undead and murderous.

There were so many of them.

Callan, Tammy, and Denny remained in human form, with no eidolghasts nearby to trigger a change that could give them an advantage. Denny hacked into the zombies with his machete. Callan and Tammy stood back-to-back, large hunting knives in hand as the horde edged in on them. Harper had her axe out, charging toward the heart of the fray.

"Harper!" *What is she doing?*

Everly wanted to run in and drag her human friend back to relative safety.

But Rylan created a barrier between the chaos and Everly. The soggy creatures swarmed him, pummeling at his pale, vampire-form skin, trying to get their jagged teeth into him. Any time one attempted to shamble past him toward Everly, he wrenched it back into melee with him.

A zombie swiped a thick, meaty arm at Rylan's face, and it hit with a terrible crack. Rylan bared his vampire teeth, covered in blood, swinging to strike back.

Darkness came again.

Everly was sorely tempted to bring out the dragon, to let it feed on these long-dead corpses—if they even still had souls. But her arms throbbed mercilessly.

She hadn't liked making the choice, but she'd let the dragon eat at Myrkur Lake, taking the lives of several of the strange, beshadowed marine creatures there. She'd hoped that would somehow help it heal, but it only made things worse.

Even what little she'd done there had taken the cracks from her forearm right up to her shoulder. She didn't like the idea of them spreading into her chest, up her neck, to her head. One more use of her powers might be enough to rip her to pieces.

As the lighthouse beam came back around, Harper swung her axe in a wide arc, disemboweling three zombies in a row. Wriggling masses of fish and worms tumbled to the ground beneath them with a wet squish.

Squealing in disgust, Harper dodged back. Even with stomachs hanging open, the fish-men didn't slow. With a wicked grin, Harper hoisted her axe again.

She twirled, and the axe sliced through one zombie's neck with such power that its head flew face-first into the living corpse next to it, crushing its skull. Their two bodies collapsed onto the third and pinned it down, letting Harper take an easy coup de grâce.

Wow. Everly had seen glimpses of Harper's warrior side, but this was something else.

They'd fought over Harper's inclusion in the dangers of Shroudhaven. Everly knew Harper had done combat and self-defense training since the doxing. She knew she was a strong woman. She knew Harper always pushed herself to do everything at the highest standards. Maybe she should never have doubted her friend.

Maybe I'm the one holding her back.

Closer to her, Rylan had incapacitated all but one of the zombies on him. He grabbed the last with both hands and lifted its full body above his head. With a rough growl, he threw the thing at a thick tree trunk where it splattered, gray chunks dripping down the bark.

Denny joined Callan and Tammy, the trio back-to-back, surrounded in a close circle. All the zombies seemed drawn there like a feeding frenzy, very few straying from the mob. Harper hacked into the edges from the outside. Everly could barely see the three in the center or the flash of their blades through the horde as it jostled them within the crush of their stinking bodies.

"Rylan, they're being overwhelmed," she gasped. "They can't change like you can. They need you."

He followed her gaze, swearing under his breath.

"I'm fine, go!"

"I'll be right back." Rylan charged, hitting the crowd like a cannonball.

There were no fish-Nazis close to Everly then, but they churned and swarmed in the mass nearby. More still fell from the U-boat. No longer a flood of bodies, just the odd straggler, tumbling down and seeking the closest prey.

Everly stepped backward, trying to distance herself from the danger so Rylan could focus on the others, as the lighthouse beam dimmed then passed away again, dropping Everly into darkness.

Something crunched through the underbrush nearby.

"Harper?" Everly whispered.

No reply.

Everly scrambled the other way, feeling her way through

the dark with her hands. A branch whipped her cheek, stinging. A stomach-churning, slurping hiss chased behind her.

She moved quickly, breaking away from the sounds of the larger battle, but her pursuer remained close at her back. Her arms felt so weak, but she grasped her long flashlight tight, ready to swing it if she had to. Damp trunks and thorny bushes blocked her path and she stumbled between them, heart racing.

Slimy hands grabbed at her, fumbling for purchase as they scraped over her back. Everly gagged as a strong, low-tide stench hit her.

"Get off me!"

She swung the flashlight like a bat, missing her target in the dark. The fish-zombie lunged. Wet, slippery hands covered in scales slapped into her chest and she went flying onto her back. Pain shot through her, and she gasped a soundless scream. The zombie didn't slow down, throwing itself upon her.

She bunched her body up, getting her legs between them before the monster could land on top of her. Her arms were weak, but she could still kick. Growling, hissing sounds helped her zero in on the thing's head. She reared back and kicked both legs up with everything she had.

Bones cracked—its neck, she hoped—and the zombie collapsed into a heap at her side. He moaned a strange, gurgling sound, and the leaves rustled beneath him as he twitched sickeningly before he stilled.

Everly lay there gasping, trying to catch her breath as the lighthouse beam returned.

A shadow fell over her face. Everly almost sobbed as she looked up, hoping to see Rylan there, or any friendly face.

Instead, another twisted fish zombie growled down at her.

Everly tried to shove up off her back, to scramble away, but pain lanced through her arms, her elbows buckling.

The zombie slammed down on top of her, crushing her back onto the muddy ground. Her head bounced off the dirt, sending brilliant lights bursting in her vision.

She kicked her legs but didn't have the right angle between them to do more than squirm beneath the fish-man's weight. Grasping her flashlight with her good arm she thrust it up at the monster. It hit soft and squelchy flesh. The impact seemed to kick the light back to life, the bulb illuminating as it sank abnormally deep into the monster's bloated, decomposing belly.

Teeth bared in disgust, Everly tried to wrench the flashlight back out again, but it had suctioned into the zombie's middle, disappearing under the torn fabric and rotting flesh, making the creature glow dull red from within.

The creature's scaly, dripping hands slid all over her,

grabbing and swatting at her weak swings as she fought to ward it away. Her legs were stuck, her arms basically useless, her only weapon gone.

"Help—"

One heavy, soggy arm pressed down over her neck, pinning her in place and cutting off her cry. She writhed and kicked, but its mushy, wet chest, glowing red, sagged down, molding over her body.

Horror and the overwhelming stench of death sent panic cutting through Everly like knives.

"Everly? Evie? Where are you?" Rylan called out in the distance.

She tried to call back, choked to silence by the weight on her throat. Tears stung her eyes as she could barely draw breath. The zombie leaned its face close to hers, jagged teeth bared. Gas puffed from its mouth, smelling of wet, decaying fish.

Everly groaned with effort, pressing her hands up against the zombie's ribcage. She shoved with all her might, her injured arms radiating agony.

The fish-Nazi snapped at her from only a hair's breadth away, trying to bite the flesh clean from her face. Slimy ichor dripped from its mouth onto her cheek. She choked on the cloying death smell as his skin sloughed away beneath her fingertips, sinking in the way the flashlight had.

But her strength held. She kept the living corpse and

its gnashing mouth propped up away from her body. She just had to hold on, keep it from biting her until Rylan got back. She just had to keep the overwhelming pain coursing through her arms from breaking her.

He'll come for me. Rylan will come and help me.

Only, she couldn't even see the battle anymore, hidden down in the thick undergrowth as she was. She didn't know how far away she'd gotten, or what was happening to the others.

The zombie shivered, moving strangely. Its mouth opened wider, then wider again, gaping open larger than humanly possible as it made horrifying gagging sounds.

For a desperate, panic-filled moment, Everly thought it was going to vomit on her face.

Then something else emerged.

Everly couldn't even scream.

A sharp, snake-like face appeared down the zombie's throat. Beady, white eyes stared at her from behind the zombie's teeth. A huge, ghostly-pale moray eel. Needle-sharp teeth snapped as it slithered out over the zombie's tongue, straight for Everly.

CHAPTER TWELVE

Jasper had been irritatingly vague on the phone.

"I need assistance with something," he'd said.

"I don't know from whom else to request support," he'd said.

"I don't want to be alone ... on this."

That was what decided Cherry to go to him. There was the smallest hint of vulnerability in those words, like an opening in Jasper's cool demeanor, a hint that maybe something had changed.

Just don't get your hopes up, he reminded himself.

The Crow's Nest was dead at that time of midmorning. Most shadyrs who stopped in for a post-patrol drink had headed home by then. Crowea herself, the old, wild-haired witch who ran the establishment, had long since turned in for the night, and her third shift bartender—a bookish woman in floral overalls—sat on a stool at the bar, paging through a fancy hardcover.

The bar remained open twenty-four seven, as a sort of haven for shadyrs, but with bare-bones staff and little service actually offered. The woman glanced up as Cherry passed into the building, eyed him as if checking he wasn't going to cause trouble or interrupt her reading, then returned to her book.

The Crow's Nest was a kitschy place of mismatched armchairs arranged around low tables. Each cluster of seating was separated from the rest by low bookshelves loaded with treasures and trinkets related to witchcraft, or that had simply caught Crowea's eye, from sparkling crystals to fairy figurines.

Antique lamps draped in colorful scarves gave the place a soft glow, and the walls and ceilings were covered in tapestries, posters of unicorns, and signs saying things like 'Witch, please.'

Cherry liked the bar, though he liked it a lot more when it was a place he could hang out with his secret boyfriend. They'd spent hours sitting in those plush armchairs, across the room but within sight of each other, chatting via text. Then they'd slip away into the shelter of the curtained back areas when the desire to be closer became overwhelming.

Seeing Jasper there now, chewing his nails as he sat waiting, brought all those memories back like a slap to the cheek.

He only chews his nails like that when he's really worried.

"Hey," Cherry said, stopping at the entrance to the two-armchair nook.

He was going for nonchalance, but the word came out semi-strangled. Loaded with unspoken regrets. His heart rate kicked up a notch and his stomach fluttered as it always did in Jasper's presence. Cherry found Jasper gorgeous, but in an understated way.

His tan cardigan gave him a sort of gentle sophistication, which perfectly matched his uptight personality and his beautiful dark skin. His ebony hair was styled back in its usual perfection. He didn't like a hair out of place, which became something of a game between them when Cherry liked to muss it up.

Jasper stood, patting at his clothes to smooth them. "Hi. Um, I really appreciate you coming. I know it's late ..."

Cherry shrugged. It was the hour most shadyrs would be getting a morning nap in. He'd been up half the night already and would have continued to the island with the others if he wasn't here. Luckily, shadyrs didn't seem to need as much sleep as regular humans.

Cherry stepped forward, sliding into the armchair directly across from Jasper. "It sounded important."

Jasper returned to his seat, rubbing his hands over his knees.

On the table between them, Cherry noticed a glass waiting for him, dark cola with a maraschino cherry dangling on the side. His lip twitched at that in-joke between the two of them. It didn't seem fair that a relationship could end but all the little details remained, left behind to hurt at inopportune moments.

He glared at the drink. "Was it actually important? This isn't some ... ploy, or—"

"No! No, I mean, it is important," Jasper said.

A zing of disappointment stabbed through Cherry's chest. "Good. Because I had to abandon *my team* on a critical mission for this."

Jasper raised his thick eyebrows. "What's happening, are they okay? I observed that Everly wasn't with you earlier, is it about her?"

"That's precisely none of your business."

Jasper's eyebrows lowered again. "Oh. Yes. Of course."

Silence fell between them. The bartender turned a page in her book and somewhere behind her, a refrigeration unit kicked on with a mechanical hum.

"Before we proceed, I wanted to be sure there wasn't too much animosity between us."

"You want to know if I'll have your back? Oh, I'm still angry at you. But I don't want you dead. Most days."

Jasper waved his long fingers at the drink. "I guess that was my misplaced attempt at a peace offering."

Cherry picked up the cola and had a sip. He needed the caffeine and the sugar, and to hide the smile that touched the corner of his lips. He wanted to hide every ounce of emotion he still felt for this man because it was a weakness. Like the longer he spent in his company, the more likely it would be that Cherry would forgive him and fall back into old habits.

Fall back into Jasper.

But that couldn't happen. They were too different. Too opposed. Howell versus Darkfrey. Jasper had proven where his real loyalties lay, and Cherry didn't want to be the runner-up, the hidden trophy, any longer.

Jasper cleared his throat. "It is good to see you."

Cherry recognized the affection glinting in Jasper's eyes, the way he leaned toward Cherry like a moth drawn to the flame.

"Don't," Cherry said, dropping the drink roughly back onto the table.

Jasper blinked. "Don't what?"

"Don't … be like that. Don't act like you still care about me."

Jasper glanced down at his shoes. "I do, though."

"Just not more than you care about keeping up appearances," Cherry scoffed, irritation and betrayal turning the cola bitter in his mouth.

The skin around Jasper's eyes tightened. "That's not

fair."

"You're right, it's not." Cherry shrugged. "But it's true."

Muscles twitched in Jasper's jaw, as though working through his reply. But nothing came. He couldn't even deny it.

Cherry sighed. "Forget about it. What did you need help with?"

Jasper chewed over his words for a moment longer, then said, "It's a mission. Something Vonny has asked me to do."

Cherry scowled. "And you need me for what?"

"She told me to keep it quiet, that I couldn't tell anyone at the estate. But she didn't expressly say I had to go on my own."

"What's the job?"

"Can't say." Jasper averted his eyes.

Cherry leaned back, folding his arms. Of course, Jasper had to follow the rules to the letter.

"Why'd she pick you for this super-secret squirrel mission? Why not go as a brace?"

Jasper's eyebrows dipped, his dark eyes flashing, troubled. "I don't know."

"And that didn't raise a red flag? Did it occur to you she might have sent you on a mission *alone* to get you killed?"

Jasper said warningly, "She's one of my brace. I trust her."

"Yeah, I suppose you're right," Cherry said, laying on

the snark. "If she wanted, she'd probably kill you herself."

Jasper snorted a soft laugh, then shook his head. "I trust her ... but I am also acutely aware of what happened to our last brace member who went off on his own. That's why I asked for your help. I didn't want to be alone."

Their gazes met, and Cherry's heart constricted. Their relationship hadn't lasted long, but it had burned bright, and Cherry would have given Jasper anything if he only asked.

"Fine," Cherry said, channeling irritation into his tone so Jasper wouldn't hear the pain he felt just sitting there, looking into his eyes, wishing things were different. "You're right that you need backup. It's the smart thing to do. I'll go to make sure you stay safe while you do whatever secret thing you need to do."

Jasper's expression smoothed into a relieved smile. "Thank you."

"Nobody should be alone in Shroudhaven." Cherry took another large gulp of the cola to try to wash away the lump in his throat. "So where are we headed?"

Jasper stood up, straightening his cardigan. "Rook's Theater."

The eel snapped.

Everly whipped her head to the side. Sharp teeth grazed her ear.

Tears spilled from her eyes as she strained to keep the undead fish-Nazi away from her face. Its arm still pressed against her throat. She couldn't catch her breath and her arms felt like they were about to splinter into a million pieces.

I should use the dragon. She could feel it, squirming inside her. Hungry, always hungry ... but weak.

Possibly still strong enough to throw the monsters on her clear away, though. But what if that shattered her entirely? What did it matter if she was going to die there anyway?

With a gurgling hiss, the eel coiled its body and retracted back into the zombie's gaping maw, tensing for another strike.

Gasping for breath, dizziness overwhelmed Everly. Blind panic pulled her in like an icy embrace.

No, don't lose control.

The eel lunged again. She turned her face the other way, and its teeth tangled in her hair.

Facing that new direction, she stared almost directly into the beam of the lighthouse, and within it, saw the silhouette of something charging her way. Bounding, speeding, *growling.*

"Everly!" the strange shape boomed with Rylan's voice. Sparks crackled and black mist swirled.

He slammed into the zombie that had her pinned, taking it and the eel with him as he dove over the top of her.

The lighthouse beam drifted away again, leaving them in darkness. The flashlight still glowed from within the zombie's stomach, casting a red aura over it and what must be Rylan. But Rylan was in a form Everly had never seen before.

He'd been fighting the shadyr transformation that Everly's presence forced on him since he woke up. Trying to keep it to a familiar vampire form. But his guard must have been down due to the fight.

Now, he was ... *everything.*

He shifted rapidly and uncontrollably as he rolled across the forest floor, grappling with the dead Nazi.

He sprouted fur as he tore the protruding eel free and flung it away, and fangs burst from between his lips as he took the full brunt of the soldier's uppercut. Then fur became scales, first shimmering iridescent, then sharp and metallic. A ripple of a translucent glow passed over his face—the shadyr's ghostly form she'd witnessed back in Gorhanmere.

Then *wings* burst from his back, bony and leathery. His shifting settled into one solid form. His body mass was twice normal. In the red glow, his eyes shone. He looked like some kind of demon, or dragon.

Without pausing, Rylan launched off the ground, taking the zombie with him. The fish man struggled sloppily in Rylan's grip, then was swiftly torn in two. Three *thunks* hit the forest floor. Top half. Bottom half. Flashlight.

Baring monstrous teeth, Rylan swooped down from the sky and flew back the way he came, leaving a gust of air across Everly's body in his wake.

She gasped that oxygen in. Shaking off the paralysis from the shock of Rylan's form, she could breathe again. With the waterlogged zombie no longer crushing every part of her, she could breathe again.

She was left lying on her back, panting, wondering what the fuck just happened.

"Hey! There you are." Harper burst through a bush in front of Everly. "Are you okay?"

Everly shook her head, then took the hand that was extended to help her up. It was covered in gray slime. The flashlight offered some illumination from where it lay on the ground but didn't extend to where roars and hideous tearing sounds came from the distance.

Everly stared wide-eyed into the darkness. "What is happening?"

Harper rested her gore-covered axe on her shoulder. "Rylan's gone full beast mode. He's mopping up everything out there."

The lighthouse beam returned, and now Everly was standing again, the area beneath the U-boat was visible. Rylan flew low, snatching zombies from the ground like an oversized bird of prey. Rotting heads were removed. Zombie bodies were flung like torpedoes, bowling over more. Dismembered legs were used as makeshift clubs.

Everly stared, eyes and mouth stuck open. Darkness came again, and when the next beam returned, it fell over a graveyard of mutilated carcasses.

Air swirled around Everly as Rylan landed in front of her. His shirt was gone, the flexible body armor beneath stretched to its limits. His chest rose and fell in huge breaths. His skin was a deep red, covered in thick, metallic scales.

With glowing red eyes, darkened by lowered brows, he stared at Everly, then tilted his head away from her.

"Everyone good?" His gravelly voice seemed an octave lower than usual.

Through the trees, Callan called back, "I think so."

"Unbelievably, yes," said Tammy.

"Right?" drawled Denny. "Didn't think we were walking out of that one."

Everly clasped both arms to her chest, shaking. Rylan eyed her for a moment, then bent down and snatched up her flashlight. He wiped it twice on his pants before handing it to her without a word.

"Um. Thanks." She shivered harder.

Callan, Tammy, and Denny picked their way through the undergrowth to join them.

Tammy's hooded sweatshirt had been ripped along the shoulder seam, exposing her body armor beneath, and the hint of red. Denny had zombie goop on his face and neck, and a nasty gash tore the thigh of Callan's pants, stained with blood around the edges. Rylan stood taller than everyone by at least three feet, and his pointed wings soared even higher.

Callan said, "So ... that's new."

"Yeah, man," Denny agreed. "*I* want to be a dragon!" Rylan growled back.

"What even is that form?" Tammy said.

"Herrelspurn?" Callan said. "I've never come up against one before but from the descriptions we learned back with the Darkfreys, it doesn't seem quite right."

"The wings are from that form, but not the rest. This feels strange, almost like more than one form." Rylan took several steps back from Everly and shook himself.

Black smoke and sparking light swirled around him, and the wings vanished. His body shrank. Then the red skin tone and scales faded, leaving only unmarred, human skin behind.

Callan smirked and poked at his brother's shredded shirt and the split seams on his pants. "Whatever it is, we can mark it down as another 'not friendly to clothing' form."

Rylan smacked his hand away, clearly not sharing the humor.

Everly tried hard not to stare at the holes. Shadyrs seemed to struggle with clothing for anything other than vasmire/vampire form, which didn't make them significantly different from their normal body shapes. And auerdax/ghost form, for which they seemed to take whatever they were touching with them onto the ghostly plane.

Their flexible Darkfrey body armor was designed for shifting, but normal clothing not so much.

Everly was surprised to see Rylan switch back to human form now, rather than vampire, given his proximity. Then, with a slight groan hidden under a cleared throat, he took a few more steps away. He seemed to be attempting nonchalance in distancing himself from her.

It didn't work.

It was painfully obvious to Everly that he neither could nor wanted to remain near her.

Harper rubbed at the side of her waist where her clothing was damp and ripped. "Do we need to be worried about zombie bites? Asking for a friend."

"Harper!" Everly gasped, reaching for her.

She lifted the bottom hem of Harper's pink hunting

jacket, peeling back layers of clothing beneath.

"I don't think so," Callan said, moving forward to inspect her wound as well. "They were beshadowed corpses, not movie-style virus-based. I mean, you'll want to disinfect it for sure, though. Short course of antibiotics couldn't hurt."

He got his flashlight back out, and after a few hits, it started working again. He shined it on Harper's skin

Everly ran a finger gently over the area to clear the gunk away. "Looks like it didn't even break the skin. Is that a scar?"

"Oh. It's nothing," Harper said, covering up again. "I'm fine."

"Yeah you are," Denny leered, eyes still on her waist as though he had x-ray vision.

"No thanks to you."

"Come on, who could resist that tempting lure?" Denny wistfully looked over his shoulder at the U-boat they'd left behind.

"Literally *everyone* except for you," Tammy replied.

Callan looked ready to tackle Denny if needed. "You're not still wanting to go in there."

"I mean ... the booty we could be leaving behind ..." Denny turned back with a sigh. "Nah man, I think I learned my lesson on that one."

"As if that's possible," Tammy muttered.

"Let's move on then," Callan said, adjusting the straps on his backpack.

Rylan took a few steps toward the U-boat and retrieved his and Everly's packs that he must have shed earlier.

Exhaustion, both physical and emotional, washed over Everly. She wobbled, and Harper caught her by the elbow with one hand, balancing her before she could fall.

Rylan's eyes flashed. "We should rest."

"We're almost there," Denny argued, pointing at the rotating light beyond the canopy.

"You can't even see that your idiocy got some of us injured, can you?" Tammy said, her eyes on Callan's still-bleeding leg. "Not that I care if I turn into a zombie. Then I could eat your brains. No wait, you don't have any."

"I was also going to suggest a bit of T and T time—triage and treatment," Callan clarified to Everly and Harper, then turned back to Rylan. "I thought you'd be keen to push on though."

Rylan's gaze flickered once more over Everly. "We should *rest*. Just for a couple of hours."

Everly nodded slowly. She wanted to keep going, wanted this done as quickly and safely as possible, but she literally couldn't move. She was frozen in place, all energy going toward reducing her interior turmoil and nothing left for external motion.

Tammy and Callan both needed first aid, and Denny,

for all his brazen arrogance, looked exhausted. Harper somehow continued to buzz around, full of energy, but Everly worried she might have other wounds she wasn't bringing to anyone's attention. Rylan's expression had grown stony. Physically, he showed no wear and tear, but his jaw twitched and he rubbed at his temples.

Rylan shook his head, the hint of a snarl on his lips. "We're all dead on our feet. And we have no idea what we're going to walk into when we reach the lighthouse."

Chapter Thirteen

They moved far enough away that the stench of zombie parts wasn't overwhelming, but there wasn't anywhere to take shelter. No cave or clearing, and no way they were using the U-boat.

They simply picked a patch of ground between twisted trees where there was enough flat dirt to sit down.

It was probably as good a place as any. If the octo-deer didn't come in there, maybe the area was safe from other beshadowed threats too, now that they'd cleared out the zombies.

The Howell team got moving quickly. Denny cleared some of the brush away with his machete and Rylan pulled a lightweight tarp from his pack and spread it out before putting Everly's blanket on top, then immediately directed Everly herself to sit down.

He quickly turned away and pulled white blocks and metal tools from his pack, which turned out to be for fire-starting.

Callan and Tammy had opened the first aid kits and were arguing over what triage meant and who got treatment first. Tammy's shoulder wound was a nasty graze, which Callan quickly cleaned and taped over with gauze as she grumbled the entire time.

Everly heard snatches of *not even worth it* and *don't bother* and *that's enough, we need to work on your leg.*

When they ripped back the fabric of Callan's pants, Everly had to agree with Tammy. His wound was far worse. Everly was surprised he was walking around the way he was. The Howell boys were tough.

But they shouldn't need to be. They are only here, getting hurt, because of me.

Rylan turned from the fire and offered to do the suturing.

"I've got it," Tammy snapped, dousing the wound with a pungent fluid.

Callan winced and mouthed to his brother, "Help."

"She's got it." Rylan grinned back.

Everly settled against the tree trunk behind her. The bark was sodden and soaked into her clothes, but as she was still wet from the storm, it made little difference. She pulled her blanket up around her, trying to fight the incessant shaking of her body.

The warm glow of Rylan's fire chased away some of the chill. Everly tipped her head back against the trunk and watched him feed sticks into the flames. She couldn't stop picturing the zombies. Their red armbands.

The way they'd swarmed her friends, almost overwhelmed them. The eel, with its dead, white eyes, snapping at her face. The ghosts, the hybrid creatures, the trees with minds of their own ... This place was a nightmare.

Her heart turned into a hummingbird in her chest.

They're only here because of me.

Tammy had her face close to Callan's thigh, moving her black hands in small, careful motions as she sutured the gash.

Callan stared at her with his eyebrows raised, wincing at each tug of thread. "You're really good at that."

She didn't look up. "And I bet that surprises you, 'cause you expect me to be a child about everything."

His lips twisted upward. "That's not it. I just thought you were going to enact vengeance on me for making you get treated first."

She paused and looked up then, completely deadpan. "You mean like a child would?"

Callan rubbed the back of his head. "Okay, got me there. Honestly, I think you're more mature than me most of the time."

Tammy only grunted in reply.

Harper warmed herself near the fire, stretching her back. "Any idea what time it is? I've completely lost track in this place."

Rylan scowled at his watch as though it had insulted him. "Later than it should be. We're moving too slowly."

Apparently finished hacking into bushes, Denny sheathed his machete and took a seat near the fire. "You're the one who called a break."

"And why do you think that was? Whose screwup wasted our time and left us in this position?" Rylan stuffed his fire striker violently into his pack. He glared Denny down as though he wanted to shove it into him instead.

Harper sighed and dropped onto the tarp beside Everly. She placed her axe on her lap like a pet.

"I told you we should have left him behind. But *no*, he's 'capable.' Isn't that what you said, Callan?"

Callan half-smiled, half-winced as he watched Tammy tie off a stitch. "I did. Can I take it back now?"

Denny huffed and reached into his pack.

"So help me, if you pull a beer can from there, you're a dead man," Rylan growled.

He rolled a log over a bit closer to the fire and sat down, keeping his gaze fixed on the man.

Denny let go of whatever he'd been holding and pulled back out empty-handed.

"Look, so what if I make mistakes sometimes? Everyone does. Even golden boy here," he added, motioning to Rylan. "He ran off alone and got himself got by a vasmire, didn't he?"

"At least he didn't get anyone else hurt in the process," Tammy said.

Rylan's jaw clenched and he turned away.

Callan pointed at Denny. "Dude, you're a human wrecking ball. You saw a Nazi submarine hanging from vines in a beshadowed forest and literally thought *I want to be in there*. Nobody in their right mind would do that."

"Yeah, well maybe you're right about that. Because nobody in their right mind would put up with this disrespect." Denny picked up a stick and threw it into the fire, shooting sparks into the sky. "I'm a damn capable shadyr, and ya'll are on my case non-stop. Denny, don't say that. Denny, don't do that. Denny, ew."

Harper squinted at him. "Have you even heard what comes out of your mouth?"

"You know, sure, I say the wrong things or do the wrong things sometimes. I'm not gonna pretend I don't. This world is hard for people like me." Denny folded his arms, frowning like a kid no one picked for their team. "I didn't grow up all woke and LGBQRTAV whatever like you kids."

Tammy groaned. "Oh my ghast, you're such a bigot."

"But you know what?" Denny snapped irritably. "I also show up. I didn't have to come to this cursed island, but I did because we're a damned team."

Harper scoffed. "Do you even know what a 'team' is? All you ever think about is yourself."

"That's not true at all, I also think about you, a lot. You and me. Together. You know what I mean."

Harper wrapped her hands around the axe on her lap and looked ready for murder.

Callan rubbed his forehead. "For ghast's sake, dude, shut your mouth before you dig your own grave."

Rylan glared at Denny from across the flames. "Seriously, how do you sleep at night?"

"Face down and naked, so ya'll can kiss my ass."

As they continued to argue, Everly squeezed her eyes shut and swallowed the pulse pounding in her throat. It didn't matter what Denny did. They were surrounded by danger. If it wasn't that fight with the zombies, it could have easily been something else. Her friends could have died, could still die, all because of her.

Her heart beat so hard it hurt, and she put her trembling fingertips to her solar plexus to massage away the knot of anxiety. Her breaths came short and fast, then shorter and faster as the group continued to argue around her.

All my fault.

It's all my fault.

She couldn't chase away memories of the skirmish, but they became twisted *what-if* versions. What if Rylan hadn't pulled that zombie and eel off her? What if Harper had been bitten? What if Callan and Tammy were crushed within that mass of dead flesh?

Every bit of fear that she'd fought back rose to the surface and overflowed. Panic consumed her in a way the zombie never could have, spiraling her down into darkness.

"Ev? Oh, hey." Harper moved closer, and she wrapped an arm around Everly. "It's okay. Remember your toolkit."

"What's happening?" Rylan said. "Is she hurt?"

"Panic attack, I think," Harper replied.

Their voices all sounded muffled behind the pulse in Everly's ears. She struggled to peel her eyes open again, trying to bring herself back into the here and now, then wished she hadn't. All the catastrophizing happening in her head was better than the look Rylan gave her. He got to his feet and stared down at her as her body rebelled against itself.

He's watching, he can see me falling apart.

She'd had panic attacks as a kid too, back when they'd been friends, but then she could disguise them. Blame it on a tantrum or simply run away and hide. She had nowhere to hide now. He could see every bit of how broken she was.

Shame screamed inside her almost as loud as the panic.

Pull it together.

She dealt with this all the time. She had her toolkit; all the breathing and grounding techniques years of therapy had given her. But everything felt so out of control right now. Everything had changed irrevocably. Even her old methods of calling her anxiety the "dragon" no longer worked because she knew now that the "dragon" wasn't just anxiety. It was the monster inside her, the light that consumed souls.

That being would escape if she lost control. And if it did, it might kill her, or kill her friends.

Everly focused on Harper's arm around her shoulders. She set her mind to controlling her breaths, counting them out. At first, they remained ragged, and she was barely able to count before it felt like her lungs would explode. But she kept going, kept counting, found a rhythm in time to how the lighthouse beam swept around them.

The rushing in her ears faded and the tightness in her chest released. Her exhalations were slow and calm, and her vision cleared to see everyone staring at her.

Shame heated her cheeks and neck, strong enough that her flight impulses almost kicked her into panic mode again.

Her voice was a harsh whisper. "I'm sorry."

Rylan's expression changed. No longer dark and brooding, it was something else, something like awe.

"Wow," he said softly. "I think I get it now."

"Get what?" Everly felt completely confused.

"How you can control that thing inside you, the dragon."

Everly shook her head. Control was the furthest from what she felt.

"You just navigated out of a panic attack in less than thirty seconds," Rylan pointed out, as though that explained things.

Callan's eyes widened. "Wow, yeah. Most people would have been knocked down for way longer. What? You think none of the shadyr kids at Darkfrey Estate dealt with anxiety issues?"

Everly's face remained scorching. "No, but, it's just ... I can't ..."

Callan shrugged. "It's nothing to be ashamed of. Not for anyone."

"Especially not you." Rylan didn't need to say why.

He knew everything she'd been through as a kid and was intimately acquainted with her nightmares.

"What you did just now, that is seriously impressive self-control. No wonder you've been able to keep the dragon locked away for so long. Why you can keep it under control. I doubt anyone else would be able to manage it like you do."

Everly gaped, close to tears.

Harper reached down to take Everly's hand and squeezed it gently. "You're a badass, and I'm not the only one who can see it."

Everly dropped her head onto Harper's shoulder. "Thank you," she said to everyone.

As her friend's hand rested on hers, Everly realized she was shaking. "Are you all right?"

Harper shrugged, a slight crease across her forehead. "Tired. More than I thought I'd be."

"You sure you didn't get hurt? Those scars on your waist, I've never seen them before. They looked new."

Harper shifted, bringing her arms back off Everly. "Well, they're not, and shut it before Denny starts picturing us naked together."

"Too late," he jeered.

Callan and Rylan also turned from the conversation as though there was something more important to see on the other side of the fire.

Tammy, however, eyed Harper. "Huh, I didn't think princesses were the cutting type."

Harper tensed. "What?"

"Scars? On places like thighs, waist, arms, where you think people won't notice? Classic cutting behavior. Not that I'd know."

Callan flashed a sharp look at her.

"You're right, you don't know. You don't know anything about me. I'm not a cutter, and I'm not a damned princess, either," Harper snarled, inordinately furious. "You all look at me and expect me to be a certain way. You don't even consider who I really am. That maybe I'm sick of those expectations."

Her anger exacerbated the shaking, and Everly sat up, turning to look at her best friend. Her hands were claw-like, wrapped around the handle of her axe and squeezing tight.

Before Everly could try to calm her, Harper surged on. "I've been expected to be perfect in every way my entire life."

Firelight sparkled in her eyes and along with her battle tangled hair it made her look like a goddess of vengeance.

"Expected to act just right and be top the class and win the pageant and marry rich but be a girl boss and be attractive but don't look like you try too hard and don't be a whore but make men want you and be smart but not so clever its off-putting and don't ever put a foot out of line or it won't matter if you did *everything else* right, it will all be over."

"You know what it's like," she flicked her chin toward Tammy and Everly. "How hard we have to work *every moment* of our lives while watching white men succeed when being entirely mediocre, or worse."

She turned her tirade toward Denny.

Then she turned her head upward, as though yelling at the universe. "How are we even supposed to know what we want, who we are, when every second of our lives we're told what to be based on how others see us?"

Nobody answered, only stared.

Harper's face changed from pure fury to confusion to shock. She covered her mouth with her shaking hand. "I don't know where all of that came from. I mean ... I do. But I don't ... This isn't the time. I just ... I'm tired."

"Hey." Everly reached for her, and Harper tensed, then relaxed into Everly's embrace. "You can be whoever you want to be. I'll still love you. I'm sorry if I ever made you feel otherwise."

Harper squeezed Everly tight enough to make her wince.

Everly looked over Harper's shoulder toward Rylan, and he turned away as though caught staring.

He grumbled, "Come on, let's get a few hours' rest. We all need it."

It was clear they did. Nerves were raw all around. It was also clear to Everly that she'd been too deep in her own mind lately to realize that Harper was going through something, too. Down in her lap, the handle of her axe had splintered where she'd been gripping it tight.

The strength she'd shown while fighting earlier ... Everly didn't want to question her friend's skill, but it wasn't normal.

What secrets was Harper keeping?

Chapter Fourteen

Tammy tried to sleep, but every time she closed her eyes, visions of beshadowed fish and squid swirling in murky water surrounded her. Within those creatures was a face, pleading and scared, and hands reaching out for her as they were drawn down into the dark. It was Blaise, then it was Callan, then it was Blaise again.

She tried so hard to rest. She didn't want to be a liability to the team. So she lay there, as still as possible, mind twisting in knots.

Maybe I need Everly to teach me some of her breathing techniques.

The few times Tammy opened her eyes over the couple of hours they rested, she checked on Callan first, who slept as easily as he did everything else. Rylan would always be there, standing alert as he kept watch over everyone, but especially Everly. She seemed to be in a troubled sleep. Harper cuddled up against her. Denny snored.

Tammy was still wide awake when Callan gently shook her shoulder. "We're moving on again. Eat and pack."

Even though her phone indicated it was early afternoon, the forest was dark as night. Even her shadyr night vision couldn't see into the deepest shadows. A symptom of the beshadowing, she guessed.

A few others had their flashlights on already, but Tammy figured more light couldn't hurt. She slapped her flashlight against her palm. The bulb flickered in and out for several seconds before it finally caught and held steady.

The fire was buried, and tarps and blankets were packed. They ate ravenously, tearing into granola bars, trail mix, and jerky. Everly nibbled at hers before she tucked the bar back into the wrapper and hid it away in her backpack. In the ambient glow of the flashlights, there were dark circles beneath her eyes.

Callan offered Tammy some of his jerky. "Did you get any sleep?"

"Yeah. Some," she lied, and waved away the offering, indicating the half-eaten nut bar she had in her hand.

"You still got water?" he asked.

Tammy's eye twitched. "Yes, I'm sleeping. I'm eating. I'm staying hydrated. I am capable of being a functional human, thanks for checking."

Callan grinned around a piece of jerky. "Sorry, I know. You're more than competent. I just wanted to make sure you're okay."

Tammy closed her eyes and turned her face away until she could return it to a comfortably blank expression.

Callan had been hovering over her every moment since they'd crawled out of Myrkur Lake. She deserved it. She'd done a crazy, self-destructive thing and nearly died for it. Almost took him with her.

And now he was treating her like she was a pet that was so pathetic it might strangle itself on its own leash.

Imagining what his attentiveness would feel like if it came from adoration or respect for her left a painful hollow in her chest for how much she wanted it. But she knew it was only pity. Poor little Tammy, disowned by friends and family, cursed, living with the guilt of accidentally killing her best friend.

She knew Callan would never have real feelings for her. But the fact that he pitied her hurt even more.

I'm nothing but a burden. Why would anyone ever want me?

With her face schooled back into its normal cool, sardonic glare, she turned back to Callan. "I'd be a whole lot better if you stopped treating me like a baby."

"Sorry, I know ..." Callan repeated.

She stood up, hefted her pack on, and walked away

from Callan's under-his-breath cursing.

With everyone ready, Rylan took the lead and they headed in the direction of the lighthouse.

Tammy expected more trouble before they reached the end of the forest, but the rest of the journey—a mere ten-minute hike—passed uneventfully.

As the trees thinned out, the lighthouse beam grew stronger and brighter. They left the thick undergrowth behind for a rocky clearing backed by a cliff, upon which the lighthouse sat perched high above. The land narrowed ahead of them, dropping off on each side into a roaring sea.

The rain had ceased. It was no longer as dark as night now that they were out from under the canopy, but bulbous, low clouds the color of ash still hung across the sky.

Tammy's steps faltered as she looked up at the lighthouse, trying to make sense of what she was seeing. It leaned out over the ocean at an angle that didn't seem possible, though the topmost portion where the light circled endlessly was still upright, balanced like a hat.

A jagged gash ran the full height of the building. It could split in half at any moment and tumble into the ocean.

The light reflected off the stormy clouds, casting an aura around the structure. Lightning branched and forked, brightening the sky and striking the highest part of the lighthouse every few seconds.

"I guess popping your wings back out and flying up there isn't an option," Harper said to Rylan.

"I'm not particularly keen on testing whether that form is lightning proof, no."

Nothing grew in the small clearing between the trees and the high cliff where the lighthouse sat. They moved closer, and Tammy dodged large boulders and fallen rocks that had sheared off the bluff.

At first, she worried they'd have to climb, but a narrow, nearly invisible staircase came into view. It zigzagged up the cliff and opened onto a surface out of sight.

The staircase was cut directly into the gray rock, with the cliff face on one side and a sheer drop on the other. Each step was carved at abnormally deep levels and covered in moss and algae, so ascending was a study in danger.

Rylan shuffled positions to be behind Everly again, leaving Callan and Tammy up front.

Callan took a step forward, then turned back. "Want to take point?"

Tammy's eyes opened wide for a moment. But then she looked back at Everly, how woozy she seemed, and Rylan on guard behind her.

Callan's probably just putting me somewhere he can keep an eye on me.

"Whatever." With a huff, she took the lead.

Tammy kept one hand against the wet wall to stay

balanced. She moved slowly and surely, testing out each slippery step for the best purchase before she shifted her weight forward. She wouldn't slip. She would show confidence. She would keep up a good speed. She would stop being a liability, a burden.

She was halfway up when she felt the first hint of an eidolghast.

Its energy pressed against her senses, and her body wavered and grew hot.

Oh no. No no no.

Tammy halted, turned her face to the wall, and clung on with both hands. She squeezed her eyes shut and focused on the sound of the waves crashing against the cliff.

Callan put a hand on her shoulder. "I feel it too."

His calm, sympathetic tone infuriated her. Every shadyr there could no doubt feel it. But she was the only one who couldn't refuse her transformation.

Don't change, Tammy snarled inwardly, fighting against the wave of magic rippling through her.

Cherry wasn't even there to make her feel better by changing as well. She'd be the center of attention. The sole person incapable of being strong.

The ghost's presence overwhelmed her senses and inky, shadyr magic burst around her, bringing the change. It wasn't a weroth or a vasmire or any familiar presence she'd experienced before. If they were out on the sea, it could have been a nyevmer, but here, up on a rocky bluff?

She'd studied all the known eidolghasts, the forms shadyrs took for each. If it was a nyevmer, she knew what was coming.

Tammy still yelped as her legs fused. The seams on her pants burst, dropping to the ground. She sagged against the wall, struggling to remain on her feet, but they vanished too, replaced by a wide, midnight-blue fin.

Her boots fell right off, dropping onto the step. She slipped, her new tail sliding out from underneath her. She wobbled, about to tumble right over the edge of the stairs, and her eyes filled with the view of the sharp rocks far below.

Callan caught her with both arms, gathering her against his chest. "Whoa. Got you."

Tammy's breath hitched in her throat. She clung to his shoulders, her skin heating from his proximity and the transformation still taking place. She hoped her top half wasn't going to change much. Her armor and hoodie still thankfully remained in place.

Her hands prickled and morphed until they were covered in delicate scales, webbed with a translucent membrane. Her nails grew sharp. But to her disappointment, her hands remained stained, shroudpool-black.

"Wow," Callan said, taking her new appearance in. "I mean, I've never seen a shadyr in nyevmer form before.

You have gills."

Startled, Tammy released one of his shoulders and touched her neck. Four raised slits had formed above her collar bones. Her studies had told her that this form let shadyrs breathe underwater, but that would be something else to actually experience.

"You guys turn into frickin' mermaids?" Harper squealed from farther back. "Are we still completely certain shadyr bites don't transfer powers?"

"Yeah, this is nyevmer form. But why here? They're water-based and we're not that close to the shoreline." Callan frowned at the ocean in the distance.

"Wherever it is, we need to keep moving."

Right. Moving. Upstairs. With a tail.

"I can ... wait here. You guys keep going." *I couldn't even lead the team up some stairs without screwing up.*

"Don't be like that," Callan said. "Come on, hold tight."

Tammy flushed even hotter. "What?"

He bent down and looped his arm beneath her tail. Tammy gasped, fumbling for his neck as he lifted her into his arms.

He settled one beneath the part of her fin where her knees would have been, then wrapped his other carefully around her back beneath her backpack so she was sitting in his grasp, fin dangling.

Callan glanced at the pants on the ground. "You got

spare clothes in your pack?"

She bobbed a small nod.

He called back down the line, "Can someone grab her boots?"

Then he straightened his shoulders and resumed the climb.

Utter shame left her speechless. Every point of contact between the two of them left a lump in her throat. The combination left her eyes hot and head spinning, but surprisingly, the touch of his skin on hers didn't send her wildly teleporting away to Dark Corner.

That was progress, at least. That was one small blessing in a world of humiliation.

He has to carry me. I have graduated to a literal burden.

It didn't help that the two human women were ogling her with barely concealed fascination. They reached the top of the stairs and stepped onto flat ground again, and Harper dashed over for a closer look. "A mermaid in a hoodie. Omigosh you're too adorable."

Everly asked, "Was the song written by a shadyr, do you think?"

Rylan shrugged. "After Harper noticed the connection, I did a bit of research into the song, but no one really knows where it came from. We're still going on pure speculation that the lyrics actually mean something and aren't entirely made up."

Everly paled.

"I mean, it's still worth checking out. Obviously."

"Okay, but we know from Rush that the lighthouse lamp is something magical, and now I know mermaids are a thing too, I think we're on the right track," Harper said, putting a hand on Everly's shoulder.

Everly half-smiled. "I can't believe mermaids were also shadyrs all along. Are there any mythological creatures you guys didn't inspire?"

Harper gasped so loudly everyone turned toward her. "Rush was a Crybel's Cove shadyr, right? She must have done this all the time, back then. Can you imagine her in mermaid form?"

She fanned her face. "I'm picturing a sunny yellow tail and all the pinup vibes."

Denny smacked his lips. "A yellow tail would be unlikely. Shadyrs take on darker colors to camouflage in the water. The scales also provide natural armor. What? I know things. Capable shadyr, remember?"

"For some reason, I keep forgetting," Harper said flatly.

Staring up at the lighthouse, Everly swayed, bumping into Tammy's tail.

"Sorry." She straightened herself up.

"Are you okay?" Tammy asked.

Everly nodded, a disoriented vagueness in her gaze

Rylan said softly, "Do you need another break?"

Everly took a few wobbly steps forward. "No. Let's keep going."

Callan readjusted his grip on Tammy and followed. The full lighthouse was within view now, and the base was surrounded by a strange growth, part smoky crystal and part slimy coral. Dark shapes reflected off the sharp edges, flitting unnaturally.

The group came to a stop. Three shallow steps with rusted metal railings led up to the front door, but the entire entrance was encased in the crystalline growth, at least three feet thick.

Rylan took a few deep breaths and shifted into the hulking, draconic form he'd taken before. Tammy's cheeks heated. There he was, able to pick and choose his shifts from Everly's interior ghast library—or however that worked— and she was stuck as the most useless possible form.

They should have left her behind.

In two giant leaps, Rylan charged at the door and the growth in front of it. The collision shook the conglomeration of coral, crystal, and shadows, but made no dent. He pushed again with his shoulder, then kicked at it, before shaking his head.

"No way we're getting in here. Not without a bulldozer."

Callan glanced at Denny. "You didn't bring any C-4, did you?"

"I wish! Lian went and confiscated my stash."

"Smart woman," Rylan said.

Harper motioned around the structure where the clearing stretched behind the building. "Maybe there's another entrance?"

The team fanned out to search, minus Tammy and Callan.

He's stuck here looking after me.

"You can put me down," Tammy told him.

"I'm not going to dump you on the ground."

"I am capable of sitting down. I can just, you know, sit down for a bit."

Or maybe commando-crawl away into a dark hole where I can hide for the rest of my life.

"I know." He flashed an amused grin. "But this isn't so bad, is it?"

Tammy's eyes widened and her cheeks heated, making him smile even more. It wasn't bad. It was nice. It was so nice but admitting that was the most horrifying part of the whole experience. That a part of her adored his attention. And that maybe, he knew.

No matter how many walls she'd put up or how rude she'd been to him, somehow, he'd seen the humiliating truth hidden deep inside. That she liked him. How dare she? Her, the burden, the cursed. How dare she want someone like him?

Something inside her was about to break and she had

no idea if that was bad or good.

Rylan continued pacing around the front door, kicking at the concrete stoop and the walls around it like he might be able to break his way in. Denny wandered about aimlessly, moving to look over the ocean-side cliff as though enjoying the view.

Everly and Harper circled the entire base, returning around the other side.

"Any luck?" Callan asked.

Everly shook her head, and Harper put an arm over her shoulder.

A gust of wind came off the sea, drowning out Denny's voice.

He put both hands around his mouth and hollered again, "Hey, didn't the Crybel's Cove shadyrs say no one comes out here?"

Rylan looked up from his study of the blocked entrance. "Yeah. They did."

Denny pointed over the edge of the cliff. "Then who's that guy?"

Chapter Fifteen

"There's a shifty-looking man scampering around on the rocks down there," Denny clarified, waving a hand into the wind that howled up from the shore below.

Skeptical expressions were shared, but the group joined him at the cliff's edge.

Everly moved slowly, fogged by pain and the effort of hiding it. By the time she'd caught up with the others, the elusive figure climbing on the rough coastline below had vanished.

"He went right into the cliff," Denny told Rylan, pointing down beneath them.

"Like a ghost?" Rylan asked.

Given the beshadowing, there was a possibility that what Denny had seen wasn't a real man at all.

Denny shook his head. "Definitely a solid dude."

"And he didn't take a nosedive into the waves?" Callan asked.

"Nah. Look, he came in that way." He aimed his finger at a small patch of dry stone on the shore, marked with wet footprints.

Rylan squinted into the gale. "Caves, maybe. Won't know till we get down there. Worth a look though."

Everly stood watch on the cliff's edge while the rest of the team attempted to find an easy way down the precarious cliffside. The one they found was a narrow goat track, far more treacherous than easy.

Callan eyed the path with Tammy still held in a princess carry. "This is going to be tricky. Can someone hold her for a second?"

Denny reached out first, and Tammy recoiled. Rylan accepted the mermaid-tailed girl.

"Here man, you can take this for me instead." Callan took off his pack and chucked it to Denny, who strapped it to his front with minimal grumbling.

Harper took Tammy's pack off her as well, and Tammy was passed back to Callan to be slung over into a piggyback position. She clung to his shoulders, and he looped one arm around the bend in her tail to support her.

The entire process left her red-faced and scowling, but she said nothing.

Everly had some idea of how Tammy felt about Callan,

no matter how much she'd tried to deny it when they'd talked at Gorhanmere. She'd joked about the two of them being hopelessly in love with Howell boys who weren't interested in them.

But from her point of view now, Callan seemed to be enjoying his mermaid-carrying role. There was a depth in his gaze and pleasure on his lips that went beyond a leader's responsibility or brotherly concern. Completely different to the growing disgust Everly saw in Rylan's frown each time he looked her way.

Callan stepped onto the rocky ribbon of path that curved down the cliff face toward the crashing waves, then slowly worked his way forward. Denny fell in line behind him, then Harper, and then it was Everly's turn to step out into empty space.

Everly leaned against the rough wall, ignoring the way the sharp, wet rocks scratched at her clothes. At least if she was tilted that way, she'd be less likely to go sailing off into the dark, white-capped waves below.

Her knees shook as she turned her attention away from the open air to her right and shuffled down the path behind Harper. On the bright side, the sheer burst of adrenaline racing through her limbs had gone a long way toward numbing the agony in her cracking arms.

Rylan was right behind her, close enough that he'd taken on vampire form again, unable to fight it. The back of her neck tingled with the weight of his eyes on her, waiting to see the next sign of her weakness, her pain, the next sign that he was right all along telling her to leave this dangerous place.

Everyone had been overly worried about her since seeing the damage from the Bane. She wanted to be okay, to have left like Rylan wanted before anyone found out, but now she was starting to get overly worried, too. She wasn't okay. The cracks inside her were spreading across her collar bone. She zipped her bomber jacket right up.

Just keep moving forward. Don't fall.

Rain spit from the roiling sky and lightning flashed all around them. Every crack of thunder sent another wave of guilt through her, especially when the ground rumbled in return.

Don't let anybody fall.

They drew closer to the jagged black rocks that poked out of the unsettled waves, carved from the cliff by eons of saltwater erosion. Every time a wave splashed against them, salt spray misted over Everly, leaving a tangy taste in her mouth.

When they reached sea level, Callan came to a stop, raising his hand to be seen in the gloom.

"Looks like something up ahead," he called back, his voice almost lost to the constant roar of waves and wind.

Everly eased up behind Harper, peering around her

tall double-backpacked frame to see Callan disappearing into the cliff face. She shuffled forward over slick, uneven rocks toward a slim opening, leading into inky blackness. The narrow entryway was a path of craggy steppingstones spread between water that churned so violently it could strip skin from bones.

"This is right about where that dude disappeared. Told you!" Denny called out.

Callan had already gone in, taking Tammy with him. "It's big in here, goes way into the island."

Denny and Harper followed next, carefully hopscotching from rock to rock.

"Careful," Harper called, pointing. "Stay to the left. That one wobbles."

Everly hesitated. Taking one step at a time was one thing. Leaping over slippery rocks was another.

Rylan moved up beside her and wrapped an arm across her back, holding tight around her ribcage and pressing her into his side.

Through vampire fangs, he said, "We'll go together."

He counted down before she could argue. Three, two, one, she jumped. He lifted. They landed and he steadied her when her knees buckled. His skin felt hard and cold.

"Again," he said, and they leaped.

The impact of landing shot pain through her arms and she cried out, biting it off too late.

"One more," Rylan said softly.

She nodded, vision blurring. She forced her eyes open as the final jump took them across to a larger ledge where the others stood. They hit the ground, and it held firm under her boots. She closed her eyes then, screwing them up against the pain. Rylan guided her a few steps and pressed down on her shoulders, seating her on a boulder.

"You're doing great. You're stronger than I ever realized." His voice was so hushed, so gravelly it could have been a crash of the waves echoing from outside.

Everly's eyes popped open at the words, but his back was already turned to her, facing the others.

Packs had been put down and flashlights were on, sweeping through the space to show a floor of choppy water that reached farther than their light sources could illuminate. Occasional miniature islands and pillars of rough stone covered in seaweed broke through.

The low cavern ceiling was smooth except for wavy lines where water had worn away at the rock over millennia.

Rylan turned to the slim crack and the ocean outside. "Is it low tide now?"

Denny reached up to the wet cave ceiling, ran his fingers across, and then popped one in his mouth. "Must be. That's not fresh water leaking in."

Everly eyed the underground lake, the way the ocean pushed in through the entrance, eddying through the deep pool in front of them.

"We should get out of here before the tide rises. This doesn't seem safe," she said. "Who knows who that guy was. Could be another zombie or something."

Rylan shook his head, pointing out into what was only darkness to Everly. "I think I can see something that way. Looks like the cave goes up, and we're right beneath the lighthouse. We need a way in."

Callan eyed the dark water. "I guess we're swimming in. We should check for underwater hazards first. I'll go."

Tammy, still clinging to Callan's shoulders, shook her head. "No, I'll do it. I'm already, you know, ready."

Callan twisted his neck to try to face her. "Yeah, but—"

"I can do it," she growled.

He nodded once. "Okay."

He carried her to the water and sat her at the edge. She unzipped her hoodie and tossed it onto the rock. In just her body armor and T-shirt, a visible shiver ran through her.

"This feels so weird," she said, then, clutching her flashlight, she slipped into the pool with hardly a sound.

Tammy swam away from the shore, slow at first until she seemed to get the hang of the tail. After several yards, she paused, took a deep breath she didn't need, then submerged.

Thunder rumbled outside, echoing through the cave like they were caught in the belly of a hungry beast. Tammy was taking a long time. Longer than a human breath. They said shadyrs in nyevmer form could breathe underwater, but Everly found herself holding her breath, too.

She got to her feet to watch for Tammy's return. Harper pressed close to Everly's side, her left hand resting on her axe and her right hand tucked around Everly's arm. The group waited in silence.

Tammy popped out of the water a few moments later, way out in the pool and almost beyond the beam of Everly's flashlight. Water glistened on her shaved head.

"It's deep," she called, her voice reverberating off the stones. "Really deep. Disturbing lack of ocean life, but … there are bones down there."

Lightning illuminated the cavern, and Callan grimaced. "What kind of bones?"

"I don't know. Big ones and small ones. I didn't get close enough to see." Tammy's voice came through chattering teeth as she swam back to them. "And I feel like, I don't know, I can sense a shroudpool down there, too. I didn't want to get any closer."

"Yeah, best if we don't," Callan said.

"Understatement," Denny guffawed.

Tammy tipped her head backward. "And Rylan's right, there's a path going upward a bit farther ahead."

"Then we follow it," Rylan said, but he didn't move.

His gaze was locked on Everly, and he shook his head.

She could almost read his mind. He didn't want her going any farther but knew they couldn't leave her behind alone.

She carefully put on a mask of 'I'm really okay and not in pain at all.' She had no intention of remaining behind, even if it was safe. They'd come to this cursed island, to this dangerous lighthouse, to this abyss of a cave, because of her. Whatever they were facing next, she'd face it too.

Callan squatted down, grabbed Tammy's hoodie, and re-arranged things in his pack. Pulling out a waterproof pouch, he put his phone, the satellite phone the Crybel's Cove shadyrs had given them, and a change of dry clothes inside.

"Sort your gear and get ready for a swim. Keep something dry for the other side." He made sure it was sealed properly, then did the same for Tammy's belongings.

Tammy had returned to the edge beside them and took her pack from Callan. It floated on her back, tipping her forward as she swam.

Rylan still hadn't moved. He stared out over the underground lake. "The nyevmer is close. Can you feel it?"

Callan and Denny both nodded.

Harper paused from taking off her outer layers. "You think it's in here with us, rather than out there at sea?"

Rylan's eyebrows drew together as a response.

"That's comforting," she said, stuffing her jacket, shirt, and boots into her pack.

She seemed to consider taking off more, then stayed in her tank top and jeans.

Callan squinted into the distance.

"It's farther inside the island. These caves must go deep, which is why we were feeling the ghast's presence up on the bluff. I don't think it knows we're here. We'll try and get across the water fast. Shouldn't be a problem once we shift. You two are going to have to swim the old-fashioned way, though," Callan said to Everly and Harper.

"Leave my tail jealousy out of this," Harper said.

"We can help you both swim faster. Cal, can you take Harper's pack as well as yours?"

Callan nodded as he stripped down to his body armor and pants. He lowered himself into the water, and after a moment, flung his soaking-wet pants back onto the shore before reaching for his and Harper's bags.

Denny didn't seem to have the same qualms, taking off all bottoms and packing them away before walking into the lake and shifting.

Everly's eyes popped wide open in pure horror.

Rylan actually chuckled. "What with changing form all the time, shadyrs have different standards of modesty."

Everly grew even more concerned as Rylan started stripping off his own clothes.

This time it's him who's going to put me into a coma.

He stopped removing clothes at body armor and pants.

He squatted down and packed the rest away, compressed Everly's smaller backpack into a tight bundle, then squeezed it into the top of his.

His starry eyes shined up at her and he reached a hand out. "Boots, jacket."

Everly stripped as quickly and un-awkwardly as she could. She had another layer under the long-sleeved top she wore, but didn't want her arms showing, so left it on. She followed Harper into the water.

It was *frigid*. Much colder than the ocean had been when they'd climbed from the rowboat onto the beach. Even the rain wasn't as cold as the cave's water. Everly sucked in a breath, holding it deep in her chest as she waded into the water, her jeans and shirt soaking through immediately.

She gritted her teeth as the cold spread over her injured arm. She'd managed to ignore the pain while investigating around the lighthouse and climbing down the cliff because she'd had other things to focus on, like fear of a short, deadly drop onto pointy rocks.

But the salty water burned like fire on her wounds, and when she left the ground behind for deeper depths, swimming with her injured arms forced out a whimper.

She heard Rylan enter the water behind them, and carefully avoided looking back as he removed his pants and shifted.

A moment later, Rylan's strong shoulders broke the

surface of the water beside her. He brushed his hands back over his shorn hair, shaking water off his face and out of his eyes. In the glow of Everly's flashlight, his dark scales shimmered like an oil slick—one moment blue, the next vivid green.

Of course Rylan's mer form would be insanely beautiful. She shouldn't have expected anything less. But it still sent a pang of yearning through her. His pack wasn't strapped on his back but held under one arm to the side, the side closest to her.

"Lean on this, and hold on," he said.

Gratefully, she did, resting her arm that held the flashlight over the semi-buoyant bag, so she could at least pretend to assist the swimming with her other hand.

Harper moved ahead of them with ease, but Rylan quickly caught up, gliding through the water even with Everly in tow.

As they reached the rest of the group, Callan said to Tammy, "Show me the bones."

Tammy nodded. She dipped beneath the surface, Callan right at her tail. Harper and Denny treaded water nearby, with Denny apparently trying to show off his tail to her, without the hoped-for response. Rylan kept him and Everly moving on.

After several moments, Tammy popped back above the water, followed by Callan.

His expression was grim. "The bones are strange, eidolghasts mostly, I'd guess. But some are human. And even worse ... Infants. Counted at least three skulls."

Harper gasped. "Oh no. *Babies*?"

A strange rumble echoed through the cave from far ahead, and the water around Everly's torso rippled from the force of it. Her heart jerked in her chest.

"Was that thunder?" Harper asked.

Her hair, which had been shiny and straight before leaping into the water, had turned dark and wavy, clinging to her skin. However, her mascara wasn't even running, despite the waves splashing against her face.

"No," Callan replied. "That was the nyevmer."

Harper gulped. "Do they ... eat children?"

"Not as far as our knowledge of them goes, but who can tell with eidolghasts?"

Everly's blood ran cold. She'd seen vasmires, weroths, and an auerdax. She didn't want to imagine the horror of what a water-dwelling eidolghast looked like. "How close is it?"

Rylan responded, "Close. But our exit is closer."

Even Everly could see it now, her flashlight beam reaching a small shore that led to a dark passageway.

They swam toward it. The current moved quickly around them, water flowing in the same direction as they swam.

It was definitely rising.

Tammy called out, "Hey. Do you guys see that? There's a light in there, up the tunnel."

They reached the shore, Harper and Everly pulling themselves out of the water first while the shadyrs who were able to shifted back to human form. The reverse process was a bit trickier than entering the water, and the three women turned their backs as Rylan, Callan, and Denny stepped out of the pool, retrieved dry pants, and put them on.

"Check it out!" Denny said.

Still at the water's edge, Tammy grumbled, "I don't think anybody here wants that."

"Not *that*. Footprints. Old fellow came this way." He wandered over beside Harper and Everly, still doing up his fly.

He pointed, and Everly shined her flashlight at the wet trail leading from the water, up into the passage in the cave wall. The marks were wide apart and too splashy to make out clear human prints from.

Harper blinked rapidly. "Oh no!"

"What's wrong?" Everly turned her light to check her over.

Harper looked her way with one bright green eye, and one brown eye, pouting.

"I lost a contact." She groaned, fishing the other one

out.

Fully dressed, Callan joined them, handing Harper her pack. "Wait, your eyes aren't green?"

"Secret's out, I guess. It's like, a whole Bellsy thing. The bright-green eyes. But no, sorry to disappoint. Just another bit of me that isn't me."

Even Everly hadn't known that. She shivered, still chilled through and unable to produce any body heat.

"You wear them every single day?"

"I wear a lot every single day." Harper shrugged.

Her face had lost the sparkle and energy she'd had that morning, and her forehead was creased. She hadn't bothered changing or putting any dry layers back on but didn't shiver like Everly.

Callan scooped Tammy out of the water like a fisherman with a big catch. He kept her at the front for the upward climb, balanced by their backpacks behind him.

Rylan had pants back on, but left his top half in body armor only, as though expecting trouble. He'd changed not to human, but vampire form, and his fingers were cold as he draped Everly's jacket over her shoulders and handed her boots back.

He didn't say anything to her, instead heading to the passage entrance where his brother waited.

Callan nodded to him. "It's a stairwell, and there's light at the top."

Rylan's galaxy gaze turned skyward. "It's got to go into the lighthouse. We're going up."

Callan smirked at Tammy. "Looks like there's going to be a mermaid in the lighthouse, after all."

Harper hummed a bar of the song. "The question is, will she be the only one?"

Chapter Sixteen

Water weighed Everly's clothes down as she trudged upward, her body growing weaker by the second. The stairs curved out of sight, toward a blue glow that ebbed softly like the sun shining through water. The dragon stirred weakly inside Everly, and its need for the light above them seeped through her being. She struggled to tell where the soul-eater's wants ended and her desire to be whole again began.

Everly trailed her fingers along stone walls covered in green algae. The cool dampness eased some of the pain crackling beneath her skin. The walls seemed to hum and pulse beneath her fingertips in time with the blue glow that illuminated the stairwell.

My love flows as deep as the ocean's black heart,
It beats in the night, it beats in the night.

The song was well and truly stuck in her head. It had always seemed so innocent when she was a kid, almost romantic. But now, the lyrics made her shiver.

As they ascended, the complete lack of sea life down in the cave transformed into an abundance of creatures moving around them. Small crabs skittered, sea snails climbed the walls, and a brightly patterned baby octopus glided away across the slick stairs to hide from their approach.

Finally, the stairwell curved one more time, and they spilled out onto the ground floor of the lighthouse.

"We made it." Denny puffed out his chest. "And we never would have found our way in if not for me. How about that?"

Nobody bothered replying to his ego.

"Everyone keep quiet," Callan ordered in a whisper. "We know we're not alone in here."

The blue glow lit the entire space, shimmering like they were underwater. Everly tucked her flashlight away in a pocket and padded softly over slick, wet floors carpeted in ribbon seaweed.

A third of the room was overtaken by the same coral and crystalline growths that had obscured the front door. An old-fashioned piano sagged against one section of wall, pouring water from its keys like a fountain, while more living coral grew out of its boxy top, covered in a horde of fingernail-sized crabs. The ceiling dripped constantly in a pitter-patter song.

No mermaids, strange men, or zombies appeared. Rylan waved them over to the curving stairwell that hugged the inside of the round wall.

"Up we go," Harper whispered cheerfully, linking her arm through Everly's.

"A million stairs is exactly what I wanted right now." Everly replied with a weak smile, grateful to have someone to lean on as the upward hike continued. Barely any warmth had returned to her body after the swim and her entire skeleton rattled with uncontrollable shivering.

Despite the bizarre angle that the lighthouse appeared to have from the outside, the interior thankfully seemed to be flat and level. Halfway to the first landing, they passed a square frame on the wall.

Everly paused with her foot on the next step, her gaze sweeping across the portrait. The walls were covered in barnacles and creeping seaweed, but the portrait remained as clean and bright as the day it was painted. It depicted a young woman close to Everly's age with midnight-dark skin and ebony hair that hung in wet ringlets around her shoulders.

Her coloring was so similar to the faceless ghost that had greeted them when they first ventured onto the island that it made Everly shiver.

The woman in the portrait sat on a lush velvet chair. Water puddled all around her, and her long mermaid tail curved around, tucked around the claw-foot leg of the furniture. She had huge sad eyes and a strangely off-putting smile that didn't sit right on her face.

Harper leaned over Everly's shoulder to peer at the girl. "Is that her? *The* mermaid?"

Callan turned back from in front of them as though noticing the painting for the first time.

He shifted Tammy in his arms to show off her tail. "Are we thinking she was a shadyr?"

"That's more likely than a true mermaid. But neither Crybel's Cove nor the Darkfreys have any knowledge of a shadyr in residence out here," Rylan said softly from a few steps down.

"Why would they? Why would anyone want to stay in this place?" Everly whispered.

"Maybe she couldn't leave." Tammy replied, her voice flat and dark.

Even in death? Everly wondered whether Tammy saw the similarity to the ghost woman too.

"Keep moving," Rylan urged softly.

They tiptoed by the portrait as though it might come to life. As the stairwell curved around, another frame loomed out of the blue gloom.

"Same girl," Callan said. "But she's just a kid in this

one, like, maybe ten years old?"

Everly stepped past it, eying it as she went. The mermaid girl was depicted lying on a wet stone floor with her tail flipped up stylistically behind her. A window overhead opened onto a stormy sea. Every brushstroke was so precise and realistic.

"She looks so sad. I mean, apart from that terrifying smile."

"Creepy, right? What's going on with that," Harper replied.

A landing beneath a tiny porthole window indicated they'd reached the first floor, where a door hung open to an empty room that was drier than the rest. A workbench lined one wall, weighed down by bent tubes of paint, ratty canvases, and multiple easels holding a variety of artworks in progress. The harsh scent of turpentine stung Everly's nose.

There was no natural light to illuminate the paintings, though Everly thought she could make out the blobby beginnings of yet another portrait of the same mermaid, rougher and more twisted than the others.

"Who do we think has been doing the painting? Self-portraits?" Everly asked.

"Or the dude we followed in here?" Denny added.

"Keep moving," Rylan said again from the back. "Our target is right up top. We don't stop unless someone or something makes us. This isn't a sight-seeing trip."

Between the first- and second-floor landings, they passed a growing collection of mermaid paintings. Her age varied from hardly old enough to be considered a teenager to possible thirties, always with those sad eyes and side-show clown smile.

Each of the portraits was eerily clean and well-maintained, while the walls around them looked as if they'd been soaking in ocean water for years.

The second-floor landing had no room attached. The wall where the entrance should have been seemed somehow melted. Streaky fingerprints of rust-red marred the surface.

The third floor did have a doorway, though if there'd ever been a door hanging in the frame, it was long gone. The round room inside was filled with narrow rows of floor-to-ceiling shelves that held glass jars in a variety of shapes and sizes.

Each was filled with cloudy, yellow liquid. In the closest jars, dead, pale fish, bleached urchins, and tangled squid pressed against the glass. There were hundreds of preserved specimens in there, maybe thousands.

"Wow. Just when I thought this place couldn't get creepier," Callan whispered.

From his arms, Tammy replied, "I don't know, I think it's kind of cool. I'm keeping a list of decorating ideas."

Callan huffed. "But in black?"

"Of course."

The whiff of chemicals followed the team as they hurried by.

Two more landings up, Callan halted at yet another portrait. "I think it's safe to say the mermaid and lighthouse connection is real, one way or another."

"And if that part of the song is true, hopefully the rest is on track to get us what we need for Ev," Harper agreed. "But if the mermaid is real, where is she?"

"With how ghost-twisted this place is, I think it might be best if we don't find her," Denny muttered.

Harper pouted like she'd been told she couldn't go see a rockstar backstage.

"Denny's right," Rylan said. "Which is something I never thought I'd say. But from the look of the portraits, this mermaid could have been here her whole life. Just look at this place. It's not a healthy environment. Beshadowings corrupt things and people."

"Speaking of, have you guys noticed the water?" Tammy said, pointing to the floor. "It's flowing up now."

Everly looked down to see the trickle of water, which shimmered in the blue glow, flowing up the stairs. She wished that same, distorted gravity would also work on her. Her breath hitched in her throat; her lungs felt like the remains of a bonfire had been shoveled inside them.

They had to be at least halfway up by now, but when

she pressed her face close to the small portal window to peer up toward the rotating light, her heart compressed. "It feels like we haven't gotten any closer to the top."

"You need a break?" Rylan asked.

"No."

His gaze pierced straight through her obvious lie.

"Maybe soon," she amended.

He leaned toward her as though ready to scoop her up into his arms like a mermaid, so she turned and put one foot in front of the other again, to prove she could keep going.

But the lighthouse was the thing that kept going, and going, and going.

Everly lost count after the eighth floor. Every landing had a new room, some of them empty, some of them bizarre enough to have them questioning their sanity. They passed a room where gravity had been turned upside down. Water covered the ceiling, waving lazily as it cast aqua refractions over the surprisingly dry floor.

Another room was missing entirely, opening directly onto a perilous drop into the ocean, as though all the other parts of the lighthouse around the hole didn't exist.

Small creatures continued to dart around them as they climbed. At first sight, most of the animals were recognizable as crabs, octopuses, or starfish, but upon closer inspection, they weren't quite ... right.

Starfish scuttled around at a much faster pace than

should have been physically possible. A few times they had to dodge plate-sized fish flopping their way down the stairs, screaming like goats. The crabs had eyes on their backs that were too human.

On the next landing, Everly paused to catch her breath by another room as lightning flashed through two windows that had no glass. A collection of fishing rods in different shapes and sizes leaned beside the openings.

Water rained from the ceiling in patches, splashing on the floor and weaving streams among the furniture. Piles of strange objects, from empty cans to ship anchors cluttered every part of the round room, creating a hoarder's labyrinth.

The furniture, however, was what caught Everly's attention.

"Look," she murmured. "Is that the armchair from the first portrait?"

It was hard to tell, as seaweed sprouted in patches and barnacles covered the legs. The armchair was one of two situated on a sodden Oriental rug that was barely visible beneath drifts of fine fishbones and large, pale-blue scales glistening like mother-of-pearl. A badly water-damaged picture book lay open on one of the chairs.

Harper moved in for a closer look.

"Come on, we've got to keep moving," Rylan grunted.

Harper ignored him and traced her fingertips over the soggy velvet. "I think you're right, Ev."

With a clatter, one of the fishing rods fell into the surrounding pile of detritus.

Everly's eyes widened. "Harper, get out of there!"

Her friend didn't move. She stared, fixated on the shadow behind one of the armchairs. Everly rushed to Harper's side to drag her out if necessary.

"Evie!" Rylan called out after her.

Harper raised a hand, waving the warnings away. "I thought I saw …"

Lightning flashed, and behind the armchair, something coiled and shifted.

And then it screamed.

CHAPTER SEVENTEEN

Harper's hand tightened on the axe at her hip.

Rylan and Denny charged in behind her and Everly, and the thing on the floor whimpered. Harper's throat grew tight. The *shnickt* of Denny drawing his machete swung her head around.

"Woah, woah, woah, back off," Harper hissed. "Can't you see she's terrified?"

The figure tucked into herself, folding smaller into the shadow of the armchair. She slipped on the wet floor and a pale-blue fin flopped into the light before being pulled swiftly back into the shadow with a soft squeal.

"Harper? Be careful," Everly called from behind Rylan, her voice desperate as Harper stepped forward.

"Shh, it's okay. We're not going to hurt you," Harper

murmured.

She slowly took off her backpack and left it behind, then moved onto hands and knees on the seaweed-slick floor.

"We don't know that it won't hurt us," Rylan growled.

He was clearly annoyed that the human had knelt to engage the strange lighthouse inhabitant, but to his credit, he remained just inside the doorway, waiting to see what happened before he decided on a course of action.

One fretful eye appeared around the chair back, framed by dark, tangled hair. Harper recognized the starry-sky of a shadyr's eyes. They gleamed with reflected blue glow and internal sparks.

With a squeak, the face vanished again.

"Who are you? Are you here to kill me?" The small, shaky voice drifted from the darkness beyond the chair.

Harper waved a hand at the others. They sheathed their weapons and stepped backward.

Everly mouthed again, *be careful*, and Harper mouthed in reply, *I know*.

"Kill you? Of course not. We won't hurt you." Harper shuffled forward on her knees, water sloshing around her jeans.

"Hey," she said softly. "My name's Harper. Who are you?"

Four scaled and clawed fingers appeared, clutching the leg of the armchair.

"Daddy said humans ... humans would try to kill me." She had a surprisingly deep voice, soft and velvety, with a tremor like water bubbling over rocks.

Harper angled her legs to the side and went down on her hip, peeking around the edge of the chair. "Why would we do that? Some of us are just like you."

The girl's face appeared again, eyes round, showing a war between fear and curiosity. Lightning lit up the room, brightening the shadow she hid within. She wasn't as young as Harper had initially thought. She looked wild—like a girl raised in the wilderness by wolves if those wolves were from the ocean.

Her curls hung to her waist, damp and matted, intertwined with seaweed, netting, and bits of coral. Her hair and skin were both a warm, russet brown, playing off her sky-blue scales.

Despite the wildness—or maybe because of it—she was one of the most beautiful women Harper had ever seen.

Careful to avoid her voice being too loud or jarring, Harper called back to the others, "Shadyr, late teens maybe. Not the same one as in the paintings."

Everly looked to Rylan. "There's more than one?"

"What's she doing hanging out in this place?" Denny yelled back.

The girl cringed into the shadows again.

Harper hushed and murmured soothing sounds.

"Don't worry about him. He's just loud, but he won't hurt you, but more importantly, *I* won't let anything hurt you, okay? Do you have a name?"

She was rewarded with a timid, "Neri."

"Neri. Nice to meet you." Harper's gaze flicked over her pale-blue tail which had unfurled a little into the light. The scales were ragged and patchy, some missing entirely. "Why don't you change back to your human form? There's not enough water for you to swim in here."

Neri blinked. "Change? I can't change, I'm a mermaid."

Callan, still holding Tammy out of sight on the landing, said, aghast, "You don't think she's been in mermaid form her whole life?"

Harper turned back to the others. Rylan had tensed up, and even Denny seemed disturbed.

"Callan," she called. "Can you bring Tammy in here?"

Rylan and Denny stepped aside and let Callan through the doorway, with Tammy still in a princess carry. She waved awkwardly, gave her tail a little wiggle, and offered Neri a rare smile.

Neri's shiny gaze took her in. Her cupid's bow lips parted, and she planted her palms on the floor, abruptly sliding out from behind the chair for a better look.

As she came into clear view, Everly covered her mouth with her hands. "Oh my."

Neri wasn't wearing a thing. Her tangled hair only

partly obscured her slim, bare chest and ribcage, visible through a thin layer of skin. Rylan and Callan averted their eyes. Everly smacked Denny until he turned around.

"Another mermaid!" Neri exclaimed with a childish kind of excitement, crawling on her stomach closer to Tammy, her smile widening.

"Umm, I'm not *really* a mermaid. Like you aren't really a mermaid. We can just change to look like this sometimes."

Neri shook her head. "No. My mom was a mermaid, and so am I."

"The paintings up the stairwell, are they your mom?" Harper asked.

Neri's smile faded. "Mm-hm"

"Why didn't they tell her what she is?" Rylan asked softly. "Her mom was clearly a shadyr too, and sounds like the dad is around, warning her off humans. Why have they let her stay here, without training? Why let her think she's a mermaid?"

Neri's eyes widened as she took in Rylan's ghostly-white skin and sharp fangs. "You're not like me, what are you?"

Harper smiled and waved it off as though having a vampire around was normal. She didn't want to go too deeply into shadyr lore and how they worked. Too much information would probably overload the girl.

"Don't worry about him, it's just a … condition he has. All of them, and you, you sort of change to look different when monsters are near."

"Like the monster that lives in the caves beneath the lighthouse?" Neri wrinkled her nose. "Daddy told me about it. That's why I'm not allowed down there."

Harper inhaled slowly, keeping her voice even. "Where can you go? Have you ever been out of the lighthouse?"

"Not yet. Daddy said he might take me out soon. There's something he wants to do that I need to be away from the lighthouse for. I don't know what it is."

Neri turned herself over onto her back so she could face Harper again, her arms displaying wiry muscles on a tiny frame. Bruises and scrapes marred her elbows, waist, and stomach. "I mostly just stay in here. Daddy says it's not safe outside my room."

Harper looked at Everly to find an identical expression of horror.

There's a mermaid in my lighthouse, and her heart belongs to me.

There's a mermaid in my lighthouse, to her I own the key.

A shudder ran up Harper's entire body. "Show her. Tammy, can you show her that you can change into a human?"

"Um, maybe? The nyevmer is farther away now, but I'm still not very good at controlling the change."

"Try," Harper growled.

She'd ask one of the guys to switch from human to

mermaid but didn't want any men stripping down in front of Neri.

Callan helped hold Tammy upright and Everly extracted a blanket from Harper's pack and wrapped it around the waist section of Tammy's tail. With a look of intense concentration, Tammy brought up the shadyr transformation mist, which slowly swirled around her.

Neri gasped and reached up to take hold of the arm of the chair. She hauled herself into the seat, presumably for a better look. As Neri's hips passed over the edge of the chair, Harper glimpsed more red welts and open sores from dragging herself around on the rough floor.

Fury made her see red.

Within a few moments, Tammy's flipper vanished and pale, human toes poked out. She stood there on two, obviously-human legs. But the mist still swirled, and she wobbled.

Tammy grunted. "I can't hold it. I'm sorry."

With a flop of a tail fin, she fell backward into Callan's arms again.

"You're doing much better. You almost had it," he said.

She rolled her eyes.

"Is this ... some kind of trick?" Neri asked in a tiny, deep voice. "Is this a dream?"

Her whole body had gone rigid, and a green tinge crept up her face. She tugged at her hair with her webbed fingers.

Harper knelt beside the chair, determination burning in her veins. "Your dad, where is he now?"

If they were going to act, she needed the info, and fast.

Neri stared at the floor, blinked, then looked at Harper with a frown. "He just got home but went up to check the light. I thought you were him at first, coming back."

"He has to be the man Denny saw," Everly said.

Harper pushed on. "What about your mother? Where is she?"

Sadness passed over Neri's shining eyes.

"She died when I was really little. I only know what Daddy told me ..." She froze, then shook her head, eyes drawn to a jumble of trash over to the side. "About her. But she sounded brave. She survived a shipwreck at only ten years old. Daddy pulled her from the sea and brought her here. To safety. Where mermaid hunters wouldn't find her. He looked after her for twenty years before I came along."

Heavy sickness settled in the pit of Harper's stomach.

He *looked after* her. A child, then a woman, who gave birth to Neri.

More thunder rumbled through the structure. Harper cringed as the whole lighthouse swayed in the stormy winds.

A knot of anger and anxiety hardened in her chest. Harper stood and moved over to Everly and Rylan, leaning in close.

"We've got to get her out of here," Harper murmured.

"She's been held captive and lied to about everything."

Everly's mouth was pinched. "Nobody's out there hunting mermaids. She wouldn't even be a mermaid if she wasn't here."

Rylan shook his head. "Doesn't mean she's safe to trust. She could be unhinged, beshadowed, dangerous."

"She's a *victim*. Plus, this Daddy guy was clearly helping himself to Neri's mom." The thought made Harper sick to her stomach. "Maybe even when she was still *a child*. He could be doing the same thing to Neri. Or if he hasn't yet, the threat is still there."

Callan leaned in, his forehead a twisted mess. "I think ... I think it could be even worse than that."

"What could be worse than that?" Harper snapped.

Callan's jaw clenched and he stared at the floor.

Rylan sighed and brushed his hand over his hair, glancing up at where the lighthouse lamp would be. "Fine. But we have to get to the top first, past that guy by the sounds of it, and figure out if the artifact powering this place can help Everly. Then we'll deal with saving the little mermaid."

Harper folded her arms. "We're not leaving her here, not for another moment. I'll carry her if I have to."

Rylan said, "We don't even know if she wants to leave, if she will leave."

"Neri?" Harper turned back to her suddenly. "Will

you come with us, out of the lighthouse?"

Neri pulled her tail up, cuddling it to her chest. "Out?"

Harper put on her best and friendliest camera-ready smile, moved closer, and crouched beside the chair. "Yeah, outside. We can show you what it's like out there."

Neri's head whipped from side to side. "It's dangerous."

Harper chewed her bottom lip. She couldn't lie to this girl.

"It can be. But I'll protect you. I promise."

Neri shifted forward, and after a few false starts, reached a hand toward Harper. Harper held her breath as the girl's fingertips lightly brushed her knee and then pulled back.

She whispered. "You really think ... I could have legs?"

Harper gave her a sparkling smile and a nod.

But Neri's gaze had slipped over Harper's shoulder, and her eyes widened.

A new voice roared through the room over the noise from the storm. "Get away from my mermaid!"

Chapter Eighteen

Harper whirled around and threw herself in front of Neri. At one point in the distant past, the … *thing* … in the doorway might have been a man.

He hunched there, bigger than seemed natural with shoulders that curved smoothly into a wide, scaly neck. If his head, neck, and shoulders had ever been separate body parts, they weren't now, as though someone had remolded his upper body into a hideous, humanoid fish, like the zombies. But he stared at them with piercing clarity.

He had the face of an anglerfish—beady eyes, uncovered nostrils, and far too many sharp teeth. What human features remained on his face were aged, lined by carved valleys and folds of dripping, gray skin. His lower appendages stuck out from the wet, fraying hems of his shorts, white and bloated with water retention.

They were less leg and more a cluster of tangled tentacles. His thick arms were covered in barnacles, his hands like meaty seal fins.

He was a walking nightmare.

"It's okay, it's just Daddy," Neri said from behind.

Harper tasted bile. She pulled her axe from its holster and held it steady in front of her. The heavy lump of metal had made swimming through the caves difficult but now, staring down the hideous monster blocking the doorway, she was very, *very* glad to have a weapon. She just wished her strength hadn't waned so much.

It runs out so fast. I should have brought the Bane with me for a top-up. But then Everly would have known, had felt it, had suffered from its presence. Hopefully she had enough power left.

"Don't come any closer!" she ordered the fish-man.

The rest of the team cleared away from the door, giving the man space.

"Who are you?" he hollered through a gurgling throat. "Did you come to steal my mermaid?"

Rylan held out a calming hand. "That's not what we came for."

Technically, Harper thought, *but it will be what we do.*

This monster had held Neri captive for years. For her *entire* life.

That stopped now.

"She's not yours," Harper spat back, disgusted. "She only belongs to herself!"

His beady eyes bulged wildly, and he stomped closer. Tiny creatures climbed and clawed around the bundle of tentacles that formed his feet.

"No, Daddy, don't hurt them. They said they're like me, look." Neri pointed across to where Callan held Tammy behind the door.

Her iridescent, dark-rainbow tail sparkled in the intermittent bursts of lightning. The man zeroed in on her with ruthless excitement, breathing audibly.

"Another mermaid?" He sloshed forward, flipper hands squeezing and releasing as he reached for Tammy.

Callan took a long stride away from him.

"Back off," he snarled, holding Tammy tight to his chest with one arm.

His other hand drew the wickedly large hunting knife from a sheath strapped to his thigh. His nebulous shadyr eyes flashed dangerously.

The old man doubled over, gasping despite being completely untouched. His wet, scaled upper body shook as he straightened, arms flailing.

"Mermaid hunters, mermaid hunters!" he screeched at Neri. "They have one already. They want you, too."

Neri curled back into the armchair, shivering all over. "They said they wanted to take me away."

"There's no such thing as mermaid hunters," Harper snarled in frustration.

This man is completely mad.

He didn't seem to know what shadyrs were and wasn't one himself, or he'd be stuck as a mermaid, too. He was just a man, twisted by the beshadowing and his obsession with mermaids. Disgust filled every part of Harper's being. She had no idea if he had ever once been any kind of good person.

Maybe when he'd saved Neri's mother's life, it had been out of the goodness of his heart. Maybe his initial intentions had been heroic.

Then why did he keep her locked up here?

No. Harper couldn't imagine that he was ever a good person.

She didn't dare imagine what Neri had been through, or her poor mother before that. They were both trapped here for ages, unable to leave this beshadowed, forsaken place.

He'd imprisoned them. Given them no other option but to be his pets.

It was too late for Neri's mother, but Harper would be damned if she didn't get Neri out of there. But now Neri stared at *her* with the eyes of cornered prey.

The rest of the team remained where they stood around the room. Everyone was on alert but in a holding pattern, waiting to see whether this could be talked out before resorting to violence. They slowly lowered their backpacks to the ground, preparing for the need for action.

When the man had his back to them, the Howell team signaled to each other with hands and mouthed words. Rylan pointed to Everly, then upstairs, and she shook her head. Denny pointed to Rylan and made a flappy bat shape with his hands, and Callan put Tammy down on a wooden crate against the wall behind him, gesturing for her to stay. She gave him two middle fingers in return.

Harper knew if it came to a fight, Rylan might be the only useful shadyr since their mermaid forms were useless out of the water. She still had some strength from the Bane, but nothing near what it was like when the cuts were fresh. Better if they could talk their way, and Neri's way, out of this.

Harper also couldn't see Neri being happy going with them if the first thing they did was murder her father.

Readjusting her grip on the axe, Harper lowered it into one hand and raised the other. "Okay, slow down. We're not mermaid hunters. We all want what's best for Neri. If you're her father, that's what you want too, right?"

The man's bloodshot gaze swung between Neri and Tammy, his hands still making strange grabby motions.

He sang in a low, surprisingly clear warble, *"There's a mermaid in my lighthouse, and her heart belongs to me."*

Since coming to Shroudhaven with Everly, Harper

had gotten to know the casually-called "mermaid song" that played nearly constantly around town. She could sing it word-for-word without issue now. But listening to the words spill from the fish man's mouth sent a chill through her. The words landed differently now. More haunting. More disturbing.

Not a love story, but one of horrific captivity.

There was a familiarity to his voice that stung Harper right through the heart.

"You ... Did you write the song?" Harper asked.

"*There's a mermaid in my lighthouse, to her I own the key*," the old man continued as if she hadn't spoken.

Everly caught Harper's eye, shaking her head. "And those portraits. I bet he painted the portraits of Neri's mom. From the time she was a child until ..."

She trailed off, letting the shadyr's death settle in silence between them.

"My muse, my muse. The greatest of muses." The man broke out of the song, his teeth gnashing wetly with every word.

His voice gargled, as though the water that soaked everything else here had taken root in his throat.

"My lighthouse. My muses. My mermaids. You will leave. All leave. Except her."

He pointed at Tammy with fused-together fingers that ended in sharp nails.

Callan raised his hunting knife in response.

From across the room, Denny spoke up. "Dude's mad. We can't negotiate with him. His mind is too broken."

"I don't think he's just going to let us leave, either. He wants Tammy now, too," Callan said.

"And we're not leaving Neri!" Harper hissed.

Everly nodded back to her in solidarity.

Neri's father shuffled sideways, sending up little swirls and eddies in the water on the floor as he skirted around Harper.

"Neri? You hear that? They want to steal you. They do. Tell them. Tell them this is your home, and no one will take you from me. This is where mermaids belong. This is where you're safe."

Harper glanced back and could see a sickening doubt in Neri's eyes. "Can't you see, he's your captor. He's lied to you your whole life. He's kept you here, like a possession, no matter how it's hurt you. He's a monster."

Neri's head turned rhythmically from side to side, tears bursting from her eyes. When Harper reached for her, she cowered back into the chair.

Harper turned to Everly and the others, desperate. "How can we make her see?"

The fish man cocked his head. His graying eyes locked onto Harper's face and a wide, sneering grin displayed his disturbingly sharp teeth.

Callan took a step forward, glaring the man down. "The human bones in the cave, where are they from?"

"Bones?" Neri asked, her husky voice broken by a shiver.

"There's no bones," the man barked, waving an arm through the air.

"Underwater, in the cave," Callan explained to Neri in slow, hard words. "We found bones, of babies."

Neri's face crumpled. "There are *baby* bones in the caves?"

"No such thing!" the fish man howled.

He barreled across the room, shouldering Harper aside, then grasped onto each side of Neri's head. His thick, fingery fins pressed over her ears, squeezing so hard that he lifted her from the chair by her head. He bounced her up and down against the cushions with the anger of his words.

"Don't listen to them, don't listen, they lie, they want to steal my mermaid. Don't listen, don't listen."

Neri shrieked, her tail whipping underneath her for some leverage against the assault.

Fury turned Harper's entire body to flame. She lunged forward and raised the axe high over her head before she brought it down with all her strength.

The man was beyond saving at this point, anyway. The power of the Bane reignited, pulsed, imagining the deadly sharp metal slicing into the monster's skull. Craving it.

"No!" Neri cried.

At the last moment, Harper turned the axe broadside so that the flat portion slammed into the old man's head instead of the sharp edge.

He let go of his daughter and tipped sideways with a small, pained grunt, stumbling several steps through the pooling water, then splashed down on his back. Thunder rumbled outside the lighthouse, and the walls shivered and creaked.

Neri screamed in horror and pitched herself off the armchair, scuttling away behind piles of clutter.

Harper strode to the man, kicking water in his face. "Why are there bones of children down there?"

The fish man lashed out with his strangely bloated tentacle legs. When she dodged them, he glared up at her, remaining mute.

Callan answered, "I suspect they're Neri's siblings. With Neri's mother being shadyr and this asshole being human—at least in the past—there's only a fifty-fifty chance that the infants will carry the shadyr gene."

Acid rose in Harper's throat. They could have died in childbirth, or during infancy. They *could* have. This clearly wasn't a safe environment for having or raising babies. That Neri survived to this age was a miracle. It could have easily been natural deaths ... and if that were the truth, it would still have been horrifying cruelty at the hands of this man.

But Callan's theory rang too true. It wasn't that, or

only that.

Harper sneered down at the monster as she said, "You *killed* your children because they weren't born with *tails*?"

Neri's tiny, scared voice arose again over the constant fall of water in the room. "You're lying, stop lying. Why did you come here? Why are you saying these things?"

Neri's father huffed like a rabid beast, then rolled to his hands and knees. With effort, the awkwardly-shaped fish-man hauled his bulk to his feet and lifted his malformed head to glare at Harper.

"There's nothing down there, Neri, only the monster," he gurgled, though he didn't look away from Harper. "They're trying to steal you from me."

Harper's lips curled away from her teeth. "Liar! You forced yourself on Neri's mother over and over, turning her into a baby factory until she gave you the offspring you wanted."

A new horror flowed ice into her veins. "Then what did you do? What did you do to her once you had a fresh new mermaid for yourself? You couldn't let her stay and tell Neri what you've done, could you?"

Neri wailed wordlessly.

Something switched in the old man's unfocused gaze.

With a wild, inhuman sound like a cow being slaughtered, he lunged at Harper, his long nails curved into vicious claws.

CHAPTER NINETEEN

Jasper stared up at Rook's Theater, hoping he wasn't leading Cherry to his death.

He rocked back on his heels as he noted all the new graffiti that had popped up in the weeks since he'd last walked past the place. The back wall was so smothered in impressive street art and illegible spray tags that it looked like an abstract art exposé on the declining modern world.

"If the thing you're after is the weird bone sculpture Callan saw, it's not there anymore." Cherry stood with his hands in his jacket pockets, eying the theater warily as though he suspected it might try to steal his wallet. "We came back and checked the next day."

Jasper knew that. They'd still been communicating back then, still been together. "No, that's not my mission target."

Cherry took one long step toward him, hovering close to his personal space. "Don't suppose you know what that thing was?"

Jasper tilted his head. Was Cherry grilling him? Was that the only reason he'd agreed to come along?

The idea brought half a smile to Jasper's lips. He always did admire Cherry's audacity.

"No, I have no knowledge of bone statues."

A deep chill rolled off the nearby river, and cold wind cut past Jasper, sending a shiver through him despite his Darkfrey armor, two layers of shirts, and cardigan. Shadows lay like a cloak over the theater, and there was a sense of despair in the air. He was glad Cherry was here beside him, whatever the reason behind it.

But there was a heaviness to Jasper's shoulders tonight that even Cherry's closeness couldn't banish.

He should have been gratified to have been given such an important mission by a superior. On any given day, he attempted to stay low-key so that nobody would suspect that he didn't exactly fit the traditional Darkfrey lifestyle, but that also meant he often felt unseen and unneeded.

More a ghost in the system than an active participant. Vonny picking him for something she considered important should have pleased him.

But Cherry's words from back at The Crow's Nest hung over him, deeper than the shadows over the theater.

Did it occur to you she might have sent you on a mission alone to get you killed?

The statement had rooted in his gut like a poisonous plant.

Was there an ulterior motive to Vonny's actions? Why had she given him so few details and demanded he go alone? Was this a real mission at all? Did she know his secret?

The possibility that this was some sort of trap, some way of ridding the Darkfreys of an unwanted member, left Jasper shaken. The possibility that he'd brought Cherry into that trap almost had him turning tail right then.

He hated that his faith in the Darkfreys had been broken enough to let those doubts in. It was ridiculous. Even if they knew he was gay, they wouldn't send him to die, surely. At worst, he'd be kicked out like Cherry.

Except Cherry had told him what Rushelle's brace did to her. Sent her into a deadly situation, alone, and left her there. Just because she wanted to write some damned books instead of hunt monsters. Cherry probably got off lightly because he hadn't reached brace duty yet. Jasper could imagine Vonny and Nilson taking his deceit as a personal insult to their brace, their status.

Despite the brisk chill, Jasper found himself sweating.

"Are we getting into this spooky joint or what?" Cherry flashed a wide, cheeky grin his way, although it didn't reach his eyes.

Jasper's heart fluttered uncomfortably. He could smell Cherry's lip gloss on the air, and the gloomy, overcast light made his red hair glow brighter than normal. He was so effortlessly, inordinately beautiful. So perfectly comfortable with who he was and what he stood for, while Jasper's own skin was ill-fitting and strangling.

This was a bad idea. Being here. With him.

But the sad truth was, he couldn't do this alone. He felt stronger and safer with Cherry at his side. Cherry's presence made him a better version of himself.

Jasper walked up to the back door and examined the rusty chains that had been wrapped through the scratched handle. A combination lock dangled from the chains, and a cursory check proved it was locked tight.

"Von didn't give me a key. Guess we're going to have to break in," Jasper said, backing up to study the building.

Most lower windows had been boarded up with plywood that had been painted like movie poster art.

Why hadn't Vonny gotten access to this place on record so she could give him a key? We should leave.

Cherry scoffed. "It's a decoy."

Jasper raised an eyebrow. "Sorry, decoy?"

Cherry's thick combat boots scuffled across the alley as he stomped up to the back door. He grabbed two dangling edges of the chain and shifted them around, then a split second later, the chains peeled away from the handle.

"The lock was already busted last time we went in. We just hung the chain up again to look like it's doing something. The place is wide open." He tossed the chain aside, then motioned for Jasper to follow him. "Come on. Let's get your mystery job done."

Beneath Cherry's fingertips, the theater door creaked like the cry of a pterodactyl. Jasper hurried in behind him as they traded the cold morning air for the dark, musty interior.

Jasper's vision adjusted immediately, and his underlying shadyr night vision kicked into gear so that he could see his path through the crowded hallway. The place was a horrendous mess, like a wave of furniture and refuse had crashed through the area.

The two of them picked their way around broken chairs, rolled-up backdrops, and dress mannequins that lay haphazardly in the shadows. A hideous jumble of life-sized doll children had been piled to one side.

"I did not notice them last time." Cherry whistled low under his breath. "I know I said I had your back, but if those things come to life, I'm out."

Jasper couldn't argue with that sentiment. Fighting ghasts was one thing; coming up against creepy black-eyed demon children was quite another. They didn't have a shadyr form for that.

"I can't sense anything, can you?" Jasper asked, then

bit his tongue.

Proximity to eidolghasts was a sensitive topic for Cherry. It didn't help that he'd been kicked out of training before he'd had the chance to master control of his shifting.

With a sigh, Cherry gestured to his still-human self. "We're obviously free from beasts of the Everdark. This place is eerie as, but I don't think it's beshadowed. Just, you know, naturally creepy."

The corridor spilled past musty bathrooms and more junk piled up along the walls on either side. Old clothing racks, strange statues—including several plaster gargoyles and creepy robed angels—plus boxes and boxes of props that exploded with feathers, rope, and gold chains. Everything that had once had a place on the stage had found a new home in the halls, giving the place an overcrowded, menacing feel.

"So ..." Cherry said, his low voice breaking the silence. "You gonna give me a clue what we're looking for?"

"A shadyr artifact," Jasper replied distractedly, his gaze sweeping the darkest shadows behind the debris. "One that's been missing from the estate for a while."

Cherry looked skeptical. "Why do they think one is here?"

Jasper shrugged. He didn't have an answer to that. But Vonny thought it was there. A number of relics had been missing from the estate for years, and the Howells' trip to

Gorhanmere had only turned out one.

Maybe the estate had decided it was time to start hunting down the others, and Vonny had info that one was at the theater. Why Jasper had to come for it alone, though, was the bigger mystery.

She'd given him a rough description of what to look for, but this place was a treasure hunter's nightmare. The clutter could take decades to search thoroughly. Jasper had to hope that if he was close, he'd *sense* the artifact.

When he'd followed Lian and Everly into the forbidden chamber at the estate that housed other shadyr treasures, he'd felt them then, a soft, thrumming magic that warmed his veins. He hoped this relic would be the same, and he wouldn't be stuck seeking a needle in a costume stack forever. Jasper pulled ahead of Cherry, sweeping the quiet building with his honed senses. Nothing. Lacking any other clue, he headed toward the center of the building.

They passed through broken doors, then through two rows of trumpeting angels that glowed demonically in his night vision. Every step he took made them move and shake, and their smooth, sightless eyes appeared a little too knowing. Too seeing. He forced his gaze to remain firmly on the path ahead, even as his skin crawled.

Cherry spoke again, breaking the loaded silence. "This place must have been beautiful once, don't you think?"

Trust Cherry to see the beauty in anything.

Jasper offered a soft grunt in reply. The ground sloped down as they left the entrance hall for the theater. The ceiling soared overhead, stretching out around them in a dusky dome, while old, broken seats stepped toward a decimated stage.

Jasper eyed the damage, noting that it looked a little too new to have rotted over time.

Cherry followed his gaze. "Yeah, the Howell boys really ripped this place up. This is where Rylan took down a vasmire, solo. When Callan, myself, and the ladies came to check it out, we also got hit by a weroth. Weird, don't you think? Two eidolghasts of different types wanting to hole up here so soon after each other?"

"We can't attribute logic to those creatures," Jasper said distractedly. "And two points of data alone can't conclude anything."

"I love it when you talk statistics to me."

A hot blush hit Jasper's cheeks and he turned away. "Let's, uh, investigate down there."

The wide path through the seats turned into a steeper decline. Jasper kept half his attention on his feet and the other half on bottling up his feelings until they reached the orchestra pit.

Cherry *tsked*. "Well, at least we know that weroth isn't still here. Otherwise, I'd be furry by now."

"Are you still training with Callan?"

Cherry took a moment before replying, "Yeah. And he's a good teacher. I guess I'm just finding it hard to focus lately. Everything has been feeling hard since ... you know."

Pop. The bottle opened again.

For one overwhelming moment, Jasper wasn't sure why his chest seemed to be heating from within and thought maybe he'd suffered some form of literal heartbreak.

Then he remembered what he'd come looking for.

Down below, where the orchestra used to play, the destruction was massive. Everything once housed there was shattered to pieces. Jasper couldn't even make out what anything had originally been. Chairs, tables, ghast knew what else, all now nothing but blackened splinters.

"Do you feel that?" he asked.

Cherry screwed up his nose. "Maybe, a little. Shadyr senses tingling, right? Not an eidolghast?"

"No, something down there. I think it's what we're after."

Jasper hopped over the wall and dropped into the pit, focusing on a far corner of the room.

Cherry landed lightly behind him. "Where's it coming from?"

"Over here." A narrow, closed door peeked out of the shadows, and Jasper could feel the artifact pulsing from within.

Cherry laughed out his nose. "You've always been

better at all this stuff than me."

Jasper strode to the door and pulled it open. The closet was empty except for a bundle of rags on the floor, but that low hum was obviously coming from beneath the tattered fabric.

Jasper knelt and peeled back the material, revealing a strange, diamond-shaped blade with no hilt. A fine filigree pattern covered its surface, and blood seemed to ooze up through the ornate shapes.

"Wrap it back up." All humor had left Cherry's face, and he stared coldly. "That's what you came here for?"

Jasper bundled the odd blade in its wrapping again and stood to face Cherry. "Fits the description Vonny gave me, yes."

"It doesn't belong to the Darkfreys. Give it to me." Cherry's hand shot out, waiting.

Jasper didn't release the bundle. "Of course it belongs to the Darkfreys. It's a shadyr artifact. I can feel the power in it."

Cherry shifted uncomfortably. "That's the Bane of Teeth and Stars. That's what we found in Gorhanmere. It belongs to us now."

"What's it doing here, then?"

"I don't know! Harper was looking after it. She must have hid it here for safekeeping because it makes Everly sick when it's near her." His dark eyes lifted accusingly to

Jasper's. "Did you know the artifact you were sent to get was the one we found?"

"No, I didn't know. I only knew it was a missing artifact." Jasper swallowed the pleading tone from his voice. "But that's all I need to know. All shadyr artifacts belong at the estate."

Cherry's open hand sped out and wrapped around the parchment-covered bundle. "Not this one. We earned this. The Darkfreys were too scared to deal with their crazy renegade brethren. We almost died to get this, and you're just going to come in and steal it from us? No wonder Vonny kept this quiet. She didn't want anyone knowing what cowards you all are."

Jasper tightened his long fingers on the bundle and yanked against Cherry's hold. "There has to be more to it than that. This must be important, or Vonny wouldn't have sent me—"

"You really think she respects you?" Cherry narrowed his eyes viciously, fingers digging in as he strengthened his attempt to snatch the artifact. "That thing is important. To us. This is what brought Rylan back, and it's our only solid lead into what is inside Everly. I can't believe you dragged me here as 'backup' to help you *steal it*."

Breath snorted hard and fast from Jasper's nose as the artifact was wrestled between them. Each of Cherry's words struck him like a blow. But he had to complete his mission.

He had to take claim over what was rightfully Darkfrey property. He wrenched back, wresting the parcel free from Cherry's grip, leaving his ex staggering.

Cherry grunted and stepped away from Jasper, shoulders slumped. "So, that's where we are? Yet again, you choose the Darkfreys over me, when I …"

Jasper stared between him and the bundle in his grip. "I didn't know anything about this artifact, or where it came from, or its connections to your team."

"But you do now." Cherry glared up from beneath a veil of bright red hair. "Are you going to do the right thing and hand it over?"

Jasper sighed, his breath coming out shakily. "You know I can't do that. This is a shadyr artifact, and they all belong to—"

"You sound like a fucking robot," Cherry cut in, hands balled into fists.

Bristling, Jasper tucked the tattered bundle into his cardigan as he replied, "My mission was to retrieve this artifact, and now I have it."

"Yeah." Cherry laughed scathingly. "Yeah, you have your artifact. And your brace. And your precious Darkfrey status. How does it feel to sacrifice everything to an institution that doesn't give a crap about the real you, who will never truly accept you or love you?"

Jasper gritted his teeth as pain billowed through his

chest like Cherry had ripped him open with his fingernails. "Move out of my way. You know you can't best me in a fight."

Cherry huffed, shaking his head. "You would, wouldn't you? You would beat me."

He backed away a couple more steps, swallowing visibly. For the first time since the argument began, Jasper caught a glimpse of Cherry's emotions bald on his face. Then his expression walled back up and he turned a penetrating glare on Jasper.

"Don't ever call me again, even in an emergency," Cherry said. "Don't expect me to ever have your back again, or care if that means you die."

As their eyes met one last time, Jasper's insides turned cold at the lack of emotion in Cherry's usually bright, expressive gaze.

Then Cherry whirled on his heel and stalked away. He clambered easily up the orchestra pit's tumble-down wall, then stomped up the aisle.

Leaving Jasper frozen on the dusty parquet. He stared into the quiet darkness for some time after the sharp finality of the theater's door slamming shut. Jasper pressed his hand against the bundle at his chest and found himself disappointed that this hadn't been an attempt by Vonny to kill him.

It would have hurt less.

CHAPTER TWENTY

Neri's father's gnarled flippers latched onto Harper before she could get her axe up between them. She had no room to move, not even an instant to try to throw up a block before his claws sank in.

He squeezed with unbelievable strength, nails digging into her arms as he threw his entire deformed bulk against her body. They went down in a tangle of cold, wet limbs. Sharp scales and seashells crunched under Harper's back. Her axe fell out of her hands.

The Howell team was yelling, and Neri continued screaming. Harper couldn't make out any words over the fish man's roars.

Harper struggled to get her hands between her and the madman. Water sloshed like a miniature ocean around them, and the waves passed over her face and head, leaving her sightless and sputtering. She flailed blindly at the fish man even as his weight pressed her deeper into the ocean-floor carpet, deeper beneath the water.

Neri's father had appeared ancient and run-down only moments before, but he was supernaturally strong in his twisted, fishy, beshadowed form. More than human. More than superhuman.

Harper knew something of supernatural strength, though. With a final slip of an elbow, she got her arms into position, leveraging against the man's chest. With a howling war cry, she thrust upward, throwing the fish man off her.

He rolled sideward, tumbling into a pile of junk.

Harper lifted her soaking head from the water for a deep, thankful breath. In the clear gap the man left behind were Denny and Callan, staring back, arms out and baffled.

"Gotta be faster than that," she told them, kipping up to her feet.

Her attempt to show her strength and capability was ruined when her legs wobbled, knees landing in a splash. The Bane's power was fading so fast. And she was capable, she knew it, even without the Bane. At least normally. But right now, she was a human who hadn't had a proper night's sleep in days and had pushed her body to the limits every moment between.

I've screwed up. I should have been more careful to rest even when I didn't feel like I needed it. I shouldn't have relied on the Bane to keep me going when I couldn't bring it with me.

But the desire to use that power, to draw it into her and revel in the strength it gave was so alluring, so irresistible. She already craved the feel of it slicing her skin again. The rush of pure, condensed energy flowing in. But that couldn't happen, not anytime soon.

Whatever was left in her would have to be enough. For Neri, and for Everly.

Harper shoved her mass of wet dark hair away from her face, grabbing her axe from the roiling water before she straightened.

Across the room, Rylan faced the fishy monstrosity, fists clenched, ready for a fight.

The man didn't let them down.

Neri's father laid into him with those heavy, clawed flippers. A windmill of blows smashed against Rylan's body. Rylan kept his forearms up to guard his head, taking the blows without fighting back. Waiting for an opening, or the man to tire.

His shadyr form gave him some protection, but even still, skin broke, then regenerated, broke, then regenerated as Rylan glared the man down with bared vampire teeth.

Callan and Denny ran to join him, but they only had their blades and their human forms to help. They sliced at the man's back, but the knives glanced off his thick, leathery skin.

Harper checked for Neri, Tammy, and Everly.

Tammy was down on hands and scaly hip, crawling herself toward the fight with a look of determination in her kohl-rimmed eyes.

Everly crouched on the floor, staring into a dark corner between a broken cabinet and a stack of old tires. A hint of sky-blue tail flicked her way.

Harper passed beneath a waterfall coming down from a split in the ceiling and swiped her eyes clear as she stumbled to Everly's side.

Everly had Neri by both arms.

"I can't hold her back much longer," she panted, her face pale and scrunched.

Harper lowered to one knee next to her, looking at the scared girl.

Neri clawed at the wet floor, tears streaming down her face. When Harper got close enough, Neri's cold, trembling hands caught hers.

"Make it stop. Please! You made him angry."

She whispered the word *angry* as though it were the worst thing in her tiny world.

Harper knew anger, too, and did everything she could to contain it.

She made her voice as gentle as possible. "He's the one that has to be stopped. What he's done, what he's doing to you, imprisoning you here, has to end."

"Please don't hurt him!" Neri's scaled hand squeezed, her eyes widening fearfully.

"If he backs down, right now, and lets us take you to safety, we won't hurt him. But do you think he'd allow that? Do you really think he'll ever let you go?" Harper begged the shadyr with her eyes to *listen* and understand what she was saying.

Neri released Harper, bringing her arms into herself. She clutched at her hair, wringing it fretfully in front of her chin. Her head shook in tiny side-to-side motions but deep, knowing despair filled her eyes.

Harper wanted to pull the traumatized girl into an embrace and hold her until everything was okay again.

She settled with placing just the tips of her fingers onto her shoulder. "Please, stay with Everly. Stay out of the way, until ... your father isn't angry anymore."

Neri didn't respond but made no further attempts to move.

"Thanks," Everly said, leaning back on the broken cabinet with a tired sigh. "I'll keep an eye on her. Are you okay?"

Harper gave her a tentative smile that probably wasn't reassuring at all. "Yeah, I've got this."

She sloshed away, unsure if she was more unsettled by what they might have to do to Neri's father, or how hard she found it to stand back up again.

She hefted her axe and raced toward the fight.

Rylan and Denny grabbed the fish man by both arms and threw him against the wall. The whole room shook, and jets of water spurted from the ceiling. The movement barely stunned the man, and he spun away from the cracked concrete on light feet, racing back toward the team with a mighty, gurgling roar.

Whip-like, Tammy's tail lashed out at his tentacle-ankles, skittling him.

Neri's father barrel-rolled, knocking Denny down on his way, then disappeared behind the chaos of waterfalls pouring from the ceiling.

Rylan growled and swiped at the blood-tinted water rushing down his white-skinned face. "We're barely touching this guy. I can hold him for a while, but he just won't stop."

Denny righted himself with a groan. "Not our fault our only options right now are being human or mermaid."

"Lucky you, you have a choice," Tammy muttered from the floor.

"They aren't your only options though," Harper said, pointing her axe at Rylan. "You annihilated the Nazi zombies in that crazy dragon-man form. Didn't you make that work because of Everly's presence?"

"Wings would only get in the way here." His starry-eyed gaze swept across the room to where Everly hunched beside Neri.

The two of them locked eyes, and strain tightened Everly's expression. She carried so much guilt and despair over what had happened between the two of them, even though it wasn't her fault. Everly never meant to drag Rylan into her dream world, and the way he'd been treating her since she risked her own life to save his grated on Harper's nerves.

Her best friend deserved better.

"Then work something else out, and maybe be grateful about what she's done for you, and continues to do for you, for once!" Harper turned to face the direction that the old man had rolled toward.

Through the film of falling water, his silhouette approached.

"All of you, pull it together. Or do you want your asses kicked by a fish?" Without waiting for a reply, Harper raised her axe and leaped at the man.

He blocked her first blow with one flippered arm. Strange black blood spurted where the blade sank into his slimy skin, but he didn't react with pain. He whirled like a waterspout and slammed into Harper.

The Bane's remnant energy flared inside her, and she held her ground. She redirected the momentum into another slash of her axe, taking several claws off the end of one flipper with a well-placed strike.

The fish man screamed, eyes rolling wildly. He darted away, trailing more black blood on the water.

Harper raced in pursuit, but a larger figure leaped in front of her. A massive shape like a werewolf, but instead of fur, the skin was covered in glistening, dark-blue scales.

It had to be Rylan. What was that? Was he drawing from part weroth and part nyevmer? Whatever it was, it was strong, and fast. He sped for the man, tearing across the room on all fours.

Rylan swiped out with claws much longer and sharper than the lighthouse keeper's ugly nails. He caught Neri's father across his deformed face and sent the old man flying into the wall with a dull *thwack*. At the same moment, a vicious crack of thunder broke over the lighthouse, and the floor shuddered under Harper's feet.

Her knees buckled and she sank quickly into the water, shooting one hand out to catch herself before she could fall in face first. A wave of exhaustion washed through her. The initial adrenaline of finding Neri and then being caught off guard by her grotesque father had begun to wear off, and fatigue was overwhelming her.

Clutching her axe with white-knuckled fingers, Harper shoved aside the woozy, pale feeling in her head. *I don't have time for being weak.*

Rylan and the fish man were in full savage mode as Harper hefted her suddenly too-heavy axe and straightened back up onto too-heavy legs—right as Rylan slammed Neri's father into the wall again.

The lighthouse shook, and a deluge of fresh water poured from overhead as if the ceiling had yawned open and dumped the storm inside.

"*Ah!*" Harper squealed embarrassingly and was thrown backward by the heavy downpour.

She hit the floor and was washed across it by the rising water. Her axe disappeared under the surge.

The wave crashed around the room. One of the piles of random objects toppled over. Broken mugs, moldy action figures, and empty cans splashed down. One bright-yellow object caught Harper's eye as it burst free of the clutter and skidded through the water—a wind-up emergency radio.

"No!" Neri gasped.

She pushed past Everly, knocking her against the tires. Everly grimaced, holding her arms into her chest. Neri threw herself belly first over the wet floor toward the radio.

Her cry caught her father's attention and his eyes bulged as she scooped the radio into her hands. "What is that? Where'd you get that?"

He swiped away Rylan's blows and stomped toward his daughter. Neri backed into shelter behind a small cupboard, tail flopping as she hopped on her hands.

Rylan threw himself onto the man, drawing the attention back to him. A flash filled the frame of the window behind them, and Harper caught sight of a huge crack in the wall she hadn't noticed before.

The lighthouse shuddered and groaned like a dying dragon. Rylan and the fish man battled like wild animals, growing closer and closer to Neri. Harper's heart lodged in her throat, and she splashed her way through the deepening pool toward the terrified mermaid. It was like being on a sinking ship that was taking on water from every angle.

More ceiling fell away on the other side of the room. A wave of saltwater sent Harper slamming into Neri.

Harper clung to the girl and yelled over the roar of rushing water, "Neri, get back, it's not—"

She didn't get a chance to finish her sentence.

Rylan and the man slammed into the wall again. Their combined weight hit the crack, and with a terrifying crunch, the side of the room fell away.

The whole building tipped, as though the interior was finally catching up to the crooked angle of the lighthouse exterior.

Water swept around Harper. It lifted her like driftwood and sent her spinning.

Neri's cold fingers tightened on her own, and the two of them clung to each other as they washed toward the hole in the wall. Harper gasped for air, thinking fast as the exit rushed at them. A large, dark silhouette clung to one side of the ruined bricks as water washed out around his bent knees. Rylan. But he was out of reach.

Harper extracted one hand from Neri's grasp, threw her arm out, and grabbed for anything she could.

She snatched at the sharp, broken concrete, catching the edge of the floor with the very tips of her manicured nails. As her nails scraped and broke along the stones, she managed to latch one leg around the wall right before the water sent her spilling into open air.

Their tumble ceased with a jarring snap of her muscles. She clasped Neri's wrist in her hand, and Neri held on. They hung far above the white-capped waves that tore at the jagged rocks below with deadly ferocity.

Neri shrieked, a raw, ragged sound that was surprisingly loud over the booming thunder and crashing waves. Her slippery fingers slid down.

Harper tightened her grip, confused over why Neri felt so heavy …

Until she saw the old man clinging to her tail far below.

"No!" Harper groaned hoarsely.

Neri's fingers dug into Harper's skin, and she squeezed her terrified, starry eyes shut. Water poured around them, obscuring Harper's vision and making it that much harder to maintain her grip. Her ankle and knee screamed from the way she clutched the wall while her arm ripped from its socket under the weight of Neri and her father.

"Let go! Let go, you're going to kill her!" Harper yelled

at the man, sputtering as salty water filled her mouth.

The man howled, wrapping his arms tighter around Neri's tail. He writhed about, and Harper couldn't tell if he was trying to climb or trying to get her to let go of his mermaid.

He slipped, flopping against the wall and taking Neri with him, smashing her side into the concrete. She cried out, whimpering.

He'll never let Neri go, even if it means tearing her in half.

Harper gritted her teeth and pulled. She grabbed an exposed metal rod with her other hand, leveraging against it. She hauled with all her strength, pulling Neri and the man back to the lighthouse floor, inch by painful inch.

Over her shoulder, she sensed Rylan trying to reach her, to help her from where he'd wedged his own body safely, but he was too far back.

"Hold on, Neri!" Harper screamed.

Neri nodded, her eyes huge and sad. Her body rocked against the concrete as her father struggled to climb her like a rope, roaring madly at Harper.

Harper yanked harder, angling her body back. Her muscles screamed and burned but she didn't give up. She could do this. She still had the Bane's power inside her, however much it had faded. It would make her strong enough.

I need to be strong enough.

She wasn't.

The old man thrashed again with a gurgling shriek, sending Neri's tail swaying wildly. In a split second, Neri's fingertips slipped away.

Then both the beautiful mermaid and her hideous captor fell down, down, down.

And the man kept hold of Neri until they hit the wild, deadly waves far below.

Then Harper lost her grip on the lighthouse as well.

Chapter Twenty-One

Everly's breath caught in her throat as Harper washed through the water and over the edge of the destroyed wall. She seized, terror turning her insides to ice-water as she imagined her best friend crashing down onto the ferocious rocks below.

In the blasting wind and backwash of rain, Everly caught sight of Harper's fingers digging painfully into the shattered concrete, one leg hooked around the wall. She was alive, but barely holding on, pelted with debris from the sloping room as the beshadowed lighthouse tilted precariously into open space.

Pull yourself up, Everly pleaded silently. *Why isn't she pulling herself up?*

The rush of water that had washed Harper and Neri

through the break in the wall had tumbled Everly across the floor alongside the fallen armchair.

She'd been thrown sideways against an unbroken portion of the wall and found herself pinned by the armchair while the water continued to cascade around her. The initial flood that poured from the ceiling had eased to a consistent stream. It rushed over the chair, strong enough that Everly couldn't get free to even attempt to help her best friend.

But the truth was, she wasn't in any position to help *anyone*. Not with her arms breaking apart from the inside. Every time she even moved her fingertips, debilitating pain tore through her and more shards broke below her skin, spreading over her shoulders.

Rylan—the strange, scaley werewolf version of him—hunched against the very edge of the broken wall, too close to falling for Everly's comfort. Callan and Tammy were tangled up on what was now the top side of the room. Tammy's arm wrapped around one side of the doorframe, securing her and Callan to the forty-five-degree angled floor while water flowed around them.

From Everly's sideways position, the whole lighthouse felt turned inside out. Down seemed up, up seemed down, and simply staring out upon the tableau disoriented her.

The old man was nowhere in sight, and Everly had lost track of Denny too until he appeared by her feet, balancing between wall and floor.

"You good, kid?" he asked around panting breaths.

Everly gestured to the chair across her midsection. "Not going anywhere. Help Harper, please. She went over."

He pressed both palms to the wall and lifted his leg to step over her and the fallen chair. "Those curves aren't getting wasted on the rocks on my watch."

Everly stared at his back, aghast. He couldn't be Harper's only hope. Her mind went into overdrive, trying to find some other solution. She couldn't take the risk to use her dragon's powers to reach out for Harper, because it liked to eat the things it reached out for.

Harper's screaming voice cut through the storm. What was she shouting—Neri's name? Was she still there, too?

Rylan leaned forward, one taloned hand reaching toward Harper's leg. He slipped, his clawed feet scrabbling against the slick stones and rushing water. He latched back onto the wall, readjusting to try again.

More screaming, three voices piercing through the waves and storm.

Denny leaped forward in a rush, landing on his chest, and threw his arms out into open space.

The screams grew quieter, rushing away into nothing.

Please, please, please have her.

"Oof! Gotcha!" Denny grunted, shuffling sideways to avoid sliding through the hole.

Once he'd anchored himself, he dragged a limp body up over the edge. Like a ragdoll, he yanked Harper away from the hole and propped her against the wall next to Everly and the armchair. "Bout learned how to fly, didn't you?"

Harper said nothing.

"That's okay, maybe you can thank me later," he added with a wink.

Harper didn't even react. Didn't even cringe. She just stared, silently, her expression one of complete desolation.

Everly made an angry sound of disgust and shoved against the chair on top of her. "Thank you for saving her. Now could you shut your gross mouth before you spoil the one good thing you've done even more?"

Denny pulled a rude face and leaned to free Everly from the armchair, but Rylan reached her first. He lifted it gently and pushed it aside into the trickling water.

"You okay?" he asked, offering her a hand.

He'd shifted back to a more manageable vampire form. His body armor held together but was scraped and dinted, and his pants hung in tatters.

Everly nodded and moved into a seated position against the angled wall.

Harper trembled. Blood speckled her fingernails on one hand, and her knees visibly shook as she lay back against the cold concrete.

"I dropped her."

Everly gasped out a sob. *The poor girl.*

Like a nightmare, she could imagine the emaciated mermaid tumbling through the air. And her best friend didn't have to imagine; she'd seen it with her own eyes.

"What happened ... it wasn't your fault. You tried to save her."

Ignoring the agony in her arms, Everly reached out for Harper's mangled hands, sweeping her gaze over the wounds. Most were superficial from where she'd clung to the stones—lacerations on her fingertips and broken, bleeding nails.

Half-moon fingernail marks had formed bloody pools on her opposite wrist, bruises already blooming under her brown skin. Harper still didn't move beyond the shudders that railroaded through her, as though too exhausted, too traumatized, to even cry.

Enough tears ran down Everly's face for both of them. "You're okay. I'm so glad you're okay."

Harper's head shook in a small twitch. "It ran out too quick."

"What ran out?"

Harper's dazed stare lifted from her hands to Everly, then she turned away, her gaze seeking out the hole in the wall. "I should have brought it with me. I should have been stronger."

"Brought what?" Everly asked, exasperated. "Harper,

you're not making any sense."

"I promised her ..." Harper's voice caught, and a sob broke like a dam from her throat. "I couldn't save her."

"You did your best," Everly assured her, reaching up to cup Harper's cold cheeks in her hands. "You always do your best."

"Look, that all went sideways, in more ways than one," Denny offered. "Blame the old bloke, not yourself."

Everly pulled Harper into her arms and looked at the others over her shoulder. "Speaking of, where is he?"

"Went down as well," Rylan confirmed.

Harper shuddered harder in Everly's arms.

Rylan stalked across the tilted floor, pushing wreckage and clutter back to clear a path up to where Tammy and Callan waited near the door. "I appreciate that we've just witnessed a tragedy, but we're on a time limit here. We've already taken way too long."

Everly shot him a warning look.

Rylan returned one as equally intense. "None of us want a second tragedy to mourn. It's time to keep moving. For Everly."

Harper nodded against Everly's shoulder and pulled away.

Everly slid an arm around her friend's waist and ducked her head, uncomfortable with Rylan's pointed gaze.

Harper let herself be guided forward as she stared at

the water running over their feet. Denny and Rylan helped them crawl up the steep incline of the slippery, seaweed-covered floor, and Callan and Tammy caught them at the top, pulling them out of the broken room and into the stairwell.

A while later, Rylan and Denny joined them, dragging the few packs that could be salvaged behind them—Rylan's, with Everly's inside, and Callan's. The others were gone. Harper didn't seem to care. Denny muttered something about how he could have done with a beer. Callan took his, then lifted Tammy as well.

Glancing back into that room filled with tragedy, Everly noticed the hole in the wall already closing over. That strange growth of coral and crystal crackled its way like a timelapse across the gap.

Everly, waterlogged and weighed down by her clothes and shoes, found every step, every movement, utterly exhausting. Coupled with the pain in her arm and the heavy atmosphere, she wanted to curl onto the floor and give up.

Rylan was right, however. They were close to their goal. Too close to give up now.

It had better be worth it.

Sparkling blue light beamed down from high above, and the stairs continued to circle toward the sky beneath that hypnotic, underwater kaleidoscope. The crooked angle of the lighthouse affected the stairs now, too, leaning them up and down, up and down as they spiraled around.

But the light they'd been following for some time finally got closer. As they reached the final level, the lighthouse straightened up again.

When they arrived at the top, there should have been more fanfare, more celebration, more relief after the disaster they'd been through. But Everly just stepped off the final stair with a long, low sigh and trudged into the room.

The stairwell spilled onto a wide landing that took up the entire topmost floor of the lighthouse. Windows lined the dome, revealing the gunmetal sky and the lashing storm outside. A metal floor encircled the all-glass container that held the magical light source, while a silver surface rotated and evenly dispersed the light into the wild, stormy night.

Everly released Harper's waist, drawn by the vivid glow of the object inside the rotating tube.

It called to her. She felt the hum of it in her core and pure glee from the dragon. She recognized the magic of it as something that had always been a part of her, even when she hadn't understood what it meant. Moving slowly, boots squelching on the landing, Everly chased the rotating light for a better look.

The twirling mechanism rolled around, coming back toward her. Light flashed, power bloomed around Everly, and she caught sight of the source.

She stumbled backward, blood draining from her face.

It was so beautiful. It was so pretty she just wanted to touch it.

She ran into Rylan, who steadied her with his hands on her shoulders. "Hey, what's wrong?"

She winced at his touch, her head shaking.

Abstract, spiraling fractals of the most delicate crystal, glittering from within.

Tantalizing, tempting. It fell from her tiny fingertips and shattered into a million shards on the hardwood floor.

It all came back to her so clearly, the memory she'd locked away, shoved deep down in an attempt to forget.

She had broken the crystal sculpture. Blinding light had brightened the room like the birth of a sun. Pure, raw energy filtering into her tiny body, coiled up within her, dug in tight.

She'd felt hungry, so hungry. And then she didn't.

And her father collapsed, eyes glazed and unmoving.

Everly gasped, choking on her forgotten need to breathe.

It was the dragon. Trapped in that crystal. That was the moment she'd taken the being into her, unbidden. And in the process, it had killed her father.

The revelation was bittersweet. She'd carried the guilt of his death for her entire life, thinking herself the terrible daughter that made her dad so angry that he had a heart attack and died.

Instead, the piece of the Beast of Teeth and Stars within

her had killed him. And it was still her childish selfishness to touch and break what wasn't hers that had freed it.

Now, another piece of that thing was the only option she had for healing the damage the Bane had done to her. The thought of allowing *more* of the soul-eating monster into her body, even if it could save her, terrified her. How much the creature inside her wanted that scared her more. Her insides howled with longing.

"Hey, is that ..." Tammy stared at the crystal, her head tilting as it spun past them.

"Looks just like the one in Barry's maze," Callan agreed, shifting her in his arms.

She looked comfortable hanging against him now, as if the two of them had become one entity, reliant on each other and preferring it that way.

Denny barked a laugh. "Well, ain't that our ghast-twisted luck. We come all this way when there was one right there back home."

Rylan let Everly go and moved toward the rotating housing, wrenching it to a stop with a pale hand. The crystal hung there before them, scintillating as it floated, suspended in mid-air behind a shield of glass.

He caught Everly's gaze. "Is it even the right thing?"

She blinked, still lost in the memory that played on repeat in her head.

Swallowing hard, she said, "That's it. It's the same as

the one ... When I was a kid. That's like what I broke when my dad died."

Harper's eyes lifted from the floor, and she stepped beside Everly, gently touching her shoulder. "The dragon has been in you since you were three?"

"Why didn't we know about it until now?" Callan asked.

Rylan answered for her, "You must have been fighting it this whole time. After seeing your dad die, you've been holding it back ever since."

"Except when I couldn't." She could see them now, the times she'd been weak and it had escaped her control.

When she was lost in the woods as a child, after the car accident, and the night Rylan was apparently killed, she'd seen its light then, before the first time she'd fully let it free at the theater.

Everly stared at her hands, at the jagged red cracks running under her skin.

Rylan snapped the latches and opened the housing. He reached in and grasped the crystal. It glowed brighter for a moment, then faded until it sparkled only from the flashes of lightning around them.

"So we break it, right? That's how we release more of the dragon into you? Help it heal itself?" He looked ready to dash the thing across the metal floor.

"No!" Everly cried.

If it worked, if it made the beast stronger, if it took control in this small space surrounded by her friends, who knew what the consequences could be.

Before it had been wounded, she'd barely kept it under control. Her whole life, she'd locked it up, starved it, leashed it, and then broke it, stole its playthings. What would it do if it were stronger?

"I, I don't think …" Everly grit her teeth and forced her words out clearly. "I don't want more of it in me."

"Are you kidding? It could be the only way to save you," Rylan growled. "There are crack marks *on your neck.*"

Everly raised her head to him, her voice hard. "And I'm still here. I'm surviving. And I'm saying I don't want any more of that thing in me. I just want to leave and forget this whole beshadowed town. Isn't that what you want?"

Rylan's chest swelled up and down with each seething breath.

The walls groaned, and another booming percussion of thunder shook the lighthouse.

Harper stepped between them. "Let's go. I want to get out of this place. We have what we came for. Can we just go now?"

"Yes," Everly said without hesitation.

She turned to lead the way down the stairs, body aching to the bone and heart stinging more. They got what they came for, had paid too high a price, and it all came to nothing.

All she wanted was to escape that cursed place without any more lives lost.

Chapter Twenty-Two

The blue glow of the lighthouse had been extinguished with the removal of the crystal, leading to a dark stumble back down the crooked stairwell. The few flashlights they had from the remaining packs offered a little light but didn't do enough to cut through the gloom.

As they went by the doorway to Neri's room, Everly noticed the growth that had so quickly formed over the hole was cracking apart.

From somewhere far below, a strange, mournful wail arose.

The desperate sound cut through Everly's thoughts and banished the agony in her arms. The team drew up short as the wails intensified. They echoed up through the stairwell, each warble repeating like a whale song of doom.

Several feet away, Denny barked, "What the ghast is that?"

Callan replied, "The nyevmer?"

In a boom of thunder, the lighthouse lurched beneath their feet, shifting again, tipping them against the opposite wall.

"Hurry," Rylan commanded. "I don't trust this place to stay together much longer."

"Right, so let me get the plan straight. We just have to escape this collapsing lighthouse, get through the underwater caves where something is howling at existence, and then hope someone comes to take us off this forsaken island," Tammy muttered from Callan's back.

"We deal as we go, now move."

Callan took the lead. "Someone will come and get us. I've still got the sat phone. Besides, we just turned off a lighthouse that's been going for decades. If the Crybel's Cove shadyrs were expecting a signal, I don't know what more we could do."

Some logic in Everly told her that lighthouses weren't really necessary anymore, that they were mostly a backup for other navigational technology. But she hated to think of anybody who might be out there on the waves in this weather, especially knowing that if they crashed to the rocks, their blood would be on her hands.

Rylan kept the crystal carefully in his hands, watching

for her to pick up pace before falling in behind her.

They circled down the lighthouse stairs, splashing and slipping as horrifying cracks and crunching noises overwhelmed the thunder. Through a portal window, a chunk of wall fell past them.

They spilled onto the ground floor, where the crystalline coral growths were changing into crumbling sand, blocking the main entrance like a sludgy dune.

The ceiling cracked and shifted.

"Run!" Callan yelled.

They bolted as one for the narrow passage that led to the caves. Callan and Tammy disappeared into the darkness, a sloshing sound rising behind them. Denny and Harper followed, and Everly hit the top of the stairs and almost tumbled face-first down them from momentum.

Rylan grabbed the back of her jacket and shoved her against the stone wall. She cried out as her shoulders stabbed with pain but was muffled by Rylan's cold chest as he pressed against her.

In a deafening smash, the thick slab of ceiling slammed against the passage entrance. Lumps of plaster and concrete sprayed through the air, pattering against Rylan's back.

Everly wiped a spatter of sand from her face, and Rylan wrapped an arm around her waist, pushing her down the stairs. "Keep going!"

The rubble above them groaned, twisting on itself

under the pressure. Then it exploded outward, filling the space they previously stood with crushing sections of floor and bone-breaking wreckage.

Rylan sped Everly onwards, faster than she could comprehend, until water splashed up around them.

The cold cave water swallowed Everly whole. She broke the surface, sucking in a breath as the chill penetrated her clothes. It hurt as much as it helped, numbing the pain but inflating it all the same.

The small beach at the base of the stairs had gone. Waves washed up into the stairwell, and Everly and Rylan swam out to meet the others around the glow of two remaining flashlights.

Tammy bobbed in the water, her tail swaying beneath her. Denny and Callan finished shifting and rolled wet pants into a bundle, putting them into Callan's pack.

The tide had risen significantly. Everly looked up, and if she had the strength to raise her arms above her head, she was sure she'd be able to touch the cavern ceiling.

"Well, we're not getting back out that way," Rylan said, tipping his head toward where the lighthouse must now be a pile of wreckage, smothering the ground above.

Another haunting howl pierced the air around them. It was strangely musical, like a hurricane trying to sing, broken by sobs.

It came from between them and their only exit.

"What *is* that?" Harper whispered.

Rylan shifted into mermaid form, then turned his galaxy eyes toward the sound. "We'll find out soon."

Everly slid closer to Harper, and shadyrs placed themselves two on either side, pulling them through the water. Everly focused on the burning in her arms to ground herself to the world. If she was hurting, she couldn't pass out. If she didn't pass out, she'd be less of a problem for the shadyrs to deal with.

Harper made little effort to swim, letting herself be towed along. Everly reached out to hold her hand, and while Harper took hers in return, there was no strength in her grasp.

Out of the narrower cave and into the larger underground lake near the entrance, the wailing was deafening, and it echoed off the rocks like a sonic weapon. The entire cavern had filled with water, the few rocky islands completely submerged except for those that rose like pillars all the way to the ceiling.

"Go, straight through and out," Callan ordered.

Harper let go of Everly's hand and broke away from the group, lurching through the water in uneven strokes toward one of the pillars where the howling sounded loudest.

"What is she doing?" Rylan muttered.

"You don't swim toward the spooky sounds!" Denny hissed.

Callan swam after her. He caught up easily, but she swiped away his efforts to pull her back.

"Look!" She splashed an arm out, pointing into the shadows.

Tammy turned her flashlight that way, and sky-blue scales reflected the beam.

Neri perched, half out of the water, clinging to the pillar like a child to a parent's leg. Her long tail trailed in the chopping waves below. She hunched over like an abused animal, cupping something small and white in one hand.

Harper picked up her pace, splashing toward her. "You're alive. You survived."

The crying ceased for a moment. Neri turned toward them but didn't seem to register what she saw. Her head shook and she screamed again.

Rylan huffed, pulling Everly at his side as he followed the others toward the girl.

Tammy's flashlight shone onto Neri again as they got closer. She held a tiny skull in her shaking fingers.

Denny grunted. "Can you shut her up? She's going to attract trouble."

After a flash of anger his way, Harper wrapped her arms around the rocky pillar beside Neri, pulling herself up to catch the girl's gaze. "Hey, shh. It's going to be okay."

Neri's wailing stuttered out between sobs. "It hurts. I can't ... I'm trying to heal my heart but it's not working."

"I'm sorry. I'm so sorry." Harper reached out a hand but hesitated to touch her.

Neri looked up, her eyes red-rimmed and wide, tears soaking her thick, dark lashes. "You weren't lying."

"No ... we weren't."

Neri's face scrunched in on itself, and her mouth opened wide, but no sound came out. She clutched the skull to her chest with white-knuckled fingers.

Harper's hand hovered in the space between them. "Hey, hey. I'm so, so happy you're okay. How did you survive that fall?"

"I missed the rocks. It hurt. The waves, the water hurt, but it's my heart that won't heal."

"Your father?" Rylan asked cautiously.

"He didn't miss the rocks." Neri's eyes welled with more thick tears. "I didn't know where else to go. I swam around and found my way in. I just wanted to go home. And I found them. I found them."

A sob racked Neri's entire body and the skull tumbled from her fingertips, sinking like a ghost back into the depths.

Neri sucked in a deep, agonized breath, and a loud howl reverberated from her mouth again. Everly had to put her hands over her ears. There was a musical quality to Neri's mourning screams—a cross between humming and crying, with a strange mix of familiar tunes, snippets of pop songs and classics from across decades, but it was too broken by pain to be a song.

In gasping sobs, Neri choked out, "What do I do? What can I do?"

Harper bent in closer. "Come with us. I know I wasn't strong enough to hold onto you, but I still want to try to keep my promise."

Neri squeezed her eyes shut, her expression twisted into one of abject despair, then she tossed herself into Harper's arms. They slipped, together, off the rock and down into the water, as Neri clung to Harper's shoulders with her bony arms.

As her wails dissolved into hushed whimpers, a new sound echoed through the tunnels, this one much less hauntingly sad.

A wicked and harrowing roar.

Where is it?

Rylan turned in the choppy water and looked back toward the tunnels they'd just left behind for the incoming eidolghast.

Only inky blackness met his searching gaze. Deep, warbling rumbles echoed all around them, and the waves against his shoulders splashed harder.

"Get ready for a fight." His shadyr senses told him the monster was close now.

But where? Rylan's gaze turned downward, toward the void-like depths of the water beneath them.

He'd never seen a nyevmer beyond sketches during Darkfrey training. He expected something the size of a weroth or auerdax. But the shape that formed from the darkness, birthed from the abyss beneath his tail, was enormous.

"Split!" he roared.

The Howell shadyrs in mermaid form dove to the sides. Everly, Harper, and Neri clung for shelter against the rocky pillar.

The water where they had just floated opened into the pit of the creature's maw.

It breached.

Whip-like tentacles lined both sides of a mouth like a bear trap, each tendril ending in sharp, three-pointed claws. Its elongated skull led to a pointed crown of bone, ringed in tiny, glowing eyes.

Its head cracked into the ceiling and shook the cavern before it turned, slithering back down into the deep again. The curve of its ridged, sea-serpent body was massive and went on, and on, until a tail of bony-points flicked the surface, then disappeared.

The ghast's sheer size was enough to kill them all.

Rylan struggled to remain upright as the creature's passing displaced tons of water. He was tossed in the waves, and his head bumped the roof of the cave.

Denny sputtered, "That thing is massive!"

"Yeah, I don't think we're taking it down." Tammy's shorn black hair speckled with droplets that dripped down her terrified goth-doll face.

They were right. It was bigger than any eidolghast Rylan had ever seen, bigger than the diagrams shown in training, bigger than a damned train.

"It must have ended up in here when it was smaller and couldn't get out again. Could have been here decades. That's why Crybel's haven't dealt with it, how it got so big. It can only be sensed on the island, and they don't go there."

Rylan thought of the shroudpool and eidolghast bones deep in the water. The nyevmer's presence here over so long would have formed the shroudpool, and the beast was big enough that it probably fed on any other ghast that came through from the Everdark. That was probably *how* it got so big.

"If it's stuck, I say we leave it and get the Everdark out of here." Denny flicked his head to indicate the opening in the cliff face.

Rain poured sideways in the show of lightning.

"The smartest thing you've ever said," Callan replied.

"Go. And go fast."

Rylan swam up beside Everly and wrapped an arm around her waist without slowing down. Harper and Neri were similarly collected by Callan and Tammy, while Denny took the lead, speeding through the water toward the narrow channel between the cave and the sea.

Rylan eyed the passage. Where they had jumped over stones to enter before, now there was only a treacherous sliver of space between the cavern roof and the waves. He tightened his grip on the crystal in his left hand, reassuring himself that he still had it.

Beyond that small hole, the storm continued to rage. Lightning flared in the cavern and thunder tore around the Howell team like a scream. The walls growled along with the nyevmer so that the whole cave was like the mouth of a gargantuan beast, about to snap closed.

The water roiled and sloshed around them, and Everly gasped for breath as it splashed continuously over her face.

Rylan had to remind himself she didn't have the luxury of breathing water like he could right now. But they also didn't have the luxury of slowing down. The nyevmer circled back like a tsunami barreling through the deep. It spiraled around them, toying with them, creating a whirlpool as it edged in closer, and closer.

They still had a long swim to the exit. Rylan took in the team.

Harper's crazy energy and bloodlust seemed to have leeched out of her system completely, but she still held Neri tightly in both arms, a fierce, protective set to her jaw.

The mermaid girl was a shadyr, but untrained and utterly traumatized.

And under no circumstances was Everly to use her powers. She looked like she couldn't even lift a finger without agonizing pain.

Denny was an asshole but had been surprisingly capable. Tammy as well had shown mettle beyond what Rylan would have guessed, and he knew Callan was up to the task. That gave him a complete brace. It would have to do.

He let go of Everly and removed his pack, letting it float over to her, semi-buoyant. She rested her arms over it like a lifebuoy.

Then he pushed the crystal from his hands into hers, indicating Harper and Neri as well. "You three keep swimming. Don't stop. We'll try and buy some time."

"What? No." Everly glared, her face white and pained, her teeth chattering.

Rylan pointed at the cliffside opening. "You're not doing *anything* except getting the hell out of here. Take Harper and Neri and get out before the water rises too high. We'll hold off the ghast."

"It's too big. The dragon could help."

"No. No way," Rylan snarled, his expression twisting with irritation. "You're in no position to use your powers right now. Don't you dare even try. Leave it to us and get the Everdark out of here!"

Her jaw set and eyes hardened. "I'm not leaving while the rest of you get yourselves killed! The dragon could stop it."

The nyevmer's head crested, then dipped back under water right behind Everly. Rylan grasped at her jacket, pulling her closer.

Fury curdled his voice, and he yelled, "And then you die instead? After all we've been through? No one wants you here, just trust me for once and leave!"

He pushed her roughly back out of his grip, toward the exit. She turned away from him, shoulders shivering. Harper, who had taken Callan's pack, reached out and grabbed Everly's shoulder, pushing her along as Neri swam at their side.

Callan caught Rylan's eye. His features were hard and judgmental, but he didn't say anything, just nodded and turned toward the eidolghast. Tammy stayed at his side. Denny swore, eyed the exit, but remained with them.

Rylan threw one more look at Everly's departing back, then he dove. He sliced through the water toward the deep, inky bottom of the pool as the nyevmer raced up toward them.

Callan, Denny, and Tammy drew up nearby, bodies arcing through the deep blue. Callan signaled and they went for the thing's head.

The closer they got to the ghast, the chillier the water became, as though it were made of living ice, or something far colder.

Its sharp-edged mouth opened, bigger than a doorway, inviting them in. The current suctioned down toward it. The water whipped, and flailing tentacles reached up for them. Rylan darted sideways as the clawed tips snipped at the water around him.

Denny and Tammy went low to avoid the whirlpool maw, tumbling into darkness beneath the beast.

Rylan waved to Callan, then the two of them fell into a dive, heading for the top of the ghast's bony head. It continued its rush toward the surface where three silhouettes swam huddled together.

Rylan latched onto the bony skull with his claws, his brother anchoring himself on the other side. Tentacles curled back at them.

The razor-tipped ends bit into Rylan's tail. He felt the crushing pressure, but they didn't penetrate his scales. He struck back with his own hands, grasping the end of the whipping limb, and tore the talons from the end. Blood spurted like a fog in the water, and the tentacle thrashed wildly, pulling Rylan off the nyevmer's head before he could let go.

Callan tumbled sideways as a clawed tentacle whipped against his chest.

Rylan wrapped the torn tentacle in both hands, pulling roughly to the side. He beat his tail against the water with all his might in an attempt to drag the creature in a different direction, but he may as well have been a flea on a dog.

They were almost at the surface, a tail and two sets of human feet right above them. Changing tactics, he went back for the head. He pushed out, raking his claws over the skull as he clung for purchase. The ring of eyes looked everywhere and nowhere, glowing faintly in the blue.

Rylan thrust a clawed hand into the closest, digging into the eye socket in a pop of inky fluid. The creature roared, twisted, and sped upward through the water. Rylan tossed his body weight aside to avoid being sandwiched between the creature and a mountain of stone.

They breached into air. The nyevmer smashed into the side of the cavern, mouth-first. The rock crumpled as if it were nothing more than Styrofoam. Then the beast pitched sideways, thrashing the entire length of its body against the cave wall.

Debris exploded outward. Brick-sized rocks lashed Rylan's body and arms, and a larger stone slammed into the side of his head, momentarily stunning him. The nyevmer crashed back down into the water.

Caught in the twirling currents, Rylan was thrown around wildly, and he couldn't figure out which way was down or up. He slammed into the ghast's slimy, long torso, then rolled out of control into the dark depths.

A giant rumbling filled the soft silence of the underwater.

Huge boulders plunged down everywhere like torpedoes, sending waves careening through the pool. Rylan swam in the opposite direction, aiming for the surface as he dodged the avalanche before it could pin him to the bottom. He fought the pull of the falling boulders all the way to the surface, where he burst through to madness.

Denny and Tammy yelled over the splashing rubble, and Callan floated between them. There was barely any light, just the dim glow of a flashlight lost somewhere deep in the water below.

Debris covered the entire side of the cavern, blocking off the tunnel to the sea. Boulders were scattered like giant knucklebones, while the tide continued to pour through the cracks.

Rylan searched for Everly, spinning a three-sixty as he surveyed the churning waves.

The nyevmer's tail flicked through the water in the far end of the pool. Everly, Harper, and Neri washed together in the new shallows created by the rockfall, gasping in the small gap between there and the cavern ceiling.

Rylan's breath caught at the sight of them. The nyevmer hadn't swallowed them whole. It hadn't smashed them against the stone.

But they hadn't made it out of the cave.

The whole team was hopelessly trapped, in that shrinking gap of air, with the nyevmer.

Chapter Twenty-Three

Rylan wanted to go to Everly, was drawn there with every fiber of his being. He wanted to hold off the rising water and destroy the gargantuan eidolghast and make everyone safe, but how could he possibly do any of those things?

Just deal. One problem at a time.

The nyevmer didn't give him a choice of what action to take next. It roared and sliced across the surface of the pool toward him.

Crashing head-on into the cave hard enough to collapse the roof around them hadn't slowed the beast down. Its bony, plated head seemed impervious. The thing was unrelenting.

Denny worked with Harper and Neri, clawing

around the rocks in an attempt to reclaim an exit. Tammy supported Callan in the water, who was worryingly still. Rylan couldn't allow Everly even an inch of time to consider using her powers.

He had to deal with the nyevmer alone.

Rylan swore at the icy water and squared himself up against the oncoming giant.

It reached him fast in a surge of fluid. Rylan ducked under, slamming and rolling painfully along the creature's sharp, scaled belly. Like grappling hooks, he flung out both clawed hands, seeking purchase.

At the skeletal tail, they finally caught. He was dragged behind as the ghast spiraled down into the depths. Then it jack-knifed its long body without warning, bringing its toothy maw and talon-ended tentacles straight for Rylan.

Three tentacles wrapped around Rylan's mer-form body. His arms were pinned, and the claws nipped at his tail, slicing clear through one fin. A roar of bubbles escaped Rylan's mouth.

The nyevmer drew him through the deep blue water on a trajectory for its tooth-ringed mouth. He fought back, swimming the other way with all his remaining strength. His damaged fin curled and flopped uselessly.

Rylan needed a plan, fast. He didn't have a weapon beyond his claws, and this ghast was simply too big.

Then a thought struck him.

He wasn't stuck with just this form. He was against a nyevmer, and shadyr forms were meant to be a match for what they fought. But what if they weren't the best option?

Could he even control the shift enough to use a different form, with the massive nyevmer so close, overpowering his senses?

Closing his eyes, he thought of Everly.

He could sense her high above at the surface like the warm glow of a campfire. Since waking up, her presence had been nearly overwhelming to him. The sheer energy—multiple energies—radiating out of her left him reeling.

He couldn't even name half of the ghast signatures he felt coming from her. He imagined that they were somehow the essences of any eidolghast the soul-eater had once consumed. Everly herself had only been around for a handful of destroyed ghasts, but at some time before that, the creature in her must have glutted itself.

Having stayed as close as he could to her over the course of that long day, he'd found some sense of balance, been able to wrangle control over which ghast energies he took in, which forms he was forced into.

He'd been able to push himself into chosen forms, even partial forms, which would give him the best tools he needed for a fight. Or been able to close himself off to her influence, which is what he'd been doing to stay in nyevmer form.

That mermaid shape wasn't going to help him in the creature's mouth, though. He had to change.

The moment he opened his senses to Everly, her power fully overshadowed the nyevmer.

Rylan cataloged the ghast essences he could feel, making a rough plan. He only hoped he could control the change. The timing would have to be perfect. If he changed to the wrong form at the wrong time, it would all be over.

Black mist swirled around Rylan's body, unaffected by the water. He no longer fought against the tentacles. He let them pull him directly into the vacuum of the massive mouth. His tail vanished.

The nyevmer's teeth snapped shut like a trap.

Rylan cringed as they went right through his body. He didn't feel a thing. They passed into his ghost-like form, mashing and gnawing in vain around his incorporeal body.

He wanted to sigh in relief but had to keep his breath held carefully. He was still underwater, inside the creature, and no longer had the amphibious features of mer form.

Darkness disoriented Rylan, and he turned, trying to gain his bearings. He caught a glimpse of light and saw teeth leading out to waving tentacles and ice-blue water. He swam in the opposite direction, straight into the solid mass of the nyevmer's head.

Eidolghast didn't always have brains or spines or hearts the way living things of Earth did. It could be hard to find a vulnerable target. Still, if this nyevmer had a skull like a steel vault, it must be protecting some vital organ within.

Using Everly as his focal point, Rylan allowed the shift to ripple over his body. His skin grew hard and red and his size doubled, expanding outward as it became whole, solid, and on the physical plane once again.

Pressure met him on all sides. Dark, gooey, heavy organs crushed against him. Rylan twisted and slammed his arms and wings outward, tearing through the vulnerable, fleshy insides of the nyevmer.

The incredible strength of this demon-dragon form shocked Rylan anew as he tore through the ghast's soft viscera. Sparks of bioelectric connections fizzing out went off around him. He held his breath and ricocheted throughout the insides of the beast's skull, still unable to break through.

But being trapped inside made the damage he dealt all the more devastating. He could feel the ghast roaring, screaming, the sound vibrating all around him as his lungs burned. He slashed and sliced the inside of the ghast to ribbons.

Finally, the nyevmer fell silent and still.

From inside the monster's skull, Rylan felt the hum of life fade away, and the draw of water and gravity pulling them down. He thrust his hands about, latching onto raw meat, slippery and cold between his fingers.

He kept pushing, kept tearing, wanting to be sure the creature couldn't survive. He hit a wall of thin cartilage and ripped through. More meat, then an armored barrier, and then the relative softness of water rushed against his face.

He burst free through the back of the nyevmer's neck.

Everything was black. They were deep, so deep. The pale glow of the creature's eyes had extinguished, and even Rylan's shadyr night vision couldn't penetrate the dark.

His dragon form sent him tumbling toward the abyssal depths as if he weighed more than a boulder. Wings tangled like sheets around him. He tried to swim for the surface but couldn't, nor could he breathe without the nyevmer gills.

His head grew cloudy and confused. Tired, more than anything, as bubbles rushed free from his mouth. He closed his eyes. The water seemed to cradle him. Maybe he could breathe it, after all. He just had to inhale.

He slammed into thick silt and sharp bones beside the nyevmer's still body. The impact brought back just enough alertness to realize that inhaling would be a very bad idea. He flailed both arms and latched onto the dead beast.

Even as a corpse, the sheer size of the thing and the physical contact forced the shadyr shift through Rylan's body on instinct. Chilled water rushed through his newly formed gills like life itself, and his eyes snapped open.

He burst to the surface, breaking into the air with a gasp. Every inch of him was battered and bruised, and it took him several moments to gather his wits. He blinked blearily around the cavern.

There was barely enough room to move without bumping and scraping against the rough ceiling at the top of his head. Water continued to rush in, rising with every passing moment. Everly, Harper, and Neri treaded water near the cave-in, tugging at the fallen stones. For every rock they moved, more crumbled into place.

At some point, Denny must have reclaimed their last flashlight from the pool's depths, but it was dim and flickering in his hands as he swam about, collecting their two remaining backpacks that bobbed on the water's surface.

He spotted Rylan, shining the light his way. "Where's the nyevmer? I lost track of it."

"Dead," Rylan coughed out.

"Yeah, good one. Where is it?" Denny laughed, then stopped. "No way you took that thing down solo."

The others turned Rylan's way, questioning.

"Except I did." His and Everly's eyes met.

Maybe not entirely solo. He couldn't have done it without her.

"Having access to multiple forms helped."

"Rylan!" Tammy called.

Her normally dry and dull tone was high and hysterical. She treaded water nearby with Callan supported against her. He was hunched-over, gasping painfully.

Fear pulsed in Rylan's gut. He dove under and swam quickly toward his brother. He came up beside them and hovered next to Tammy in the water.

Callan was conscious but grimacing as he pressed his hand against a gaping slash in his chest armor.

Rylan swore, lifting Callan's fingers for a better look. His body armor was torn right through to the skin beneath. The wound stretched from his collar bone to his solar plexus, the edges raw and red.

For a moment, he wanted to tell his brother to shift into vampire form so he could regenerate. But the other shadyrs didn't have that connection to Everly like he did. He grunted, hands balling into fists so tight his claws dug into his palms. They couldn't offer any first aid in there, being almost completely submerged.

"We need to get out of here. Try ... try and keep some pressure on it."

Tammy shivered. She probably knew just as he did how futile that would be, with the length of the wound and the saltwater smashing around them. But after a brief hesitation, she pressed one black, webbed hand there, shifting her other arm around Callan's back.

"What are we going to do?" Water splashed over Tammy's chin. "This place is filling up fast."

Callan hissed and jerked against her touch. His long

dark hair clung over a face that was turning white.

He stared at his Rylan with red-rimmed eyes. "With the nyevmer dead, we can hold these forms for maybe twenty minutes, max."

Tammy's mouth moved but said nothing. She was probably doing the math in her head like Rylan was, and realized that nothing added up.

She shook her head in denial. "No. Longer if we get close to the corpse. Like we did for you with the vasmire bits. We could swim down and stay near it."

"Yeah, but what are they going to do?" Rylan turned and flicked his head toward Everly and Harper.

They still fumbled madly at the stones. Whitecaps splashed around them, and the humans tilted their heads back for clear breaths of air. Denny and Neri resurfaced beside them, shaking their heads. There must have been no other way through below, either.

"Keep him afloat," Rylan told Tammy.

He saw tears rush into her eyes as he turned away. He left them, streaking across the water as fast as possible toward the cave-in.

Rylan came to a halt behind Everly and gripped her by both shoulders. "Enough. You're going to hurt yourself."

He pulled her away from the rubble. He would take her place digging, although he had little hope that it would help.

Before he could get a grip on the rocks, Everly splashed

back up against him and shoved him with all her might, crying out painfully.

Her shove barely did anything at all beyond making him aware that she was *very* angry.

"You ... jerk!" she hissed, swiping an arm feebly through the water. "If you'd let me use my powers to kill the nyevmer, maybe we'd have gotten out of here before the whole cave collapsed!"

She lashed out again and Rylan caught her hands in his, careful not to squeeze. Her fingers were too pale, with bright red crack-lines mosaiced all over.

Rylan growled, "If you had, you might be dead already."

"And now we're going to die anyway! All of us!" Everly jerked away from his grasp and sank beneath the rising water momentarily.

He grabbed her by the waist and hauled her sputtering back to the surface.

"You're going to hurt yourself," Rylan said evenly, but his heart raged painfully in his chest.

This, all of this, was a nightmare.

"Better that than everyone dying for me." Her features hardened and she pushed herself out of his arms, turning to face the collapsed exit.

A chill ran up Rylan's back as her energy surged. "Evie, no!"

Pale light burst through the cavern, glittering over the

waves. Rylan threw up an arm to shield his dilated eyes, too late.

"Stop, no!" Harper screamed.

Bodies splashed around in the water. More cries.

The light sputtered and strobed, and with a gurgling crackle, it went out instantly. Everly screamed. Her agonized shriek ended with a gurgle.

Terror overwhelmed Rylan. His vision swam with bright-colored globs, burned into his retina. He blindly swam forward, sweeping the water with both arms. Everly had been right there in front of him, hardly an arm's length away, but now, she was nowhere to be found.

Rylan dove underwater, silently begging his eyesight to right itself. Purple flares painted the focal point of his vision, and beneath the surface, he couldn't see any form or substance through the imprinted light.

Hair tangled into his fingers, and he swam to meet it. His hands found Everly's jacket, her curves. Looping an arm around her waist, he dragged her to the surface with his heart beating out a wild rhythm in his throat.

They burst through into the steadily dwindling air. She sank into his arms, her face dipping toward the surface. Rylan's vision cleared to just a couple of stars floating across his sight. Nearby, Harper surfaced. She must have gone under for Everly, too.

"Is she okay?" Harper said from behind her fingers.

"I don't know," Rylan replied.

Everly's head rolled limply against his chest, but she gasped a breath.

Harper cried, "You idiot. You could have killed yourself."

Everly's shoulders convulsed, and Rylan pulled her closer.

"Bring her over here." Harper waved a hand in the water, showing a shelf near where a flat boulder had fallen just below the water's surface.

Rylan swam over, lifted Everly, and floated her onto the shelf like it was a bed.

He supported her head so that her face remained above water.

Everly squinted her eyes shut.

"I can't feel my arms," she said, her voice high and frightened.

Rylan swallowed hard. Her arms were the least of his concerns. The cracks had spread right up onto her face and across her chest, meeting between her collar bones. Her breaths were shallow and uneven.

"We can't wait any longer," Rylan said firmly, trying to keep his voice calm and even so his own fear wouldn't exacerbate her terror. "Where's the crystal?"

"I have it," Harper said.

She reached down to where her axe used to hang at her

hips, bringing the crystal back up. Rylan took it carefully.

Everly jerked, trying to back away from him, but the cave ceiling was at her nose and the wall blocked her other side. "No! We can't."

"We don't have a choice." A wave of water washed around Rylan, and his scalp bumped into the ceiling.

Everly shook her head, struggling to keep her eyes open. "I can't ... risk it. I need to be somewhere ... Somewhere alone, away from you. All of you. It might hurt you the way it hurt my dad ..."

Rylan held the crystal up, prepared to smash it anyway.

Everly turned her face toward him, panting hard. "Don't you dare. If you try to force that on me, I will burn through every last bit of the dragon's light before you have a chance to smash that thing."

Rylan's arm stayed, his teeth bared. Harper stared at him with eyes showing white all around the unfamiliar brown irises. Neri cowered behind her, clinging to her shoulders.

Tammy moved closer, swimming slowly with Callan supported in her arms, her hand still pressed into his chest as though she could hold him together.

Rylan's fingers shook around the crystal. What if Everly was right? What if saving her meant losing Callan, his own brother? And Tammy, Harper, Neri ... even Denny?

Could he live with that? Maybe he wouldn't have to.

He could be gone as well. The whole mess ate at his heart.

Either way, Everly wasn't giving him a choice.

Rylan lowered the crystal but kept it tight in his hand.

Harper shook her head and whimpered, moving away, closer to Neri. Denny continued to dig against the rocks. His movements were slow, his face resigned, but he kept going.

Even if they could keep up their mer forms until the high tide passed, they couldn't get out without help. They were buried. They might survive this high tide, but the next? And the next? No one would know where to look for them. They might start the search at the collapsed lighthouse, but they were a long way down.

Rylan's shoulders slumped. This really was it. On some undeniable instinct, he looped an arm under Everly's neck and pulled her closer. Their eyes met.

Warmth flushed through Rylan's body. Every inch of him wanted to protect her. He wanted to take away the pain in her shattering body. He wanted to take back what she'd done to herself in order to save his life. He wanted nothing more than to make sure she walked out of there intact and unharmed with the lighthouse crystal in hand.

He clutched Everly to his chest, racking his mind for any solution to this problem. The stones were immovable, the cavern filling up fast. Everly's powers were out of the question, and Rylan had nothing. No answers.

They'd come this far only to die. All of them.

Cold water closed around his neck and pinned his head to the ceiling.

"It won't be much longer," Everly whispered calmly. "When I'm gone, when Harper and I are gone"—her face wrinkled with emotion— "swim down with the nyevmer and wait for the tide to go out again."

He pressed his forehead against hers, words hard to force out of his throat. "Don't say that."

She turned her face away weakly. "That's what you want, isn't it? You want me out of your life, and soon I will be."

"That's not ... this isn't how I wanted it."

"You hate me. You didn't even want the poster." Her voice was flat, eyes delirious.

Rylan frowned. "The what?"

"You took it down. You don't want anything that even reminds you of me."

The one in my old room? Three thousand years ago, he had taken the poster down last night. He shook his head, forehead wrinkled.

"No, that's not ... The ... the silverfish were getting to it. I put it away to keep it safe."

When he had walked back into his childhood room after so long away, that poster more than anything reminded him of her, and their time together as kids. That time—their entire relationship—was so special to him. He didn't want to see it get destroyed, so he packed it away, out of sight.

Just like he did to Everly.

He'd forced her away when he joined the Darkfreys. He'd been sure he was making the right choice. Keeping her safe. But in doing so, he was the one who destroyed what they had. Or could have had.

Now, facing the end, he knew that it hadn't been worth it.

All those years they'd been apart when he'd wanted her near. All those times he'd thought of her and refused his feelings. It all felt wasted.

She shivered in his arms, and he turned her face gently back toward his. "I just wanted you to be safe. And I thought I could do that by keeping you away. But I have missed you, every single second. Keeping you safe wasn't all I ever wanted. I wanted *you*. I don't want to push you away any longer."

Everly blinked hazily at him. "I see how you look at me, you hate me."

"Not you." He had stared at her with growing disgust, but it was at himself. "Every moment you remained here, every time you were hurt, or put in danger, that was my failure, that was me I hated."

He hadn't been able to stop it or fix it.

"You can't keep me safe, not from everything. That's

not your fault."

Rylan knew she was right. He'd thought he couldn't be with her if he wanted her to be safe. But if he couldn't keep her safe, why couldn't he be with her? Even if for only their very last moments.

The water slipped higher, cresting over his chin.

Rylan cupped her face in his hands. "Don't think that I hate you. Don't ever think that. How could I hate you? I love you."

Her mouth opened in a shaky O. "You love me?"

He leaned in, whispering against her ear. "I've always loved you. All I've known my entire life is loving you. I never wanted to lose you, Everly. The dumbest thing I've ever done in my life was pushing you away."

Everly turned to face him. Her eyes closed and she pressed trembling, deathly-cold lips to his.

Chapter Twenty-Four

Jasper stomped toward the Darkfrey Estate entrance, glowering at his surroundings as though they were to blame for all his pain inside. The gates opened with an electric hum and the driveway ahead was gloomy and foreboding.

The perfect atmosphere to match his emotions.

A blood-red sun sank behind the wooded hills. Storm clouds crowded in the distance and a harsh wind blew dust and leaves around.

Jasper had taken the long way home from the theatre, meandering through Shroudhaven to buy enough time to drown his thoughts and worries. Along with trying desperately to wipe the visage of Cherry's betrayed features from his mind.

Have I lost him for good now?

The artifact—the "Bane," Cherry had called it—was wrapped in its tattered parchment and shoved beneath his right arm, bulky and pulsing with that low energy.

Jasper couldn't wait to dump it on Mordan's desk and be done with it. The thing had ruined everything and chased Cherry even further away.

In actuality, though, Jasper knew *he* had done that. Not the Bane. His choices. His mistakes.

The sports complexes surrounding the estate buildings were all quiet beneath their floodlights at this time of evening. Training was done for the day and shadyrs who were part of braces generally took some downtime around sunset before patrols started. He walked the grounds undisturbed and then took the stairs to the main building two at a time.

One of the admin staff clicked off lights to a room on the side as she stepped out, then jumped, caught off guard by Jasper's passing. She took in who he was and gave him a respectful nod.

That was what being part of a brace meant at Darkfrey Estate. They were the top of the pecking order. Every other service and role at the estate, from paperwork to cleaning, existed to serve them and their mission. He could see even in this staffer's eyes that he was important. What he did meant something.

But did that mean that everyone else *wasn't* important? That's how many Darkfrey shadyrs behaved.

It was something Cherry always hated about this place.

Jasper returned a nod to the woman, imbuing it with his thanks for everything she did. She seemed taken aback by his acknowledgment of her existence. She gave a shy smile, then clicked away in her heels with a bundle of paperwork clutched in her arms. Her footsteps echoed into nothing, leaving a hush over the building.

What am I doing? What do I want? Jasper rubbed his forehead, his mind a noisy mess.

The answer was easy in the past. To be a Darkfrey. To be the best shadyr he could be, to give everything he could to the cause, and receive the respect that came with that role.

Now, those goals felt hollow.

He let his feet lead him blindly forward. He was still down the hall from Mordan's office when a voice broke the silence.

"You sure took your time."

Jasper whipped his head up, unease snaking through him. Vonny leaned against a doorframe between a suit of armor and a gilded painting.

Jasper blinked at her and brought himself into a pose of attention. Although she never was his brace leader, she always held superiority over him.

Jasper delivered his half-truth with the ease of everyday practice. "The mission was more complicated than anticipated."

Vonny muttered under her breath. "Did you even get what I sent you for?"

"Of course I did. I was heading to Mordan's office to return the retrieved artifact now." He tugged the bundled-up Bane from beneath his arm and held it up as evidence.

"Why would you do that? He didn't give you the mission, I did."

He hesitated, grip tight around the ancient parchment. "Because the relics belong with the estate, that is how it should be."

Ghast damn it, Cherry is right. I do sound like a brain-washed robot.

Vonny straightened and traipsed his way. Something about standing in the empty hallway with Vonny Mesman staring him down left Jasper cold inside. That chill grew when another form loomed through the shadowy doorway behind her.

Kole Mesman. Vonny's husband.

Like most at the estate, Jasper typically gave the man a wide berth. He was ... strange. Possibly unhinged. The loss of their son affected them both, but it had twisted Kole beyond recognition of his former self. He was prone to violent outbursts, which were terrifying given the bulked-up state he'd built his body into. A brick wall of corded muscle, barely contained beneath his clothes.

The couple stopped in front of Jasper as a single unit. Kole reached over his wife's shoulder, holding out a meaty hand.

"We'll take it from here."

Were they trying to take the credit for the find? That explained the secrecy to some extent, but something else felt off.

Jasper eyed the older man's palm. It was scarred and covered in a sheen of sweat. His own hand, which held the Bane, twitched and withdrew back toward himself.

"I don't mind conveying the artifact to Mordan. I'd like to know the relic reaches the place it belongs."

Kole's eyes narrowed dangerously, and Jasper worried he'd overstepped.

Vonny tilted her head, blond bob swinging. "Of course it will go where it belongs. Don't you trust us? Or do you just want to go and get your pat on the head from your master for a job well done?"

Jasper blanked his features and spoke evenly. "I'm sure Master Darkfrey will give credit where it is deserved. I simply thought delivery jobs were a duty below your standing."

Clearly tired of waiting, Kole reached out and snatched

at the bundle. He yanked it from Jasper's fingers, then sneered at him. "You haven't got the faintest understanding of my duties."

The couple turned their backs on him, marching away.

"What does that thing do?" The words fell from Jasper's lips before he could silence himself.

They kept walking, and Vonny called back, "You don't typically make a habit of asking questions. One of your very few qualities."

"Cherry said it was related in some way to Everly, that it makes her sick, or—"

Damn it, shut your mouth.

They didn't need to know what he knew. He wanted to know what *they* knew.

Vonny stopped and turned back with a raised, pale eyebrow. "*Cherry* said?"

Ghast damn it, get it together!

Jasper's thoughts swirled and he couldn't grasp onto the point he was trying to make, why he was daring to rile up the Mesmans. The mission was done, what did it matter? But it all felt wrong. He wanted answers. And he wanted those answers from a superior he should be able to trust.

Jasper lifted his chin. "That artefact belonged to the Howells. It was the one they reclaimed from Gorhanmere. You didn't give me that information when you sent me on the mission. Why not?"

Vonny stalked toward him and shoved the point of her fingernail into Jasper's chest so hard it bruised. The action was at odds with the sweet smile on her face.

"Listen to me carefully because you seem to be extremely confused right now. Your job isn't to ask questions, and certainly isn't to question me. Your job is to keep your mouth shut and do as you're told. Do you hear me?"

Jasper swallowed against his heart in his throat, but he didn't lower his gaze. He tried to channel Cherry's bravery, even as he knew he fell short.

"I want to know why you sent me for it, why alone, and what you're going to do with it."

His heart stopped beating as Vonny's faux good-natured expression faded away, replaced by fury. "The last time someone didn't keep their mouth shut and do as they were told, they found themselves alone and afoul of an eidolghast. The same could easily happen to you. Except this time, hopefully *you* would stay dead."

Jasper's carefully-crafted blank expression vanished.

"Rylan?" He choked the name out, shock making his fingertips numb.

Vonny's expression didn't change. She stared him down, while Kole looked on with cold, hard eyes.

"I'll go to Mordan," Jasper stuttered.

Vonny and Kole exchanged amused glances. Vonny pushed her nail into him one last time before pulling it back like a gun.

"Go ahead," she said, shrugging. "Do you think I care what happens to you if you go down that path? Think what you want, say what you want, but at the end of the day, you're just another replaceable nobody. Raise your voice and find out how quickly you'll be on the other side of the fence, sleeping on the streets."

Jasper gaped, unable to form words.

She reached out and patted him on the cheek. "Poor thing is so confused."

"Then let me clarify for him," Kole growled, face lowered in shadow. "Get your act together. The cause is what matters, all that matters. We would do anything for the cause. Anything. You would too if you were truly loyal."

Anything? Jasper barely heard his own voice over the hum building in his skull. "I am loyal, I've done everything, given up everything for the Darkfreys."

"Prove it." Kole rolled his head, cracking his neck.

Vonny smiled at him sweetly. "The way you 'associate' with that queer is a black mark on your record, Jasper. You'd be better off if he were out of the picture, permanently, don't you think? To avoid any ... temptation, or the spread of rumors. Prove you are loyal."

The blood drained from Jasper's face.

Do they know? What do they know?

Vonny and her husband turned away and left him

paralyzed there, as lifeless as the empty suit of armor beside him.

Nausea bubbled in his stomach as Jasper watched the two of them fade down the hallway. Once they were out of sight, his body gave in, buckled over, and he dry-retched.

They had been involved somehow in what happened to Rylan. And Mordan Darkfrey as well, he had to know. They were too unconcerned about Jasper going to the estate's leader. They were too unbothered by his questions. They didn't even need the silence they could buy with what they clearly knew about him.

They had everything they needed against him, and what evidence did he have? Guesses? Worries? Vague admissions of guilt witnessed by no one but him?

Nearby, doors opened and closed, and voices penetrated the stone-cold silence of the hallways. Braces prepared to leave for their night patrols, as they had done every night of his life at the estate.

But now ... everything had changed.

He had believed in their mission. He had been loyal. He had worked so hard and sacrificed ...

But now, he couldn't look at the Darkfrey crest or his fellow brace members without questioning everything about *how* they achieved their goals. It was wrong, it was all wrong.

Cherry had been right. The one right thing in his life.

He should have listened earlier. He shouldn't have been so scared to lose something that never belonged to him anyway—the acceptance of this place.

Darkfrey Estate was broken, and it broke him, and his friends had been hurt in the process. Even worse, Jasper himself was complicit in the betrayal.

He clenched his hands into fists and whirled on his heel. Regardless of what he'd done before this moment, he knew now what he had to do. What he would have to find before his time at Darkfrey Estate ended forever.

Evidence. Even just a scrap of evidence. That was what he needed.

Those nights that Rylan had spent sneaking about alone before he went missing, is that what he'd been searching for too? Is that what got him almost killed? And if one of the best shadyrs Darkfrey estate had ever seen had failed on that mission, what chance did he have?

Chapter Twenty-Five

The water rose shockingly around the gills in Tammy's neck as she tried to keep Callan afloat. Every particle of her energy was focused on him and her screaming thoughts of oh-ghast-what-are-we-going-to-do-with-his-wound-if-we-even-survive-the-incoming-tide, which was how she found herself inhaling a lungful of water through her nose.

Her brain confused the signals between her human side and her shadyr side, and she didn't know whether to breathe the quickly diminishing oxygen or the water.

She attempted both at once, nose and gills gulping.

Tammy slipped beneath the surface as icy saltwater filled her lungs. She choked and gagged, eyes stinging. Her body flickered unstably and the fear of vanishing to Dark

Corner beat out her fear of drowning.

Don't go, don't go. You can't leave them like this. She flailed for the surface, slamming into Callan's tail in her desperate bid to find air.

Callan's hands found hers and he pulled her up. He latched an arm around her waist and held her head above the water as she coughed in a way that felt like vomiting directly from her lungs. She spat out the excess water and wheezed painfully at the air.

"I'm sorry," Tammy gasped the words out, beating her tail against the water to back away from him. "Are you okay?"

"You're choking on water, and you're worried about me?" Callan's eyes moved lazily, unlike his normally alert gaze, but he still managed a smile.

Somehow, he always managed to smile. Tammy's heart ached.

She moved quickly back to his side to help support him. He wasn't yet incapable of swimming on his own, but she could tell too much motion would put dangerous strain on his wound. Her breathing screwup had already hurt him too much.

Tammy focused on her shadyr form and dragged in a deep breath through her gills. She could taste Callan's blood in the water. For the fiftieth time, she blinked away tears. For all her nihilistic talk of looking forward to the moment when she was freed from the burden of life, Tammy was shaken to her core in the face of death.

The thought of leaving scared her. The thought of Callan leaving her terrified her more. He couldn't die. She couldn't lose someone else she cared for.

A sob escaped, and her body flickered again, trying to drag her away to the place of her nightmares, her personal hell. She set her jaw and held on with everything she could to existing in this place only, there beside Callan.

He looked back at her with widened eyes. "I'm an idiot. Of course ... You can go."

"What? No."

His head lolled in the waves that beat against his ears. He tipped his face upward to speak above the water.

"You can get out of here. You can live. Tell Mom where to find us."

"You *are* an idiot. You know we wouldn't get back out here and break through into the cave in time. You're bleeding out! Everly and Harper, they can't ..."

Callan's eyes closed in a slow blink. "The other shadyrs might be able to hold nyevmer form until the tide goes down."

"Great, so I can save fucking *Denny*."

"And my brother. And Neri. They must almost balance out having to save Denny."

Tammy half laughed, half sobbed against Callan's

cheek. "I'm not going anywhere. If this is it, if this is the end, I deserve front row tickets more than the rest of you."

Wincing, Callan turned in the water and wrapped his hands around her upper arms. "You *have* to let go of this guilt!"

Surprised by the vehemence in his tone, Tammy stiffened. She wanted to back away from him, but she couldn't leave him swimming without her support.

Since they'd arrived at the lighthouse and she'd been trapped in mermaid form, he carried her, never once complaining. She had to stay and carry him now. She would stay and look him in the eye, no matter how his hands on her muddled her mind so that she couldn't think straight. No matter how she wanted to hide, and scoff, and roll her eyes.

She carefully wiped the emotions off her face. "You don't know what you're talking about."

"You think I don't know anything about survivor's guilt? I know you're suffering. I know how much it hurts. I know how it makes you blame yourself. You internalize *everything* that goes wrong around you. You blame yourself even when a situation has nothing to do with you."

"I do not," Tammy said hotly, her cheeks burning with shame. "I blame myself exactly the right amount!"

"Remember when you and Everly set off that weird mini-beshadowing at The Crow's Nest?"

Tammy flushed hotter, despite the cold water creeping up her cheeks.

"You blamed yourself for that, entirely."

She lifted one blackened hand up between them. "Of course it was my fault."

"No," Callan said firmly. "It was some kind of reaction between you *and* Everly, that no one could have predicted, that you didn't choose to do, or choose to have happen to you. You do this *every* time. You're so absolutely certain that your existence causes everything around us to go wrong."

Tammy wanted to cover her ears with her cursed hands. She hated that he could see all her failings so clearly.

"Because it does."

"It doesn't. Life just fucking sucks sometimes but you're not some omnipotent deity making that happen! It just … happens. It's not your fault." His thumb brushed over her cheek, then he locked gazes with her. "Transport yourself out of here. You can leave and save yourself. And even if it's only yourself that you save, *it's worth it*."

"I don't deserve to get out of here while you die," Tammy said hotly, the words thick with withheld tears.

"You think being here to *watch* us die, and die alongside us when you don't have to, is what you deserve?" Callan pulled her closer, enveloping her in an embrace. "No one deserves that."

Their tails bumped beneath the water. Their chests

pressed together, and Tammy tried to pull away, worried she was hurting him more. He held her still with surprising strength. But his hands were shockingly cold.

Callen pulled back enough to lock eyes with her. "Blaise fell through the shroudpool, and you couldn't save him."

Tammy flinched as though he struck her physically.

"Do you know why that hurts so much? Because you care, so deeply." He kept holding her tight. "You carry such immense guilt *because* you love so strongly. You love with your whole heart and soul. That's something that takes great courage. It's something to be admired. You have to stop trying to hide from that. You have to let yourself live."

Sobs rushed from Tammy's chest so thick she couldn't breathe.

The water pressed them higher, ducking them under, but Callan didn't let her go.

They surfaced again, and Callan dropped his voice to a whisper at her ear. "Don't argue. Just go. I want you to live. Mom would want you to live. You are loved. You're worthy of being loved the same way you love your friends and family."

"No, I'm not," she gasped, voice small and lost beneath the waves.

"You are. Nothing will ever make me believe otherwise." Callan grunted as his upturned cheek hit the ceiling.

"Have we reached the point we're all doing declarations

of love?" Harper sniffed and sobbed out a giggle from close by. "Because I love you, I love all of you. I know I've only known you a while, but I do. Except maybe Denny."

"That hurts like you punched my heart in the dick," Denny replied, nose pressed against the stone above them.

The water lapped at the side of Tammy's face, obscuring her vision and washing away tears. Part of her was mortified that the others no doubt heard everything she and Callan had said to each other, but that part was drowning beneath the fear of losing any of them.

She felt Rylan reach out and wrap one arm around his brother, drawing him close and bringing Tammy with him.

"You still hanging in there?" he asked.

"Pssh, it's just a scratch." Callan still smiled.

Rylan frowned deeply as he took in his brother's wound and pallid skin. Everly was cradled tight at his other side, eyes bloodshot and unfocused. Harper and Neri bumped up behind them, bobbing in the water. Even Denny moved in. They'd all floated closer, coming together in their final moments.

The water had officially reached the top of the cavern.

Time was up.

Mere seconds later, the waves closed over Tammy's head.

When she had been thrown out of the Darkfreys, all she had were the clothes on her back, a dead best friend, and fresh enemies of his parents who had once treated her like their own daughter.

Lian had taken her in with open arms when nobody should have wanted her. It was her, Lian, and Rushelle at first, then the family grew with Denny, Cherry, and Callan. She didn't think they could love her, that they did anything other than tolerate the burden of her, her curse, and her attempts to push them away.

But she did love them. Quickly and completely. They became her family. She loved them. All of them. And if she could dig past her issues and trauma and yes, survivor's guilt, and trust that Callan had spoken the truth—they loved her, too.

She floated under the water, cut off from the surface. Cut off from safety.

She could breathe, for now. But she couldn't watch anyone else die.

Tammy opened her arms and grabbed for her teammates.

Her friends must have thought she was going for one last embrace. One last goodbye beneath the waves. Because all of them drew in, arms looping around one another. One tug from her brought the whole team into a group hug.

Then Tammy pictured Dark Corner.

The place had haunted her nightmares. Every time her "ability" had dragged her back to Dark Corner, she'd hated it more and more. Now, though, she needed the shroudpool to be their salvation.

I can do this.

I have to do this.

She closed her eyes, concentrating so hard it hurt as she opened herself to the pull of her curse and its destination. This had to work. Everly and Harper had already taken their last breath and wouldn't last much longer.

Tammy clenched her hands tight, crushing her friends, her family, close to her. She wasn't going to let them go. She wasn't going to lose them like she lost Blaise.

Opening her eyes, Tammy zeroed in on Callan's face.

He stared at her through the water, his eyes wide open, a small smile on his lips as they shaped the word, "Go."

"I will." She nodded and mouthed back, "And I'm taking you with me."

The world changed in an instant.

The cold press of water vanished, and her body slammed into solid ground, feeling much, much heavier than it had been while floating. Splashing water pattered down all around.

Tammy groaned as dried grass and twigs crackled beneath her back. Her eyes scrunched closed with the pain and shock of the impact. The familiar sulfurous stench, laced with several layers of decaying leaves and undergrowth, met Tammy's nose.

She was back at Dark Corner.

She was terrified of opening her eyes, to find out whether she was back at Dark Corner alone. She'd lost her grip on her friends somewhere before or after the impact with solid ground, and felt no one in her hands.

Please, please. They have to be here too.

CHAPTER TWENTY-SIX

Everly's blurred vision tried to take in the change of surroundings. For a few moments, she thought maybe she had died or fallen into delirium.

She wondered when that delirium had begun, whether Rylan had really told her he loved her, whether they had shared that kiss tasting of salt and long years of yearning.

The pressure on her lungs eased, and she coughed up a splattering of seawater before taking a deep breath.

Bodies slammed against her in a tangle of tails and limbs, followed by grunts and sighs and giant, gaping breaths of air. Salt water spattered around them like rain. Confused voices surrounded her.

"What happened?"

"What is this place?"

"Is this Dark Corner?"

"How in the Everdark did we get here?"

"Tammy? You're incredible."

"Did everyone make it? Is everyone okay?"

Everly counted out each voice in turn. Rylan, Neri, Harper, Denny, Callan, and Tammy. Everyone was there. Everyone was okay.

Then the pain hit her, and Everly knew she had to still be alive because she experienced the blazing agony through every fiber of her being. Breathing hard and fast, she curled on her side, screaming silently. Her vision blanked out completely for a moment, then wobbled back.

Rylan leaned over her with his expression set like stone. "Evie? Hey, it's all right. Just breath."

"Is she okay?" Tammy crawled closer, her mermaid tail flopping behind heavily in the dirt.

Tammy. They were at Dark Corner.

She'd done this.

Somehow, for the first time, she'd carried other people with her to the shroudpool.

Vaguely, Everly wondered if Tammy had that power in her all along. She knew the kid didn't like being touched, that she generally kept her blackened hands out of reach.

She'd probably never transported while touching anyone else before. But the way Tammy had pulled them all in when Everly had thought it was the end, the way she'd clung on so tight, she must have been attempting to do exactly this, and she'd succeeded. She'd saved them.

Turning her head, Everly took in the entire team, dazed, drenched, but alive. A mess of mostly mermaids scattered across the ground, far from the sea.

"You did it. We're all here." Everly wriggled her fingertips closer to Tammy.

She had been so scared for Harper's life just moments before, but they were all safe. "Thank you."

Tammy frowned at Everly's hand, eyes roaming to Everly's face with naked concern. "Please tell me that we still have what we went to that ghast-forsaken island for, that it came with us too."

"The crystal? I've got it," Rylan said.

Tammy's eyes glistened, red-rimmed. "Good, because she's not looking so good. Those cracks ..."

Everly attempted a smile, and her lips ached like they could split into a thousand pieces. Everything about her body felt heavy and brittle.

"I'm okay."

"You're not." Rylan leaned close to her on his stomach, raising the crystal for her to see. "But you will be."

Everly swallowed, unsure whether she was more scared of having another portion of the soul-eater inside her, or of the death she felt herself teetering on the edge of.

Rylan's face twisted, and he grunted in frustration as

a dark mist enveloped him. The influence of the nyevmer over him and the others must have run out. All around, shadyrs were swapping tails for bare legs. Rylan put the crystal down beside Everly, then rolled away in a haze of dark magic.

Tammy squealed, "Pants! We need pants!"

Denny had the remaining packs—Callan's, and Rylan's, with Everly's inside it—hanging from straps on one arm. "Bet you're all glad I hung on to these. While ya'll were being all sappy and sentimental, who was being the capable shadyr? This dude! You might even say that I *saved your asses*."

Rylan jumped to his returned feet and snatched the bags. He tore through the contents, hauling out the shredded pants he'd worn earlier, and pulling them on still soaking wet, before the black swirls faded. Everly blushed, the rush of blood painful in her cheeks, and turned away.

"How many pairs have we got left?" Denny asked.

"You can have my spare set," Rylan said. "Callan, here are yours."

"I had an extra pair in my bag," Everly croaked. She heard more rummaging, and Tammy called out a thank you.

"Do we have something for Neri? She's not changing yet, but, you know," Harper said.

"Here."

As flies were zipped up, Everly turned back. Harper helped direct Neri into a man-sized T-shirt. The girl poked at it curiously like it was the first piece of clothing she'd ever worn.

As soon as it was on, she clung back onto Harper like she was drowning. She stared at the foreign world around her as though gigantic mermaid hunters were about to crash through the trees and crush her under their heel. But there was no sign of change on the girl, no sparks or dark clouds of magic.

Denny buttoned up his pants and eyed Rylan strangely, a smirk forming on his wide mouth. "So, when you changed from mermaid to dragon form to beat the nyevmer, you were going pants-less that whole time, right? Nice one, taking out an eidolghast with your—"

"Denny!" Harper scolded.

"—dick out," Denny finished with a grin.

"Rylan? Chuck me a first aid kit, too, if it's still any good," Tammy said.

Everly's pants swam on the goth girl's tiny frame. She took off her hoodie to tie around her waist like a belt, then knelt back down beside Callan. He had the pants draped over his lap but hadn't been able to get up to put them on.

"How's he doing?" Rylan's gaze cut between where his brother lay and Everly.

"I can hold on a bit longer," Callan said, weakly flopping

a hand at him.

Rylan turned the pack upside down and dumped the contents at his feet. The first aid kit tumbled out and he unzipped the rubber cover.

"Damp, but not too bad." He under-armed the kit and Tammy caught it neatly, quickly laying out dressings, sutures, and shears.

Rylan nodded to her in thanks, then snatched up a waterproof pouch and stuck his hand inside. He swore as he removed a phone that had been snapped nearly in two.

"Try mine," Callan said, as Tammy cut the flexible straps of his broken body armor with the shears and removed the pieces.

"No luck." Rylan held up the other pouch to reveal a gash down the side, water pouring out. "Did anyone's phone survive?"

In Everly's periphery, she could see Harper lean back to fumble in her jeans pocket. She tugged her cell from her pants and tapped at the screen. "Mine's good. Better be, considering how much I paid for the waterproof model."

"See if you can get a signal and get in touch with Lian. We need assistance, fast," Rylan told her.

Harper got to her feet and said to Neri, "I need to move around to try to find a good spot for this to work. I'll be right back."

Neri stared up at her with dinner-plate eyes, her head

shaking and tail hugged to her chest.

Pouting, Harper bent down and scooped her into her arms. "Fine, you can come with me. It's okay, you don't weigh a thing."

Rylan came and knelt beside where Everly lay on her back, staring up at the sunset. She had been trying to slow her breathing, gain some control over her body, but her inhalations remained short, sharp shivers. A dimness clung to her thoughts, and her body was going blessedly, horrifyingly numb.

"You're ... yourself," Everly mumbled, staring up into Rylan's face.

There was no monster there, not vampire or werewolf or any combination of forms. Just human. Just Rylan, as beautiful as he ever was.

He grunted softly. "It's taking a bit of effort, but today has been like one seriously intensive training program. I'm getting a handle on how you ... affect me."

"Show off," Tammy muttered.

Harper wandered in an ever-widening circle, staring at her phone that was held in the same arm that Neri's tail hung over. "I'm not getting any bars here."

"I don't normally get any reception until I'm near the gate. It's a bit of a walk, out that way." Tammy pointed.

Harper's face scrunched up. "How long do we have?"

Rylan brushed a finger through Everly's hair. "Not

long enough. I don't think we can wait for anyone else to get here and help. Everly needs the crystal *now*."

She tried to shake her head, but that made the whole world slosh around her.

Rylan picked up the crystal and placed it with infinite gentleness onto her chest, then lifted her hands, draping them over the top. "No excuses. We don't know what will happen if you use the crystal, but we know what will happen if you don't."

I won't last much longer. I'm fading fast.

Rylan's voice was low and rough, reminding her of the waves that still echoed in her ears. "And I'm not strong enough to lose you. I never have been—that's why I pushed you away. I suffered being separated from you because I could survive that. I could survive, as long as you lived. So please, you have to survive now, for me."

Everly swallowed a lump of pain. The last time she had broken a crystal containing part of the Beast of Teeth and Stars, it had killed her father. But she'd also been a child. She knew what she was dealing with now and had learned to control it—mostly. She could only hope she would maintain that control.

Everly took a deep breath and forced out scratchy words. "Move everyone away, *far* away."

Rylan turned, signaling to the others. "Everyone get clear. You've seen the dragon's light in action—double that reach and take up position."

Denny helped Tammy lift Callan and their makeshift med station back to the farthest boundaries of the clearing.

"Good luck. I'll see you again, strong and healthy soon, okay?" Harper hovered on the spot for a moment, biting her lip, then backed away with Neri.

Rylan put his hand against Everly's cheek. His touch was soft, and the hard look on his face had fallen away to concern.

"Do you want me to stay close? I will, if you need me."

Everly stared down at the gently glowing, deadly shard under her chin. "No. Get safe."

Rylan kissed her forehead, leaving behind a hot brand on her skin, then stood. She listened to his footsteps fade away across the cracked dirt, then shivered as a cool breeze passed over her. Above, swathes of scarlet slashed through the parting storm clouds, tinting the thin mist on the ground around her with a bloody cast.

The forest fell silent. She tilted her heavy head and glanced around for a glimpse of her friends, but her eyesight had grown too blurry, showing only faded smudges of gray.

Hopefully, the others were all far enough away to be safe.

She wrapped numb fingers around the crystal, and her head swam as she forced her remaining energy into raising the sparkling item. Her shattered arm turned to an inferno. It was too heavy, the crystal, her own arm. A strange, crunching, chinking sound echoed up through her body, bringing a raging pain along with it.

But she didn't have to lift far. She cried out as she pushed her arm up straight above her head, and then with a rush of exhalation, let her arm drop to the side like a dead weight.

Pain exploded across her every nerve ending. The crystal hit the rocky ground beside her. And the world was engulfed in light.

Chapter Twenty-Seven

Harper shifted Neri in her arms, holding her phone out as high as she could and glaring at the wavering lack of reception.

"Come on, come on!"

Everly was hurt and exploding with light and everyone was wrecked, and Harper loathed the thought that Shroudhaven's awful phone network would be the reason someone didn't survive.

She'd walked all the way to a boundary fence before even the hint of a bar showed up. A text requesting help was already locked and loaded, just waiting for the magic of technology to whisk it away. She'd tapped the details out fast as Neri watched the bright screen in awe.

Whole team at Dark Corner. Need med assistance and

transport ASAP.

"What is it doing now?" Neri asked.

"I just need ... no, it's too complicated and I don't even really understand it myself. See those little bars? We want more of them."

Neri nodded under twisted brows, but glared hard at the screen as though doing so would make it work better.

An icon spun, and a little green tick appeared. Harper let out a whoop.

"We did it," Neri said, wide eyed.

A second later, the phone buzzed in her hand. Lian calling back.

"How—get—*shhchshh*." Lian's staticky voice cut in and out on the line.

"We're at Dark Corner," Harper enunciated as loudly and clearly as she could, even though she'd shared it in the text already.

Any other details were almost impossible to convey over the dodgy network. Harper winced as she tried repeating herself the third time, and kept glancing anxiously over her shoulder, back to where her best friend lay close to death.

"I—" *screech*. "—my way." *Shh. Shh. Screech.* "—the road."

"See you soon. Hurry," Harper said, though the line cut out before she finished her sentence.

She turned around to see the spot where Everly lay lit

up like a fireworks factory that had caught ablaze.

Oh, Ev. Please be okay.

Neri stared wide-eyed at the light and clung tighter around Harper's shoulders.

"Hey, it's okay. It's just something Everly does sometimes. All good ... as long as you don't get too close." Harper readjusted her hold around Neri and headed back to the others.

All the energy from the Bane had now faded from her system but carrying the mermaid girl was still something she could do with her tired, human arms. Neri really was tiny, and bony. Harper shuddered to think what kind of diet the poor thing had in the lighthouse.

She shuddered to think of *anything* that had happened in the young woman's life until that point. Including the violence of that day. Neri seemed to have calmed down slightly, progressing from near-catatonic to trapped-rabbit. But she hadn't shown any violence, hadn't shown any signs of the beshadowed madness her father had succumbed to.

Maybe he'd always been mad.

If anything, Neri seemed to have decided she could trust Harper, and Harper's suddenly fierce, vengefully protective heart was okay with that.

Rylan, Denny, and Tammy were all bent over Callan. Everly's light cast harsh shadows around them through the trees. Denny stood to the side and kept a watch over the bright tendrils that drifted and whipped around Everly, but none could reach far enough to touch them. He also turned his gaze to the woods, which Harper knew could be equally dangerous.

Rylan's attention was all for his brother now. Considering how he'd shadowed Everly incessantly all day, that made Harper concerned for several reasons. She picked up her pace.

"Lian's on her way," Harper informed the team.

She moved closer, kneeling near the others and settling Neri in her lap.

"Oh thank ghast." Tammy's shoulders slumped.

She crouched on a bed of dead leaves next to Callan, who was on his back, face pale and eyes closed. She had the suture needle in her trembling hand and had managed to close half of the wound. But it had gaped wide open in the time since the flesh was torn, the edges white and ragged from saltwater.

"He needs a hospital. He needs ... I don't know. More than this. He's lost so much blood, and he's barely responding."

"I can help."

The voice was so small, Harper thought she'd imagined it.

Neri's grip around her shoulders tightened just enough to gain her attention, and again she said, "I can help. Maybe.

I want to try."

Tammy and Rylan shared a skeptical look as though the wild girl had proposed she perform surgery.

"Umm, how?" was all Harper could say.

"I'm a mermaid," Neri said as an explanation, letting go of Harper and sliding down off her lap to be closer to Callan.

"You're not a mermaid," Harper corrected, but her tone was weak.

She tried to come up with a valid argument, but the truth was, she didn't know why Neri hadn't transformed back into human form yet. Even though the rest of the shadyrs had regained their legs when they crash-landed at Dark Corner, Neri had not. She looked entirely out of place in the spooky forest with her limp, sky-blue tail and ill-fitting T-shirt.

Rylan took a hesitant step forward, as though ready to protect his brother from the tiny girl, but she didn't attempt to touch him. Instead, she inhaled and opened her mouth wide.

Neri sang.

Harper exchanged glances with Tammy at the first few notes. Harper shrugged. If this was all Neri was going to do, at least it wouldn't harm Callan further. Tammy frowned and returned with a sniff to her stitching.

"She's going to draw in trouble again," Denny muttered.

"Like Everly's light show isn't already a beacon the entirety of Shroudhaven could see," Tammy said back. "Let her sing. It's steadying my hands."

Rylan frowned and clutched his brother's wrist, keeping fingers on his pulse point and eyes on his watch.

And Neri sang.

Harper recognized the strange, haunting tones that had filled the cave when they'd found Neri crying over the infant skull, but this was clearer, less shaken by anguish.

The tune was familiar, a strange combination of a few popular nineties songs.

Without the cave echoing Neri's voice into a disembodied cacophony, it was beautiful. Goose bumps rose on Harper's skin as she knelt behind Neri and listened.

The song filtered through her senses, down into her bones, and had a strangely calming effect on her. She closed her eyes and swayed to the music, growing lighter and less achy as Neri went on.

"What in the ghast-blighted Everdark?" Tammy hissed.

Neri's voice faded away.

Harper's eyelids flew open.

Callan looked up, bright and alert. His bloodless pallor had turned back to its normal light tan, and the wound on his chest was gone. Flecks of blood still marked his skin, and a fresh pink scar lay where the injury had cut across his pectoral muscle and collar bone.

But it had closed completely. The stitches lay loose on the surface, as though expelled by his body.

Tammy's jaw hung open comically as she gaped at Neri. "*How?*"

Neri flinched as everyone stared at her, then covered her face in her hands. "I ... I'm a mermaid."

"That's not an explanation!" Tammy snorted. "And you're not a mermaid!"

Harper pulled Neri in close. "Shh, you're scaring her."

"I ... I am. I didn't get legs. You said I would, and I didn't."

"What if she really is a mermaid?" Harper asked. "Weirder things have happened, right? And can any of you shadyrs siren-song away a bloody gash?"

"I've never really considered trying," Tammy deadpanned, paired with an eye roll.

"She's not a mermaid," Rylan said, although he didn't sound certain. "But she has lived as one her whole life, in a beshadowing. I'm not surprised there are some side effects. I'm more surprised she's not completely insane."

Callan probed his chest with his fingers in awe, then sat up.

"Maybe she kept herself sane with her singing. I certainly feel refreshed." He reached out a hand toward Neri but didn't touch her. "Hey, thank you. I feel so much better now."

Neri peeked out from behind her fingers.

"Mermaid songs heal. Well, they're supposed to," she added as she touched her fingers to her own chest. "It still hasn't helped my heart hurt less."

The odd, mashed-up tune still filled Harper's head. Neri had grown up so isolated, with just a madman to learn from. But there had been a few picture books in the room, and for one moment during the fight, Harper thought she saw a radio.

When it got knocked on the floor, Neri had rushed out of safety to reclaim it. Maybe it was more than singing that kept the girl sane. Maybe she'd had a secret connection to the rest of the world.

Harper spoke softly, "Where did you learn those songs? I thought I saw a radio in your room. Have you been listening to it?"

Neri shook her head fearfully. "I wasn't supposed to have it. I wasn't supposed to hear anyone else. Daddy only liked that one song. I wasn't supposed to sing anything else."

"It's okay, you won't get in trouble from us."

Neri's mouth clammed shut.

"I really liked the way you combined songs together, it was beautiful. And I'm glad you had something to listen to. It must have been lonely for you."

Neri emerged from behind her hands and checked each of the faces around her, as though looking for signs they were about to pounce. Her voice was confessional quiet.

"It came up to me one day from the sea when I was fishing. I liked the songs it played. So many beautiful songs. I wanted to sing them all at once. But sometimes the people talked about *news* and *traffic* and *sports* and the world outside seemed so scary. I knew I wasn't supposed to listen. I knew I wasn't supposed to have it. But I couldn't throw it back to the sea. I knew that's what Daddy would make me do, would have …"

Her tiny frame was racked with sobs.

Harper's mouth twisted. That man was a monster, inside and out. There was little doubt he killed his offspring, and probably Neri's mother, too. But he was the only living company Neri had her whole life.

"I'm so sorry. I'm sorry you lost him. I'm sorry everything has changed so quickly, how scary that must be."

Neri curled herself tighter against Harper's chest and Harper wrapped her arms around her. The girl's wet hair shimmered in the flickering glow cast by Everly, who still shone too bright to look at. Harper stared anyway, her vision swimming with globs of color. The brightest point was a few feet off the ground, hovering as Everly often did when the dragon emerged.

The others had also turned back to watch. After Callan got his pants back on, Rylan put his arm over his brother's shoulder and faced the light, muscles around his jaw twitching and his eyes desperate. There was nothing they could do.

They couldn't risk getting any closer until the scintillating tendrils receded. The tendrils whipped out and were drawn back, over and over, as though some great internal battle was being fought. Everly spoke often about how she had to fight so hard to control the Beast of Teeth and Stars. And now, it looked so much stronger.

"Is your friend going to be okay?" Neri asked. "I can try to heal her, too."

Harper swallowed. "I think Everly's alone on this one."

CHAPTER TWENTY-EIGHT

The flash was blinding in its intensity. Everly didn't have a chance to cry out or close her eyes before a shockwave of energy slammed into her. Pure white power surged through her body, searing her veins. It filled her senses, erasing her ability to see, hear, or feel anything exterior to her own thoughts.

She floated in total sensory deprivation for several seconds, too shocked by the sudden absence of *everything* to react.

Her senses returned slowly. First, the sound of dripping met her ears. Not like water, but thicker. More of a *pat, pat, pat* sound, like something thick and viscous.

Then goose bumps rose on her skin as a chilled wind rushed around her. Not the same breeze she'd felt sitting on the ground next to the shroudpool in the woods. This wasn't natural. It tasted like power, control, and blood.

Something gleamed and roiled far ahead, a star in an empty sky. She focused on the light as if it were a life raft in a void-like sea. It bobbed and wove, moving closer.

Everly could feel her body, but she couldn't seem to *move* it. Her limbs felt like phantoms, as invisible as the air she was suspended in. The effect of being indistinguishable from the void around her sent a sharp thrill of terror through her.

"I'm dreaming, this isn't real."

She said the words like a prayer—that this wasn't death, that she could reclaim control. A shiver ran through her, opening her senses back up through her body. She had toes and fingers she could feel again, arms and legs she could move.

A breezy weightlessness filled her. All the pain that had saturated her being was gone. The agony of her body cracking to pieces had ended.

The light grew closer, moving with incredible speed. A scintillating, rippling body of complex, fine-boned patterns spiraling into each other swam through the air like a ribbon.

Her dragon.

It was larger than she'd ever seen it. It had eyes now, sparkling like stars, and a long, treacherous mouth, forming a face so alien, it hurt Everly's mind to gaze upon it. It came to a stop several feet away, turning in circles in the void as though gravity were a concept it despised.

"The Beast of Teeth and Stars," Everly murmured.

"Not that. Not that," the dragon returned in an echoing whisper.

Everly tensed. *It spoke.* It had never communicated before, not in words. Only in urges, hunger, or wrath.

"What are you? Soul-eater?"

"Not Beast of Teeth and Stars. Not soul-eater." Its voice was the crackle of fire, the burst of a supernova. It made Everly's ears ache and left them ringing.

"But you do eat souls," Everly shot back warily. She'd experienced it. She counted them like tally marks scratched in her heart. Starting with her father.

"Souls equate sustenance. Take you *your* name from what is consumed? Beast of Teeth and Stars. Soul-eater. Simple names. Gifted by quarry in fear. I am so much more."

Everly winced, trying to make sense of the being's words. "Then what are you?"

Its long body undulated as it hissed, "The Coruscare."

The dragon, the *Coruscare*, seemed strong, too strong. Between that and the absence of pain in Everly's body, she had to hope that breaking the crystal had worked. That this dreamlike void was her way of processing those new powers flooding through her.

Pressure clouded her senses, as though her mind and body were trapped in a vice. One of contested power. She could feel the dragon needling her will, testing for weaknesses, pushing for control. Whoever won the battle in this space would decide which of them would emerge back into the real world in command.

She could sense its tendrils seeking hungrily all around out there. They had not yet been satiated by the soul of one of her friends, which comforted Everly. She used that relief to strengthen her resolve, to pull back against the dragon's reach, to try to contain it, lock it back away. She had to emerge the victor.

"That name means nothing to me. But I know what you are, soul-eater, and I won't let you control me."

The void shivered and the creature's words dripped venom. "Nothing? You know nothing!"

It rushed at her, straight through her, blinding her with its light.

Everly fell. Not physically—there was no sensation of falling, no dip to her stomach. But the void around her flashed by as if she were falling down a star-filled tunnel, straight into another world.

Her surroundings stopped abruptly, and she shook her head to clear away the disorientation.

Everything around her was bright, glaring white.

A vast realm of pillar-shaped mountains and rippling plains stretched out under an egg yolk-colored sky. Alien, crystalline plants grew in geometric patterns, and directly ahead, a transparent pyramid soared over the land.

My realm.

Time and space passed with a fast-forward sensation. Everly was inside a vast room that cradled a throne within a kaleidoscope of diamond-cut ornamentation.

The throne was mammoth in size, a sharp-cut circle, hollow through the center. Within that gap, the Coruscare floated, its glow setting every surface in that gleaming space ablaze.

Other creatures moved nearby. Much smaller, humanoid but unlike anything Everly had ever seen. Except for their eyes. They had shadyr eyes. A line of them trailing into the distance, dragging in squirming bodies of eidolghasts, and sometimes their own kind, injured and chained shadyrs, all brought toward the Coruscare.

My servants.

The Coruscare lashed out with a white tendril and consumed the prisoners. All other shadyrs fell forward in supplication.

The throne room vanished.

Something large, hulking, and dark flashed by. A black void, smoky and oozing malice. Everly shuddered.

She had dreamed of that thing before. Everything it

touched turned into *nothing*. It rushed for the Coruscare.

The Bane appeared, flew through the darkness, and slammed into the light. Tremendous, overwhelming power split the dragon into pieces. Agony burst through Everly like a thousand dying worlds.

My enemy.

Her surroundings went into hyper-speed again. Images of war, eidolghasts and shadyrs fighting as they fled that dimension and found a balance in the human realm. Three shining crystal pieces were separated, swallowed by the chaos. Vanished. Lost.

Then her father's face. He opened a cabinet, smiled as he placed a crystal on the shelf. A moment later, Everly saw herself as a small, brown-haired child, hand grabbing at the latch to the cabinet. Standing on tiptoes, the very edges of her fingers shoving against the pretty crystal. Her dad loomed behind her, she dropped the crystal, the Coruscare emerged.

Sensations of freedom and confusion washed over Everly. The thing of light did not know this realm, could not exist in this new dimension in its true form. So it took shelter in the closest being.

Hunger.

The Coruscare's fractured piece entered Everly's tiny body, merging with her like a parasite, and then eased a hunger of thousands of years by consuming her father.

It didn't expect this new beast it inhabited to lock it away again. That it would tangle in the small creature's thoughts and become trapped by them.

Fast forward again. Familiar woods. Everly, pale-haired, still small, angry, crying. Lost.

Weak. Weak enough for the Coruscare to taste freedom.

Everly felt the Coruscare's fear that its human host would die in those woods, and it would be lost entirely.

Then Rylan found them.

Confusing dream and reality, Everly tried to cry out to the young boy, tell him to run, before his soul was consumed.

No. The Coruscare didn't consume Rylan that day.

But something happened.

The thought snapped Everly out of the barrage of flashbacks.

She fell violently back into the present moment. Her limbs flailed as if she'd left her body and returned.

The Coruscare stared at her with twinkling, ageless eyes, satisfied at the utter terror on her face.

"What did you do to Rylan?" Everly said. "That day in the woods, when I was lost."

The dragon bristled and hissed. "Sought subordination, succor, from descendant of my changelings."

Subordination? Succor?

"What did you *do to him*?" Everly snarled.

The Coruscare's light strobed like a heartbeat. "Partial consumption. Connective tether forged. Bondage to create a guardian. Protection was required more than sustenance. My being was held captive to your fragile form ... Couldn't allow host to perish. Could not lose any piece of resplendent self."

Everly's hand fluttered to her lips. Nausea bubbled in her stomach. All those years they'd been close. All the times he'd watched over her, stood up for her, took care of her ... He'd only done so because the Coruscare had forced him against his will. He'd been tethered to her like a *pet,* against his will.

Her voice broke as she said, "You *enslaved* Rylan to me?"

The dragon's expression remained stoic and unmoved. "To *me.*"

That's why Rylan had been in her dreams since they'd met. A literal piece of him had been within her that entire time. It was never fate. It was never love. It was this creature, this hateful, emotionless alien's enthrallment.

Almost unable to breathe, Everly whispered, "Zozo too?"

"The four-legged beast? Accident. Desired sustenance. Host regained control too soon. Only partial consumption achieved."

Everly exhaled sharply. She'd made no emotional bond with the big cat. It had only been protective of the thing inside her, lashed to it in servitude.

The flashbacks she'd witnessed churned like curdled food through her mind. *My realm. My servants.*

"And the shadyrs ... their ancestors in the Everdark. They weren't feeding you their own kind because they wanted to. You forced them to."

The Coruscare made no reply. The pressure on Everly's mind built, crushing her thoughts and feelings.

Everly pushed back.

"They're free now. They're all free of you now!"

She'd seen to that. She'd almost died for it.

"You have no more servants. You have no realm."

"This realm. Eidolghasts should rule instead? No. They stole my last. This realm will be mine."

Everly gritted her teeth against the waves of power washing over her, trying to drown her. "You'll have *nothing* that I don't allow."

"Resplendent self is stronger. Two of my thirds exist here now. Find my third. Give it to me. Make us all." The Coruscare moved close to Everly's face, swirling before her eyes in a mess of sparkles and teeth. "*Our* realm."

"No. I don't want that. And I don't want any more of you." Everly extended her senses, feeling out into the real world for her body, for consciousness, for the tendrils that lashed around her. She focused on bringing everything back.

The dragon reared up, body snapping in violent motions. "Still strive to control? I ruled realms. I am god. How does fragile form hope to dominate?"

Everly took a long, solid breath. "I have so far."

With a great heave against the boundaries of her dreamscape, Everly broke through to consciousness. She opened her eyes to the arching limbs of the twisted, dead tree beside the Dark Corner shroudpool.

There was no longer any pain, although her fingertips tingled slightly. All the agony and dizziness she'd known were gone. Other than a faint bleariness from having just awoken, she felt good. Healed.

But at what cost?

Pale beams of light shone down over her, rushing back into her. The dragon—the *Coruscare*—growled from within its cage. She was holding it back for now, but she could feel the bend and push of its will against her own, wrestling for control.

How long will I be able to keep that thing at bay?

Singing flowed to her from nearby, and then sounds of a discussion. Everly lay there for a moment listening, counting the voices of her friends, too afraid to open her eyes and see one of them gone.

She smiled as she heard Tammy, Denny, Harper, and Neri. Then Callan spoke, too. Her smile faded as Rylan's voice reached her.

He said he loved me.

It had meant everything to her, that moment between them in the caves. Now she worried that it meant nothing. Rylan had been freed from the Coruscare's enslavement, but he'd lived with that forced need to protect her his whole life. He'd barely known freedom. How could she accept that the love he professed was real?

Sighing, Everly opened her eyes and lifted her hands before her face. The skin was smooth and clear, completely unmarred by the cracks that had spread there before. She was whole again, but the Coruscare was also stronger. She hoped it would be worth it.

"Hey, Ev's moving!" Harper called out.

Rylan was the first to reach her side, kneeling to check over her. "How do you feel?"

He'd protected her for so long, Everly imagined that it would be a hard habit to break. She shifted to sit up, withdrawing from his efforts to help.

"I feel good," Everly said, brushing back her pale gray hair.

Her clothes were still wet, and the sunset had only a small tint of red remaining as it faded into night.

"How long was I out?"

"A minute, maybe two." Rylan reached a hand for her as she prepared to stand.

She ignored it, leaving him frowning.

Footsteps crunched as Harper trotted over to her side, Neri in her arms.

She made a couple of abortive attempts to hug Everly without dropping the mermaid girl.

"Screw it!" Harper huffed and pressed herself toward Everly with Neri in between them.

Neri squeaked.

"I was so worried about you!" Harper cooed, pressing her cheek to Everly's. She shuffled back to give everyone more room as they gathered around.

Tammy's lips turned up in a rare smile. "You look so much better!"

Everly pulled up the sleeve of her jacket, revealing smooth, unbroken skin.

"Yeah. My arms are back to normal, cracks all gone. Even all the little scrapes and bruises I got in the lighthouse are gone."

"Did Neri heal you, too?" Callan asked.

"Huh?"

Harper chimed, "Neri has healing powers! With her voice!"

"Yeah, check this out," Callan said, showing off the fresh pink scar where his open wound had been.

Tammy tsked. "All that excellent stitching I did, wasted."

"I still appreciated it," Callan said, beaming.

Everly blinked. "Wow. Okay. Um, I don't think it was her that fixed all this, though. I heard her singing, but it only started after I woke up. I was already better by then."

Rylan had shoved his hands into his pockets, glowering. "You think it came from the crystal? That it healed you?"

Everly nodded.

Harper said, "I mean, we were hoping for a power-up. But more like it would fix the dragon so the cracking stopped spreading and you could heal normally. You got the full regen package. So cool! If you got that from the crystal, do you think Neri's healing could have something to do with her living near it for so long?"

"I have no idea," Everly replied. "But anything is possible at this point. The dragon powered up in a few ways. It talks to me now. And it has a name."

Harper gave her a questioning look. "A name?"

"The Coruscare."

Harper's expression remained the same, but a sharp inhale came collectively from the shadyrs.

Rylan's eyes sparked like lightning. "The WHAT?"

Chapter Twenty-Nine

"The thing ... the thing inside you is the Coruscare?" Rylan growled, rubbing the remnants of seawater off his chin with the back of his hand.

Every shadyr stared wide eyed at Everly in a way that made her want to shrink away and vanish.

"No way!" Denny said.

Tammy's dark hands covered her mouth. "Oh my ghast. *The* Coruscare?"

Everly winced. "You know it?"

"It's literally a class at the Darkfreys," Callan said. "The Coruscare and Pre-Transition Mythology."

Everly's memories itched, taking her back to sneaking through the estate grounds with Lian. She'd seen that on a projector screen as she peeked into classrooms. They studied the thing inside her as though it were a myth?

Rylan's gaze grew intense. "Shadyrs have a rich history, but myths from before coming to this world are pretty sparse. We know the Coruscare was worshipped as a god and some histories speak of the gods being literal. Like they actually existed as tangible entities. But when early shadyrs came to the human realm, the gods didn't come with them."

He shook his head at some inner thought. "After a while, shadyrs questioned their existence, gave up their worship, and they kind of faded into obscurity. They're no more part of current shadyr culture than, say, Babylonian gods are to modern humans."

"The Coruscare is real," Everly said softly.

She tapped her chest and raised her gaze to his again.

"It's the Beast of Teeth and Stars."

It only took a couple of minutes for Everly to relate everything she'd learned while unconscious. The shadyrs listened raptly.

When Everly was done with her tale, Callan shook his head and let out an astonished laugh. "Wow. It never occurred to me to connect the Coruscare to 'the light' in the Everdark."

"I don't even get how you're making that connection now," Denny shrugged.

"The Everdark wasn't always dark," Callan explained.

"We were always told that it was when the eidolghasts took over, destroying the light, that the entire realm became beshadowed and the shadyr ancestors had to leave."

Everly grimaced. "The Coruscare ate eidolghasts. It held them back from taking over the realm until it was broken by the Bane. The Coruscare was the light that was destroyed."

"Huh, I always assumed the light was like, daylight, and the eidolghasts took over. No wonder our 'god' didn't come over to this world with us." Denny made a *squicky* noise and dragged a finger across his neck.

Everly kicked at the remaining crystalline shell that had shattered on the ground beneath them. "Well, it did come to this realm, just broken and trapped in three pieces."

"Two of which now exist inside you." Rylan shook his head, laughing breathily. "The god of the shadyrs."

Tammy, Callan, and Denny also stared at Everly, each of them with expressions that were borderline awed.

She turned away and stared at the ground, crushing one of the broken shards beneath her boot. "Yeah, well, I can guarantee you it wasn't a benevolent god."

"This is still huge news. Like, huge." Callan squatted down and picked up a few of the larger pieces of crystal, putting them in his pocket.

Tammy glanced over her shoulder. "Hey, we should get moving. Lian's going to beat us to the pickup point."

Everly nodded and strode forward quickly, avoiding Rylan. She didn't like the new way he looked at her, how they all looked at her. None of them seemed willing to believe her whenever she tried to explain that the thing inside her was. Not. Good.

They passed out of the clearing and through the chain-link fence, then waited on the dirt road until headlights appeared in the distance.

Harper bumped a shoulder into Everly's, offering a kind smile. "You're the real goddess here, don't ever forget that."

Everly rested her forehead against the cool glass window and watched Howell House grow closer.

The sight of the homestead chased away the pain and horror of the last day. There were times while on the island when she'd been certain she wouldn't make it out alive, that maybe none of them would. Seeing the welcoming lights that lined the wide veranda was like the best kind of victory prize. This place was more her home than the house she'd grown up in.

She wasn't sure she'd *actually* won. Not while the Coruscare was still a part of her.

But she'd come home intact, with all her friends—and

a new addition—and for now the world felt whole.

Lian put her SUV into park, then glanced back at the team. "Rush will no doubt have a big dinner laid out for you. Our stakeout on Vonny didn't get far. She holed herself up at the estate and wouldn't come out. We can debrief after you're all fed and recuperated."

"I don't know what any of that meant," Neri whispered, eyes wide.

Everything was new to Neri, and her learning curve was going to be steep. Getting her into the car had been a struggle and required a lot of coaxing. The poor girl was terrified of *traffic* from her radio-only education.

"That's going to happen a lot. I'll catch you up as we go." Harper reached over and opened the car door.

At the same instant, Neri screamed.

Everly jumped in her seat and whipped her head toward the young woman, who was sitting between her and Harper.

Neri stared down at her legs, her eyes so wide the whites were visible all the way around.

She had legs.

Naked legs.

Rylan, who was in the front passenger seat, had turned around at the first scream.

He whipped back to the front with a "Shit! Sorry!"

"Woah!" Harper squeaked, throwing both hands to

grab the hem of Neri's T-shirt and pull it over her lap.

Everly leaned forward and tugged her bomber jacket off, laying it over Neri's thighs. Harper grabbed the sleeves and tied them around Neri's waist to create a makeshift skirt.

"What is *happening*?" Neri screeched.

Harper took her hands. "Looks like you are human, or shadyr, after all."

There was a scuffle in the backseat, and Everly glanced around to see Callan holding Denny in a headlock.

Tammy cringed away from the wrestling men beside her. "One minute, he's saving our lives. The next, he's trying to sneak looks at naked girls."

"Sounds about right," Everly said wryly.

"I was just ... reaching ... for the seat release ... thingy." Denny wrestled himself free from Callan, brushing off his disheveled clothing indignantly.

"Nobody believes you," Tammy said.

Denny huffed. "I know you all think I'm the world's biggest asshole, but at least *I* didn't enslave multiple generations of women to be my mermaid harem."

Callan scoffed. "Wow, talk about setting a low bar."

Lian hummed and eyed Neri with interest. "You said she lived above a nyevmer her whole life?"

Rylan nodded. "Yeah, a big one. It was trapped in the caves beneath the lighthouse."

"She must have had one heck of a shadyr hangover,"

Lian explained. "Almost two decades in contact with the ghast and completely untrained? Took her body a while to catch up."

Neri clawed at her thighs and twitched her toes. "I don't know what to do with these. They feel so *strange*."

"It's okay. I'll help you. Don't worry." Harper leaped out onto the gravel driveway, then turned to help Neri from the seat.

Neri moved her legs weakly, and even with Harper supporting her, she collapsed the moment she tried to stand.

While Harper held Neri up, Everly hopped out behind and adjusted the jacket-skirt. Then she took one side, tucking Neri's arm around her shoulders, and Harper took the other. Together, they coached Neri on how to move her brand-new legs, while keeping the majority of her body weight on their shoulders.

Denny flipped the car seat forward and the rest of the team piled out after them, groans of relief and exhaustion all around.

Callan asked, "Is Cherry back yet?"

Lian shrugged, casting her eyes toward the lights of the town. "Got a message a while ago saying he was on his way. Taking his time though."

Halfway to the door, the excitement on Neri's face became contagious. She didn't really get the hang of it— Everly and Harper were doing most of the work. But she marveled at her newfound ability like a child discovering how to walk for the first time.

With a little practice, Everly figured she'd be ready to go at it alone. Both girls found themselves grinning as they carried Neri up the porch steps and into the house, where she declared, "It's so *dry* here."

Lian ducked up the stairs ahead of them and returned with a long cotton dress that she offered to Neri. "It might be a little big. But it'll keep you warm until we can get you some clothes of your own."

Neri ran her fingertips over the fabric like a pet.

"It's for me?" She pressed it against her cheek. "It's so soft."

Lian's stoic face melted, and she blinked glossy eyes at the young shadyr before waving her and Harper off to help her get changed.

Lian held Everly back in the hall as the others passed them toward the kitchen. "You did good, saving that poor thing."

Everly shivered. They almost hadn't.

Lian nodded solemnly as though she could read minds. "All of you are going to need recovery time after this, not only Neri. I hope you're not still planning on packing up and leaving."

"I ... hadn't really had time to think about it."

"Forget what my blockhead of a son has said," Lian

muttered, flicking her head in the direction Rylan had gone.

Everly inhaled a wobbly breath. What he'd said to her in the caves was *All I've known my entire life is loving you. The dumbest thing I've ever done in my life was pushing you away.*

Lian reached out and took her hands, squeezing them. "You're wanted here. I can support you if you're here. Neri can recover here. And if that thing inside you is the Coruscare, that's of huge significance to shadyrs."

Rylan's words, what she'd seen the Coruscare do, to others, to him, left Everly's heart cold. "Maybe having the Coruscare inside me is exactly the reason why I shouldn't be around. What it's capable of ..."

"Just ... think about it. This old woman isn't fond of saying goodbye to family. Okay?" Lian pressed her fingers, then left toward the kitchen.

Harper and Neri returned from a side room, and Harper handed Everly back her jacket. It was still damp from their underwater adventures, like the rest of Everly's clothes. She longed for a hot shower and bed, and Harper looked equally tired.

But Harper's grin glowed as she said, "I smell bacon! Wow, Neri gets to eat bacon for the first time. Are you okay with eating animals?"

"Like fish?"

They followed their noses down the corridor.

As Lian had promised, Rushelle stood in the warm

kitchen, flipping bacon in a cast-iron skillet. She glanced over at the three of them as they entered, and when her gaze found Neri, her eyes lit up.

"Oh, you brought home a new friend! Omigosh, omigosh, look at you! Oh honey, let's get some food into you!"

The rest of the team was at the table already. There was an empty space beside Rylan, and the vulnerable look in his eyes almost broke Everly. She turned from him and sat on the other side, keeping her gaze down.

Tammy hovered for a moment. She often didn't join them at the table, instead perching on a nearby cabinet or lurking in a corner. But she shuffled forward, taking a spot beside Callan with inaudible mumbles and a halfhearted eye roll.

Harper helped Neri into a chair at the table and set to work making a plate of food from the various platters awaiting them, doing her best to explain what went on it.

Bacon (Neri knew pigs from her picture books), chips, quiche, cauliflower gratin (white vegetables were an obvious novelty). One of the more surprising things that amazed Neri were the simple bread rolls. She'd heard of bread, but the way her eyes lit up at the first nibble made Everly's heart ache and swell simultaneously.

Lian said, "Just go slow, kid, your stomach won't be used to all this."

Rushelle bustled around on sunshine-yellow stilettos, taking orders for hot drinks. She reached Neri.

"Hmm. No coffee for you, yet, but I'd love to see if you like a chamomile tea with plenty of milk and honey." As she returned to the kitchen, she asked Lian, "Is little duck going to be joining us here long-term?"

Lian leaned back in her chair and addressed Neri. "We've got plenty of room. You're more than welcome."

Neri shot a wide-eyed gaze at Harper. "Is this where you live?"

Harper shook her head. "No. Me and Everly have been staying at another house nearby. But ... we don't technically live around here, in Shroudhaven."

Neri listened intently, fiddling with the sleeves on her borrowed dress, and frowning at every other word. Even when other people spoke, she looked almost exclusively to Harper, leaning toward her in her chair as though her presence was a protective bubble.

"She can stay with us," Everly said. "I think she should stay with us."

Harper pouted. "And where are we staying?"

Everly kept her gaze carefully away from Rylan. "We can stay here, at the Boderleth house. However long is needed for Neri."

"Wonderful," Lian said like a sigh. "Whatever support she needs, whatever support you need, I'm here for you."

As Everly looked up to offer her a smile, her gaze flickered over Rylan. His face was set like stone, cracked down the middle with a line of confusion. She turned away again.

Harper beamed and mouthed *thank you*.

"Yeah, it's better if she doesn't stay here," Tammy scoffed, then smirked. "I mean, we want her as far away from Denny's influence as possible."

"Hey, I was a damned hero today!" He threw a chip at her across the table.

Tammy snatched it, popped it in her mouth, and crunched it between her teeth. "Okay, I'll admit, you saved a life or two. Let's balance that against how often you've endangered lives, and *whomp whomp*, still in the negative."

"I think Tammy here is winning the hero game at the moment." Callan chuckled.

"Maybe we shouldn't be keeping score," Tammy groaned.

She flicked her hood up over her head and sunk into her chair.

The team ate, and laughed, and took turns relaying every perilous moment on the island. By the time all the details of their harrowing journey had been told, their plates and glasses were empty and most of the eyes around the table had begun to droop.

Everly got up to take her plate over to the kitchen, and

when she turned from the sink, Rylan was right behind her.

He leaned in and spoke under his breath. "Can I talk to you? Alone?"

His piercing warm-green eyes held a painful vulnerability.

All I've known my entire life is loving you.

The world seemed to stop turning. She'd dreamed for so long that Rylan would admit that he wanted to be with her. As a girl, she'd been *convinced* that Rylan was her soulmate, that they were fated to be together.

She knew better now. But how could she tell him? How could she explain that the feelings he'd confessed weren't his own? That they were a leftover symptom of having been enslaved to the malevolent deity within her?

Once Rylan shook off the remnants of protective nature he'd been conditioned to feel, he'd figure out that he didn't want to be with her. She just had to wait for that to happen.

"I ... I'm not ready."

She turned to rejoin the others in the kitchen.

He grabbed her arm, gently pulling her back toward him.

"What's going on? You've been avoiding me since we got back."

Everly shook her head. She couldn't speak. She desperately longed to forget what she'd seen, what she'd learned, and just *be* with him. Being with him would have been proof that fate existed, love existed, that this dark, difficult life had meaning.

But none of that was real.

She took a slow step back, releasing herself from his grip.

His jaw worked, twitching as he swallowed. "Please talk to me. I—"

The screen door slammed, and footsteps stalked down the hall.

Callan got to his feet. "Cherry, you okay?"

Cherry stopped at the entrance to the kitchen, blinking as he took everyone in. His cheeks were streaked with dried tears and his eyes were a red that matched his hair.

"You're all back." Eyeing Neri, the torn, damp clothing, and Everly standing upright and looking healthy, he sniffed. "Looks like I missed out on a lot."

"Adventure of a lifetime," Denny crowed. "There was a fucking U-boat full of Nazi zombies, dude!"

"You say that like it was a good thing," said Tammy.

Callan frowned, moving to Cherry's side. "Are you okay? What did Jasper want?"

Cherry laughed bitterly. "The Bane. He wanted the Bane."

Harper rose to her feet, knocking the chair over behind her. "He what?"

Neri squeaked and put her hands over her ears.

"Vonny sent him on a mission to find it. He took me as backup, to Rook's Theater," Cherry explained, giving Harper an apologetic grimace.

"Vonny wanted it? What is she up to?" Lian asked.

Harper groaned and grabbed fistfuls of hair at her scalp. "Ugh, I thought it would be safe there!"

Everly stepped beside Harper, placing a hand on her shoulder. "Hey, it's okay! It might be better if it's not near me, anyway. We'll work something out if we need it again."

Harper smacked Everly's hand away. "It's not okay! You have no idea ..."

Everly's mouth hung open at the alarming look in her friend's eyes. Brown eyes she was so unfamiliar with. She'd thought the two of them shared everything, but she hadn't even known her true eye color. Her best friend, who'd scolded her for keeping secrets, clearly had some of her own.

Cherry shook his head and slumped into a seat at the table. "I'm sorry, once I knew what he was after, I tried to stop him."

"Did you really?" Harper spat. "Or did you just let him walk away with my blade?"

"Your blade?" Everly asked.

"What, you think I gift-wrapped it for him?" Cherry's dark eyes grew glossier.

"I have to get it back." Harper started pacing, glancing at Neri, then toward the front door, back and forth, over and over. "I need it back."

"I told you, it's okay, we—"

"I NEED IT!" Harper roared. "I can't be strong enough without it!"

Neri whimpered and Lian rose to her feet to comfort her.

Harper clutched at her head again. "I'm sorry. I'm sorry. I ..."

"What's going on, what do you mean you need it?"

Strong. The word echoed in Everly's mind.

What was it, the shadyrs in Gorhanmere said? *Our family is strong.*

And they had been. Unnaturally strong. And covered in scars. Like the ones on Harper's waist that Everly knew hadn't been there up until recently. Harper was too fond of mid-riff tops to deny that.

She had cut herself with the Bane the night Rylan was freed. She must have discovered then what the Gorhanmere shadyrs knew. The way she'd been so full of energy ever since ... Everly felt like a fool for not having realized earlier.

"You've been cutting yourself with the Bane," Everly accused, her voice hushed.

Harper scoffed. "That's ridiculous. Why would I do that?"

"Because it makes you strong."

Harper's eyes flashed.

Everly took a step back. "It's true? Why would you do something so dangerous?"

All eyes in the room were focused on Harper, and she turned a slow circle like a cornered animal. "You have no idea what you're talking about."

"And you have no idea what consequences there could have been. You could have ended up like the shadyrs up in Gorhanmere. All so you could be stronger? You didn't *need* that."

Harper snarled. "Of course I did! None of you know what it's like to be the only human in the group of superheroes. I know you don't think I can keep up, that I'm not good enough, never good enough. None of you would understand why it's necessary."

"Because it's not!" Everly shot back.

"What does it matter now? It's gone!" Harper glared at her. "It's gone, and you're not going to help me get it back, are you?"

Everly's lips tightened into a thin line.

Harper's shoulder slumped and she turned to where Neri watched from Lian's arms with wide eyes. "I'm sorry. I'm ... tired. I'm going home now. You don't have to come with me ..."

Neri reached a hand out and said, "I have ... big feelings sometimes, too."

Harper just nodded slowly and walked them toward

the front door.

"I'll drive you." Lian grabbed her keys, though her expression told Everly in no uncertain terms that she wasn't happy with this new revelation, either.

Everly brushed past Rylan and followed them out, feeling like even though her body was no longer shattering into pieces ... her heart was.

CHAPTER THIRTY

Harper's campervan, which contained most of their belongings, was still parked at Crybel's Cove docks. Rushelle and Lian returned it to the Boderleth house the next day.

Unpacking into the house Everly thought she'd said her final goodbye to wasn't as hard as she thought it would be. They had cleaned and banished so many of its ghosts that Everly was able to treat it as a simple roof over her head, nothing more.

It hadn't yet started to feel like her home, though.

Harper barely spoke to her. She took to helping Neri acclimate to her new life like a project to perfect. That hyper-focus also doubled as a great way to block Everly out.

Neri woke up screaming every night for her first week. She would dream of the "monster below" coming up through the ground and swallowing her. Taught her whole life to stay up high for fear of the nyevmer in the caves beneath, even sleeping in a bed on the first floor left her terrified.

Everly dreamed most nights of the Coruscare. Of it telling her its desires, wanting to be made whole, trying to seize control. Being woken from that wasn't so bad.

Harper tried to hide it, but Everly could see she was drawn, pale, and shaky. Whatever withdrawal she suffered from the absence of the Bane, she pushed through it, for Neri.

Everly wondered whether her disconnection from the Bane would have been different without the responsibility of the new shadyr there with them. She wondered a lot of things about Harper's use of the Bane. But Harper didn't give Everly an opportunity to ask, or to apologize.

After another sleepless night of Neri screaming, they decided that being higher up would make Neri feel safer. There would no doubt be more screaming, more trauma to heal, but they wanted to work with what they had, and they knew Neri wanted a space for herself farther from the ground.

Everly thought back to her vague, dusty memories of the house. She didn't like the attic or the basement here in her childhood home. But she recalled the attic being a fairly large-sized room tucked under the roof beams.

As morning fog drifted like a pale tide outside the windows, Everly descended to the kitchen. She set some coffee to brew, then gathered some necessities for cleaning—multiple trash bags, a basket of sprays and wipes, a broom and mop. While she was waiting for the coffee machine, she stared out the window into the early morning air, lost in her thoughts.

Movement drew her attention, and she moved closer to the window, staring out wide-eyed, hoping to catch a glimpse to prove it was Zozo. But whatever had been there had already vanished.

Everly didn't really expect the cougar to stick around as close as he had. For two days now, the meat she placed out in the backyard hadn't been eaten.

Maybe the cougar had fully recovered from its forced attachment to her. Maybe that meant Rylan would recover soon, too. Maybe he already had. He'd stopped trying to call a few days back, after several attempts that Everly didn't answer.

Harper appeared at the kitchen door wearing hot pink yoga pants and a man's-sized T-shirt with the sleeves cut off. She'd taken to only wearing her green contacts when doing photoshoots because the change had confused Neri, so her brown eyes took in the supplies Everly had gathered but didn't make contact with Everly herself.

Lian and Tammy had picked up Neri a few moments

earlier. They were taking her shopping to continue filling out her wardrobe and personal belongings, and to keep her out of the way while Everly and Harper prepared the attic for her as a surprise.

"I'll take these up." Harper hefted the basket of cleaning supplies to her hip.

She left the room before Everly could offer her a coffee.

With a sigh, Everly poured hers into a travel cup and followed with the rest of the gear.

Harper had the attic stairs pulled down, and she vanished through the hole in the ceiling.

"Not much room up here. There's a load of stuff right at the top of the stairs," Harper called down.

Everly climbed and once her head and shoulders were through, saw what Harper meant. It looked like her dad had received a shipment of boxes and left them all there, half-opened, spread over the floor. She vaguely remembered that he was always up and down between the attic and antique store. He must have kept overstock and new purchases up there.

Harper shimmied between the boxes to make more room for Everly. There were two windows at either end of the oblong room, but they were covered in dust, only letting a weak yellow illumination filter through.

"Light switch is over there, I think." Everly pointed and climbed the rest of the way.

Harper found the old-fashioned toggle and flicked it. With a low hum, two bare bulbs popped to life. Evenly spaced through the center of the room, they revealed mountains of dusty boxes, wooden crates, old suitcases, and smaller items of furniture.

Harper set the basket of cleaning supplies on top of one pile and whistled. "We might need to call in for backup."

Everly analyzed the space as she took a slow sip of coffee. The room was dusty, but dry, with no scent of mold or mildew to worry about. There was a lot up there, but they didn't have to deal with it all right away. Most were stacked neatly to the sides.

The main issue was the boxes scattered on the floor. If they could be sorted and stacked somewhere else, there would be more than enough space to get a single bed in and lay out a small bedroom.

"I can hang some curtains across the middle beam there to section off this end for Neri, and we can clear the rest out later if she wants to expand. I think we can manage to clean up half the attic ourselves. We managed with the rest of this sty of a house." Everly offered a small smile, which Harper returned briefly before she seemed to remember herself, returning her expression to carefully neutral.

Harper squatted beside one of the opened boxes that cluttered the floor to inspect its contents. Everly frowned and set her coffee down on the floor as she checked the box closest to her. She was glad it was just her and Harper. But Harper didn't seem quite ready to talk yet.

They worked in silence as they checked the boxes, taped them back up, and stacked them on the other end of the attic. Most had what appeared to be the contents of an elderly woman's home.

Pretty lamps and teapots, ornamental plates, and a teaspoon collection. Then Everly opened one that had some kind of body armor, similar to what the Darkfreys wore, but a much more old-fashioned design. It was made of steel and rubber strapping rather than carbon fiber and high-tech elastics.

Everly dug deeper, sifting through Darkfrey uniforms and binders until she found something black, sharp, and shiny at the bottom.

"Woah!" Harper exclaimed, robbing the word from Everly's mouth. She sat across the floor, shuffling papers that she'd pulled from one of the boxes.

"What is it?" Everly replied.

"I think I found something you'll be interested in." She turned the sheets outward for Everly to see.

"An invoice, for all of these boxes, purchased at the estate sale of Portia Darkfrey." Harper flipped over to another document, a long list stapled together.

She jabbed her finger at a line, shuffling closer so Everly could read.

It seemed to be a catalog, and Harper's manicured fingernail underlined the words "Starry crystal."

"Do you think that's the Coruscare crystal? Where he got it from?" Everly exhaled the words. "From a Darkfrey, but how? Why would they be selling things like that at an estate sale?"

Harper's lips drew thin, and she flipped another sheet of paper to the front again. This one was a yellowed sheet of newspaper, torn rough down one side—*The Shroudhaven Post*, classifieds section, with an ad circled.

"Your dad kept good records. He found all this through her estate sale and has her obituary circled here. It says here she had no surviving next of kin and was given a state burial."

Everly raised an eyebrow. "But … she was a Darkfrey. I mean, there's only *one* Darkfrey family in the area."

Harper handed Everly the papers to inspect herself. "My best guess is that Miss Portia was disowned by her family, the same way they cast out anyone who doesn't fit their definition of good soldier material."

"I wouldn't be surprised. Maybe Lian wasn't the first to start the tradition of absconding with precious relics." Everly smirked, shaking her head as she flicked through the documents.

It was just conjecture, but it made a weird kind of sense. Portia Darkfrey had died, separated from her kind, and Everly's father had bought up a large portion of her belongings after the fact.

Including the crystal. Everly breaking the crystal, her father dying, her life falling apart so that she ran away and met Rylan, the Coruscare bonding them ... all happened because the Darkfreys didn't care enough about that one family member to deal with her estate after her death. Even Everly had given her mother that courtesy.

Everly shook her head and let the papers fall to her lap. "Maybe if the Darkfreys weren't so keen on kicking people out for being different, none of this would have happened."

"Maybe we can ask Lian if she knows any more about it, but I would bet my top social account that Darkfrey bigotry is behind this." Harper's eyes sparkled at the prospect of gossip.

Everly smiled back, and for a moment, things felt good. Sitting there talking with her friend had felt almost normal again.

They stared at each other for several moments as the house creaked and settled around them, and their expressions dulled.

As one, they both gasped out, "I'm sorry."

"No, what are you sorry for?" Harper asked.

Everly took a deep breath, then expelled her thoughts. "I feel like, I've been so worried about your safety that I must have seemed like I doubted you, that I made you feel like you were somehow lesser. That I pushed you into wanting to use the Bane."

Harper's eyes turned down to the dusty floorboards. "No. It wasn't you. It wasn't even the Howell team. Honestly, they accepted me as much as could be expected. It was always me. It was my own insecurities."

Everly pulled her plait of pale gray hair over her shoulder and worried it between her fingers. "I can totally see how hard it must be though, being the sole human. I understand—"

Harper shook her head. "It's not just being a human in Shroudhaven. It's something I've dealt with my whole life."

She lifted her brown hands up on display. "The standards I live by aren't what the majority has to live by. I always feel like I have to push the limits and fight to be *the best*. Be more, do more, be better. If I'm not excelling, I'm falling short, and the world will be ready to point it out and crush me back to where it thinks I belong."

"I hate that you've experienced that," Everly said softly. "They're the problem, not you. You're enough, exactly as you are."

Harper's long lashes fluttered as she met Everly's eyes. "I'm working on accepting that. That other people's biases are *their* flaws, not mine."

Tears flooded Everly's eyes, and her heart swelled. "You're kind of my hero."

"Oh, you've got that *way* backwards," Harper said, her voice cracking.

She leaned in and pulled Everly into a tight hug.

"You're *my* hero." Her voice was small and muffled against Everly's shoulder. "I'm sorry that I took such a risk trying to be stronger. I'd used the Bane for barely twenty-four hours, and this week without it ... Ev, I can hardly explain what it's been like. I feel like I'm barely clawing free of the cravings now. I think about what things might have been like if I still had it around, and it terrifies me."

Everly squeezed Harper tighter. It scared her, too.

Harper leaned back out of the embrace. "My drive to be perfect, and everything it's rooted in, it's something I'm working on, and will keep working on."

Everly smiled. "Seems to me having Neri around will be good for that."

Harper quirked an eyebrow.

"I mean, you saved her when you'd lost your green contacts, your hair was tangled from swimming, the strength from the Bane had worn out—although *somehow* you still had some makeup clinging on."

Harper chuckled. "I have the best cosmetics sponsors."

"Still, you didn't need any of those things, or shadyr abilities, or superpowers, to save Neri. You just needed your amazing heart. And Neri needs that. She's clearly attached especially to you. She doesn't need perfection from you, she just needs you."

"Yeah, she is helping." A pink flush tinged Harper's cheekbones.

She avoided Everly's eye as she admitted, "She's helped me in other ways too."

"Other ways?"

"Finding myself again? Finding ... who I am and what I want." Harper bit her lower lip. "I haven't felt a lick of attraction to anybody since the absolute circus of my last relationship. But I feel things ... *romantic* things. For Neri."

Everly laid her hand on Harper's knee, palm up.

She waited until Harper took it and entwined their fingers before she said, "Is this new?"

"Liking girls? I don't know ... I've wondered recently if I was only dating guys because it was the thing I was expected to do—get the man, get the ring, get the house, get the kids. Like I had to follow that path to uphold an image of perfection, and I never even questioned that path until recently."

"Hey, whatever path you want to take, I'm here for you. Thank you for telling me."

"Just ... don't tell anybody else yet, okay? I'm not ready to ... I'm just not sure who I am right now. I don't want word to get out to my followers and then I'm caught up in some scandal accusing me of trend jumping or attention seeking."

A soft smile formed on Harper's lips, steeped in sadness. "I like Neri *a lot*, but ... she's been through so much. Obviously, I can't, and won't pursue more from her. It's just nice to feel something real again. I want that to just be for me, for now."

Everly placed another hand over Harper's. "You don't owe me or anyone else an explanation. Your secret is safe."

Harper took a deep breath and squeezed Everly's hand in return.

Everly wiped her eyes but couldn't wipe the smile from her face. She leaned in and gave Harper another crushing hug.

"You know, I found something I think you might be interested in, too."

Turning around, she dug down into the bottom of the box with the Darkfrey paraphernalia. She wasn't entirely sure what to expect when she drew the shiny black object from the depths, but knew it had to be some kind of weapon.

An ornate hilt of silver and obsidian-like material led down to a long, flexible, whip-like sword. The segmented pieces of the blade were also of dark, smoky crystal, and wickedly jagged.

Harper gasped audibly. She took the grip carefully from Everly, inspecting it as the length lay on the floor. She frowned and twisted something near the pommel.

"I think this might—" *shnickt*, the length retracted, locking back together as one solid blade. Harper's eyes glittered.

"Whip sword," she whispered in awe.

She got to her feet, giving the sword a few slow twirls. "Hot damn, I'm in love!"

"I can't wait to see you kick some ass with that." Everly chuckled, then added, "Just be careful not to cut yourself with it."

"Oh, hardee har har," Harper mocked back. "Like we've learned nothing from playing with ancient dark magics. Don't worry, I will report any and all weirdness that may result from my new toy and suspend use of it if needed."

Everly's eyebrows knit. She hoped that having found the weapon in the same box as other Darkfrey armor and gear meant it had been one that was used by Portia, safely, in the past.

"Lian seems to get along well enough with her blade. We can get some shadyr eyes on it soon too, just in case. But yeah, we'll be careful, and we'll work it all out together."

"Together," Harper echoed with a glowing smile.

Everly glanced back down at the invoice for the "starry crystal," hoping this new weapon would bring no drama with it.

Whoever cataloged the estate must have known nothing about what they'd sold but had gotten the starry part right.

The crystal had belonged to the Beast of Teeth and Stars.

And there was another crystal out there, powering Cardboard Box Barry's magical box maze. The Coruscare had told her it expected her to retrieve the final piece, but she knew she couldn't do that. What Barry did for Shroudhaven was way too important to take the crystal away from him.

Not to mention, what would happen to her if the Coruscare was whole again? Anytime she'd allowed the light to take control, she'd barely managed to rein it in before killing anybody around her. She was already struggling to maintain control.

A fully intact Coruscare might be more of a danger to Shroudhaven than anything else they'd faced.

"It's mine?" Neri stared wide-eyed at the space.

The front half of the attic was transformed. Cleaned glass let bright afternoon light in through white lace curtains. The golden sunshine landed on a simple bed that Harper and Everly had bought flat-packed, hauled up the ladder together, assembled, and made with fresh sheets and a fluffy comforter.

Harper arranged a scattering of plush cushions, rug,

and nightstand, while Everly hung drapes to separate off the rest of the storage area. They'd found a couple of smaller cabinets and tallboys in the antique store, and slowly but surely carried them to the top of the house, together. They moved Neri's few belongings in, ready for her to add more.

"Do you like it?" Harper asked. "It's okay if you don't, or if the ladder is a problem."

Neri did a slow turn all the way around, then sat on the bed. Her eyes widened and she bounced up and down a few times, smile widening. "It's like from a picture book. All soft and warm."

Everly grinned. "I think she likes it."

"You two did good work here today." Lian carried in shopping bags full of clothing.

She was followed up by Tammy, who placed a plush pink seahorse toy next to Neri on the bed.

"Did you buy that for her?" Harper pried cheekily.

"Maybe? So what if I did? It was cute. Whatever. Ugh."

"The shops were fun, like seeing friends you only know from sounds." Neri hummed a few bars of the nearby mall's radio ad jingle.

"My legs are very tired now though." She leaned over and touched a hand against Harper's thigh. "How do I get legs like *yours*? They're so strong and perfect."

Everly bit her lips together to avoid giggling at Harper's deer-in-headlights expression.

"Okay, come along everyone. You're all coming over for dinner tonight," Lian said, taking the lead down the stairs. "No excuses this time."

Harper grinned. "Ooh, sounds good! I can show off … I mean, get my new sword checked over."

Everly smiled wryly. She had been avoiding the daily dinner invites, often using Neri as a reason, that she wasn't ready, needed quiet time. But it was Everly who wasn't ready to see Rylan again so soon. She wasn't ready to know if he'd realized how he really felt about her yet, or if he hadn't.

"I'll give you all a lift over now," Lian called back to them like an order.

Given no other option, they loaded into Lian's SUV, and she drove them around the block toward her home. The sunlight was warm with sunset shades, breaking the sky into a thousand shades of pink and orange as they coasted slowly up the long, tree-lined drive. Dust motes chased the light like sparks of gold in the cool air.

Everly was staring into the nearby overgrown field, lost in daydreams of her childhood spent out there, when Lian slammed on the brakes.

From the briars beside the road, a figure stumbled onto the laneway, right in front of them.

"Jasper?" Harper said from the front passenger seat as the figure collapsed in the dirt.

The women were out of the car in an instant, hurrying

to his side.

Lian put a hand on him, and he opened bruised eyes, cringing away from them.

"It's us, we won't hurt you," Harper said.

"What happened to him?" Everly asked, kneeling.

His lips were split and knuckles raw. He looked up with wild eyes and clutched at his cardigan-covered chest. Something crinkled beneath.

Neri clung to the car door, peeking around it. "Can I help?"

"Let's get him to the house first, we don't know what's out there," Lian said.

She nodded to Everly, and the two of them got their arms under his shoulders and lifted.

Back on his feet, Jasper groaned and coughed. "It's the Mesmans."

"They did this to you?" Lian hissed.

He shook his head weakly. "At Darkfrey Estate, they ... they're trying to create their own ... They're trying to open a shroudpool."

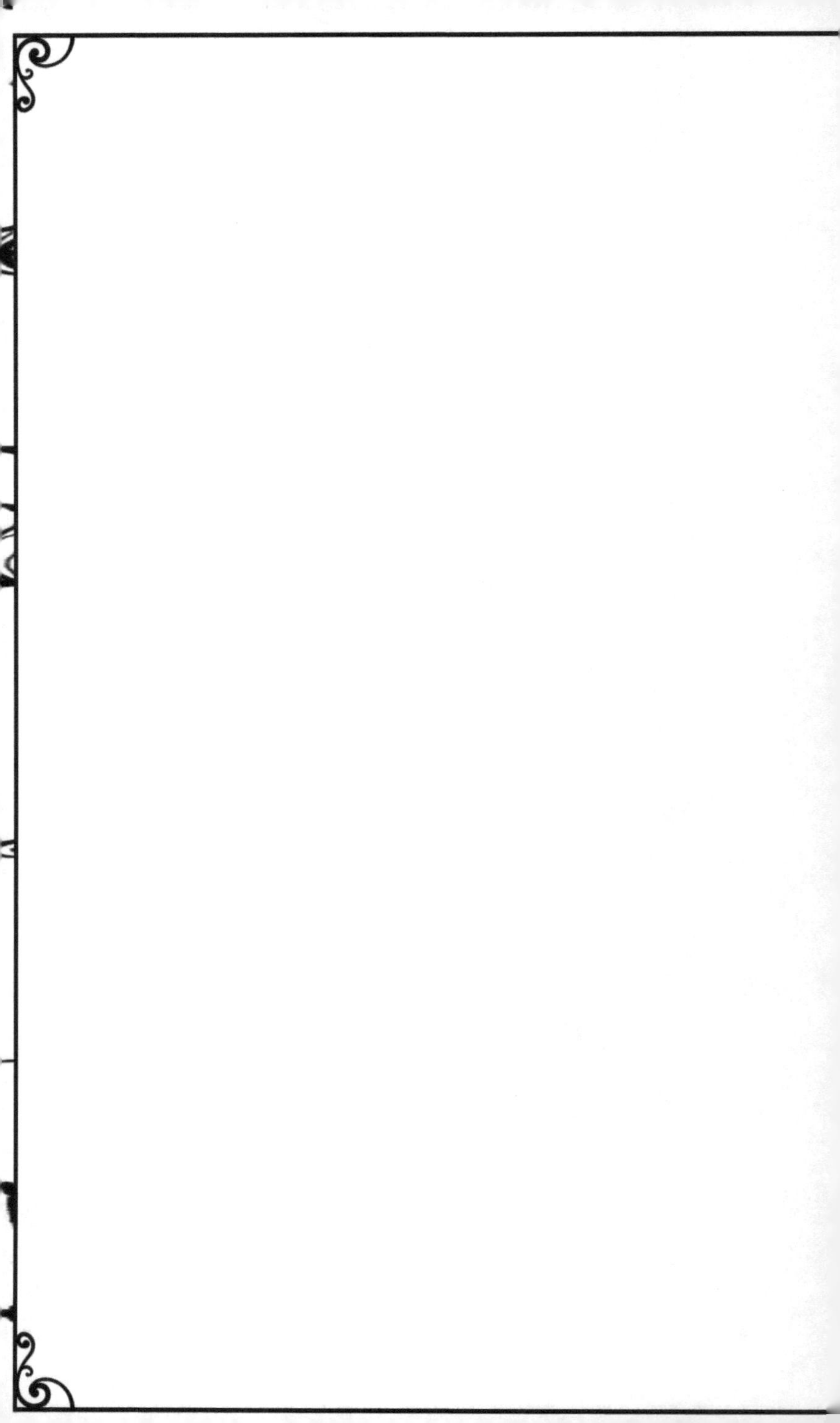

No one comes back from the Everdark alive

The Howell team has discovered the true plot brewing at Darkfrey Estate, one that requires a terrible sacrifice to be put into action. When it comes down to saving the people they love or saving the world, what will the Howell team choose?

When darkness descends on Shroudhaven, it may not even matter.

Because the creature inside Everly has already made its choice.

Discover the fate of the shadyrs in Everdark Cursed, book four of the Beshadowed series by Selina A. Fenech.

More Books by Selina A Fenech

Shadow Dragon Saga
Into a haunted realm a creature unlike any is born, and must be protected. Diverse young adult epic fantasy with dragons and magic

Memory's Wake Trilogy
A modern girl lost in and hunted in a fairy tale world. An illustrated young adult portal fantasy with Arthurian and Victorian themes.

Empath Chronicles
Teenagers with superpowers fueled by emotions ... what could go wrong? A young adult superhero romance.

Fairy Tale Wishes
Romantic fairy tale retellings with a twist. Young adult, standalone paranormal romance in urban and epic fantasy settings

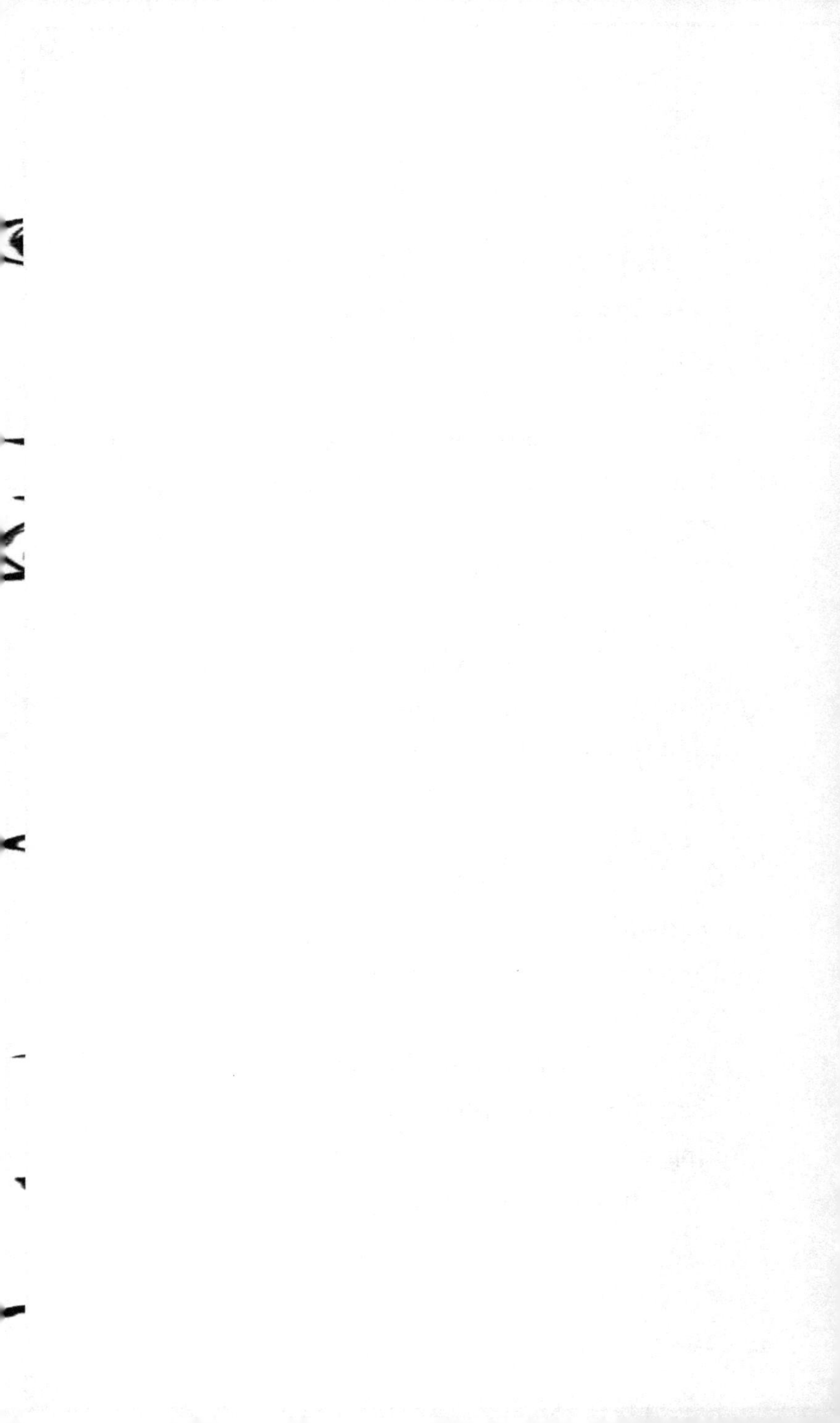

About the Author

Professional daydreamer, Selina A. Fenech writes "adorably dark" Epic and Urban Fantasy for teens and adults. Filled with sweet and quirky characters, laugh out loud moments, and perilous adventures, her magical worlds are perfect for readers who love daring twists and happily ever afters.

A cancer survivor determined to live life to the fullest, she is an escape room enthusiast, avid gardener, foodie and self-proclaimed geek, residing in Australia.

In addition to literature, Selina applies her unique take on the dichotomy of light and dark as a professional fantasy artist working under the name Selina Fenech and has published many illustrated books, oracle decks, and colouring books.

Find Out more About Selina

OFFICIAL WEBSITE:www.selinafenech.com